THE SUICIDE CLUB

GAYLE WILSON

D0018171

MIRA®

ISBN-13: 978-0-7783-2469-0
ISBN-10:   0-7783-2469-9

THE SUICIDE CLUB

www.MIRABooks.com

Printed in U.S.A.

Praise for the novels of
GAYLE WILSON

"A writer who combines impeccable craft with
unsurpassed storytelling skills. Her books are
dark, sexy and totally involving."
—*New York Times* bestselling author Anne Stuart

"Gayle Wilson is a rising star in romantic suspense."
—*New York Times* bestselling author Carla Neggers

"Gayle Wilson will go far in romantic suspense. Her books
have that special 'edge' that lifts them out of the ordinary.
They're always tautly written, a treasure trove of action,
suspense and richly drawn characters."
—*New York Times* bestselling author Linda Howard

"An exhilarating continual action thriller
that never slows down."
—*TheBestReviews.com* on *Double Blind*

"Wilson gives her readers just what they want: more
thrilling adventure and heart-wrenching suspense....
Inspiring. Wilson is destined to become one of the
suspense genre's brightest stars."
—*Romantic Times BOOKreviews* (4½ stars) on
Wednesday's Child

"Gayle Wilson pulls out all the stops to give her
readers a thrilling chilling read that will give you
goose bumps in the night."
—*ReadertoReader.com* on *In Plain Sight*

"Writing like this is a rare treat."
—*Gothic Journal*

"Rich historical detail, intriguing mystery, romance
that touches the heart and lingers in the mind.
These are elements that keep me waiting impatiently
for Gayle Wilson's next book."
—*USA TODAY* bestselling author BJ James

For all the wonderful "nifty-gifties" I taught through the years. The bad guys in this one aren't you, my darlings, but the good guys surely are.
Enjoy...and remember that it's just fiction.

Dear Reader,

Thank you so much for picking up a copy of *The Suicide Club*. I spent the major portion of my life as a high school teacher, and many of those years were spent working with highly gifted students. I have never enjoyed anything more than associating with those bright, eager, funny and endearing kids. And despite the fact that I've now written over forty novels, I still consider myself to be a teacher first.

This book examines the relationships between teachers and their students, as well as the friendships that form within the teaching corps. Trust me, the villains and the unsavory parts of this story are all imaginary, but the rest is based on a reality I lived daily for a number of years—the joys of teaching, the camaraderie, the demands of a profession that is, to me, one of the highest callings. I hope you enjoy a peek into that world, although one distorted by the expectations of the suspense genre.

This book truly started as an experiment with "What ifs…." Gifted kids are indeed the same as their peers in so many ways. They are subject to the same adolescent stresses, and they react, for the most part, exactly like others of their age. However, in thinking about what a high intellect combined with a propensity for wickedness would be capable of, the concept of an evil genius let loose in a small Southern town—and, more specifically, in its high school—was born. I added a generous dose of the kinds of teen behaviors I see talked about every day in the media, and *The Suicide Club* was born.

And although the gifted kids here are indeed an "evil genius," there is a dedicated teacher who remains exactly what she should be—an advocate and a protector of her students. I hope you'll cheer her on as she and an equally committed policeman attempt to unravel the mystery and survive the dangers that lie at the heart of this story.

Enjoy!

With love,

Gayle Wilson

Prologue

"*It was already starting to get boring. I mean, how many times can you do the same thing?*"

"*Boring? You mean compared to the excitement of just sitting here?*"

"*You know what I mean.*"

"*I know you're so full of shit your breath stinks. You weren't bored. You were a lot of things, dude, but you were not bored.*"

"*I'm bored.*" *The girl beside him reached for his beer.*

"*Because* you *have no imagination,*" *he said, releasing it.*

He watched as she took a draw, tilting her head back so that he could see the movement of her throat in the moonlight. The pale column of her neck looked thin. Fragile. Vulnerable.

"*So what do we do now, Mr. Imagination?*" *she asked when she finally lowered the bottle.*

"*Time delay,*" *the boy in the back seat said.* "*We rig some kind of incendiary device and a trigger. Something that lets us be far away when it goes up.*"

The boy in the back was his friend. The only person he had ever considered in that light. That gave him certain privileges. Including, he guessed, making stupid suggestions.

"You got that kind of device, bozo? And something to use for the trigger? Like what, man?"

"I don't know what it would take, but I can find out. You can find out how to do anything on the web. Just Google nuclear bomb and you could build one."

"Because if you don't have it already," he went on, ignoring the crap-spew, "then you'd have to go out and buy it. All purchases are traceable, but something like that... Besides, all of that's gonna to leave behind evidence."

"In a fire—"

"Because that is the key to success in any criminal activity, my friend. Leave nothing behind. Nothing they can play their little CSI games on."

In the resulting silence, he retrieved his beer, draining it in one swallow. Stolen bottle by bottle from his father's basement fridge, there was never quite enough to get a good buzz going. Especially not when it had to be shared.

"As if," his friend said. "That's shit anyway. Maybe up North they do all that, but not down here. You think the pissant state labs here have got stuff like that?"

"The feds do."

"The feds?" the girl repeated.

"ATF. They're the ones who broke the other case."

"People saw 'em, dude. They left tire tracks, for Christ's sake. It doesn't take a genius—"

"Maybe it does."

Another silence as the other two tried to figure out what he meant. And since he wasn't exactly sure...

"What does that mean?" the boy in the back finally asked.

"All you have to be to carry out any crime is smarter than the cops, right?" He glanced back, pressing for agreement.

His friend shrugged. "Yeah. I guess."

"Actually, you've only got to be smarter than the smartest cop. He doesn't figure it out, the rest sure won't."

"You want to give the cops IQ tests?" The girl laughed, a sound that was beginning to get on his nerves. "We see which of them is the smartest and...what? Plan to do something criminal that even he can't figure out?"

She was being sarcastic, what passed for wit in her narrow world. Like that saying about the mouths of babes, the simplicity of it seemed to loop over and over inside his head.

See which one of them is the smartest and do something even he can't figure out.

And if he couldn't outsmart the local constabulary, he needed to reevaluate his life goals. They thought they were so fucking smart with those patrols. He'd love to be able to circumvent them. Set one more fire, just to prove he could.

But the risks were too great. He wasn't going to risk his future. He had that all planned out, and it didn't include any of the things a conviction would entail. Whatever he did to prove to those bozos that he wasn't defeated would, like the fires, have to be something that they could never trace back to him. Or to anyone associated with him.

He'd had lots of time during the summer to think about the way to set those fires without leaving evidence. And he'd been right about all of it. The cops had nothing.

With school started, he'd have less time. So...something simpler. But without the risk, would the satisfaction be the same?

There had to be a way to feel the same exhilaration he'd felt watching through his father's binoculars as those churches went up in flames.

"Exactly," he said. "Something he can't figure out. Or trace back to us. Something like the fires. Only better."

"Like what?" the boy in the back asked.

"I don't know yet," he answered truthfully.

Lower risk. Same exhilaration. Raise the stakes in the game with the cops without raising the stakes for himself.

To do that meant that the risk would have to be very high for somebody else. But after all, that really wasn't his problem.

One

Lindsey Sloan hesitated, her knuckles hovering just beneath the metal plaque on the door. David Campbell and then below the name in smaller letters, Principal.

Although it was unusual for Dave to leave a message with the school secretary asking her to come to his office, Lindsey believed she knew what her boss wanted to talk about. Randolph-Lowen was for up for accreditation review this year. He probably wanted to ask her to head up the school committee.

That wasn't something she wanted to do, but she knew she would end up saying yes to his request. Which was why she was standing outside the door to his office as if she had been called here for punishment.

Taking a deep breath, she tapped lightly and then, following Melanie's instructions, turned the knob. Dave, who was seated behind his desk, looked up.

"Melanie said to come on in," Lindsey offered.

Although she'd followed the instructions she'd been given, as Dave stood, he seemed slightly annoyed by the interruption. Or maybe, she realized as she continued to study his expression, he was annoyed because of the presence of the dark-haired man seated on this side of his desk. He, too, got to his feet as Lindsey stepped inside the office.

He was no one she recognized. A parent with a complaint about something she'd done? Since it was only the second week of school, she'd given out no grades. If he *was* here to complain, it must be about an assignment. She mentally ran through the ones she'd handed out to her classes, but she couldn't imagine why any of them would bring a father to the school. Not in person.

"That's fine, Lindsey," Dave said. "Want to close that?"

The frisson of anxiety she'd felt when she realized there was someone waiting with Dave escalated. She used the excuse of securing the door to hide it. When she turned back to face the two men, her "meet the parents" smile was firmly in place.

"Lindsey, this is Lieutenant Nolan. Detective, Lindsey Sloan, our gifted coordinator."

"Ms. Sloan."

That thin, hard mouth probably didn't do much smiling, Lindsey thought. And he obviously didn't intend to make an exception for her. His eyes, as dark as his hair, continued to study her as she attempted to retain her own smile.

"Detective?" she questioned.

"With the sheriff's department."

"And…you want to see *me?*"

"The lieutenant's in charge of the investigation into the church fires," Dave interjected.

Lindsey's gaze automatically shifted to her principal as he made his explanation. Almost immediately she refocused it on the detective. She realized that his eyes had never left her face, undoubtedly because he was noting her reaction to what Dave had just said.

Three rural black churches in the county had been torched

on separate nights last July. Although no additional fires had occurred during August, the initial three continued to get top billing in both the state and national media.

"I'm sorry. You must think I'm very slow," Lindsey said, "but I still don't understand why you want to see me."

"We've been working with the FBI to develop a profile of the people who set those fires." Nolan's voice was deep, its accent decidedly not local.

Nor was his appearance. The dark suit was too stylishly cut. And probably too expensive for this setting. His hair was a little long. Not nearly conservative enough for someone associated with local law enforcement. She wondered how the good old boys in the department related to Lieutenant Nolan.

Of course, her idle curiosity had no relevance to this discussion. And based on the intensity of the detective's gaze, she had the distinct impression that she'd better get focused on what Nolan was saying rather than on what he looked like before something important slipped by her.

"And that profile led you to me?"

She thought she'd figured out where this was going, but she wanted him to put it into words. At least she now understood Dave's uneasiness.

"Actually, it led us to the students you teach."

Randolph-Lowen wasn't the only high school in the county. It was, however, the one designated to provide services for the gifted. A few kids even came from outside the county because they didn't have access to appropriate resources at the schools to which they were zoned.

"Are you saying your profile indicates the arsonists have high IQs?" All those old wives tales about that supposedly thin line between genius and insanity reared their ugly heads.

Before she could begin to dispute them, Nolan added, "And that they're young. White. Male."

Lindsey glanced at Dave, wondering why he wasn't objecting to this. Profiling wasn't a science. The description the detective had just given with such an air of confidence might be wildly inaccurate.

Besides, even if there *were* something to what he'd just said, there was nothing the school could do to help him narrow his search. She wasn't going to start suggesting that one child or another might be involved in something as high-profile as this crime. That would be a quick way to a suspension followed by a lawsuit.

"I'm sorry, Lieutenant. I don't think I can help you." She'd already turned toward the door when Dave stopped her.

"Lindsey, this isn't what you think."

"Then what is it?" She looked from one to the other.

"The people who developed the profile believe this is a thrill crime," Nolan said. "Something designed to get the adrenaline pumping."

Despite her doubts about the methodology, she thought that was probably an accurate description. She just didn't see what it had to do with her. Or with her students. "And?"

"Once they've experienced that rush," Nolan said, "they're going to want it again."

"And you think other churches will be burned."

Even given her animosity toward the investigative process he'd described, she didn't want that to happen. Not only did those small congregations suffer a huge emotional and financial loss, the entire region had received yet another black eye through the lawlessness of a few individuals.

"We can almost guarantee it."

"Even if I had a suspicion that any of my students were involved—and I assure you I don't—I wouldn't feel comfortable discussing those with the police."

"Those churches were all within a twenty-five mile radius of this high school. If you take a map—"

"I'm sure you have. Believe me, we all understand that the people of this county are suspects. But even if this community is at the center of the area where the fires occurred, that doesn't mean any student from this school set them. Nor does your profile, no matter who composed it."

"Profiling gives us a place to start. This is it."

Lindsey looked at Dave, wanting him to defend the kids of this community. It wasn't that none of them had ever been in trouble. Or that she thought they couldn't be. Not after ten years in the profession. But she also wasn't stupid enough to believe that just because the school sat in the geographic center of the area where the arsons had occurred, that meant the people involved in them attended it.

Dave shrugged, seeming to indicate he was bowing to what he saw as inevitable. Maybe Nolan had shared more information with him. Considering what he'd shared with her, however, Lindsey wasn't willing to be sucked in. Not until one or the other of them leveled with her.

"Anything other than that profile and the proximity to the fires that makes you think my students might be involved?"

There was a flash of something in those dark eyes. The emotion was quickly masked, but not fast enough that she didn't wonder if he was laughing at her reluctance to believe her kids could be involved in something like this.

"Those aren't enough?" His tone was devoid of sarcasm.

"Not for me, I'm afraid. Look, if I thought any of my students were involved, I might feel differently. But as of now I have no reason to think they are. I've had no reason to even think about the possibility until you showed up this morning."

"And if you *did* have a reason?"

"I'd talk to someone I trusted about it."

"Like Dr. Campbell?"

Although Dave hadn't finished his doctorate, neither of them corrected him. "Only if I couldn't resolve those feelings in my own mind." Lindsey said.

"My best advice, Ms. Sloan, is that if you develop 'those feelings,' you don't try to resolve them. Here's my card. I'd appreciate a call if you have any reason to…shall we say…reflect on the possibility that our profile has merit."

The phrasing was careful, perhaps intended not to offend. The look in his eyes was not quite in keeping with it.

"Of course."

Lindsey accepted the card he held out, making a show of looking down at it. The first thing she noted was his first name. Jace. The second thing she noted was something far more disturbing: the fact she had been wondering about that.

Jace Nolan. Who was very obviously from somewhere far from here. And very much outside the norm of men she knew.

She raised her eyes from the card, again finding his on her face. "Is that all?"

"You can call me if you think of anything I should know."

Not exactly what she'd meant, but clearly a dismissal. She quickly took advantage of it. "Thanks. I'll do that."

She turned and walked to the door, conscious that they were both watching her. When she'd closed it, she leaned against its solid wood, releasing a breath as she thought about the interview that had just passed.

Before it seemed possible that either of the men inside the room had had time to walk across it, the door opened behind her. Slightly off balanced, she tried to get out of the way of the man who emerged.

"Sorry." Jace Nolan put his hand under her elbow in an attempt to steady her.

"My fault. I should have moved out of the doorway."

Now try to explain why you didn't.

"No harm done. Have a good day, Ms. Sloan."

With a slight nod, the detective moved past her and walked into the main office. She continued to watch as he disappeared through the door that led out into the lobby.

"Cops after you, Ms. Sloan?"

She turned to see Steven Byrd lifting the American flag off the top shelf of the hall closet where it was kept. One of her seniors, Steven was responsible for putting the stars and stripes up the outside flagpole every morning and taking it down and folding it properly every afternoon. For most of Randolph-Lowen's students, even some of those in her gifted program, that single act was enough to classify him as a nerd.

"You know him?" she asked, wondering how Steven could be familiar enough with the local police to recognize Nolan.

"I was sitting in my car when he got out of his. County tags. Besides, he looks like a cop. Glad to know my powers of observation are as well-developed as I thought." Steven grinned at her, blue eyes shining through his glasses.

"So you were guessing."

"Only until you were kind enough to verify it. What'd you do? Run a red light?"

"Something like that," she hedged.

Neither Dave nor Nolan had cautioned her to keep what they'd told her to herself, but it wasn't the kind of thing she would ever share with a student. Not even one like Steven, whom she considered trustworthy.

"Naw, they'd send a uniform for that. So it's probably not about you. That means it's about us."

"Us?"

"Students. Maybe *your* students? And if I had to guess—"

"I think you've done enough guessing," Lindsey said, putting a hint of classroom firmness into her voice.

It wasn't lost on Steven. "Okay. I can keep my mouth shut. You know that. I'm not surprised they showed up here."

Unable to resist, Lindsey asked, "Why?"

"The usual suspects. They always focus on kids for something like that. Especially if the fires are copycat things like the news says."

The previous spate of fires had been the work of a few college kids without a political agenda. Although those had not focused exclusively on black churches, that was probably a geographical consideration more than anything else. And the three buildings that had been set on fire in this county were the only ones so conveniently isolated.

"Is that what you think?"

"I think this is just as stupid as those were. The only difference is that in this case, they knew when to stop."

That was part of the local speculation. That the arsonists had simply run out of churches they could torch without getting caught. And apparently they'd learned something from the earlier fires. According to the papers, there had been little physical evidence found at the recent ones.

"You hear any talk about the fires?"

"Sure," Steven acknowledged, holding the folded flag against his chest as he closed the closet door with his elbow. "A lot of talk. A lot of guessing. Nothing that made me pay attention. Got to get this up."

She nodded, moving aside to let him go by her in the narrow hallway. As she watched him follow the route the detective had taken, Lindsey thought about what both had said. She almost turned back to Dave's door, but the first bell sounded, reminding her that her room was locked.

The school day had officially begun. Any other discussion

with anyone about the surprise visitor she'd had this morning would have to wait until after it was done.

For a few select members of the staff, the teachers' lounge was a refuge at the end of the day. Surprisingly, today the room was empty.

Lindsey glanced at her watch to find that it was only twelve minutes after three. Like her students in last period, she'd been more than eager to put this day behind her. She'd had her things gathered up almost before the last of the stragglers had left.

She set her canvas tote down on the table beside the nearest sofa and went over to the coffeepot. The liquid in the bottom of the glass carafe looked black and strong, which was exactly what she needed.

Picking her mug out from the dozen or so residing on a plastic lunchroom tray on the counter, she poured some of the thick liquid into it, relishing the slightly scorched smell. Before she could bring the cup to her lips, the familiar squeak of the outer door caused her to lower it again.

She turned to see the person she was closest to on the staff enter and drop her briefcase on the table by the door. Shannon Anderson was the Junior/Senior counselor. Although she was a few years younger and undeniably more hip than Lindsey, the two of them had struck up a friendship almost as soon as Shannon had been assigned to Randolph-Lowen.

"Any more of that?" she asked.

Lindsey turned back to locate Shannon's mug on the counter and fill it. She held it out to her friend.

"Thanks." Shannon took the cup with her right hand. With her left, she hooked a curling strand of long, dark hair behind her ear before she sipped the coffee. "I think I made this third period." She pulled a face at the bitterness.

"How can you tell?" Lindsey asked with a laugh.

"Tastes like third period." Shannon walked over to one of the couches. She sat, tucking long, boot-clad legs under her. Her colorful skirt spilled around her, almost touching the floor. She leaned her head back and closed her eyes. "I hate the beginning of school. I'm *so* frigging tired."

"You're a twelve-month employee. You're supposed to be used to working." Counselors didn't get the nearly three-month summer break teachers did.

"It ain't work if the little darlings aren't here."

Lindsey laughed. Shannon loved interacting with their students more than almost anyone else on the faculty, but she was right. It was dealing with teenagers and their raging hormones that put the stress in all their lives. Shannon dealt with them on a much more personal, one-on-one basis, unlike the relationship in the classrooms.

"Who's giving you grief now?"

"No one in particular." Shannon raised her head from the back of the couch to take another swallow of her coffee. "Little darlings *en masse,*" she said, giving the words their correct French pronunciation. "'Can you change my schedule, Ms. Anderson. I didn't mean to sign up for Algebra II.' Translation, I did, but now I don't want crazy old Ms. Brock."

"Can you blame them?"

"Well, no, but somebody's got to be in her class."

"She needs to retire. She was here when I was in school." Fourteen years ago, which wasn't quite as long as she'd just made it out to be. "We called her old Ms. Brock then, too."

"Was she as bad as she is now?"

"I don't know. I didn't have her. I don't remember that kids talked about her the way these do. But, I don't remember kids talking all that bad about any teacher back then."

"You hung with the wrong crowd."

"Or the right one."

They drank their coffee, the silence that had fallen companionable and unstrained. Shannon leaned her head back, her fingers making that habitual rearrangement of her hair.

"Something weird happened this morning," Lindsey began.

Shannon straightened, her eyes interested. "In class?"

"Before. Melanie told me when I signed in that Dave wanted to see me. Some detective with the sheriff's department was in his office. He said the FBI has developed a profile of the arsonists in the church fires." She hesitated, wanting to see if Shannon reached the same conclusion she had.

"And they wanted to talk to *you*? They think your kids are involved?"

"Apparently. I've been thinking about it all day, getting more and more pissed."

Shannon didn't respond, but Lindsey could almost track the thoughts moving behind her green eyes. She knew the counselor was running through the individuals in the gifted program, just as Lindsey had been all day. The fact that she had been was a large part of her building anger.

"He give you any idea who?"

"He wanted *me* to give *him* ideas."

"Well, that sucks. You think…?"

Lindsey shook her head. "But I admit it ate at me. I kept trying to think of anyone who might be involved, but… You *know* them. Who the hell would do something like that?"

"I told you. Little darlings. They aren't any different from the others except they're probably smart enough not to get caught."

That, too, was a thought that had occurred to Lindsey at some point. She had wondered if that's why the profilers had zeroed in on the students in her gifted program—simply because of the lack of evidence, something law enforcement officials had openly acknowledged.

"I think that might be exactly what they're thinking."

"That they must be geniuses because the cops can't catch 'em?" Shannon asked. "Isn't *that* convenient."

"They can't admit that some dumb, redneck yahoo can outsmart them, burn three black churches, and get away with it. So, stands to reason, this has got to be somebody else."

"Who was the detective? Anybody I know?"

Shannon had dated a sheriff's deputy a couple of years ago. Surprisingly, they'd managed to maintain a friendship after the romantic relationship had ended. *If,* Lindsey amended, knowing her friend too well not to have wondered if all aspects of that particular relationship *had* come to an end.

"Jace Nolan."

"Doesn't ring a bell."

"I don't think he's from around here."

"Want me to ask Rick why they're looking at your kids?"

"Would it get back to Nolan if you did?"

"Not if I tell Rick to keep his mouth shut."

"Would he?"

"Sure. Why not?"

Why not, indeed, Lindsey thought. And as Shannon said, what could it hurt?

Two

"So I hear you got finally somethin' on the fires."

Jace raised his eyes to find one of the county deputies looking down at the papers spread out over on his desk. He resisted the impulse to push them together. After all, the man was a fellow law enforcement officer.

"A profile. From the Bureau. We're working from that."

"Yeah? I always thought those were pretty general. You think this one's helpful, then?"

"A place to start." The words echoed inside Jace's head. Exactly what he'd told the two at the high school yesterday.

The transition from that realization to the next was almost instantaneous. Before today, few of the deputies had bothered to speak to him, not even when passing him in the halls, much less visit his desk to ask questions. Not that he gave a damn whether they did are not. Still…

A glance at the name bar above the man's shirt pocket provided the name. Had Deputy Carlisle attended Randolph-Lowen? And if so, did he have ties to any of the people Jace had talked to there yesterday?

Like maybe the redhead who'd been so determined to question the validity of his interest in her kids?

He didn't blame Ms. Sloan for her skepticism. She had every right to question why he suspected the students in her gifted program might be involved.

"So who are we looking for?"

"Thrill seekers," Jace said, watching for reaction as he rolled out the now-familiar list of characteristics the Bureau had given him. "Young. White. Male."

"How young?"

"Probably teens. Possibly early twenties. The profile isn't that precise."

"College age. Like those others."

"Maybe. But since there isn't a college in this area—"

"Junior college over in Carroll. Another near Bedford. Hell, thanks to old George Wallace and Lurleen, we got a junior college or trade school on about every other corner."

"And neither of those is in the geographic center of the arsons. This community, and its high school, are."

"Sounds like you got your mind made up."

Despite the beginnings of what would soon became a paunch, Deputy Carlisle looked as if he might be a few years younger than Jace. Early thirties or so.

Old enough to know better.

As he waited for Jace to respond to that accusation, the deputy shifted his weight from one foot to the other, displaying what might be a hint of nervousness. The movement was accompanied by the creak of his utility belt, reminding Jace that whatever else he was, the man was a fellow officer.

"Like I said," he said softly. "It's a place to start."

"I heard you were out at the high school yesterday."

At least this approach was more honest than the previous one. Maybe he could even work it to his advantage.

"That's right. Since I didn't talk to many people there, I'd be curious as to who shared that information with you."

The deputy grinned. "In a town this size, *all* information's shared. Half the department probably knew you'd been over there before you got back in your car."

"I'll remember that. I thought maybe you had a friend who'd asked you to see if you could find out why I was there."

The grin wavered so that Jace knew he'd struck a nerve. It hadn't taken a lot of deductive reasoning to figure out the reason "Deputy Dawg" here had stopped by to chat, no matter how subtle Carlisle thought he was being.

"So you're a friend of Ms. Sloan's," Jace went on before the man had a chance to think up an excuse.

"Sorry." Carlisle shook his head. "Don't believe I know her. That the teacher you talked to?"

"The gifted coordinator. I'm not totally clear what that means, but I'll find out."

"Yeah? Me, either. They didn't have one of them when I was in school."

"You go there?"

"Everybody around here did."

"Know anybody there now?"

"I might. You looking to talk to people? Unofficially?"

"Something like that."

"Kids?"

"I don't care. Just somebody who'll be candid."

"I'll think about who I know. You believe whoever's doing this is a genius."

"They burned down three churches without leaving physical evidence. Does that make them a genius?"

"Might just make 'em lucky." Carlisle's grin was back.

"That's what I figure."

"'Course my daddy always said it's better to be lucky than good."

"Eventually luck runs out."

On Jace's orders, the remaining black churches in this county and the adjacent ones had been under patrol since the last fire. So far it had worked, but if he was right…

If he was right, something else was going to happen. Sooner rather than later. And he intended to be on top of it when it did.

The slight headache Lindsey had been conscious of when she'd awakened this morning, after another night of less-than-restful sleep, had become full blown. It was the Friday afternoon pep rally, and the entire student population was crammed into a gym that had been too small to hold it for at least three years. The band blasted away on the fight song, the sound of the drums throbbing through the prefabricated building like a toothache.

She had thought about retreating to the quietness of her room until the dismissal bell, but faculty was supposed to supervise assemblies. As a compromise, she had moved to one of the two pairs of open double doors, so that she was actually standing out in the hall, looking back into the gym. Not only was the noise less out here, so was the heat and the claustrophobic press of bodies.

In any case, this one was almost over, with only the obligatory speeches by the game captains and Coach Spears remaining on the program. After those, even the cheerleaders would give up, trailing out of the gym after the transported students, who'd be off to catch their buses.

As soon as the fight song ground to a halt, the football coach, who had held his position for more than twenty years, took the microphone and began introducing the two boys standing diffidently beside him. Lindsey took a deep, calming breath, savoring the fact that the week was almost over. She could sleep in tomorrow morning. Right now, she couldn't think of anything more appealing.

"Will they win?"

In spite of the brevity of the question, the accent was distinctive enough to allow her to identify the speaker even before she looked around. Detective Jace Nolan was beside her, his dark eyes focused on the three people standing along the midcourt line. When she didn't answer, he turned his head, peering down at her.

From this angle his lashes looked incredibly long. A hint of stubble that hadn't been there Tuesday morning darkened his cheeks. The knot of his tie had been loosened, although the pale blue dress shirt still managed to look crisp. As did his midnight hair, which in the humidity was displaying a surprising tendency to curl.

"What are you doing here?" Lindsey asked.

"Watching the pep rally. I thought that was permitted."

Parents and others from the community always showed up at assemblies. At Randolph-Lowen they'd never imposed the strict security measures other schools now took for granted, given today's climate of fear. At this moment dozens of outsiders lined the court, mingling with the faculty and staff.

"It is. I just didn't think you'd be interested."

"I'm interested in anything that goes on around here. It's part of my job."

He refocused his eyes on the trio at center stage, appearing to listen to the senior captain's stumbling rhetoric. Lindsey's gaze followed his, but she heard nothing of what the football player was saying. She was examining the implications of Nolan being back at school so quickly, as well as those inherent in him once more singling her out.

"And you're on the job now?" she asked, without taking her eyes off the boy holding the mike.

"Since the county's paying me for a full day's work."

"Why here? Why today?"

"The fires occurred on a weekend. I'm trying to get a feel for what these kids do outside of school."

"So you came *to* school?"

He glanced down again, a slight tilt at one corner of what she'd once thought of as a hard mouth.

"Doesn't make much sense, does it? What would you think about showing me?"

"Showing you what?" As soon as the words were out of her mouth, Lindsey knew what he wanted. Despite that, she was unprepared when he put the request into words.

"What these kids do on a Friday night."

She looked back toward the center of the gym, watching Ray Garrett pass the microphone to the second captain, their junior fullback. She eased a breath, unobtrusively she hoped, and then raised her eyes to Nolan again.

His were on her face. Waiting.

"They go to the football game," she said.

He laughed. "Yeah, I figured that. And afterward?"

"That depends on the kids. They go out to eat. Or to a party." She didn't particularly want to discuss with him the myriad other actions she knew students this age engaged in.

"Couples? Or groups?"

"Both."

"Yours, too."

"Mine are like all the others. They date. They hang out. They drive around. They stay out too late—"

"They burn churches."

She closed her mouth, fighting to control her surge of anger. She was pleased with how rational she managed to sound when she was able to respond. "Not in my opinion. And I've yet to hear any credible evidence to the contrary."

"Normally we don't share that kind of evidence."

"But you have it?"

She could hear the blatant need for reassurance in her question. Tuesday she'd been convinced that he was bluffing. Fishing for information. In the intervening days, for no reason she could pinpoint, that conviction had weakened.

"Despite the acknowledged charms of Ray Garrett's recent pep talk, why else would I be here?"

And that was what bothered her. His surety. She could probably put that down to an inherent arrogance. A sense of self-worth that might have been born of success, but one that might also be based on nothing more than a mistaken belief in the superiority of anything not native to the region.

Like Jace Nolan himself.

"You caught me off guard on Tuesday, but since then... I've been thinking about what you said."

She sensed that his attention had sharpened. The sensation was so strong it was almost physical.

"And?"

"And in all honesty," she said, each word carefully enunciated, "none of my kids would do anything like that."

"You just said they were like all the others. I've been doing a lot of research into the annals of youthful offenses around here. Despite the bucolic nature of the environment, these kids appear to get involved in the same kinds of criminal activities that they do in any other locale."

"In the ten years I've been here, I can't remember one of my students being mixed up in anything like that."

"How would you know?"

"What?"

"Juvenile records are routinely sealed. Parents are under

no obligation to tell the school about any charges or probations imposed on their children."

"You've forgotten where you are, Detective Nolan. *Everybody* knows *everything* about *everyone* around here."

"Except nobody knows who burned those churches. Or don't you believe that?"

"Do you?"

"It doesn't match my experience. Kids talk. Unless there's a very strong reason *not* to."

"Like a fear of prosecution. Or going to jail?"

"I meant talk among their peers."

"As angry as people in this community are, whoever burned those churches would have to be very stupid to do that."

"Bingo," Nolan said, turning back to look into the gym.

The cheerleaders were gathering up their megaphones for a last cheer at center court. After that the band would play everyone out with another repetition of the fight song.

A few teachers and some of the parents were already making a break toward the two pairs of double doors. Although the other adults might continue to the parking lot, most of the faculty would do what she was doing: stand near the entrances to supervise the dismissal.

The fact that Lindsey was talking to the chief detective in charge of investigating the arsons would be noticed. It would undoubtedly cause comment and maybe even questions, neither of which she was eager to deal with.

"If that's your so-called evidence for thinking my kids were involved—"

"It *does* make sense, doesn't it?"

A couple of people had reached the doorway where they were standing, providing Lindsey with an excuse to move off to the side. After nodding in response to the curious stares of departing parents, Nolan followed.

"You and Carlisle seem to be right."

"I'm sorry?" Had Shannon's ex actually approached him?

"You said everybody here knows everybody's business. I guess they know every*body,* too. They seem to be trying to figure out who I am and why I'm here."

"We've all been warned often enough about strangers in the school."

"Except I had no trouble walking right into the building. Not on Tuesday. Not today. Apparently your administration doesn't take those kinds of warnings very seriously."

"The curiosity you admit to arousing is, in itself, a safeguard."

"Against outsiders. Statistically, however, that isn't the real threat in any high school."

He was right, of course. The school tragedies in this country had almost all been student-directed.

That didn't mean that the students here posed a threat, she reminded herself. Just as the fact the arsons had occurred in this general vicinity didn't mean anyone from this community had been involved.

The 3:00 p.m. bell rang, preventing her from having to formulate an answer. Kids poured out of the gym in a wave, the sound of the band seeming to add to the general sense of chaos. In response to the flood of students, Nolan grasped her elbow, directing her away from the doors.

She had been conscious of the feel of his hand on her arm when he'd attempted to steady her outside Dave's office. Today, the warmth of his fingers seemed to burn into her bare skin. She was aware of their strength and hardness. Sensitive to their callused roughness. Totally masculine and yet surprisingly pleasant.

Surprising. Like the length of his lashes and the sensual

appeal of that five-o'clock shadow. Even his voice, despite the unfamiliarity of the accent, was intriguing.

Realizing that she was in danger of being *overly* intrigued, she pulled her elbow from his grip. "I have to go back upstairs and get some papers from my room."

It was a lie. She had decided she wasn't going to do any grading this weekend. She was working the gate at the game tonight, and she intended to sleep in tomorrow. The few essays she needed to finish for her fifth period class could be done during her free period Monday.

"So I take it you aren't interested in being my guide to Friday night in Randolph."

In the unfamiliar rush of emotions she'd forgotten his invitation. She didn't intend to accept. Not until she'd had time and space to control her physical response to Jace Nolan.

"I don't think so. Not when you seemed to be so tightly focused on my kids as the perpetrators."

"I'm willing to have you change my mind."

"I'm not willing to try. You're wrong. Sooner or later you'll figure that out without any help from me."

As exit lines went, it wasn't particularly powerful. Nolan didn't argue, tilting his head as if acknowledging the possibility. The quirk she'd noticed before at the corner of his lips occurred again and was once more controlled.

"If you change your mind, you have my card."

It was the perfect opening to respond with something rude. Deny that she'd *ever* change her mind. Defend her kids.

She did neither. The attraction was strong enough that she couldn't be sure that if he kept on, he wouldn't wear her down. She wasn't going to give him a chance.

She'd learned early in her professional life not to make a threat unless she was willing to carry it out and that the fewer words she said in any situation, the fewer she would have to eat if things didn't work out as she'd anticipated.

With Jace Nolan, she had a feeling that things not going as she'd anticipated was a distinct possibility.

Three

"Think we can go ahead and shut down?"

Shannon's question caused Lindsey to look up at the scoreboard. It was nearing the end of the third quarter, which was the traditional closing time for the booth. Tonight only a handful of tickets had been sold since the half. They'd already counted up the money in both cash boxes, keeping only a few dollars out to make change.

"I don't see why not." The score was lopsided enough that people were beginning to eddy out of the stadium toward the parking lot. That movement was unlikely to reverse.

"Me, neither. If Coach doesn't like it, he can get somebody else next week."

Although the faculty members who manned the booth and the gates each game were paid minimum wage, this was mostly volunteer labor. Those who normally worked were mostly hometown products who perhaps felt a stronger loyalty to the program as a result.

The aspirin Lindsey had taken and the cooler night air had banished her headache, but not her tiredness. And although she'd been raised to finish whatever task she started, closing a few minutes early wasn't going to break the bank.

"How much?"

The question brought her head around. Jace Nolan was standing in front of her window, opened wallet in hand.

At her hesitation, Shannon replied, "We don't charge after the third quarter."

Jace looked at the scoreboard and then back to Shannon. "Consider it a contribution. I'd just as soon not wait."

"I didn't mean you had to wait. You can just go in."

"You sure?"

"This isn't that much of a game."

Shannon was obviously in flirt mode. Despite her initial dislike of the detective, Lindsey had admitted he was an attractive man. Why should she be surprised her friend had reached that same conclusion?

"So what do you do when you close?"

For the first time since he'd questioned the price of admission, the focus of those dark eyes was on Lindsey. Since it was clear to which of them the question had been addressed, Shannon kept her mouth shut, leaving it up to her to answer.

"We turn in the money and go home."

"Not interested in watching the coup de grâce?"

"Not tonight."

Shannon's sneaker-clad foot made contact with the side of Lindsey's ankle. Although she, too, might have been attracted to Jace, Shannon was smart enough to have picked up on the obvious undercurrent between them. The kick had clearly said, "What the hell do you think you're doing?"

An attractive man. A single woman on the wrong side of thirty stuck in a town this size. An invitation.

To Shannon—and to anyone else in Lindsey's situation—that should spell "yes," rather than such a definite "no."

"You go on," Shannon urged her before turning to smile at Jace. "I'll take the money up to the press box."

"If you aren't interested in the game," he said, again speaking directly to Lindsey, "maybe we could get something to eat. It's been a long day, without any chance to grab dinner."

For her, too. She'd spent the couple of hours between the end of school and her duties at the game lying down while she waited for the aspirin to work its magic. Because of her headache, she hadn't eaten much lunch.

Apparently Shannon sensed the weakening of her resolve. "Friday night special at The Cove is hard to beat."

"The Cove?" Jace's gaze swung back to her.

"Out on the highway," Shannon said helpfully. "One of our better restaurants. Who am I kidding? It's the only decent food within thirty miles. And Lindsey's favorite."

"I appreciate the information. Ms. Sloan?"

Avoiding Shannon's eyes, she met Jace's instead. They were amused. And slightly challenging.

"I'm not dressed for The Cove."

"On a ballgame night?" Shannon asked. "Honey, you'll fit right in." Her tone implied, *And you damn well know it.*

"You look fine to me," Jace said.

The dialogue—the entire scenario—was so hokey, it was humiliating. And becoming more so by the second.

"Look—"

"Dinner," Jace said. "No tour guiding involved."

A reference to their conversation outside the gym this afternoon. At least Shannon had sense enough to keep her mouth shut, despite her almost palpable curiosity.

"Then…dinner."

Why the hell had she agreed? Had she lost her mind? The man wanted to prove that one of her students was a criminal.

And if that were true? Wouldn't she—and everyone else in this town—want to know?

"You sure you don't mind closing up by yourself, Ms...?"

"Anderson. Shannon Anderson. I don't mind. It's a matter of walking up the stadium steps and handing in the cash at the press box."

"You have a security escort?"

"Uh... Not in Randolph," Shannon said with a laugh. "Everybody in the stadium knows what we're doing. Believe me, nobody's gonna try to make off with the money."

"Then if you're ready, Ms. Sloan."

"Lindsey." Again she wondered if she'd lost her mind.

"Lindsey."

Sitcom dialogue. She looked at Shannon, daring her to laugh at the silliness of it. Surprisingly, her friend was looking exceptionally pleased with herself, but not amused.

"I'll see you Monday," Lindsey said to her.

"Y'all have fun."

God, could this possibly get any worse? Lindsey stepped to the back of the booth and opened the door. She stood there a moment, trying to control her sense of unreality.

"Ready?" Jace had walked around to retrieve her.

"It doesn't have to be The Cove. There are a couple of places that are nearer."

"In a hurry to get home?"

She wasn't. She was just a little out of her element.

Which had nothing to do with the restaurant and everything to do with the man she was going there with. The man half the town would see her with, which would inevitably create more gossip. And after the pep rally today...

"Compared to most places around here, The Cove is expensive. And likely to be crowded."

"Then maybe if we left now..."

Jace's suggestion was logical. To keep resisting would only make her appear more immature than she did already.

"My car's here."

"We can pick it up after we eat."

On the way to where? she wondered. That had sounded as if dinner wasn't the only thing he had in mind.

"Ready?" Once more Jace took her elbow, guiding her toward the parking lot. It was beginning to be a habit. One she discovered she was in no hurry to have him break.

"Jace. That's an unusual name," Lindsey said. "I don't think I've ever heard it before."

Since he'd made this same explanation dozens of times, Jace didn't even have to think about what to say. "Probably because my family made it up."

They were headed out of the restaurant, where the food had been as good as advertised. Not his preferred style of cuisine, but definitely eatable. Which was more than he could say about some of the meals he'd had down here.

"Made it up?"

"My great-grandfather was James Christian Nolan. He was called James. My grandfather was James Christian Nolan, the second. Jimmy. They called my dad Trey, because he was the third. When I came along, somebody got the bright idea of calling me J.C., which became Jacey when I was a toddler. At some point, that got shortened to Jace. By the time I started to school, I thought that *was* my name."

"Sounds like a story someone around here might tell."

"What does that mean?" he asked opening the car door for her. He waited as she slid into the passenger seat.

"The whole name thing. We're big on family down here. It just… I don't know. It sounded…Southern."

"Yeah. Well, I don't think my family would qualify as

Southern by any stretch, but for what it's worth, we're big on family, too." He returned her smile, but the ease they'd found over the meal—talking about everything from football to food—seemed to have evaporated into the same sense of awkwardness that had marred the drive over from the stadium.

Jace closed the door and walked around the front of the car, trying to decide if it was worth doing what he'd planned. Probably better to play it by ear and see how she reacted.

He opened the driver's side door and slid in behind the wheel. As he inserted the key into the ignition, Lindsey turned to look at him. He met her eyes, his questioning.

"Thank you for dinner."

"My pleasure." It had been, Jace acknowledged.

Once the initial awkwardness had dissipated, he'd found her easy to talk to. Of course, he'd avoided the subject he knew would set off all her defense mechanisms. That wasn't something he could continue to do, not if he was going to get any of the information he believed Lindsey Sloan could provide. If she wanted to.

Decision made, he put the car into reverse. When he reached the highway, instead of turning back the way they'd come, he headed in the opposite direction. As if on cue, Lindsey offered the protest he'd been expecting.

"This isn't the way to the stadium."

She didn't sound alarmed. It was more as if she thought that he, as a newcomer, might be confused about the location.

"I wanted to show you something."

"Look—"

"Relax. Your virtue's safe with me."

He was no longer entirely sure of that. His original intent in asking to meet Ms. Sloan that day had been strictly business. He'd never expected to be attracted to a teacher.

Auburn hair should mean at least a few freckles. Instead,

flawless ivory skin overlay a classically beautiful bone structure. The copper-colored eyes were open and direct.

So why the hell was she available on a Friday night? And,
judging by her friend's eagerness to push her to come with
him tonight, most other nights as well?

"It's been a long week," she said, her voice no longer
relaxed. "I enjoyed dinner, but I'd really appreciate it if you'd
take me back to my car."

"This won't take five minutes. We're almost there."

He knew that as soon as he turned off the highway and
onto the two-lane road, she'd recognize their destination. He
could imagine her reaction.

Still, this had been the purpose of the entire exercise. He
wasn't about to let the fact that the prelude leading up to the
main event had been enjoyable keep him from doing his job.

She didn't bother to argue, which he also liked. In his experience, it was a rare woman who knew when to keep her
mouth shut. The silence lasted exactly as long as he'd anticipated it would.

"I've seen the church," she said flatly.

"I'm sure everyone around here has. I just need to check
on something."

"If this is intended to make me more willing to concede
the possibility—"

"It doesn't matter to me whether you believe what I told
you or not. Your opinion isn't going to change the course of
the investigation."

She turned her head away, looking rigidly out the side
window as he pulled into the unpaved area in front of the ruin.
He couldn't tell if she was studying the burned-out shell or
if she simply couldn't stand to look at him.

He stopped the car directly in front of the church, turning
off the engine. After a moment the headlights went out.

Gradually, in the moonlight, what remained of the church was silhouetted against the lesser darkness behind it.

"Walk with me."

Without waiting for her agreement, Jace opened his door and climbed out of the car. The sound of its closing echoed through the stillness of the clearing.

He headed toward the ruin, not looking back to see if she was following. Finally—and with a sense of relief—he heard her open and then close her door. Her footsteps made no noise in the soft dirt, but when he turned his head, she was beside him, her gaze focused on the building.

After a moment, she looked up at him. "It's tragic, and I hate more than you can imagine that it happened. For the people who went to church here and for the rest of us. But I don't know anything that can help you find out who did this."

"You may not know that you know."

"I've thought a lot this week about what you said. I looked at every kid who came through my classroom and wondered. And after all that, the answer I came up with isn't any different from the one I gave you on Tuesday. I don't believe any of my kids was involved." She turned to look at the ruin again. "I don't believe any of them are capable of this kind of… I don't know. Senseless destruction."

Except Jace knew it hadn't been. It had been premeditated and deliberate and very carefully thought out.

That wasn't what the media had suggested with their spur-of-the-moment copycat theory. At that point he'd seen no reason to correct their impression.

He still didn't. He had just wanted the people involved to be aware that as far as he was concerned, this wasn't over.

"Maybe… Maybe they're through with it," she went on. "You said they were after the adrenaline rush, but maybe all the attention scared them away."

"The only thing scaring them away is irregularly spaced patrols of all the other isolated churches in the area."

"Then why don't they go somewhere else? There are plenty of places in this part of the state—"

She stopped abruptly, making it obvious she'd made one of the connections he had hoped she would. He didn't say anything, preferring to let her work it out herself.

She turned to look at him again, the perfect oval of her face revealed by the moonlight. "They have a curfew."

"And somebody who waits up for them. Maybe even somebody who checks the mileage on the car they drive."

"The fires are on the weekend because they aren't allowed out on a school night," she said, continuing to put it together. "That's why you're convinced they're students."

It wasn't the only reason, but it appeared to be enough to make her buy in to the theory that the task force had devised. Once she did, he should be able to use her to get into the heads of her students.

Just as he'd used plenty of other people to succeed at what he did. He'd misled them. Tricked them. Any cop who said he'd never done those things was a liar. They all did them on occasion because it worked. And because it served the ends they sought. The right ends. Justice.

"They're probably out there tonight," he said. "Driving around. Thinking about what they could do instead of this."

"They haven't done *anything* since the last one."

Seven weeks. Or rather seven weekends. They'd all waited, diligently patrolling any spot that was particularly vulnerable. And Lindsey was right. Nothing had happened.

"That doesn't mean they're through."

"You don't know that."

"I know about the rush. I know it's addictive."

"Is that what made you a detective? The rush?"

Maybe it had. Maybe that's what had kept him at this job when any sane person would have moved on to something else. Anything else. Instead of doing that, he'd come here—a south Alabama county as alien to him as the face of the moon.

At least he was doing something constructive with his addiction, he thought, pulling his mind away from people and places he couldn't bear to remember. All these punks were doing was destroying. And he knew in his gut, as strongly as he'd ever known anything, that whoever or whatever they were, they weren't through with their destruction.

Four

"Ms. Sloan's got a boyfriend."

The comment came out of the blue during the last seconds before the tardy bell for second period. Lindsey looked up to see who'd made it, but half the class was sniggering.

The masculine half, she realized. And the voice that had made that announcement had definitely belonged to one of them.

"Ms. *Sloan!* Have you been keeping secrets from us?"

Renee Bingham was the prototype for the American cheerleader. Blond, blue-eyed, and slightly buxom, she was also enormously popular. And one of the nicest people Lindsey had ever known. No matter where someone ranked on the school's rigidly established social ladder, Renee was friendly to them.

That same friendliness extended to her teachers, whom she was apt to treat with a familiarity that had nothing to do with disrespect. Since Lindsey was aware the girl's taste in literature ran to supermarket celebrity magazines, she knew any gossip pertaining to a teacher's love life would be irresistible.

She was grateful when the tardy bell sounded, bringing the

last few stragglers to their desks as well as giving her an excuse to ignore Renee's question. She opened her grade book, willing the telltale flush in her cheeks to subside.

"Paul Abbott."

"Here."

"Ms. Sloan, you aren't just gonna call roll and not tell us." Renee's tone was indignant, as if an injustice had been done, to her and the class.

"Tell you what, Renee?"

"About your *boyfriend.*"

"I don't have a boyfriend. And if I *did,* that would hardly be something I'd discuss with y'all."

"He's the new detective in the sheriff's office. From somewhere up north."

Lindsey was surprised that Steven Byrd had been the one to share that information. He seemed to have little use for the rumors that ran rampant in the high school—who was dating whom, which couple was breaking up, which was reconciling.

"When I first saw them together," Steven continued, his eyes shining mischievously behind his glasses, just as they had when he'd seen her and Jace that morning in the office, "I thought Ms. Sloan was in trouble with the law. Lucky for her, that wasn't what the detective was investigating."

There was a masculine chorus of "ooohs" from the back of the room in response to his slightly suggestive statement. Lindsey could feel the color rising in her cheeks again.

"That's enough." Lindsey looked down at her grade book in an attempt to gather her composure. "Leslie Arnold."

"Here. Is that the guy you were with at the game?"

"I sold tickets at the game," she said evenly. "I wasn't *with* anyone. And I'll repeat for those of you who don't seem to get it, my social life isn't any concern of yours."

By now she realized she'd bungled this. If she'd made a joke, said something clever, claimed to be smitten, they would have let it drop. Instead, she'd stupidly added fuel to the fire by trying to quash it. Then she'd fanned the flames by letting them see that she was embarrassed by their teasing.

"We're just glad to know that at your age you can still get a date." Roy McClain's comment drew laughter, still good natured, despite her mishandling of the situation.

Maybe it wasn't too late to rectify that mistake. These were her seniors. She'd taught most of them for the last two years. Their interest in her social life was misplaced, but after all that time together, it was also pretty natural.

"I'm delighted to have relieved your mind about that concern, Roy. You may now consider yourself free to worry about your *own* social life." The laughter that greeted her response told her she'd struck the right note. Maybe one that could carry them safely into today's lesson. "Can we *now* concentrate on *Beowulf* rather than me?"

"Is he cute?" Renee's lips were slightly parted as she looked up at Lindsey from the front row, blue eyes rapt. And she wasn't referring to the hero of the Anglo-Saxon epic.

"As a little ole bug," Charlie Higginbotham drawled. Coming out of the mouth of the biggest defensive lineman on the football team, the phrase provoked more laughter.

"I don't think cute is the right word." Although Lindsey had pointedly looked down at Renee as she answered, there was another outbreak of catcalls from the guys. "But we're not going to spend class time discussing what might be."

"Ms. Sloan, are you sure you want to date some Yankee?" Charlie asked. "Aren't there enough good ole Alabama rednecks around here to keep you occupied?"

"Y'all were the ones worrying about my social life. I was perfectly content with it. I still am, by the way. So…with your very kind permission, ladies…" She nodded toward Renee. "*And* gentlemen…" she said to Charlie, who laughed. "I'd like to finish the roll. You should know by now you can only distract me so long before I crack the whip again."

"He's into that, is he?" Justin Carr's question had not been asked in the same teasing tone of the rest.

Even the other students seemed to sense the difference. The mood in the room changed immediately.

One of the brightest kids in her program, Justin had never quite fit in. An Army brat, he must have attended a dozen schools before his father retired here to be near the facilities at Fort Rucker. Justin was respected for his intellect, but he was not well-liked.

"The roll," Lindsey repeated softly, picking up where she'd left off. Thanks to the inappropriateness of Justin's remark, this time she was allowed to finish.

Even the discussion of the section of the epic they'd been assigned to read last night went well, although she was aware the entire time that Justin's eyes were fastened on her face. She ignored him, as she'd ignored his comment, concentrating instead on the elements of the heroic poem she knew would appeal to her teenage audience. Still, she was relieved when the bell rang.

As the other students left the room, Renee approached the lectern. "So how long have you been dating this detective?"

"I'm not. It's nothing, Renee. Really. He invited me to get something to eat after the ball game. There's no romance, I swear to you."

"So…what is he?"

"What?"

"You said cute wasn't the right word. What is?"

"I'd say the right term is…an *acquaintance*." Lindsey emphasized the last word pointedly.

"Ms. *Sloan!*"

"Go to class, Renee, before you're tardy again."

"I'm just next door. What's his name?"

"James Nolan."

"James. Oh, that's nice. Don't you think so?"

"Yes, I do."

"Is *he?*"

"I don't know yet." She had thought he was until he'd taken her by the church. In fairness, he'd had a point to make in doing that. One that had been successfully driven home. "Honestly, Renee, you need to move on. Nothing to see here," she said, repeating the familiar *Star Wars* phrase her students used to stop discussion.

In a further attempt to end the conversation, Lindsey turned, laying the senior anthology on the corner of her desk. Next period she would have her juniors. The atmosphere would not be as relaxed as it had been this period. Even if any of them had heard about her evening with Jace, they probably wouldn't have nerve enough to tease her about it.

"When are you going out with him again?"

She wasn't sure whether Renee was unwilling to take the hint or whether she honestly didn't realize she was being too personal. "He hasn't asked me."

"But you'd go if he did, wouldn't you?"

"Do I grill you about who *you're* dating, Renee?"

"No, but if you did, I'd tell you. I even tell my mom."

Lindsey laughed at the confession, provoking an answering giggle from the girl. "There isn't much to tell with this one. We went out to eat. And he didn't ask me out again."

"Did you kiss him?"

"*Renee.*"

"But he tried, didn't he. That's a good sign."

"Oh, *please*. Surely you've got something besides this to talk about."

"Nope. I can't think of a thing."

"Well, then bless your heart. I hope you find a more interesting subject than my love life during next period."

"In Ms. Miller's class? I don't think so." Renee laughed again.

Agnes Miller had taught calculus for the last thirty years. Having been her student, Lindsey knew Renee was right.

"Well, go try," she ordered, moving away from the lectern to retrieve the eleventh grade lit book from the stack on her desk. Her juniors were beginning to filter into the room, and she didn't want the discussion to carry over.

"Okay, I'm going," Renee said, "but I'm warning you, I'm not done with this. I've just got a couple of problems to finish before the bell rings."

Which she intended to copy from someone else. Right now, if it got rid of her, that was okay with Lindsey.

One of the students coming in approached her desk, giving her the opportunity to turn her attention from Renee. Lindsey was conscious when the cheerleader finally left.

Two classes down and two to go. If they were all like the last one, this was going to be a very long day.

It had taken him until lunchtime to be able to think through the implications. Anger and anxiety had delayed his reaching any kind of rational conclusion, but when he had finally fought through the distraction they represented, he knew the one he'd arrived at was correct.

Ms. Sloan was being used. Any single woman her age was vulnerable to flattery and masculine attention. And he had no doubt the detective was laying it on heavy in hopes she'd help him finger students she believed would be capable of setting the fires.

Which was a pretty shrewd move on Nolan's part, the boy acknowledged. There were few people here who would know the kids smart enough to pull those off better than the gifted coordinator did. Maybe Ms. Anderson, but she didn't seem the type to be manipulated.

And that was what Nolan was doing. Manipulating Ms. Sloan to his advantage.

His mouth tightened as he pushed his books into his locker and fished out the notebook he'd need for his next class. Maybe it was time to let both of them know that nobody was going to roll over and play dead because some outsider thought he'd found a slick way to get inside information. His lips relaxed into a slight smile at the unintended irony of the phrase he'd just used.

He wasn't stupid enough to take Nolan on straight up. He wouldn't catch someone with the cop's level of training and experience off guard. Ms. Sloan, on the other hand…

If he was wrong—if the detective wasn't playing her for a sucker—then maybe Nolan would back off out of concern for her safety. And if he was right about what was going on, then he had no doubt she'd get the message. After all, she was too intelligent not to.

"So how was it?"

Shannon settled onto the couch opposite the one Lindsey was sitting on. The counselor slipped her shoes off and put her feet up on the coffee table between them.

"Typical Monday. Half of them asleep. Half revved up just to be here." That enthusiasm was not because of the opportunity to learn, but because they were again with their peers, feeding off the energy produced by all those hormones.

"Oh, for God's sake, Lindsey. I didn't mean *today*." Shannon's voice was rich with disgust.

She meant Friday night. She meant Jace Nolan. There was a good ten-years difference in Shannon's and Renee's ages, but her friend's curiosity was no less intense than her student's.

"We went to The Cove. We talked over dinner. Then he took me home."

"That's *it?*" Shannon looked at her over the rim of her cup, waiting for an answer before she took a sip.

"What did you expect?"

"I dunno. *Something.* Something besides that."

"Well, that's what happened."

"You like him?"

"I don't *know* him. He seemed pleasant enough. He can carry on a conversation." Lindsey shrugged.

"You seem just a little too blasé about this whole thing. I take that as a good sign."

"Of what?"

"Of interest. If you *weren't* interested, you'd be telling me what was wrong with him. You aren't, so I figure there must be a degree of interest there."

Lindsey shook her head, eyes focused on her cup. "There's nothing to tell. Nothing happened. That's it."

"End of story."

"Maybe."

"He ask you out again?"

Déjà vu all over again. Shannon seemed to be channeling cheerleaders.

"Nope."

"Shit."

Lindsey laughed. "Hey, I managed to survive life pre-Jace Nolan. I'll survive post-Jace Nolan, too."

"What kind of name is that? Jace."

"He was J.C. as a kid. Some kind of family thing. It got shortened to Jace." Lindsey shrugged again.

"He tell you all that?"

"I asked about his name."

"Polite conversation 101."

"Something like that."

"Anything else interesting?"

"We talked about the fires."

"He tell you who it is they suspect?"

"I told you. My kids. I swear, Shannon, I've thought about everybody in my program since he told me that, and I just don't see it. I can't see any of them being involved in setting fire to those churches. Most of them grew up attending ones very much like those. Burning any church would be an act of blasphemy to them. And they're too smart, for another thing. They have too much at stake to risk it all on something so mindlessly stupid, for another.

"My juniors and seniors have worked hard to raise their test scores. The seniors are already filling out college applications *and* applying for scholarships. They've taken every AP class we offer. Why would they take a chance on blowing all that to burn a couple of tiny black churches? These kids didn't grow up during the Jim Crow years."

"That doesn't mean they don't know about them. Or that they couldn't be racist."

It didn't, of course. There was still the occasional undercurrent of black/white tension in the school, despite forty years of integration.

"Do *you* think that's why those churches were burned?" Lindsey asked. "Race? You think they were hate crimes?"

Although most of the staff would have jumped to deny the possibility, Shannon seemed to be thinking about the question.

Finally she shook her head. "I don't. I didn't from the beginning. I don't think it has one thing to do with those congregations being black. Except maybe they knew the act would get more attention."

"More bang for the buck."

"I hadn't thought about it that way, but… Yeah. More exposure. More distress."

"More danger," Lindsey said, remembering Jace's comment about thrill seekers.

"More *danger?*"

"A higher-profile crime. More people want them caught and are willing to work to bring that about. It ups the odds they *will* be caught. If they'd vandalized a car or burned a vacant house, do you think someone like Jace Nolan would have been assigned to the case?"

"Do *you?*"

Lindsey shook her head. "He thinks he's put a stop to that particular brand of mischief."

She hesitated, unsure she wanted to articulate the conclusion she'd come to some time in the middle of a nearly sleepless Friday night. But this was Shannon. And there were few secrets between them.

Like how attracted you are to Jace Nolan?

"He says they're going to find something else to do," she went on. "Something that will give them that same rush. *That* scares me."

"Because you think he may be right?" Shannon asked. "About it being your kids, I mean."

"It terrifies me that he might be. He seems so damn certain."

"Then in all likelihood, he knows something he hasn't told you."

"Like what?"

"Something that brought him straight to you."

"I've thought about this for almost a week. I still can't fathom any of them being involved."

"*None* of them?"

"What does that mean?"

Shannon shrugged. "I guess I just don't believe they're all as lily-white and innocent as you do."

"Pun intended?" Lindsey's sarcasm didn't faze her friend.

"Maybe."

"Who? If you've decided it's possible, then you have to have thought about who might be involved."

Shannon shook her head.

"Oh, for God's sake, Shannon, you can't say something like that and then clam up. Who do you believe would be capable of doing that?"

"If I tell you, you'll never think about that person again without remembering my suspicion. That's like accusing them. I don't have any reason to do that. It's just…" She shook her head again. "I don't know. Gut reaction."

"Female intuition," Lindsey mocked.

"Maybe. *Whatever* I'm feeling is academic. I know what's at stake. So I'm not going to tell you. Or Nolan. Or anybody else. As your friend, I'll just tell you that you shouldn't completely discount what he's told you."

"Has Dave talked to you?" That seemed to be the only explanation for Shannon's willingness to embrace the detective's theory. That she knew more than Lindsey.

"*Dave?* No. What made you think that?" There was the slightest bit of defensiveness in Shannon's answer.

"I thought maybe the two of you had discussed possible suspects."

"The only person I've talked to about this is you. And you're the only one I *will* talk to about it."

"Unless the police ask your opinion."

"Even if they did, I've told you how I feel. I would never want to accuse someone—especially a kid—based on a hunch that he *might* be capable of doing something."

"So it *is* a he?" Just as the FBI profile had indicated.

"I would think that's a given. Arson doesn't seem like the kind of thing a girl would do."

It didn't, Lindsey admitted. "It also doesn't seem like the kind of thing any of my kids would do."

Shannon shrugged, her expression saying as clearly as the gesture that she didn't necessarily agree. For the first time in Lindsey's memory the silence between them wasn't relaxed.

"Well," Shannon said, finally breaking it, "I've got a ton of stuff to do to get ready for PTA tomorrow night and the usual flood of parents we won't see the rest of the year."

"You're not complaining about that, I hope."

It was the kind of remark that would have normally provoked Shannon's ready laugh. Instead, as the counselor got to her feet, her expression was serious.

"I shouldn't have to tell you this, but...don't be too trusting. You see them an hour a day. And some of them are adept at hiding whatever they're thinking or doing during the other twenty-three."

"You know, that sounds like a warning."

"It's meant to be. You said that Nolan believes they'll find something else to give them the rush he's cheated them out of. He's probably right. And frankly, I don't even want to imagine what that might be."

Five

The turnout for the PTA meeting and the Open House following it had been one of the largest Lindsey could remember. The main attraction was the new field house, of course, which brought in people who hadn't darkened the door of the school as long as their kids had been in attendance.

As usual, most of her tenth grade parents showed up and almost half of the upper class parents as well. Since many were accompanied by their children, she'd found herself thinking about the kinds of homes the kids Nolan was accusing of arson came from. Homes very much like the one where she'd grown up—loving, religious, with intact families. Because of that, she was still having a hard time reconciling the crime with the so-called criminals.

She inserted the key into the lock on her front door and turned it. As the door swung open, the interior of the house appeared totally dark. She would have sworn she'd left the kitchen light burning, but in her hurry to get back to the school, she must have forgotten.

The porch light illuminated almost half of the foyer. She stepped inside, setting her purse beside her tote bag on the hall table. She reached for the switch, but her hand hesitated halfway there. The familiar scent of home had been replaced by something strange. Chemical. Unpleasant.

She breathed through her nostrils, attempting to identify the smell. Something she should recognize, but, perhaps due to its unexpectedness in this environment, didn't.

Finally she flicked the switch upward, her eyes narrowing against the resulting influx of light. The hall appeared exactly as she'd left it more than four hours before.

Her gaze swept the adjacent living room, but nothing there seemed different, either. Reassured, she secured the lock and the dead bolt on the front door before she slipped the end of the safety chain into its slot.

When she turned back, she raised her chin, slowly drawing air in through her nose again. The odor seemed less distinct than when she'd opened the door. Either the smell was fading or she was becoming accustomed to it. Still, she hovered in the hall, strangely reluctant to go farther into her own house. That scent, along with the absence of light—

Only with the juxtaposition of the two did she realize what must have happened. She knew from school that when a fluorescent bulb failed, its dying was accompanied by a distinctively unpleasant smell.

Relieved to have arrived at an explanation for both, she crossed the foyer and headed toward the kitchen. Although she didn't have a replacement bulb on hand, she could at least verify that the old one had gone bad.

When she reached the entrance, she could see moonlight shining through the glass half of the back door. She normally pulled the café curtains across it at night, but that was something else she must have forgotten.

Without bothering to test the fluorescent, which had been her intent in coming here, she walked across the pale tile, her heels echoing with every step, and drew the fabric over the glass. Then, through force of habit, she checked the lock and the dead bolt. Both were secure.

She turned, the burned-out bulb almost forgotten now that her eyes had adjusted to the darkness. The familiarity of the room was reassuring. A little exasperated with her initial unease, she started back across the tile.

Although she'd brought papers home this afternoon, she decided she was too tired to mark them. All she wanted to do was crawl into bed and go to sleep. She'd already taken a shower before she'd dressed for the meeting. She wasn't going to take another. At least not tonight.

She turned off the light in the front foyer and then, in the darkened house, moved down the hallway to the bathroom doorway. She reached inside the small room, flicking the switch up. She resisted the urge to put away the few items of makeup she'd left out on the counter as she'd gotten ready. Wasted effort since she'd use them again in the morning.

She continued down the hall to her room. Without turning on the overhead, she slipped off her heels and carried them to the closet. The carpet seemed to massage her tired feet.

She'd hung the hangers for her suit and the silk shell she was wearing over the top of the door. She took them down, dropped her shoes inside, and then stripped down to her underwear, carefully re-hanging each item as she took it off.

Finally, she took out a nightgown and carried it with her to the bathroom. As she entered the room, she again caught a whiff of something that didn't belong.

Whatever it was, it was so faint she forgot about it as she walked over to the counter. She leaned forward, peering into the mirror. Although her skin had always been one of her best features, especially for someone with her coloring, it looked sallow. Tiny lines had begun to form at the corners of her eyes, and the delicate area beneath them was dark.

Too many nighttime hours spent thinking about what Jace Nolan had told her. And a few spent thinking about Jace Nolan himself. Which was sad. And a little desperate.

No wonder Shannon and her students were interested in pairing her up with him. The words "last chance" flickered through her mind before she ruthlessly denied them a place.

She straightened, reaching behind her back to unfasten her bra and lay it on the counter. She took off her panty hose, standing on one foot and then the other, and put them into one basin of the double lavatory. She set the stopper before she turned on the water and added a squirt of shampoo.

Only then did she push her panties down over her hips and thighs, allowing them to fall to the floor. She scooped them up, placing them on top of the discarded bra.

After she'd slipped on her nightgown, she used baby oil and tissues to remove her makeup and then brushed her teeth. As she was turning to go back to the bedroom, the small pile of underwear caught her eye.

She grabbed the panties and bra in one hand, carrying them over to the wicker clothes hamper. More decorative than utilitarian, it held less than a week's worth of laundry.

Intending to lift the lid with her left hand and toss the clothes she was holding in, she bent over the basket. Again that hint of something unpleasant assailed her nostrils.

Although it was definitely stronger over here, the smell was still faint. Not chemical, she thought, as her fingers grasped the edge of the top. This was something earthy. Slightly rank. Like mushrooms. Or decay.

She had already begun to raise the lid of the hamper when she became aware of the sound inside. A sizzle, like bacon frying or like someone rustling papers—

Rattles. By the time her brain had put it together, it was too late to stop the muscle contraction in her arm, which had continued to lift the lid.

The split second of realization *had* been enough, however, to cause her to jerk her upper body backward, allowing the top to fall as the body of a snake exploded out of the hamper.

Stumbling backwards, she felt rather than saw it strike. Too quick to be seen by the naked eye, the power of its momentum seemed to literally disturb the air between them.

Despite the lid she'd dropped on top of it, the rattler's ugly, triangular-shaped head had easily cleared the top of the basket. Before she could think of a way to prevent it, the rest of the squat, powerful body trailed over the rim.

She knew enough about snakes to know this one didn't have to be coiled to try for her again. And that the range of its strike could be as much as half its length. Despite the panic clawing at her chest, she continued to put distance between the rattlesnake and her bare feet and legs.

By now it had flowed down onto the tile. As Lindsey backpedaled, it began to re-coil. Head now erect, the snake's cold, black eyes seemed to fasten on its prey. At the same time, the tail lifted and began to tremble, its ominous warning echoing off all the hard surfaces of the bathroom.

Unable to tear her eyes away from the deadly, seductive movement, Lindsey located the edge of the bathroom door with a hand that shook. She stepped out into the hall, pulling the door with her so that it slammed shut before the snake could make another attempt to reach its warm-blooded target.

The episode had occupied only seconds. One of those "life flashing before your eyes" moments, when you knew with absolute certainty you were going to die.

Despite the seeming safety of the wooden barrier between her and the snake, Lindsey's breath sawed in and out through her open mouth. Somehow she had managed to escape. And, as incredible as it seemed, without being bitten.

Before she had time to fully relish what a miracle that was, her eyes focused on the crack of light beneath the door. A gap big enough for the rattler to slither under?

She had no idea how wide that would need to be. But she couldn't take a chance.

The only thing worse than knowing there was a venomous snake inside her house was knowing that and *not* knowing where it was. If she followed her instincts to put more distance and more doors between them, and the rattler got out of the bathroom, they might never find it.

And she would never again spend another night here.

Realizing she still held the wadded underwear in her hand, she bent and began gingerly to stuff them into the crack under the door. It quickly became apparent that was not enough fabric to fill its length. Even if it had been, those wisps of nylon didn't seem substantial enough to create a strong enough obstruction if the snake tried to push through.

There was nothing else close enough that she could reach it without taking her eyes off the ribbon of light at the bottom of the door. She fought a renewed sense of panic as she tried to figure out what she could use to keep the rattler trapped in the bathroom.

The comforter on her bed would be both large enough and heavy enough to block the opening. To get it, she'd have to leave the hallway. Could the snake get out in the few seconds it would take to retrieve the spread and bring it back here?

That was a risk she would have to take. Otherwise, she might still be out here in the dark hall when she discovered that there *was* room enough for him to work his way through that crack. That possibility was enough to end her paralysis.

She bolted for the bedroom, throwing the light switch at

the end of the hall as well as the one in her room. She grabbed the comforter and sprinted back, her eyes searching the gleaming hardwood floor in front of her as she ran, looking for a darker streak than those revealed by the grain of the wood. *One that moved.*

When she reached the bathroom door, she threw the spread down in front of it. Then, on her hands and knees, she crammed the thick, quilted material into the crack.

Even when she'd blocked the last bit of light escaping from the bathroom, she wasn't convinced she'd created a sturdy enough barrier to keep the snake confined. Once more she made the trip to her bedroom.

As her bare feet made contact with the carpet, she had a flashback to the first time she'd entered this room tonight. Her feet had been bare then, too, except for her hose. And she hadn't turned on the overhead light.

What if the snake had been in here, rather than in the hamper? What if she'd stepped on it in the darkness? Even as she looked for something to reinforce her makeshift barricade, she shivered at the thought.

And then she froze at the next one. Her rational mind had, in the last few minutes, given way to the far more primitive part of her brain, the one that viewed the creature in her bathroom with the same primordial fear her ancestors had.

Admittedly, this was snake country. One Alabama city held a rattlesnake roundup each year, capturing hundreds from among the scrub. It was certainly not unheard of for snakes to get inside a house. *But inside a closed hamper?*

There could be only one explanation for that. One she didn't want to think about.

Someone had *put* the rattlesnake inside that basket, where, angered by the confinement, it had waited until she'd come into the bathroom. Highly sensitive to the body heat of prey, it had been coiling to strike even while she'd hesitated, her hand on the lid of the hamper, trying to identify what she smelled.

And she'd been right about that, too. It had been something far more alien than a burned-out fluorescent bulb.

In spite of not wanting to take the next step in this chain of logic, its conclusion was already inside her head, impossible to deny. If someone *had* put a snake in her laundry hamper, then it was possible the one she had trapped in the bathroom wasn't the only rattler inside her house.

As her terrified gaze swept the cream-colored carpet surrounding her, she knew that if there were others they'd be hidden, as the first had been.

In the drawer she'd taken her nightgown from? In the closet where she'd hung up her clothes and put her shoes? Or somewhere she would never think to look until it was too late?

She had to get out of here until somebody could conduct a thorough search of the entire place. *Somebody...*

Who the hell did you get to search your house for snakes? Whoever it would be, she owed it to them to complete the containment of the one whose location she did know.

Hurrying as much as her growing paranoia would allow, she began to take books off her bookshelf, expecting another triangular-shaped head to dart out of the space left by each one she removed. Then, arms full of the heaviest volumes the shelf had contained, she returned to the bathroom door and laid them end-to-end on top of the comforter.

With the placement of the last book, she stepped back to check once more for any light seeping underneath the door. It would have been easier to do that with the hall fixture turned off, as it had been before, but she couldn't bring herself to throw the switch.

When she was satisfied with the barrier she'd con-
structed, the need to get out of the house was irresistible.
Her cell was in her purse, which she'd left on the front hall
table. She'd go out that way, picking it up as she went
through the foyer.

She turned on lights in front of her as she ran, eyes again
searching her path. She grabbed her bag off the table, slinging
the strap over her shoulder to free her hands so she could deal
with the locks.

Only when the door was open, and the heavy heat of the
September night rushed into the coolness of the house's
interior, did she think about the danger of stepping out into
the darkness barefoot. It wasn't that she hadn't done that
before—to get the weekend paper or to cut off the sprinkler.
But all that had been before she'd had a firsthand experience
with something whose deadliness she'd recognized—and
taken for granted—all her life.

She put on the porch lights as well as the spotlights on the
corners of the house. And then she stepped outside, closing
the door behind her.

The porch tiles were cool and smooth under the soles of
her bare feet, the brick steps below them incredibly rough in
contrast. Once she reached the sidewalk, she turned to look
back at the front of her home.

For a moment she wondered if she would ever again feel
the same way about it as she had before tonight. That it was
a sanctuary. Somewhere safe. Security from the threats of the
outside world.

She shook her head at the disconnect those words evoked,
given what she'd just gone through. In spite of her escape,
she knew this wasn't over.

Her first impulse was to call her dad. He would come, of
course, bringing one of the guns he kept locked in the tall,

glass-fronted case in the hall. Armed with that, he would open the door and step into her bathroom—

She shook her head again, acknowledging that as much as she wanted him here, she wasn't going to allow him to do that. Not at his age.

This wasn't his job. She wasn't sure whose job it was. But right now, she didn't much care.

At least she knew where to begin finding that out. She reached inside her purse and dug out her phone. She flipped the case open and, for the first time in her life, dialed 9-1-1.

Six

It had taken only minutes for a county cruiser to respond to her call. The deputies had listened to her story and then radioed its details to the sheriff's office.

After almost a half hour's wait, a hard-bitten, older man had shown up. He wasn't wearing a uniform, but he had come equipped with a forked metal pole and a heavy vinyl bag.

Without so much as an introduction, he and the two deputies had disappeared inside. From then until now, maybe an hour later, no one had bothered to tell her anything about what they were doing or what they'd found.

In this close-knit neighborhood, it hadn't taken long for a couple of neighbors to join her on the front lawn. Especially since the cruiser was still parked along the curb. Both had expressed disbelief at her assertion that someone must have put the snake into her hamper.

"That thing probably just crawled in there while you were at PTA," Betty Savage had said.

"And closed the lid behind it?"

"Lindsey, you don't honestly believe somebody broke

into your house and put a snake in your clothes basket, do you? Who in the world would *do* somethin' like that?"

"Maybe it was in some gardening clothes you brought in out of the yard," Milt Trump suggested. "You just didn't see it."

Faced with their disbelief, Lindsey hadn't continued to argue. Maybe their determination to deny what she was telling them was based on an unconscious realization of how much believing her might change their view of this neighborhood.

That was okay with her. She no longer had any doubt what had happened tonight. And now, after more than an hour of having nothing to do but think, she also had an idea of why.

The three of them turned when a second police cruiser pulled into the drive, lightbar flashing. When Shannon's friend Rick Carlisle climbed out from behind the wheel, Lindsey walked over to meet him.

"Heard about your snake on the scanner as I was heading home," he said. "You think somebody put it in your hamper?"

She hadn't thought about how quickly her accusation would spread when she'd made it. Still, it's what she believed had happened. And no matter how unpalatable that belief might be to anyone else, she wasn't going to back down from it.

"That rattler didn't crawl in there by itself. The basket was closed, Rick. Somebody had to put it there."

"That's a serious accusation, Linds."

"Yeah? Well, it was a 'serious' snake. A pissed-off one."

"You got an idea who might have done somethin' like that?"

"A few."

"You want to tell me?"

"I can't. Not specifically."

"What the hell does that mean?"

"I don't have a suspect, but…"

"But?"

"I think I might know what this is in relation to."

"You make somebody at school mad at you?"

"Shannon told you that Detective Nolan thinks some of my kids might have had something to do with the church fires. I think this may have something to do with that."

"Like *what?*"

"Nolan took me to dinner after the football game last week. He just wanted to pick my brain, but some of my students made a big deal out of seeing us together."

"A 'big deal'?"

"Like it was some kind of romantic relationship."

"Is it?"

"I don't even *know* the guy, Rick. After we ate, he took me out to Rohanna to show me the ruin."

Rick's mouth pursed. "To prove what?"

"I'm not sure. Maybe just to make me more aware of the destruction. He doesn't think they're through."

"Whoever burned the churches?"

"He believes that since they can't do that anymore, they'll turn to something else. Maybe this is it."

"You think this is what they're doing because we've got patrols on the churches? Putting snakes in clothes hampers."

Rick sounded amused, which she resented. "Not exactly." She hesitated to put into words what she *had* been thinking. But since she'd started this… "I think when they saw me with Nolan, they thought I'd sold them out."

"You know something about the fires you haven't told us?"

"Of course not. Until Jace said it, I'd never had any reason to think about my students in connection with them."

"Jace?"

"Nolan," she amended, catching the look in Rick's eyes. "I had dinner with the guy. During the course of the meal, we exchanged first names. It's…" She shook her head, realizing she'd gotten off track. "Look, I probably wouldn't have put any of this together except yesterday my seniors made such a thing about seeing me with him."

"Give me some names, Lindsey."

"I'm not saying there's a correlation with the kids who brought it up. They were just the ones who saw us. But you know how things like that get talked about. And then tonight… Tonight, when every kid in that high school knows where I'm going to be and when I'm going to be there, I come home and find a rattler in my laundry basket. I can't help thinking—"

The front door opened, and the deputies and the guy with the sack and the pole came out. Although she didn't want to look at the bag, Lindsey could tell there was now something inside.

As the older man headed toward his pickup, one of the deputies started across the lawn to where she and Rick were standing. On the way, the deputy nodded to her neighbors, slowing to answer a question one of them asked, before he continued toward her. Neither she nor Rick said anything as they waited for his arrival.

"I don't think you've got anything else to worry about, Ms. Sloan. We poked around in there pretty good."

Despite the cringe factor inherent in having people look through her closets and less-than-orderly cabinets, she had pleaded with them to check out the rest of the house. While that wasn't as reassuring a message as she'd hoped for, they'd probably done all they could tonight. Whether that made her comfortable enough to go back inside and crawl into bed…

"She thinks somebody put the snake into that hamper." Rick raised his brows, shrugging slightly. "I don't see how it could have got into a closed basket otherwise."

In spite of her own conviction that that's what had happened, hearing him put it into words created a sickness in the pit of Lindsey's stomach. Never in her life had anyone deliberately tried to hurt her. To think that one of her students might be involved in this made her question every day of the ten years she'd spent in the classroom.

"You see any sign of forced entry?" Rick asked.

"No, but we weren't looking for them, either. You got any idea who might have done something like that, Ms. Sloan?"

She remembered what Shannon had said. In a town like this even the suggestion of wrongdoing could taint a kid's life.

"No." She didn't dare look at Rick.

"Lindsey."

She turned her head, meeting his eyes. "I don't. I told you I don't have a name. Anything else is just speculation."

"I'd say it's a little more than that."

"Not really. Besides, what I'm willing to tell you as a friend is very different from what I'm willing to put into a police report." She looked back at the deputy who'd responded to her call. "Thanks for taking care of the snake and for searching the house. If I think of anything, I'll call you."

"You teach at the high school, don't you?"

"That's right."

"Think this could have been some of your students? Some version of the old puttin' a frog in the teacher's drawer."

She should have expected the question, once the subject was broached. "I can't think of a child I teach who'd do something like this."

She heard Rick's snort of disbelief, but she wasn't being

dishonest. Whether she bought into the idea that her students were involved in the fires or not, she couldn't believe any of them harbored this kind of animosity toward her.

And toward Jace Nolan?

"Okay, then," the deputy said, sounding relieved. "If you think of anything else or if you want us to check out the whereabouts of any of your students tonight, let us know."

She knew where her kids would *say* they'd been. Either at school or at home, while she and their parents had been at the PTA meeting. And very few of them would be able to produce any witness who could verify their presence there.

"Ma'am." The deputy touched the brim of his hat before he turned to join his partner who was waiting in the patrol car.

"You want me to come in with you?" Rick asked.

The idea was appealing, but Rick had obviously just finished his shift. He was probably tired and wanted to get home to his own bed. It must be nearly midnight by now. If the other deputies and the snake hunter hadn't found anything…

"I'll be okay. But thanks. I appreciate the offer. And thanks for coming by. I appreciate that, too."

"You call me if you need me, Linds. I mean that."

"I will." She leaned forward and hugged him.

His arms closed around her, squeezing hard. When he released her, there was an awkward silence. Despite the number of times she'd been around Rick while he and Shannon dated, she'd never thought of him as a friend. He had been tonight.

"It's gonna be okay," he told her. "We'll get to the bottom of this. I'll do some looking around on my own. Talk to a few of the kids."

"I don't want to accuse my students and then find out I was wrong. Something like that can follow a kid for the rest of his life. Shannon will tell you that."

"Maybe you and Shannon ought to be more concerned

about yourselves. That wasn't a frog in your hamper. You remember that."

She nodded, unable to dispute his assertion. She was lucky she wasn't at the emergency room being treated for snake bite. And she knew it. "Thanks again."

"I meant what I said. Call me if you need me."

"I will."

"You going to school tomorrow?"

"It's a little late to get a sub."

"If I were you, I wouldn't say anything about this. Not to the kids. Just watch how they act around you. See if you see anything that sets off alarms."

"Like what?"

"Someone who seems a little strange. They may not, but you never know. Especially if *you* act like nothing happened."

"You know how long it will take for this to get around," she said, glancing back at her neighbors who were still standing in the middle of her yard.

"Not by tomorrow morning. Just keep your radar up. Whoever did this is probably going to be looking to gauge *your* reaction. Maybe you can tell which kid that is."

She nodded, even though she wasn't convinced she'd be able to tell anything by the way her kids acted. Between hormones and football, anything approaching normal was a crapshoot.

"You want me to let Nolan know?"

Rick's question caught her off guard. It was logical that he'd want to tell the guy in charge of the church fire investigation that she was wondering if this were related.

"Do what you think is best," she said finally. Jace had a right to know. And he was bound to find out anyway.

Was letting Rick tell him the coward's way out? Maybe. But right now she didn't want to have to face Jace and confess that she was wondering if he'd been right. Let Rick convey her doubts. In the meantime, she needed to try to get some sleep and get ready for tomorrow.

"You gonna be okay?"

Rick's question brought her eyes up. "Of course," she said with more conviction than she felt.

And if she wasn't, she would deal with it in private.

Although she'd resisted the impulse to pack a bag and spend the remainder of the night at her parents' house, she hadn't been able to just crawl into bed and go back to sleep.

She'd settled down in the den instead, the light beside her recliner on so she could see most of the room. And if she occasionally thought she caught motion in one of its shadowed corners, that was only to be expected.

She had always functioned okay in college after pulling an all-nighter. She'd be all right at school. Then if she still felt that she couldn't sleep here tomorrow night—

The doorbell interrupted the endless cycle of trying to deal with this. She looked down at her watch and found it was almost two. If they thought she was going to be stupid enough to open the door after what they'd done—

The bell rang again, strident and demanding.

Maybe the deputies had come back. Maybe they'd already discovered something. As appealing as that thought was, she was still reluctant to face anyone right now.

When the bell rang once more, she righted the recliner, slipping her feet into her shoes. As she headed toward the front door, she turned on the lights in her path.

"Who is it?"

"It's Jace. Let me in."

She wasn't prepared to deal with him right now. That's why she'd agreed to let Rick tell him what had happened.

"Lindsey? Open the damn door."

The air of command she'd previously classified as arrogant was suddenly appealing. Jace sounded furious. As if he were prepared to kick someone's ass. And right now, that was exactly how she needed him to feel.

She slipped the chain out of the slot, then threw the deadbolt and turned the handle. The porch light verified her initial impression. Jace *was* furious.

"May I come in?"

"Of course." She stepped back, allowing him to enter. Before she turned to face him, she secured the locks on the door. The process not only occupied her trembling hands, but it gave her a moment to get her act together.

When she'd seen him standing outside, she had wanted to throw herself into his arms. It was a feeling that made no sense. If anything, she should be angry at him for putting her in this situation. If he hadn't singled her out, both at school and at the game…

Taking a steadying breath, she turned to face him. It was the first time she'd seen him in casual clothes.

The black T-shirt emphasized the muscles of his chest and upper arms, which had up until now been camouflaged by the suits he normally wore. The worn material of his faded jeans was almost as revealing as the knit shirt. And the five-o'clock shadow she'd noticed Friday night was much darker now, giving him a hard, almost sinister appearance.

"What happened?" he demanded.

Without any hesitation, she told him what she believed. "Somebody put a rattlesnake in my clothes hamper."

"Somebody?"

She'd already been through this with the neighbors and the deputy. As convenient as it might be to accept the theory that the snake had enclosed itself in that basket, the explanation didn't fly. And she was tired of trying to convince people who should know better why it wouldn't.

"Somebody," she repeated. "They came into my house while I was at PTA and dumped a snake where they knew I'd find it."

"Any signs of forced entry?"

"No, but I found a window in the study that wasn't locked. They may have used that."

"So how could they be sure you'd open the hamper?"

"Chances were good I was going to undress tonight."

"You always put your clothes in the hamper."

"Of course."

There was a visible relaxation of his tension. "Most people don't, you know."

"Don't put their dirty clothes in the laundry?"

"The snake might have died of old age at my place."

"Anybody who knows me—"

"Knew full well you'd open that hamper tonight."

She nodded and then realized she'd made his point.

"You want to show me?"

"The hamper?"

"Eventually. The window first."

"All right."

She moved past him, leading the way toward the back of the house. When she'd bought the place, she'd turned one of the two generous-size bedrooms into an office, which was where she'd discovered the unlocked window. It was one of the few that hadn't been painted shut.

When she'd worked in there last spring, she had opened the window and turned on the ceiling fan, allowing it to pull in the scent of honeysuckle along with the cooler night air. It had been too hot and humid to do that this summer, of course, and although she found it hard to believe the window had been unlocked for months, she couldn't deny the possibility.

"In here."

Jace stood in the doorway of the room she'd indicated, a hand on either side of the frame. "They dust for prints?"

"I didn't find this was unlocked until after they'd left."

He walked across the room, looking intently at the carpet, which, chosen for its tight weave and durability, didn't show footprints. Then he leaned forward, making an inspection of the sill. "I'll get someone out here."

"What for?"

"To dust for prints."

"Does it have to be tonight?"

He turned, eyes examining her face. "Were you asleep?"

"No."

"Why not?"

She laughed. "Call it residual snake phobia."

"You don't like them."

"No better and no less than the average person."

"Yeah? They give me the creeps."

His honesty surprised her. Most men she knew, even if they felt that way, would have been reluctant to admit it.

"He strike at you?"

She nodded, crossing her arms over her body as she remembered the near miss.

"So how come he didn't hit you?"

"I don't know. I heard him. But first..."

"What?" he asked when she hesitated.

"I remembered something my grandmother told me when I was a little girl."

"Your *grandmother?*"

"We used to pick blackberries every summer when we went to visit her. Snakes love to hide in the vines. They stink—like goats, my grandmother told us—and that if we ever smelled that, we should run."

"Goats?"

She shook her head. "I don't know what goats smell like. This was…rank. Unpleasant. I smelled it when I leaned over the hamper. Actually, I smelled it when I came into the bathroom, but I didn't know what it was. Not until I heard the rattle. By that time…" She shivered, the image of that lethal, arrow-shaped head shooting out of the basket in her mind again. "In the middle of lifting the top off the basket, I just suddenly knew what was inside. I jumped back and let go of the lid. It fell on the snake. I don't know whether that distracted him or whether he wasn't long enough to get to me. And I didn't stop to figure it out."

"At least he warned you."

"I wondered if that was deliberate."

"On the part of the snake?" Again, there was that hint of amusement in his voice.

She found she didn't mind it, even if it was at her expense. "On the part of whoever put it there."

"You think…they didn't intend for you to get bitten."

"Wishful thinking?"

"Maybe. If this was a prank, it was a dangerous one. And they went to a lot of trouble to carry it off."

"I don't think it was a prank."

"Yeah? Neither do I. For what it's worth."

"My kids knew we had dinner together."

"So?"

"It was discussed in my senior English class yesterday."

"And you think this is related."

"Don't you?"

"You first."

"Maybe I'm too prone to look for symbolism, but…" She

took a breath, steeling herself to say it. "I *do* believe it's related. Somebody thinks I'm helping you."

"So they put a snake in your house."

"Snake in the grass," she said softly.

"What?"

"They're saying I'm a snake for helping you."

"Sorry. A little *too* much symbolism for me."

"Even the kind of snake they used, notorious for warning about its intentions to harm."

"So…you think this was a warning?"

"Don't you?"

He shrugged, his eyes tracking back to the window that had probably given them access to her home. Her sanctuary.

"If it *isn't* a warning," she prodded, "what is it?"

"It's exactly what I told you before."

"I don't understand?"

"A new way to get that rush. You know. The one that, before we stopped them, they used to get from setting fires."

Seven

"No fingerprints on the window or the basket. Other than yours." Jace flipped the page, eyes scanning the report he'd received shortly before Lindsey arrived at his office this afternoon. She'd given him a key to her house last night so that he could get a crew out there this morning. "And no footprints in the ground under it."

It was exactly what he'd expected. Actually it was almost satisfying, although he didn't think Lindsey Sloan was going to see it that way.

"So what you're saying is you have nothing."

"There's also no sign of forced entry, and this time they checked every inch of the place. So…"

"*So?* I don't understand."

"They were careful to leave no evidence."

"You think I'm right." She sounded surprised.

"I think you might be. And I owe you an apology for getting you involved."

"If you *were* right, I was already involved."

"Because they're your students?"

"As hard as it is for me to believe. And even accepting that…" She stopped, shaking her head.

"It's harder to believe that they'd invade your home and threaten your life."

And what had occurred was nothing less, Jace thought. This had not been the action of some unthinking kid. It had been a well-planned attack, vicious and cold-blooded.

Although snake bites were rarely fatal when treatment was available, they were extremely painful and carried a danger of infection and tissue loss. If Lindsey's students were as smart as they were represented to be, they would know that. Or they would have taken the trouble to find it out.

They hadn't meant to kill her. If they had, they would have chosen some other method. So she was probably also right about the symbolism.

"It's hard to explain the connection that exists between you and students you've taught for a couple of years," she said. "You've mentored them. Disciplined them. Encouraged them. Loved them."

"Loved them?" It sounded maudlin and emotional, and he hadn't pegged her as either. Unless…

She laughed. "Not all of them. But certainly some."

"That ever go beyond the classroom?"

"I'm sorry?"

She sounded at a loss about what he meant, but everybody had seen those stories on the news. Maybe there was something more to this than the fact that he'd tried to make her an ally.

Looking for a Get Out of Jail Free card, Nolan?

Maybe he was. Although he was usually able to put mistakes out of his head as being part of the process, he'd been feeling guilty since last night. This morning, he amended.

He didn't relish the thought that there might have been something going on between her and a student, but it was an avenue he needed to explore. Not only because of what she'd just said, but because the attack had taken place at her home rather than at school or somewhere else. That made it personal.

"I'm talking about your relationship with your students. Has that ever gotten a little *more* than professional with any one of them?" He watched the realization of what he meant form in her eyes. Just before they grew cold.

"When I said that I loved them, lieutenant, I mean like a parent. I've never had an affair with a student, if that's what you're implying."

Her indignation struck him as genuine. After more than fifteen years in this business, his radar was well-honed for cheats and liars. He didn't believe Lindsey Sloan was either.

Just some innocent who got caught in your drive to explore every angle of those fires.

"It's my job to ask the hard questions," he said. "Consider that one asked and answered. And I guess I owe you another apology."

"Right now I'm more concerned with where we go from here."

"For one thing we'll add your address to the list of regular patrols the deputies are making. Ever think about installing a security system?"

"I've never *had* to think about it. Not here."

He let her words rest between them without a response.

After a moment, she turned her head, looking at the door to his office. "I guess all that's changed now, hasn't it?"

"It changed with the first fire. Randolph isn't immune to the kinds of things that happen in other places. Those burned churches were proof of that."

"Do you still think they'll do something else?" she asked, meeting his eyes again.

"To *you?* I'm going to do everything in my power to see they don't. If this was a reaction to your being seen with me, then they may well be satisfied with their warning. You might indicate somehow that you got the message."

"Indicate that to the *kids?*"

"You're the one who said people talk. Let it be known that you're not going to talk to the police anymore."

"You think that will convince them to leave me alone?"

"That and a patrol of your neighborhood."

"For how long?"

"As long as it takes."

"How will you know when that is?"

"When I know who they are."

Jace had set up the patrol he'd promised, but despite that, he wasn't comfortable with the situation. When Lindsey's place was being searched, he had made sure there were no more unlocked windows and that the dead bolts were strong. All of which meant less than nothing if someone was determined to get in.

Which was why he was sitting in his car on the street behind her house. He was convinced that whoever had put the snake in Lindsey's hamper had gotten in through that study window at the back. The front of the place was too exposed. You'd have to be an idiot to attempt a break-in there. And no matter what else he thought about the people involved in this, they were far from idiots.

He reached for the thermos he'd brought, pouring the last of the coffee into the plastic top. It was almost two. If these kids had parents who enforced curfews as he suspected, they wouldn't be out at this time of night. He should go back to his apartment. Get some sleep like a human being for a change. Lack of rest wasn't going to help him solve this case.

The kids had delivered their message. They were probably home in their beds, in that near-comatose state only teenage boys seemed able to achieve. And if he were smart—

He didn't finish the thought. The same vague restlessness that had driven him to undertake this vigil wouldn't let him abandon it. Call it cop's intuition. Call it whatever the hell you wanted, something he needed to know about was going on.

He shifted in the seat, trying to get comfortable. The change of position didn't relieve the ache in his spine. That was better at some times than others, but obviously this wasn't going to be one of them.

As he brought his cup up to his mouth, his gaze lifted to scan the back of Lindsey's house. Before the rim made contact with his lips, he straightened, his eyes narrowing as he focused on a faint light that moved waveringly behind Lindsey's curtained windows.

He watched for perhaps five more seconds, verifying his initial impression, before he opened his door. He threw the coffee on the street and then pitched the plastic cup back onto the passenger's seat.

By the time he was standing, he'd drawn his weapon. He eased his door closed, not bothering to fully shut or lock it. And then, staying low and taking advantage of the abundant cover the heavily planted yards provided, he skirted between the houses of Lindsey's neighbors and slipped into her backyard.

The wavering light he'd seen from his car had disappeared. Maybe Lindsey had been watching television in the dark again. Maybe she was having trouble sleeping, too. If so, she probably wouldn't mind a little company.

Providing she didn't already have some.

* * *

After hours spent tossing and turning, Lindsey had finally decided she'd be better off up doing something productive. She certainly had enough that needed doing.

She couldn't bring herself to go into the office to work. Although she knew the window was now locked, there was something about sitting in that room that kept her mind off whatever she was trying to concentrate on.

She picked her tote up off the hall table where she'd put it in preparation for the morning. Its familiar weight didn't ease the feeling that something in her world was very wrong.

She sat down on the couch, digging through the canvas bag for her American Lit anthology. Maybe trying to come up with enough essay questions for Monday's tests and their makeups would carry her through to dawn. If it didn't...

She took a breath, lifting her eyes from the book to fight an unexpected burn of tears. She hadn't allowed herself to cry since she'd found the snake. She'd had a feeling that once she started, she wouldn't be able to stop.

As she blinked away the unwanted moisture, a shadow moved between the light from the streetlamp and her front windows. A chill began in the middle of her chest and then dropped like a rock into her stomach. Hardly daring to breathe, she laid the anthology down carefully on the coffee table and eased up off the couch, intending to call the police.

As she started toward the foyer, she realized that her cell was closer since, like her bag, she'd laid her purse on the hall table in preparation for tomorrow. She tiptoed across the room, bare feet making no sound. She slipped her phone out and flipped open the case. Her finger hovered for a few seconds over the nine before she lowered the cell.

She was calling the cops because she'd seen a shadow?

Something that could have been nothing more than a play of light? Or a tree moving in the wind? A bird or bat flying directly in front of the streetlamp?

All she needed right now was to be sending up false alarms for help. That would make the police less likely to respond quickly in case of a real emergency.

Phone in hand, she tiptoed over to the front door and put her eye against the peephole. A human shape was silhouetted against the glow from the street.

She reached out and located the switch for the porch fixture. If she turned it on, she knew whoever was out there would run—a result she wasn't exactly opposed to. If she could get a glimpse of him before he did, all the better. Even size and build would give her something to work with. Decision made, she pushed the switch, flooding the porch with light.

Her recognition was instantaneous; her relief so great that she didn't even stop to wonder what Jace was doing outside her door in the middle of the night. Fingers trembling from the flood of adrenaline, she undid the chain and then the other locks, throwing open the door.

"You okay?"

She nodded automatically, although she didn't understand the question. Or why his gun was in his hand. "What's wrong?"

"I thought I saw a flashlight moving around inside."

"A flashlight?"

"Something dim. Maybe in the back hall."

Where her office, the bedroom and the bath were located. The hall she'd walked down not five minutes ago. "When?"

Jace shook his head. "I don't know. Maybe…four or five minutes ago."

"I was back there—"

Jace didn't give her time to finish. He brushed by her, gun still drawn, and headed toward the back of the house. Not sure what she was supposed to do, Lindsey followed.

She stood at the end of the hallway and watched as he turned on lights and searched each room. In the heavy silence of the sleeping neighborhood, she could hear him opening the cabinets under the bathroom lavatory and then the closet door in her bedroom. It was not until he started down the hall toward her that she realized what he had seen from outside.

"The night light has a motion sensor. It must have come on when I got up. When I moved far enough past it, the light went out again."

He glanced down at the small bulb attached to the wall plug, which was still burning. He took a few steps toward where she was standing. Just as she'd said, the light went out.

"Sorry. False alarm." He shoved his gun back into the holster under his arm. "At least I didn't wake you."

"I was in the living room. I saw something move in front of the windows and thought…" The burn was again at the back of her eyes, and she hated it. She strengthened her voice to go on. "I thought they'd come back."

"Yeah. So did I."

"I looked out through the peephole and saw a shape. I thought maybe if I turned on the porch light, I'd be able to see enough to identify them."

"Sorry."

"For what? Looking out for me? That *is* what you were doing, wasn't it? Watching my house."

He looked almost embarrassed by her realization. Despite that, he nodded.

She knew by gauging the density of the stubble on his cheeks, something she was becoming adept at, that he hadn't gotten up early to stand watch. He had been there all night.

"Something didn't feel right," he added.

Maybe Jace hadn't been able to sleep, either. In spite of their obviously overdeveloped sense of impending danger, nothing had happened. And in another couple of hours, it would be morning.

"I can make coffee," she offered tentatively.

Did that sound like an invitation to something else? Even if it did, she didn't regret having made it. She wanted company. And she wasn't opposed to that company being in the form of an armed detective.

"Or I could make it while you go back to bed," he offered.

"Even if I did, I wouldn't sleep. Everything keeps running through my mind like some kind of endless looping."

"You have an internist? Somebody who could write you a prescription for sleeping pills?"

She had a family doctor. The one who had delivered her, actually. And she didn't intend to ask him for drugs to help her cope with this. "I'll get over it."

"There's no shame in taking medication to help you deal with trauma."

"I didn't say there was. I just…" She shook her head, crossing her arms over her chest.

For the first time she was conscious of how thin and short her nightshirt was. Maybe that's why Jace had suggested she go back to bed. Maybe she was embarrassing him.

"It also wouldn't hurt to talk to somebody about what happened. A psychologist. Someone to help you deal with the possibility of PTSD."

It took her a second. "Post Traumatic Stress? You think I'm going to get PTSD from finding a snake in my house?" Despite the fact that she hadn't slept since that had happened, she managed a short laugh. "This is snake country. Every time I went into the woods as a child there was the threat of running into one."

"Which you knew and accepted. That's not the same as having someone put a rattlesnake into your laundry hamper."

It wasn't. Still, she didn't really want to hear his analysis of how poorly she was dealing with this.

"I don't need medication. And I don't need counseling. I *do* need coffee. You're welcome to stay if you want some."

She was acting like an idiot. She hadn't slept in two nights, other than in snatches interrupted by nightmares. So, yeah, she was coping just fine, thank you very much.

They were still standing face-to-face in the hall, with every light in the back of the house blazing. She watched his lips thin and a muscle in that dark jaw tighten.

"I'll let you get back to work," he said. "Enjoy your coffee."

Although Jace's tone had been neutral, she was experienced enough at reading emotion to know she'd made him angry. Maybe even insulted him. And for what?

Because he was sitting up all night so he could make sure you were all right? Or for offering advice that made perfect sense?

"Look—" she began, but by that time Jace was already moving past her toward the front of the house.

She attempted to grab his arm, but he shook her off, continuing to stride purposefully in the direction of the door. All she could do was follow.

"Jace, I'm sorry. What I said was stupid. I really appreciate the fact that you—"

"Lock up." The command was punctuated by the slam of the front door.

Lindsey closed her mouth, still hanging open from her unfinished apology. Then she closed her eyes, once more welling with tears.

Idiot. Idiot. Idiot.

Frustrated with herself and more than a little annoyed with Jace for refusing to listen, she turned on her heel, furiously blinking the moisture away.

She had said she was going to make coffee, and she was, damn it. Then she'd come up with at least ten essay questions before it was time to dress for school.

She had bragged that she didn't need help in coping with what was happening. Now seemed to be a good time to prove it.

Even if she would only have the opportunity to prove it to herself.

Eight

"Do you have a minute, Ms. Sloan?"

Lindsey looked up from stuffing things into her tote bag to find Andrea Moore, one of her juniors, hovering in the doorway of her classroom. "Can it wait, Andrea? I'm running late for Scholars' Bowl practice."

Assuming the girl's agreement, she remembered to add her grade book to the other material in her bag. She had to send out mid-six weeks' warning notices on Tuesday for the kids who had a "C" average or lower in her classes.

Although few of her upper classmen would fall into that category, more of her tenth graders than she wanted to think about might. She was giving them a test tomorrow, a last-ditch effort to raise their scores, but she'd wanted to take a look tonight at how many of them were in the danger zone already.

"Oh. Okay. I'll catch you tomorrow."

Something in the girl's voice belied her easy agreement, making Lindsey feel guilty for not taking time to talk. She'd sent the team to the auditorium to set up tables on stage for the two sets of buzzers they used for competition. They would be ready to start practice for Tuesday's meet by the time she got there.

Was it possible Andrea had heard about the snake? If so, she would be the first person to mention it.

Lindsey had followed Rick's advice, watching for anyone who seemed to be acting strangely. So far, no one had. Unless Andrea knew something about what had happened—

Even as the thought formed, Lindsey rejected it. Of all the kids she taught, this shy, quiet girl would be among the last she'd suspect of being involved in something like that.

So was this a boyfriend problem? Or something more serious? Trouble at home, maybe. In her experience, those were the two things girls generally wanted advice about.

"You want to walk with me down to the auditorium?" Lindsey offered. "We can talk on the way."

"No, really, Ms. Sloan. It's okay. I don't want to keep you. I know y'all have got a match coming up."

"Is something wrong, Andrea?"

Andrea was a diligent student, but by no stretch was she among the brightest in the program. Lindsey hated to turn her away, especially since she couldn't remember the girl ever making a similar request.

"I was just going to ask you about the test on Monday."

"Colonial period literature." Lindsey added the anthology she would need to draw those questions from to her bag.

She should have pulled some old tests from her files and done some recycling of the short-answer questions. Since she was already late, she would have to come back by the room before she left school in order to do so. After practice she'd weigh whether or not it would be worth the effort.

"I know," Andrea said. "I just wondered if it was going to be essay or short answer."

"Some of each. Like always."

Despite having been in the accelerated program for a year, Andrea, like the majority of her students, would no doubt prefer that she stick to multiple choice and fill in the blank. If so, Lindsey thought with a touch of uncustomary impatience, *they* should stick to the general track.

"So…anything else I can help you with?" Lindsey had bent to take her purse out of her bottom drawer. When she looked back up at the girl hovering in the doorway, she was surprised by the bleakness in her eyes. "Are you sure you're okay?"

"I'm fine. I've just got a lot of tests coming up. I wanted be certain of exactly what to study for in English so I could start tonight."

"You'll do fine, Andrea. You always do. You always have." Lindsey's smile was intended to add reassurance.

"Things just seem to be so much harder this year."

"In my class?" Something nagged at her about this. Some problem she obviously wasn't getting at with her questions. "Or harder in general?"

"Everything, I guess. There's just a lot more stress than there used to be."

Welcome to my world, Lindsey thought.

She'd tried all day not to think about having to go back to her house tonight to face more of the same tossing and turning. Her parents would welcome her if she decided to sleep there. In addition to the fact that would necessitate an explanation she didn't want to make, she also didn't want to do that. Despite growing up in a town the size of Randolph, where everyone tended to live in one another's pocket, she needed her own space.

Even if you have to share it with a rattlesnake?

"Honestly, Andrea, you'll do fine," Lindsey comforted briskly as she closed the drawer and took one last look at her desk to make sure she wasn't forgetting something.

"Well, thanks for telling me about the test."

"You sure you don't want to walk with me?"

"No, I'm gonna go on. Try to figure out how to get everything I need to do done before Monday."

"If I know you, you've kept up in your classes. Just review thoroughly and get a good night's sleep. Come back tomorrow and let me know how the day went."

She almost added some platitude about how much she cared, but she knew how awkward that could make a conversation. If Andrea didn't know after a year in her class that she cared, then Lindsey needed to turn in her grade book.

"I will. Thanks, Ms. Sloan."

"You bet. See you tomorrow." With a wave, the girl disappeared from the doorway.

Lindsey took a breath, wondering why everything seemed so damn hard lately. *Welcome to Andrea's world,* she thought, mocking her earlier surge of self-pity.

She slung the strap of her purse over her shoulder and picked up her tote bag. If she had time after practice, she'd come back for a quick search through her test files. If she didn't, maybe she could pull some short answer questions from the files during her prep period tomorrow. After all, she'd have her two classes of sophomore papers to mark and grades to average over the weekend.

As she crossed to the door, she picked a couple of wads of paper up off the floor and tossed them into the garbage can. She pushed the light switch up with her elbow, but left the room open. The janitor would lock up after he swept.

Another day, another dollar, her dad would say. If she averaged all the hours she spent on her work, that was about what her salary amounted to.

And you wouldn't change it for the world.

The reminder was automatic. Something that up until

Tuesday night she had truly believed. She had once thought she would always feel that way. Now...

She swallowed the lump in her throat, positioning the strap of her purse more securely on her shoulder. No rash decisions, she told herself. And no more self-pity.

She had the greatest job in the world, and no one, not even some teenage genius with an adrenaline addiction, was going to take it away from her.

"We'll leave from the north parking lot at ten of three." Lindsey raised her voice to be heard over the sound of the tables being broken down and put away. "If you need a pass out of sixth period, it's your responsibility to ask for it."

She tried to think if there was anything else she should tell them about the meet. There were only two sophomores this year, both recommended by the Scholars' Bowl coach at the junior high. They would know how all this worked.

"Any questions?"

"Can we ride with you, Ms. Sloan?"

Tammy Evans was one of the new members. Apparently she was speaking for the other tenth grader, Jamie Rouse, as well. That would surely be the arrangement their parents would prefer.

"Sure. I have room for one more. Anybody need a ride?"

"I'm good. Paul and Stewart can go with me."

Roy McClain was one of her four seniors. Paul Dabbs and Stewart Reynolds were juniors, so that probably took care of everyone who didn't have his or her own car.

"What about the rest of you?" Lindsey called to the boys who had taken the tables off the stage to return them to the rack. "You have transportation on Monday?"

"Providing it starts," Steven Byrd said. "And that's never a sure thing. If it doesn't, I can ride with Mary."

The best player on the team, Mary DeWitt possessed an encyclopedic knowledge of minutiae. Lindsey wished she could take credit for any of that, but Mary was the daughter of another of the military retirees who had settled in the area. Before she'd arrived at Randolph, Mary had lived all over the world and attended a dozen schools. Most of the local guys were intimidated by that, as well as by the fact she made no effort to hide her ability.

The boys on the team, and most of those in the gifted program, tolerated her brashness and lack of social skills because they recognized how bright she was. Another reason, in Lindsey's book at least, for the kind of accelerated academic track this high school offered. It gave a place for the Marys and the Stevens and even the Justin Carrs of the world to fit into the landscape of rural Alabama.

"Todd? Dale? Jean?"

"I'll need a ride over," Todd Bates said. "My dad's picking me up."

"You can come with me," Steven said. "Or in case of a lack of ignition, I guess we'll all go with Mary." As he put both hands flat on the edge of the stage to vault up onto it, Steven smiled at the girl he was clearly attempting to flirt with.

Lindsey hadn't been aware of Steven's attraction, but they would make a good couple. Smart, polite, and probably destined to spend their lives somewhere other than the Wiregrass.

"You said you have room for one more?" Jean Phillips' thin body tilted as she slung her backpack over her shoulder.

"That's right."

"Okay if I come with you?" Jean secured a strand of straight fair hair behind her ear as she waited for an answer.

"Of course," Lindsey said.

"And I'll ride with Steven. If you'll take me home?" Dale Carter, another junior, was one of the students who came to

Randolph-Lowen from outside the county in order to be able to participate not only in the honors and Advanced Placement classes here but also in the activities like this.

"The more the merrier." Steven drew the final word out, so that it sounded like "marrier," obviously a play on Mary's name.

Roy shook his head, catching Lindsey's eye and grinning. The look said that as a senior he was beyond that kind of silliness, but being good natured, he didn't see any need to openly embarrass Steven's fledgling efforts.

"All right. Then I guess we're set. Quarter of three in the north lot," Lindsey repeated, knowing once was never enough.

"You said ten till," Jean corrected.

"Let's aim for quarter of and maybe they'll all be there by ten till," Lindsey said, smiling at the girl. "Okay?"

Jean nodded. "I won't be late."

And she wouldn't. Lindsey had no doubt of that.

She watched as the team began to leave the auditorium, Steven trailed Mary, talking as they crossed the stage toward the stairs leading down to the auditorium. The two sophomore girls had already disappeared. The other boys had their heads together as they walked down the central aisle, probably discussing plans for the weekend.

Relieved the day was over, Lindsey went backstage to retrieve her purse and tote bag. As she picked up the latter, she remembered that she'd planned to go back by her room to go through the test files.

That thought triggered the next, a nagging sense that she'd missed something important in her conversation with Andrea. As she walked toward the control panel to shut off the lights, the memory of the girl's expression haunted her. She pushed the switch, throwing the backstage area into darkness.

When she walked back onstage, she realized that daylight was still flooding into the auditorium from the double doors, open at the back. Her body canted to balance the weight of the book bag slung on her back, Jean was trudging down the aisle toward them, sneakers squeaking on the tile floor.

If the rest of the kids hadn't disappeared in the minute or so that she'd been backstage, Lindsey would probably have let it go. Jean was a senior, but Lindsey had seen her talking with Andrea a few times in the hall last year. Maybe their lockers were close to one another. Or maybe…

"Jean?"

The girl turned, her brown eyes narrowing as she tried to see into the darkness. "Yes, ma'am?"

The thought of shouting her question across the auditorium was unappealing. "Wait up a minute, please."

Obediently the girl swung her backpack off her shoulder, lowering it to rest on the floor. After taking a last look around to make sure they'd left the stage as they'd found it, Lindsey hurried down the stairs, choosing the narrower side aisle to make her way toward the front.

Jean's eyes tracked her progress. She was probably wondering what this was all about. And now that it was time to broach the subject, Lindsey was wondering if doing so was a good idea.

"Something wrong?" Jean sounded apprehensive.

"I wanted to ask you something."

"Yes, ma'am?"

"You're friends with Andrea Moore, aren't you?"

Something shifted in the girl's eyes. "You couldn't call us friends exactly. We don't have a lot in common."

"Oh. Sorry, I thought I'd seen the two of you together."

"Maybe last year. Not anymore."

Hardly promising, but Lindsey was in so deep it seemed she had nothing to lose by pursuing this. "Do you know if she's having problems this year? Something at home? Guy trouble?"

Jean's eyes seemed unwilling to meet hers. "Sorry, Ms. Sloan. I really wouldn't know. We don't talk."

"Okay. I just—" Lindsey hesitated, aware that she had already stepped beyond the bounds of her own personal guidelines concerning student confidences. "I guess it was someone else."

Jean nodded. "Is that all you wanted?"

"Can I help you carry some of those?" Lindsey nodded toward the overstuffed backpack.

"I can manage," the girl said, again hoisting the bag to her shoulder. "You've got your own stuff. I'm used to this."

"If you're sure…"

"Quarter of three in the north parking lot. Right?"

"That's right. Have a good night."

"You, too."

Jean turned, heading in the opposite direction from that Lindsey would take to her car. Her mother would be waiting to pick her up, but Lindsey would circle the school and make sure that everyone had a ride home.

Home. At one time the thought of going there, taking off her clothes and her shoes and sitting down to dinner in front of the TV would have seemed like heaven. Now, however…

Even as she wondered if Jace would be keeping his vigil tonight, she knew the answer. That was a bridge she'd burned pretty effectively. A tendency on her part. Unlike Shamon's on-again-off-again relationship with Rick Carlisle, once Lindsey knew something wasn't going to work, she didn't see any reason to belabor the point. Usually she had no regrets. In this case…

In this case, it was going to be another long, lonely and sleepless night. Plenty of hours to revisit every word she'd said to Jace last night.

And this time, at least, plenty of regrets.

Nine

Friday morning, after a third nearly sleepless night, Lindsey set her tote bag down on the office floor and picked up the ballpoint chained to the sign-in sheet. She scrawled her signature, glancing up at the clock behind the desk of the school secretary before writing 7:02 beside her name.

"Did you hear?" Melanie leaned across the front counter to whisper the words.

Obviously, whatever this was about, Lindsey *hadn't* heard. Given the secretary's air of secrecy and the events of the last few days, she wasn't sure she wanted to.

Only a couple of faculty members had asked her about the incident with the snake. Both had heard it from one of her neighbors, who'd stuck to his theory that the rattler had gotten into her house and her laundry hamper in some gardening clothes.

Lindsey had downplayed the whole thing, mostly because she didn't want to answer endless questions about what had happened. School, with its demands on her intellect, had become the one place she didn't have to think about the damned snake.

"Heard what?"

"About Andrea Moore."

Although she had no idea yet what this was about, a knot of dread formed in the pit of Lindsey's stomach. "What about her?"

"Suicide," Melanie whispered, lifting her brows. "Last night. The police are with Dave right now."

"Oh, my God."

Nausea so powerful she literally had to put her hand over her mouth surged into Lindsey's throat. All she could think about was Andrea standing hesitantly in the doorway of her classroom yesterday, assuring her she'd only come to ask about the coming test.

What she was feeling must not have been apparent to Melanie. Her voice still lowered, the secretary continued to add details. "Nobody else knows. Not yet. The county's gonna send out grief counselors today. I just thought staff should be aware, so they can be prepared when the kids do find out."

"Excuse me, ladies."

Lindsey automatically stepped to the side, at the same time turning to see Walt Harrison, who taught honors history, set his brown-bag lunch on the counter as he picked up the pen.

"Have you heard, Walt?" Melanie asked him.

"Heard what?"

"About Andrea Moore."

"Andrea? What about her?" Walt asked as he wrote his name.

"She killed herself. Cut her wrists."

"Who the hell told you something like that?"

The anger in Walt's voice made the registrar pull back. After a second, she recovered. "The sheriff's department. That's who. They're in there with Dave right now."

"Son of a bitch."

"She was a junior. You must have taught her last year."

It was obvious Walt was shaken. Lindsey realized belatedly that he had a son in that same class. Suicide always brought home the terrible vulnerability of this age group.

"I had her this year and last. Son of a bitch," Walt said again, his voice softer.

"Bad family situation?" the secretary prodded.

"I don't know. Tim might, but… She was just…I don't know. One of those kids you like. Never said much. Worked hard. Listened. Cared."

Tim was also in Lindsey's Honors English. His father's words about the dead girl might have as easily described him.

"You taught her, too, didn't you, Linds?" Walt asked. "She was in your program."

Lindsey nodded. "She came by my room yesterday afternoon. She wanted to talk about a test. At least that's what she said. I had no reason…" Regret choked off the faltering words. When she'd regained control, she went on, trying to make them both understand. "I had Scholars' Bowl practice. I told her she could walk down to the auditorium with me, but…"

"Don't," Walt ordered into her sudden silence. "This has nothing to do with you. It never does."

"Maybe if I'd made time to listen to her. If I'd brought her into the room and closed the door—"

"Stop it. You tried to listen. Maybe her original intent was to talk to you about whatever was going on, but for some reason, she didn't take the opportunity. Her choice. And there was *nothing* you could do about that."

How about be five minutes late to practice? Sit down and take the trembling hand of a girl who was obviously upset?

"So she was what?" Melanie asked. "Sixteen?"

"Yeah. I guess so," Walt agreed, turning his attention back to the secretary. "Sixteen. What a screwed-up world. God, as a parent you never can rest easy. Not with teenagers."

And as a teacher, Lindsey thought. Even though she'd sensed Andrea's anxiety, she'd never dreamed it was intense enough to make her take her own life.

"I don't think you have anything to worry about," Melanie said. "Not with Tim."

"I wouldn't doubt Andrea's mother thought the same thing." Walt picked up his lunch and turned to look at Lindsey again. "We have them an hour a day. We aren't responsible for whatever's going on in their lives. Or for how screwed up those are. Everybody here knows how much you care about your kids."

"I should have cared enough about this one to sit down with her for five minutes."

"You offered your time. She turned you down. If that's what she came to you about…" Walt hesitated. He swallowed before he went on, fighting an emotion that was palpable. "Then it was a testament to the fact that she knew you would care. She could have come to anyone at this school, but she chose you."

"And I let her down."

"Like hell, Lindsey. You aren't a mind reader."

"Maybe if I'd probed a little deeper…" She took a breath, replaying those few minutes in her head.

"It just brings home to you how goddamn fragile they are. Even the ones you think have it made."

Lindsey nodded, unsure if that reminder was supposed to be a comfort. Maybe it was a simply personal reflection, since Walt himself had a teenager.

"Any word on the arrangements?" Walt's question had

been directed at Melanie, normally a font of such information.

"They've not made any yet. They have to do an autopsy."

"God," Walt said under his breath. "Let me know when you hear something."

"I will," Melanie said. And she then added, as she did every morning, "Have a good day."

Walt didn't respond, walking out of the office. As he disappeared, Melanie's eyes came back to Lindsey. "You need to go tell Dave she came to see you."

Tell Dave. Did that mean also telling whoever was in his office from the sheriff's department? "Now?"

"Want me to buzz in and ask? That detective that was here before is the one handling the investigation."

As Melanie walked over and picked up the phone to ring Dave, a dozen questions formed in Lindsey's mind. What about a teenage girl's suicide did the sheriff's department need to investigate? Even if that was something they did routinely, why would this one have become Jace's investigation?

Because he's already investigating things that he believes are connected to the school, she realized. Was it possible the authorities were thinking Andrea's death had something to do with the church fires? That Andrea was involved?

Out of all the students she taught, Andrea would be among the last she'd suspect of that. Still, the fact that the girl had come to see her shortly after the incident with the snake—

"Dave said to come. They want to know everything you do."

Although he could guess how little sleep Lindsey had had in the last few nights, Jace was a shocked by her appearance. The discoloration beneath her eyes was to be expected. The lack of color in her cheeks was not.

"Come in, Lindsey," Dave Campbell invited.

As he had last time, the principal had agreed to anything Jace wanted as far as the investigation was concerned. His only caveat was that the grief counselors, composed of all those in the county with training in this sort of thing, be allowed to meet with the students before Jace questioned any of them.

That was okay with him. The time for asking those questions would come later. Right now, he wanted to be an observer. Gauge reactions. Feel out the faculty members about the girl. He just hadn't expected to start with Lindsey.

He'd known he would have to talk to her, despite what had happened between them Wednesday night. According to the girl's mother, Andrea was in her program.

"Melanie said I should tell you—" Lindsey began.

"Sit down," Jace suggested, indicating his chair.

Both of them had stood as she'd entered. She was still hovering near the door, looking fragile enough that something moved in his chest. An unfamiliar tightening he wanted to deny.

In response to his suggestion, she crossed the space between them. Before she sat down in the chair he'd offered, her eyes met his. In them he could see exhaustion and pain.

When she was seated, Jace took the back of one of the other chairs in the room and moved it parallel to hers. Only when he sat down again did Campbell retake his seat behind the desk.

"What is it you want to tell us, Lindsey?" Campbell asked.

"Andrea Moore came to see me yesterday afternoon. She said she wanted to talk about the test I'm giving on Monday." She hesitated, as if only now realizing that every plan any of them had made for the next few days might now be put on hold. After a moment, she moistened her lips and went on with her story.

"I had Scholars' Bowl practice. I asked Andrea to walk

with me down to the auditorium because I was late. She said what she wanted to talk about wasn't that important. We talked a little about the test. I tried to reassure her that it wouldn't be anything she couldn't handle. She said that everything was harder this year. More stressful. Even with her saying that, it never crossed my mind that she'd…" She shook her head.

"Nobody could have anticipated this," Campbell offered. "For God's sake don't start blaming yourself for not knowing what was on her mind."

"What kind of stress?" Jace asked.

Lindsey turned, her eyes widening. He'd already acknowledged her fragility, but he had to ask these questions. What she'd just said made him curious about what was going on in this girl's life. And more curious about what she might have been involved in.

"Her classes. That's what we were talking about."

"Did she mention anything else?"

"Just that everything was more stressful this year."

"Good student?"

"She was a hard worker," Lindsey hedged. "Things didn't come as easily for Andrea as they did for some of the others. That's why she had such good study skills. I tried to tell her that. To reassure her that she'd do fine."

Lindsey seemed to run down all at once, dropping her eyes to the strap of the tote bag she twisted in her hands. Since Jace didn't believe Andrea Moore had slit her wrists because she had a test coming up, closing the subject was fine with him. There were other things to consider, and as long as Lindsey had it in her head that the girl was overworked and stressed about grades, she'd be reluctant to consider them.

According to her mother, the girl had a history of depression, which had brought on previous episodes of cutting.

She'd been in therapy for a couple of years and seemed to be doing much better. Then the mom had walked into her bathroom last night and found her dead.

"Did you know she was being treated for depression?"

Lindsey's eyes came up. "Maybe if I had—"

He cut her off. "Did *you* know that, Dr. Campbell?"

"In all honesty, I had to pull Andrea's record this morning when you called to remember what she looked like. I confess I knew very little about her."

"She didn't do things to bring attention to herself," Lindsey explained. "Dave knows the worst among our students and the most outstanding. The ones who never make waves…"

Get ignored? Jace knew that's what she was feeling right now. That the girl's coming to her had been some kind of cry for help. One she had ignored.

"Any hint she might have come to apologize?" he asked.

"Apologize?"

"Like maybe she had something to do with the snake."

"What snake?" Campbell asked.

"Ms. Sloan didn't tell you?"

"Obviously not."

"And you haven't heard?"

Campbell shook his head. "What happened?"

"Somebody broke into Ms. Sloan's house to put a rattlesnake into her laundry hamper."

"*What!* Lindsey? Why the hell didn't you tell me?"

"Because I didn't want to have to talk about it. I know it's stupid, but…I just didn't want to answer questions."

"When was this?"

"Tuesday night. While I was at PTA."

"You weren't hurt. No, I guess not," Campbell said. "My God, that's insane. Why would someone do that? You've always had such a good rapport with your students. Did something happen that I'm not aware of? Some disciplinary problem—"

"I made the mistake of approaching Ms. Sloan in public," Jace broke in. "The community knows that I'm in charge of the arson investigation. Some of her students became aware she was talking to me. Apparently one of them didn't like that."

"Is that true, Lindsey?"

"They knew I'd talked to Jace. At least my seniors did. I imagine they could figure out what he wanted to talk to me about. Their powers of deduction would be up to that. Whether that had anything to do with what happened..." Lindsey shrugged.

"And now, detective, you're suggesting Andrea may have come to see Lindsey to...apologize for the snake? That she may have had some role in what took place?"

"It's a possibility. On Tuesday night someone plays a dangerous trick on Ms. Sloan. Yesterday afternoon, Andrea Moore shows up at her door, says she wants to talk, but decides not to. Then she goes home and cuts her wrists. Seems to me there might be a connection between those events."

"You didn't know Andrea," Lindsey said.

"You don't think she was involved?"

"Frankly, she'd be the last person I'd suspect."

"Who'd be the first?"

"I'm sorry?"

"If you have people you'd *never* suspect, then you're bound to have some you might. I'm asking you who those are."

"And I've already answered that."

"But you're convinced it couldn't have been Andrea." Jace didn't bother to hide his sarcasm.

"Yes. And I'm *not* convinced the two are related."

"So you have stuff like this happening around here all the time? Dr. Campbell?" Jace demanded of the principal when it was clear Lindsey didn't intend to give him an answer.

"It's Mr. Campbell," the principal corrected, "and of course, we don't. I don't believe we've ever had a student commit suicide. Not in the twenty-three years I've been here. We've had deaths, of course. Most of them driving mishaps—"

"Then you're lucky," Jace said shortly. "Remarkably so."

"I know. And since we can't predict how the kids will respond, the county's sending everyone they've got out to talk to our classes. It can become epidemic, you know."

"Suicides?"

"Some from grief. More often because they long for or are jealous of the attention the victim's getting," Campbell said. "Kind of a 'look how everyone will miss me when I'm gone' syndrome. It seems we're dealing with a variety of issues today, detective. Although what happened to Lindsey is both shocking and unforgivable, it isn't going to be our top priority right now. I'm sure you understand."

"If you think Andrea's suicide on the heels of the attack on Ms. Sloan is coincidence, you're ignoring the obvious."

"Like Lindsey, I'm not convinced these things are connected. Not any of them."

"But you admit it's a possibility."

"Right now, since we have no idea what precipitated Andrea's suicide, I'll have to. Maybe when we know more—"

"The autopsy results should be back early next week."

Campbell's face changed, his expression conveying his emotional reaction. Jace felt Lindsey stir in the chair beside his, bringing his attention back to her.

"Is that necessary?" she asked. "They know how she died…"

"Her mother gave permission. Given the department's concern that this school might be connected to the arsons—"

"Don't you mean *your* concern?"

Her copper-colored eyes were filled with bitterness, and Jace found himself regretting that. Still, he had a job to do. One he was going to do to the best of his ability. Even if Lindsey Sloan didn't approve of the way he went about it.

What he had asked for was well within the boundaries of his investigation. He could appreciate her feelings about the autopsy, just as he'd been sympathetic to the reaction of the girl's mother. That didn't mean he regretted asking for it.

"You're right. It's my call. And my responsibility. One I take as seriously as you take yours, Ms. Sloan. Now if you'll both excuse me," Jace said, getting to his feet, "I'll let you get back to dealing with the impact of Andrea Moore's death on your school and its students. And I'll get back to dealing with its impact on my investigation."

Ten

"I hoped you'd be here," Shannon said, as she came into the teacher's lounge. Dropping her belongings on the table behind the couch she sat down, using the fingers of both hands to push her hair away from her face. "I went by your room to convince you to drop by if you weren't already planning to."

"God, I thought this day would never end."

Lindsey had also wanted to talk about Andrea's suicide with someone with whom she could be completely honest.

"Yeah, me, too. Any more coffee?"

Lindsey turned, picking up Shannon's mug and filling it. She walked over to the couch, holding it out. As one of the counselors, Shannon had probably had more to deal with today than any of the rest of the staff, including her.

"I feel like I've taken a beating." Shannon took the cup, cradling it between her palms as if to warm her hands.

"Was it awful?"

Shannon ignored the question, maybe considering it rhetorical. She took a swallow of coffee before she raised her eyes. "You meet with Nolan?"

Lindsey nodded. "He talked to everyone who taught her."

"And with me. I don't know what the cops think we can tell them. Talk about the last-to-know."

A small silence fell as Shannon took another sip from her mug. Lindsey sat down on the opposite couch, mentally preparing to share the burden of her guilt.

"She came to see me yesterday afternoon. She said she wanted to talk about Monday's test, but… Maybe if I'd given her the right opening, she would have told me how she was feeling."

"And maybe if I'd been the kind of counselor who was close to the students I'm assigned, she would have told me what was so wrong she had to go home and slit her wrists. You sure you want to play the blame game with me, Linds?"

Shannon's tone was savage, but Lindsey knew her well enough to know that was caused by a regret equal to hers.

"The tragic thing is," Shannon went on, her voice still caustic, "there probably wasn't all that much to whatever it was. Somebody said her thighs were too fat or something. Insult *du jour*. Let's all go cut our wrists."

"Don't."

"I know. It's just… God, why don't they think?"

"They do. Just not like us."

"I know. I know," Shannon said tiredly. "Jay Burke said it perfectly today. Their brains aren't done. I've read all those studies about their control centers not being fully functional. The impulsiveness. Not realizing consequences. But doesn't that just say it all—their brains aren't done."

"You ever talk to her about the depression?"

"Nope. Nor did Beth." Beth Taylor was the tenth grade counselor, who would have dealt with Andrea during the previous school year. "I mean obviously we both talked to her about her schedule. What classes she wanted to take. I saw her this summer at registration. You know what a zoo that was."

Beth and Shannon were both conscientious about their duties. It was just that they had so many of them now. Scheduling. State-mandated testing. And the same Mickey-Mouse, everyone-takes-a-turn crap like monitoring the halls and sponsoring clubs and chaperoning after-school activities.

"Jace said she'd been in therapy for a couple of years," Lindsey offered. Maybe that would help with Shannon's guilt.

"Had there been other attempts?"

"I don't know. If Jace knew—and he'd talked to her mother—he didn't say."

"Maybe she didn't mean for it to happen. Sometimes they don't. They just want everybody to feel bad about how mean they've been."

"If she wasn't serious, wouldn't she have had time to call 9-1-1 before…? I mean it wasn't immediate. She must have had a few minutes when she realized what she'd done."

"One of the kids said she was in the shower. How the hell do they know things like that when we don't? Don't answer that. We don't know because nobody tells us. Sometimes I wonder why we're even here."

Shannon put her forehead against the rim of her mug. When she looked up again, the anger seemed to have drained away. Her eyes reflected exhaustion and despair.

"Maybe with the hot water—" she began. "Shit, I don't know. I'm no expert. God knows I don't want to be. I hope we never have another suicide as long as I'm here."

"Dave said there hasn't been one during his twenty-three years."

"You think that's religion? The lack of suicides. Because all of them go to church? Do they still teach it's a sin?"

They didn't *all* attend church, but a huge portion did. This was the heart of the Bible belt, and that still meant something in a place like Randolph, Alabama.

"I don't know. I feel like I don't know anything. You think having the grief counselors here helped?"

Lindsey's gifted kids had not been impressed. The people the county had sent out, many of them elementary school personnel, had not related well to that particular segment of the school's population. After hearing the comments her students had made, Lindsey had wondered if they had related to any of them well.

"Who knows? We keep saying that, don't we?"

"I just keep thinking that if I'd pulled her into my room and closed the door and then sat down with her…" Lindsey's now-familiar litany ground to a halt.

"Maybe she really did just want to talk about the test. Whatever triggered this could have happened after she left school. You can't know. You probably won't ever know."

That was the problem. She would always wonder what difference it might have made if she'd given Andrea more of her time. More concern and attention. Instead, she'd been thinking about what she needed to take home and hurrying to practice.

"What are your kids saying?" Shannon asked.

"They're as shocked as we were. I don't think Andrea was all that close to many of them. Which in itself is kind of sad."

"It's all sad. So much potential lost. What's that old saw about suicide? Permanent solution to a temporary problem."

"Now we have to prevent any of the rest of them from thinking it's *any* kind of solution."

"Guidance should probably work up a list of warning signs for the faculty. Do you know when the funeral is? The most dangerous time for a copycat will be immediately following. The drama, the tears, the whole focus on her death."

"Dave said this morning arrangements hadn't been finalized. They're doing an autopsy."

"Oh, God." Shannon again made that habitual sweep of her hair back from her face. "The thought makes me ill."

"Jace suggested she might have had some part in the thing with the snake. He said that otherwise, her coming to talk to me seemed too much of a coincidence."

"You buy that?"

"No. Do you?"

"I wish I could say I knew Andrea well enough to have an opinion one way or the other. Granted, she doesn't seem the type, but… Frankly, I didn't get that much of a psychological profile going from talking to her about whether she should sign up for chemistry or AP biology."

"I knew her." *Just not well enough to know about the depression or the possibility of suicide.* "At least I taught her last year. I just can't see her being involved."

"Maybe she came to your room not because she was involved, but because she knew something. You said Jace was convinced that, too, was done by somebody in your program. Kids talk. Maybe Andrea overheard something. She's the type no one would notice. And that's also a sad commentary on this place."

The familiar squeak of the lounge door warned them their conversation was no longer private. They both turned, waiting for the intruder to clear the partial partition that created a small anteroom adjacent to the seating area.

Lindsey was surprised when Walt Harrison walked into the lounge. Although she and Shannon usually stayed later than anyone else in the afternoons, there was a crew of semi-regulars who came by for end-of-the-day coffee or to wait until the traffic had cleared. Walt wasn't among them.

"Hey," he said, nodding to them. "I thought I might find somebody here today."

"Join us," Lindsey invited, sliding over to make a place

for him on the couch. "Want coffee? I can make another pot."

"Not for me. I can't drink it this late. So what do you know?" Walt eased down on the end of the sofa, looking from one of them to the other.

"Not much more than I did this morning," Lindsey said. "And I've still heard nothing about the arrangements."

"Burial on Tuesday, is what I heard. Pending the coroner releasing the body."

It sounded cold and clinical. Something out of one of the TV forensics shows rather than the reality of this community.

"Well, obviously you know more than we do," Shannon said. "The kids say anything to you about a possible reason?"

Walt looked uncomfortable, but clearly he had wanted to talk or he wouldn't be here. After a moment's hesitation, he answered. "They say she was pregnant."

"Pregnant?" Lindsey repeated in disbelief.

Even here that wasn't an unprecedented occurrence. And normally not grounds for suicide. That might depend on Andrea's home situation, of course, something she knew too little about.

"By whom?" Shannon asked.

Walt shrugged.

"I didn't even know she had a boyfriend," Lindsey offered.

"Not a necessity," Shannon said. "Not these days."

Dating had not yet been completely replaced by "hooking up" or whatever the current teen term for casual sex was, but despite the religious values of the region, the kids at Randolph-Lowen weren't immune to the messages bombarding them from the national culture. It would be naïve to believe that just because they were in church on Sunday morning, they weren't out having sex, often unprotected, on Saturday night.

"Is Tim okay?" Shannon asked.

"I don't know. That's why I'm here. I thought I'd wait for him to get his instrument and music together and talk about this on the way home."

Lindsey realized that she'd forgotten about the game tonight. The customary Friday-afternoon pep rally had been cancelled, but due to the tightness of the season and the playoff structure, it would have been difficult if not impossible to cancel the game. Unless she could think about some way to get out of it, she would be expected to work in the ticket booth.

"That's probably a good idea," Shannon said. "Just let him 'debrief.' Let him tell you everything he's thinking and feeling, Walt, no matter how hard it is to hear. That is, *if* he'll tell you."

"Tim's a good kid. And we talk. I didn't want him to hear a lot of garbage from the guys he usually rides home with."

Wanting to be with his son after a day like this was reason enough for Walt to play chauffer, but Lindsey didn't quite understand his last comment. "Garbage about Andrea?"

"About the suicide. Cutting. The whole nasty bundle."

"Cutting?"

"She had a history of that. It seems a lot of the kids knew about it. You never noticed she always wore long sleeves?"

The image of Andrea standing in her doorway, fingers nervously plucking at the wrist of a long-sleeved knit top, played through Lindsey's mind. In spite of the September heat, she'd thought nothing about the girl's attire. The building was air-conditioned, sometimes uncomfortably so. Lindsey always kept a sweater over the back of her own chair.

"A manifestation of her depression," Shannon said.

"I've read about cutting, but… I always thought that was something that would go on somewhere else. Somebody else's kids. Pretty stupid, huh?" Walt's smile was self-mocking.

It would probably have been comforting to believe that. Especially if you had a sixteen-year-old of your own.

"You know, you'd think parents would make us aware of stuff like that. How are we supposed to help kids if we don't know what the hell is going on with them?"

Shannon's complaint was valid, but there was still a stigma attached to mental illness, even depression. No teen was going to want that kind of information blazoned across his permanent record. Most parents would probably agree.

"She told me everything was more stressful this year," Lindsey said.

"We aren't a month into school yet," Walt said. "How much stress could there be?"

"If what the kids are saying is true…"

"Whether there was a reason for it or not, she was obviously *feeling* a lot of pressure," Shannon added. "She probably went home yesterday afternoon and gave in to the urge to cut. Supposedly, the act itself relieves tension. And if she *were* in therapy, then after she'd done it, she probably felt as if she'd failed. Lost control. Regressed." Shannon shook her head. "It would have made her feel even worse about herself than she did before. Maybe at some point the thought surfaced that with just a couple of slightly deeper cuts she wouldn't have to feel that bad ever again."

"Surely, when she realized what was happening—" Lindsey stopped midway through the sentence. She could have no idea what the girl had been thinking. None of them could.

The only thing she would ever know for sure was that Andrea had showed up at her door the day she'd killed herself, and Lindsey had told her she didn't have time to talk. That was something she would have to live with the rest of her life.

"Pretty much shoots my theory to hell," Shannon said.

"I don't know." That phrase again. "Maybe... Maybe she'd talked to the boy and he didn't believe her. Or didn't offer to help. Her mom's at work, so—"

"You know, I can't do this anymore." Shannon stood up abruptly. "Maybe tomorrow I can figure out what went wrong in Andrea Moore's life, but right now... Right now, I need to go home and think about mine." She crossed over to the sink while Lindsey and Walt sat, stunned to silence. She rinsed out her mug and put it back on the lunchroom tray upside down. "See you guys Monday morning."

"Shannon—"

"No more. We're just picking at the carcass here." She gathered up her belongings from the table. "None of us has got a clue what was going on with that girl. We need to admit it."

She started toward the door to the hall. From outside came the sound of young voices, obviously students. Shannon stopped as if she'd hit a physical barrier. "Shit."

"Tim and company." Walt rose, walking toward her. He put his arm around her shoulders. "I'll get rid of them. Go home and have a drink. Then get into bed and sleep in tomorrow."

Lindsey didn't remind either of them about tonight's game. Walt was right. Shannon needed to get out of here. Away from the whole mess.

With a final squeeze, Walt brushed by her to go out the door. They listened as he greeted his son and whoever had been with him. After a moment the voices faded down the hall.

Shannon's eyes cut back to Lindsey's face. "I'm sorry. That tirade wasn't directed at you."

"I know. Walt's right. You need to go home. Get some distance."

"You okay?"

She nodded, although that was far from the truth. "I'm fine. I'll see you Monday."

"This wasn't your fault."

"Or yours."

Her friend's smile was as mocking as Walt's had been. "Yeah. You're right. Then why do you suppose neither of us feels any better?"

Without waiting for an answer, Shannon turned and walked out of the lounge.

Eleven

"We just want to go out in the middle of the field at halftime, before the band comes on. Or right after. It doesn't matter which. We bought all these candles." Renee lifted one of the overstuffed bags the cheerleaders each carried in their hands. "There's enough for everybody, and we'll just hold them while they shut off the stadium lights. We thought you could read a poem or something. Maybe say a prayer—"

"Have you cleared all this with Mr. Campbell?"

Renee and a couple of the others had approached Lindsey as she was unlocking the ticket booth. Their faces expressed the same need to do or say something, without knowing what, that she'd seen on all the other faces in the halls today.

Somewhere in the back of her mind she'd had the idea that the game would serve as a respite from grief. That it would get the kids' minds off the tragedy in their midst. Still, the candlelight ceremony they proposed would probably be seen as an appropriate way to pay tribute to one of their own, here in a place where almost everyone in Randolph spent Friday night.

"He'll let us. Especially if you ask him, Ms. Sloan."

Valerie Jacobs wasn't in the gifted program, but she hung out with a lot of Lindsey's students, including Renee.

"I'm not sure I *want* to ask him, Val."

Renee's eyes revealed her puzzlement at Lindsey's lack of enthusiasm. "But why? You're our teacher. And Andrea's."

"Because I'm not totally sure it's a good idea. That it will be good for the school. Or for y'all."

Lindsey racked her brain trying to come up with a reason that would make some sense of her reluctance. Since it was more a gut reaction than anything else, she was having a hard time articulating her reservations about this impromptu memorial.

"It's just a way to say we care. And that we'll miss her. We *have* to do something," Renee pleaded.

The girls' earnestness made it hard to belittle the gesture. Candles and a prayer. During their lifetimes, they'd seen this sort of thing on every occasion from Princess Diana's death to 9/11. It was all they knew about expressing grief.

"I can't be the one to speak, Renee," Lindsey capitulated. "Maybe Mr. Campbell will."

"If you think that's better. We just need somebody to say something. Oh, and be sure to tell them to cut out the lights after we get out on the field."

"What about Coach? Have you talked to him about this?"

"About letting the team stay on the field, you mean?"

"No, I meant..." Lindsey didn't bother to finish.

She'd realized nothing she said now would break through their determination. And maybe it was better this way. Let them do this here, away from the school. The funeral next week would be bad enough. Maybe if they got to carry out this public expression of their grief, offer their goodbyes, it would speed the healing process.

"I'll ask Mr. Campbell, but if he says no, that's it. Okay? Everybody is upset enough. We don't want to cause trouble or make Andrea's family feel any worse."

Renee's eager nod assured Lindsey that she didn't question the logic of that. Of course, Renee wouldn't buck authority. She usually just found a way around it.

"Will you ask him now so we can hand out the candles and tell everybody what to do before the game?"

"If I can find him," Lindsey promised.

"Thanks, Ms. Sloan. We knew you'd understand."

"Y'all come back and check with me in fifteen minutes, okay? Right here. And don't do *anything* until I tell you it's all right with Mr. Campbell."

If Dave were here, he'd be in the field house. In the meantime, if Shannon showed up, she could open the booth. If she didn't, it wouldn't hurt to be a few minutes late. The gates to the stadium were still locked.

As Lindsey walked toward the new cinder-block building, the first cars were beginning to pull into the parking lot. Volunteers from the Boosters Club directed them with flashlights, although it was still twilight. She was relieved to see that most of those early arrivals were disgorging band members, who always assembled on the practice field before they marched into the stadium.

The door to the field house was ajar, but no sound came from inside. By now, the team and the assistant coaches would probably be in the dressing room under the stadium.

Dave usually picked up a pizza or something quick on his way over from the school. He and Coach Spears shared the meal in the coach's office, a ritual that had developed early in their long relationship.

She stepped inside, pulling the door closed. She wasn't sure what Dave's mood would be after the day they'd all had.

If he was going to chew her out for not thinking this proposal through, she'd just as soon no one else heard him.

As she turned the corner to the hall that led to Coach Spears's office, she heard voices. They were low, but definitely masculine. She couldn't decide if having Coach there while she explained the cheerleaders' plan would be a plus or a minus, but there wasn't much she could do about it now. She'd made the commitment to the girls that she'd ask.

The voices grew louder as she approached. Still trying to frame the request she was about to make, she paid little attention to what was being said.

The door to the office was also ajar. She raised her hand to knock, for the first time becoming aware of the words being spoken inside. As she did, she stopped the motion she'd begun.

"It's out there. I thought you should know."

"And just what am I supposed to do about it?"

Dave's voice. She hadn't recognized the other one, but it didn't sound like Coach's low rumble.

"Not a goddamn thing, Dave. I didn't come here to get you to *do* something. I came because I consider you a friend."

"Yeah, well, you've got a hell of a way of showing it."

"You've been around long enough to know how this works, so don't try to pretend you don't."

"What does that mean?"

"That there are no secrets in a place like Randolph. You should remember that." The voice Lindsey hadn't yet identified grew louder on the last phrase.

Before she could lower her fist or move away from the door, it swung away from her, opening inward. Walt Harrison's eyes widened when he saw her standing on the threshold.

"I—I need to see Dave," she stammered. "Is he here?"

Walt said nothing for a moment, his eyes searching her face. She tried to pretend she hadn't overheard, but guilt at having eavesdropped on what was clearly a private conversation was probably written all over it.

Finally Walt tilted his head toward the office. Then he stepped by her and continued down the hall.

She waited until the echo of his footsteps against the concrete walls faded before she again raised her hand and tapped lightly on the wood.

"What?"

The barked question was not the most auspicious opening. Given that she'd interrupted what could only be described as a heated exchange between her principal and a coworker, she couldn't blame Dave for being less than thrilled to have to deal with her right now.

Despite that realization, she stepped inside. Dave's head was between his hands. After a moment, he looked up.

"Lindsey?"

"I'm here to convey a request from the cheerleaders."

"What kind of request?"

"They want the student body to go out on the field at halftime holding candles. They want you to offer a prayer or read a poem or say something about Andrea."

"Good God," Dave said, taking a deep breath.

"I know." She did. She knew exactly how he felt.

The endless day at school had been surreal. They were all trying to get through the game tonight, hoping everyone could regroup during the weekend and then make it though the emotional trauma of the funeral next week.

"You think that's a good idea?" he asked.

"I didn't, but… I don't know. Maybe it will help them cope. I'm not sure how much it can hurt."

"You don't think it will just get them all stirred up?"

"Look, if you don't think it's smart, just say no. I only agreed to ask. I didn't come up with this. The cheerleaders bought the candles and are waiting for permission to hand them out. And they want the field lights off while they do this."

"An invitation to disaster right there."

Normally she would have agreed. When you have several thousand people congregated in one place and turn out the lights, you're asking for trouble. But for something like this…

"I doubt anyone will take advantage of the situation."

"It's not *your* job that's on the line." Dave ran his hand though his hair. "You hear what Walt was saying?"

"Not enough to understand what he was upset about."

"Is that the truth, Lindsey?"

"Of *course*. I heard the two of you arguing, but not the gist of it. I was too busy trying to figure out the best way to ask your permission for what the kids want to do. If you have doubts, maybe you could call the superintendent."

"It's still *my* school. You think this will go all right?"

She figured Dave wanted to let the kids have their tribute. He just wanted someone's assurance it was the right thing to do. All she could do was to give him her honest opinion.

"I didn't. Not at first, but…I think maybe it will give them some closure. They had to listen today to people they didn't know or particularly like tell them how they should feel and what they should think about Andrea's death. This is something *they* want to say. Something they want to do for someone they cared about."

Dave's eyes held on hers a moment. "Okay. Tell them we'll have a minute of silence. And tell them to get on and off the field as quick as they can."

"They want you to say a prayer."

"I don't want to get sued as well as fired. A moment of silence, and we'll kill the lights. That's the best I can do."

"I'm sure they'll be very grateful."

Dave nodded, tiredness etched on his features.

"You okay?"

"Are you?"

"No," she said truthfully.

"Me, either. And I didn't even know the girl. You hear the rumors?"

"About her being pregnant? I heard."

"Anything else?"

"About Andrea?"

"About the pregnancy."

"Just that she might be."

"Okay." He seemed relieved. "Tell them I said okay, but with those stipulations."

"Thanks, Dave. You need to get some rest."

He nodded again. After a moment she left him there alone, the desk lamp shining down on his bowed head.

As the second quarter wound down, the team was behind, but not far enough they couldn't rally in the second half. *If* they could manage to get their minds on the game.

Almost everyone who had come to the ticket booth wanted to talk about the suicide. A lot of those had been worried parents, looking for a reason for Andrea's death that would have nothing to do with anything their own child might feel or think. Some had been her former students, home from college, who'd heard about the suicide as soon as they'd arrived in town. To all of them, Lindsey said the same meaningless sentence. She had no idea what had caused the girl to take her own life.

At the end of the first quarter, Jim Wells, whom she'd

roped into replacing Shannon, had gone back to his normal duties at the concession stand. She'd thought a couple of times about calling Shannon on her cell, just to check on her. She hadn't because she hoped her friend had cut off her phone and taken a couple of sleeping pills. And if Lindsey had any, she would have done the same thing as soon as she got home.

As the play clock ticked down on the first half, she thought about locking the booth and walking through the gate of the stadium to watch the ceremony. Maybe if her emotions had been more controlled, she would have. Instead, she opted to stay where she was and listen to whatever Dave said over the public address system. No court ruling could prevent her own prayer for Andrea.

She forced a smile for the man approaching the booth, two little boys in tow. "Can I help you?"

"We still need tickets to get in?"

She couldn't remember seeing them before. The little boys' eyes shone with such excitement as they looked up at her, she suspected this might be their first time at the stadium. And if money was an issue…

"Tell them at the gate Ms. Sloan said to let y'all in. The band's about to perform. Want to see the band march out on the field?" she asked the youngest child, who nodded solemnly.

"You sure it's okay?"

She smiled again at the father. "It's fine. Just tell them I said to let you in."

"Ms. Sloan?"

"That's right."

"Thanks."

"I'll never forget the first game my dad took me to."

"Thank you," the man said with an answering smile. "Okay, let's go, guys. Stay close to me, now, you hear?"

She almost called after him to warn that the lights would go out soon. The two little boys had run ahead to the gate. She watched as the dad caught up with them, taking each by the hand. She waved at Albert Markham, who allowed the trio to go through before he waved back at her.

The people who had been milling around outside all seemed to have disappeared into the stadium for the halftime show. Of course, the band was part of the spectacle, and many parents came as much for this as for the game itself.

Lindsey blew out a breath, and then glanced down at her watch. Almost eight-thirty. Another thirty minutes and she could legitimately close up shop and head home. She couldn't remember a night when she'd looked forward to that more.

As the band played on in the background, she thought about having to unlock the door to her house, after being away for several hours, and walking inside. She hadn't been comfortable there since the incident Tuesday night, no matter how many times she told herself she was being ridiculous.

She could always spend the night at her parents, who would welcome her with open arms. And of all the people on earth, she could be surest of their response to her worries about how she'd handled Andrea's request yesterday afternoon.

She suddenly realized that the music had been replaced by the PA system. Although she strained to hear, she was unable to distinguish Dave's words, distorted by the amplification and by the bulk of the stadium between.

She could visualize what was going on, though. In response to the invitation to join the band and the cheerleaders on the field, students would be pouring out of the stands, candles in hand. And as soon as they were all lit, Dave would announce the moment of silence.

The stadium grew quiet as the crowd waited. She felt isolated and alone here, second-guessing her decision to stay in the booth. Maybe she, too, needed the kind of closure publicly saying goodbye to Andrea would provide.

I'm so sorry. Tears blurred the familiar scene through the ticket window. *I didn't know. I didn't understand. If only you'd told me…*

The lights blinked out, eliciting a drawn out ahhh from the crowd before silence again fell. As it did, Lindsey realized that not only had the switch for the field lights been thrown, someone had cut off the lights outside the stadium as well.

Across the parking lot, the glow from a streetlamp glinted off the tops of the rows of cars. Here, in the shadow cast by the overhanging bleachers, it was as dark as pitch. Then, in that overwhelming darkness, she became aware of the smell of smoke.

She turned from the open window, looking toward the door at the back of the booth. Although she couldn't see the smoke she smelled, there was a flicker of red visible along the crack at the bottom of the frame. *Fire?*

She tried to picture the area behind the booth. There was nothing back there but the steel Dumpster where the clean-up crew put the trash left in the bleachers after the games. No grass or weeds grew in the mixture of sand and dirt around the small wooden building.

Wooden, she realized with a sense of horror.

And by now there was no doubt it was on fire. She could not only hear the crackle of the flames, but the smoke she'd smelled was seeping inside the booth.

She glanced back toward the window. Although the opening was large enough for her to crawl through, at some time in the past steel bars had been installed three quarters of the way down it. The space left under them was sufficient for money and tickets to be passed back and forth, but it was not nearly large enough to offer a means of escape.

Which meant the only way out was the back door. The one that seemed to be on fire.

A moment of silence. That's what Dave had said. Which meant that in sixty seconds, the lights would come up and someone would notice what was happening.

There was no need to panic. There were thousands of people within shouting distance. Somebody would look around. Or somebody would smell the smoke and come out to investigate. Somebody—

With one last glance through the ticket window, she ran to the door. She put her hands around the knob, its metal already heated from the fire outside. If she opened it, the flames would come in. And there were a lot of combustible items stored inside the building.

It would be better just to wait. To go back to the window and breathe the air that was still pouring in. And start screaming for someone to extinguish the fire and let her out.

Despite the logic of all that, she couldn't force her fingers to release the knob. She wanted out before the fire got any bigger. If it was just at the bottom of the door, she could jump it. Even if she got burned a little it was better than taking the chance that someone might discover what was going on before it was too late.

She turned the knob and pulled. The door moved slightly inward and then caught. It refused to open wider even under her repeated and increasingly frantic efforts, until finally she came to the only possible conclusion as to why.

Someone had slipped the padlock she'd unlocked earlier back through the hasp. Someone—clearly the same someone who had started the fire—had locked her inside the burning booth.

Twelve

Jace watched the sea of candles waving slowly back and forth in time to the sole trumpeter's mournful rendition of "Amazing Grace." Someone in the stands had begun singing the words to the hymn, and the sound spread around the stadium as more and more of the crowd joined in.

Although the principal had announced there would be a moment of silence, either the band director or the kid with the trumpet had taken it upon himself to extend the tribute. And in spite of his self-avowed cynicism, Jace had to admit the whole thing was moving. And far too late to matter to Andrea Moore.

Did you tell her you cared while she was alive? Or did you make fun of her because she didn't wear the right kind of clothes or was ten pounds over the latest anorexic standards of Hollywood? Or maybe you didn't do any of those things. Maybe you just ignored her as unworthy of your attention.

Recognizing that even for him, that kind of thinking bordered on sacrilege, at least right now, Jace turned away from the tiny, wavering flames dotting the field to look across the sea of people standing in the bleachers. Although his eyes had adjusted to the darkness, he couldn't make out individuals, simply a mass of humanity silhouetted against the night sky.

He wasn't sure why he'd come. To get a feel for what the community was thinking? Or to find out how the students were reacting to the suicide? Or because his gut continued to tell him that Andrea's suicide wasn't what it seemed?

Or rather, not *only* what it seemed. Up until the moment when she'd walked in from work and discovered her daughter's body, the mother had thought the girl was doing well. They'd both been proud of her progress. Reassured that finally she had turned things around. Even her therapist, with whom he'd talked this afternoon, had agreed with their assessment.

Which had left Jace with a question he couldn't answer. On a day when everyone at Randolph-Lowen had assured him nothing out of the ordinary had occurred, why had Andrea Moore gone home from school and slit her wrists, watching as blood pooled in the bottom of the shower until she passed out and died?

He took a breath, trying to push the image that had haunted him from the time he'd been called to the scene last night out of his head. And then he took another breath. This one deeper. Longer. With purpose.

Something was burning. His first thought was the candles. His gaze returned to the field, sweeping the mass of flickering lights, looking for anything that might explain the smoke. No blaze, other than that from their small, individual wicks.

He raised his eyes to survey the guest stands on the opposite side of the stadium. Made of wood, both smaller and lower than the concrete bleachers provided for the home crowd, they, too, offered no explanation for what he smelled.

With the lights out, it should have been easy to spot a fire large enough to produce smoke. His eyes searching outside the stadium, Jace became aware that not only had the flood-lights illuminating the field been extinguished, so had every light around. The entire area was black as pitch.

He turned, reassured that the streetlamps on the main road were burning. Those would provide light for the parking lot, the most likely area for mischief. And one that would be especially vulnerable while everyone's attention was concentrated on the field.

He began to push his way through the spectators who'd crowded the area between the concession stand and the front gate to watch the ceremony. As he neared the fence surrounding the stadium, he saw that no one was collecting tickets at the gate.

It was only halftime, yet when he'd come to the game last week, Lindsey's friend had told him tickets were required until after the third quarter.

Tickets.

Lindsey had been working the ticket booth again tonight. Shannon Anderson hadn't been there, her place taken by a man Jace hadn't recognized. In the pregame rush, the guy had taken his money and pushed the ticket under the burglar bars without making eye contact.

Although Jace had deliberately chosen not to go to the window where Lindsey was working, he'd watched her while he'd waited for his change. She, too, had been focused on the crowd lined up in front of her, her face pale and strained in the shadow of the fluorescent light above her head.

Remembering that moment, Jace began to run, unable to explain his sense of urgency. In his hurry to get outside the gate, he bumped into someone he hadn't seen in the darkness. Child, he realized, as he caught the little boy by the shoulders to right him before he fell.

"Sorry. You all right, big guy?"

"I'm okay."

"Sorry about bumping you. Okay now?"

"No harm done. I told you to stay with me, Nathan," a man Jace assumed to be the kid's father said. "Thanks."

"My fault. It's hard to see out here."

"That's why we stopped. I didn't want to take a chance on losing them in the dark, but he just had to see the band."

Behind Jace, the last notes of the trumpet faded away into stillness, as the voices of the crowd, now several thousand strong, sang the final word of the hymn. In the momentary silence between that and the rustle of the spectators once more taking their seats, Jace finally heard the screams.

"Help. Somebody help me."

"Call 9-1-1." Jace said to the man with the boy. "Tell them there's a fire at the stadium." He didn't wait to see if his orders were obeyed. Even if they were, it might be too late by the time the fire trucks arrived.

As he ran, he yelled over his shoulder at the people who had begun to follow him toward the exit, "I need a fire extinguisher."

On his right, someone said, "Maybe the concession stand."

"Get it."

By that time, Jace was through the gate. He didn't stop at the barred window, although he could see Lindsey leaning down to yell through the narrow opening at its bottom.

The front of the booth wasn't on fire. A reddish glow came from its back, which was under the bleachers and thus hidden from the crowd. As was undoubtedly the intent.

He rounded the corner of the small building, stripping off his blazer as he ran. When he reached the back, the flames were already so high they licked at the roofline. And the door to the booth, the one at which he'd met Lindsey to take her to dinner last Friday night, was at the heart of the conflagration.

Hand shielding his eyes, he tried to see what was fueling

the blaze. Although it was obvious something was piled on the ground right in front of the door, he couldn't tell what.

Using his coat to beat back the flames, he tried to get close enough to the building to kick whatever was there away. The intensity of the heat drove him back.

Where the hell was that extinguisher? He glanced over his shoulder. In the light from the fire, he could see several people watching him. None of them seemed eager to help.

"Extinguisher," he yelled again. Someone broke away from the crowd that had begun to collect and disappeared around the corner of the booth.

Jace turned his attention back to the blaze. He could wait for the fire trucks, but once the wooden wall really caught, it might be too late even for them to get Lindsey out.

Besides, the heat and the smoke were as dangerous as the fire itself. Once it burned through to the inside of the building, the air from the windows at the front would only fuel the growing inferno.

He beat at the flames again with his coat, dropping it when the material flared up in his hands. Unless he could push whatever had been piled in front of the door away, he wouldn't be able to put this out. And in a matter of seconds the wooden wall would be fully engaged.

Stepping back from the heat, he scanned the area under the bleachers. He needed a board or a pole of some kind.

Just as he decided there was nothing like that to be found, someone pushed past him. A man, a rake or a shovel in his hands, rushed toward the flames. Braving the heat, he thrust whatever he carried into the pile at the bottom of the door. After several attempts, he succeeded in pulling part of the burning debris away from the building.

"Here." Someone from the crowd finally put an extinguisher into Jace's hands.

Although it wasn't standard size, intended to be kept in a car or a truck rather than a building, it was better than nothing. Pulling the seal, Jace directed its contents against the door. As the extinguisher began to beat back the fire, he saw that the padlock had been inserted into the hasp of the door and snapped shut.

If there had been any thought in Jace's mind about the possibility that this was an accident, that single, cold-blooded act destroyed it. Someone had locked Lindsey in the booth and then stacked something flammable against the door.

Although it smoldered, smoke rising from the charred wood, the door itself was no longer burning. And the man with the rake continued to maneuver whatever had fueled the fire farther and farther away from the booth.

Reversing the empty extinguisher, Jace used it to pound on the hasp. The lock itself held, but after a few blows of Jace's makeshift hammer, the nails holding the hasp pulled free from the charred frame.

He dropped the container and retrieved his ruined jacket from the ground. Wrapping it around his right hand, he gripped the edge of the door, jerking it open. Smoke billowed out from the interior, driven by the cross draft created by the ticket window. In the darkness, he could see nothing.

"Lindsey?" He took the single step up into the booth, the smoke eddying away from him as he moved inside. "Lindsey?"

He never saw her, but suddenly she was there, her arms wrapping around him as if she didn't intend to let go. The strength of that embrace reassured him about her safety. And reminded him of how close a thing this had been.

He pulled away, putting his arm around her back to direct her outside. As they emerged from the booth, the lights around the stadium came on, revealing those who had looked on as he and the man with the rake fought the fire.

Jace's eyes went immediately to his helper. White haired, heavyset, and wearing a county maintenance uniform, the man leaned against his rake, trying to catch his breath. A few feet away the remains of what appeared to be a blackened crate stuffed with refuse continued to smolder.

"You okay?" Jace asked.

The man nodded, air wheezing in and out of his mouth in labored gasps. "You two?" he managed.

"We're fine. Thanks to you."

"I told 'em they needed to fix those." The man nodded toward a melted tangle of wires dangling from the charred roof.

Before they'd been damaged by fire, they must have run from the building to one of the poles holding the stadium lights, Jace realized. The power supply for the booth?

"Must have overheated and set off that trash sittin' there," the worker went on. "Told 'em a dozen time it was dangerous to have that much stuff plugged into a jury-rigged source like that."

Even if it was possible that had been the cause of the blaze, it didn't explain the locked door. Opportunistically locked? Jace didn't buy that. Not for a minute.

In the distance he finally heard the wail of sirens. As the sound grew louder, more and more people came crowding into the space behind the small building.

Jace realized why it had taken so long for anyone to become aware of the fire. The booth had been built to extend beneath the concrete bleachers. Only when the smoke had risen high enough to drift over its roof had the smell reached inside the stadium. Even then, if he hadn't heard Lindsey's screams…

He looked down, realizing that he still had his arm around her. She was leaning against him as if exhausted.

"You all right?"

She nodded, her hair brushing against his chest. The movement seemed to set off a fit of coughing. When it was over, she lifted her hand, touching the side of his face.

"You're burned."

If so, he hadn't been aware of it. Given the ineffectiveness of using his coat to beat out the flames, he wasn't surprised he'd suffered collateral damage.

Collateral damage. The words reverberated unpleasantly.

He moved his head so that her fingers no longer made contact with his cheek. Reflex rather than a conscious rejection of her concern, but he knew from her expression how she'd taken it.

He'd been raised in a family of four brothers, where the cardinal rules for dealing with injuries had been ingrained from an early age. If it was a scrape or a bruise, you rubbed dirt on it. Anything internal, you walked it off. And as long as you could do either of those, you kept your mouth shut. He still wasn't comfortable talking about his pain. Not any of it.

Lindsey's body stiffened slightly before she straightened, breaking away from his hold. "Thank you. I was terrified that... I didn't think anyone was ever going to hear me."

He nodded, aware once more of the press of people. Soon the paramedics would arrive to check them both out, which wouldn't be a bad idea. As the adrenaline began to fade, Jace became conscious that the burn Lindsey had noticed on his face wasn't the only one he'd suffered. He'd been oblivious to pain as he'd fought the fire, but now injured nerve endings clamored for attention. If he ended up in the hospital tonight—

He had turned his head, speaking low enough that only she could hear. "No matter what he says about the wiring, this was set. They locked the door," he went on, because she needed to understand, "and then they piled trash in front of it and set it on fire."

Eyes bleak, she nodded, the movement tight and controlled.

"You see anybody around here before the lights went out?"

She shook her head before she remembered. "Some man with his little boys. Maybe three and five years old."

"They come from behind the booth?"

"I watched them walk up from the parking lot. And then I watched them walk in through the gate. I wanted to be sure that whoever was taking tickets admitted them. I didn't charge him because he asked if he still had to pay, and I thought maybe it was a strain..." She stopped, seeming to realize that had nothing to do with the information Jace was looking for. "There was nobody else out here. I think most of the crowd had heard about the candlelight service and wanted to get inside to see it."

"When was that decision made?"

"About the ceremony? Maybe...forty-five minutes before the game. I asked Dave to okay it myself. The cheerleaders wanted time to tell the students and to give out the candles."

So a good half hour before the game most of the people in the stadium would have known the lights were going out at the half. Plenty of time for someone to put this into play.

As for why the lights were out everywhere instead of just the field, he'd have to take that up with whoever had set this in motion. From what Lindsey had said that would be Campbell.

"You folks all right?"

Jace glanced up to find that the fire department had finally arrived. The paramedic who'd asked the question moved them aside so that the firemen could get close to the building.

"You need to check out the guy with the rake," Jace said. "He seemed to be feeling the smoke and exertion. Older man in a maintenance uniform. White hair."

"I'll do that. How about you, ma'am?"

"Just a sore throat from the smoke."

"We'll check you all out. Can you two make it to the truck?" He tilted his head in the direction of the emergency van that had been pulled up onto the inner edge of the parking lot. "Wait there and I'll see about the other gentleman."

"I'm fine," Jace said.

"You got burns that could be deeper than you think. Let us take a look at them to make sure."

Lindsey's hand slipped into his. "Let them look."

"Tell them not to do anything with the crate and that trash over there," Jace instructed the EMT. "I'll send someone to pick them up."

The paramedic turned his head, looking at the smoldering pile Jace indicated. "What for?"

"Evidence," Jace said tightly.

The man's eyes swung back to his face. "Of what?"

"Arson for a start. Then we'll go from there."

Thirteen

The paramedics had insisted on taking all three of them to the regional medical center. Although Jace had protested, Lindsey hadn't argued.

Maybe they would keep her overnight, she reasoned. That way she wouldn't have to face her empty house *or* explain to her parents why she wanted to sleep at theirs.

Besides, her throat and chest really were raw from the smoke she'd inhaled. Maybe they could give her something for that. And something that would help her sleep.

"Everything looks fine," the doctor who'd examined her announced as he came back into the treatment room where he'd asked her to wait.

He was younger than she was, but that difference hadn't prevented him from flirting. After Jace's reaction to the feel of her hand on his cheek, the resident's attraction had been balm to her battered ego.

"Lung function's good," he went on, thumbing through the results of the tests he'd asked for. "The coughing and rawness are the result of smoke irritation. It should clear up completely within twenty-four hours. If they don't, you can make an appointment with your regular physician or come back here. Got any questions?"

"What about the man who was brought in with me?"

"Guy with the burns? Superficial. You were both lucky. Of course, I'd say that's par for the course for him."

"I'm sorry?"

"A little ER humor. You want to see him?"

"Is that okay?"

"No reason why not. They're putting dressings on a couple of the places, but you can go in and watch. Give him a little moral support. I'll show you the way."

He offered his hand to help Lindsey off the table, his fingers closing firmly around hers. He waited to release her until he was sure she wasn't lightheaded.

He and the nurse watched as she gathered up her purse and the papers they'd given her, including the prescription for the sleeping pills she'd asked for. Then the resident led her out of the room and down a long, glass-walled corridor.

He opened the door to another treatment room without knocking and ushered her inside. "You got company."

A nurse was putting a square of gauze over an angry-looking patch of skin on Jace's left shoulder. His *bare* shoulder, Lindsey realized, her mouth suddenly dry.

Jace Nolan, fully dressed, was a force to be reckoned with. And he was undeniably more impressive without his shirt.

His skin was darkly and evenly tanned, the chest it covered broad and firmly muscled, like that of a well-conditioned athlete rather than someone who had lifted weights to achieve that look. Her eyes traced along a defined six-pack, bisected by a dark arrow of hair that disappeared into the top of his khaki trousers. Despite the fact that he was sitting on the end of the examination table, bent slightly forward as the nurse worked on his burns, there wasn't a hint of fat around his waistline.

It wasn't until she raised her eyes from her unthinking assessment that she understood what had elicited the doctor's remark about luck. The scars were on the opposite side of Jace's chest from where the nurse was working, one just above the bulge of his pectoral, the other near the top of the rib cage. Red and puckered in contrast to the smooth, brown skin that surrounded them, even to a layman's eye it was obvious the marks had been made by bullets.

"You okay?" Jace asked, his dark eyes concerned.

"Just some smoke irritation. What about you?"

"A couple of cinders burned through my shirt."

"I can give you one to wear home," the resident offered.

"I'd be grateful."

"There you go," the nurse said, pressing the last of the tape across the bottom of the pad. "Don't get 'em wet for a couple of days."

"Thanks."

"You got somebody to call that can come get you?" the doctor asked.

They'd ridden over with the paramedics. Lindsey hadn't even thought about her car back in the stadium lot. She assumed Jace hadn't either. "I could call my dad."

"The department will send a car," Jace said, obviously reading the lack of enthusiasm in her voice. He eased down off the table, rolling the shoulder the nurse had just bandaged.

"If the burns don't seem to be healing when you take off the dressing in a couple of days, you need to come back."

"They'll be fine."

"You get those on the job?" the resident asked, nodding toward the reddened scars on Jace's chest.

"You said you had a shirt I could borrow."

"In my locker. I'll get it."

"Thanks."

The nurse had gathered up the materials she'd used to treat the burns. She handed Jace a tube of ointment. "You might as well have this. It's just going in the trash."

"Thanks."

The nurse smiled at Lindsey. "Keep him out of trouble. Not that that'll be easy from the looks of him."

"I will," Lindsey agreed, feeling like a fool as she said it. "Thank you."

The nurse followed the resident out the door, leaving them alone. Obviously, the medical personnel believed their relationship was very different from the one that existed between them. One strained by the argument they'd had the night Jace thought someone had broken into her house.

Another time Jace had come to her rescue, she realized. As he had tonight. "Thank you."

She couldn't remember if she'd told him that at the stadium. He'd been too intent on grilling her about who'd been around the booth before the fire. Still, he *had* probably saved her life, and she needed to express her gratitude.

"Somebody else would have broken down that door."

"Maybe. Eventually. But you were the one who did." And at no small cost to himself. She suspected from his earlier behavior that he prefer she not make reference to the burns. Just as he'd ignored the resident's question about the scars. "I am truly very grateful."

Jace was saved from having to respond when the door opened again. In his hand the doctor held a faded black T-shirt.

"My workout shirt. Old, but clean. Actually, it's just out of the dryer."

"I'll send it back to you."

"Doesn't matter. Like I said, it's old."

"Thanks." Jace took the shirt and slipped his hands into the sleeves.

Lindsey was close enough that she heard the intake of breath when he raised his arms to pull it over his head and then down across his chest. The thin knit, which was probably loose on the lanky frame of the young doctor, clung to Jace's body, emphasizing all the attributes she'd just mentally catalogued.

She pulled her eyes away to smile at the resident. "Thanks for everything."

"Y'all take care now." He opened the door of the exam room, allowing them to precede him into the hall. "Go to the end and take a left. That will get you back to the ambulance entrance. You can make your call from there."

Jace nodded, putting his hand against the small of Lindsey's back. His touch sent a shiver up her spine, although she knew the gesture was meaningless.

She was probably reacting so strongly because she'd just been treated to the display of his rather blatant masculinity. Or maybe it was gratitude he'd been the one willing to brave the flames. In any case, she was aware of him as a man in a way she hadn't been since the night he'd taken her out to dinner.

All you are to Jace Nolan is a component in his investigation of the church fires. No more and no less than you've ever been. Just because he happened to be the one on hand when the fire was discovered tonight doesn't make any of this personal. He's a cop. Protecting people is his job. And you're an idiot if you take any of this any differently.

The automatic door to the emergency entrance the resident had described opened before them. Jace stepped aside, allowing her to go through. Once the panel slid closed behind them, he took a deep breath, filling his lungs with the humid night air.

"I can't stand that smell."

"Of a hospital?"

"You have your cell?" he asked without answering. "Mine was in the inside pocket of my blazer."

Which meant it had met the same fate as his jacket. Something else she owed him for. She fished around for her phone in the bottom of her purse and held it out to him.

"I really can call my dad," she offered again.

"You up to dealing with that tonight?"

She wasn't, she realized. She didn't even know what to tell them about what had happened. Although Jace might be convinced someone had locked her in the booth and then set it on fire, that entire scenario was still hard for her to grasp. It would be even harder for her mom and dad.

"I should probably call them anyway. They may hear about the fire from someone else."

"Calling them is one thing. Having to replay what happened is another."

"Actually..." She hesitated, reluctant to confess that she was coward enough to have been thinking about staying with them tonight. "I'm not looking forward to going home. I mean, if you're right about what happened at the game—"

"I'm right." Unequivocal.

"Then that's twice someone has targeted me."

"It makes you wonder, doesn't it?"

"Wonder what?"

"What you know. Or what they think you know."

Before she could protest the conclusion he'd come to, Jace flipped open her cell and punched in a number. After a moment he put the phone to his ear, clearly waiting for a response.

As he did, she looked out over the parking lot, trying to figure out what she was supposed to know that had made her a target. Something about the church fires? Or about Andrea?

"This is Nolan. I'm at Grace Regional Medical Center, at the ambulance entrance in the back. I need you to send a squad car to take me home." He listened again, before he closed the case with a snap, holding it out to her.

She took it automatically, her mind still working at the puzzle he'd given her. "I don't know *anything*. And I don't know why anyone would think I do."

"One, because you've been seen with me on a couple of occasions and I'm in charge of the arson investigation. Two, because as far as anyone knows, you were the last person associated with the school to see Andrea Moore alive. And, in all likelihood, the last person to talk to her before she died."

The last person to talk to her before she died. For some stupid reason, she hadn't realized that.

"That doesn't mean I know anything about either."

"Someone obviously doesn't believe that."

"It's the truth."

"Maybe not."

Which meant Jace thought Andrea might have told her something important. "We talked about the test. She didn't confide in me. If I'd had any idea what was in her head—"

"I came to you. So did Andrea. Obviously that's making somebody uncomfortable."

"Uncomfortable enough to want to *kill* me?"

"I'm not sure either incident was intended to do that."

"Then… What does that mean? Exactly?"

"As attempts at murder, they were pretty inefficient."

"They didn't feel inefficient to me."

"Snake bites are rarely fatal. Painful and dangerous, yes. But rarely fatal. And tonight… Why pull that stunt in front of thousands of people?"

"It *wasn't* in front of them. And it almost succeeded. If it hadn't been for you and a couple of other people—"

"Who were *there.* A lot of people were there. I can't see how anyone could believe that was going to be a successful attempt on your life."

"Then what was it?"

"Another warning about keeping your mouth shut. Or an act of revenge."

"*Revenge?* For what?"

"For talking to me."

She still was. She had been tonight in front of all those people. Actually, she'd stood at the back of that smoldering ticket booth with his arm around her.

If Jace was right, and she was being targeted because of her relationship to him, the smartest thing she could do would be to have nothing else to do with him.

She'd given him the analogy of the rattlesnake being a warning. If he was right about the fire—

"Andrea didn't tell me anything, Jace. I don't have any idea why she killed herself."

"Would you be willing to try and re-create that conversation for me? As close to word-for-word as possible?"

"I told you most of it this morning at school. There's really nothing in what she said…"

She hesitated, trying to think if she might be mistaken. Had Andrea given her a clue as to what was wrong? If so, she hadn't picked up on it.

"Don't try to force it," Jace advised. "We'll sit down and talk about it when you're rested."

She laughed, thinking how little sleep she'd managed this week. Despite having a prescription that might help, there was no way to get it filled tonight. She wasn't going to drive to the Wal-Mart out on the highway. Not alone. Not at this time of night. Especially not after what Jace had just suggested.

"Something funny?"

"That whole idea of me being rested. I can't remember the last time I slept for more than a couple of hours at a stretch. I doubt that after this tonight will be any different."

"You aren't sleeping?"

"Not since Tuesday."

She'd never before understood the psychological implications of sleep deprivation as a punishment. She did now.

"You want me to stay with you tonight?"

She admitted the offer was tempting. Despite his earlier rejection. Despite what had happened the last time he'd been at her house. Despite her unexpected reaction to the sight of his bare chest tonight.

"My neighbors would talk," she said finally.

"Mine won't."

Which sounded like an invitation to spend the night at his place. Only, she wasn't sure what the invitation included.

"You're suggesting that I spend the night at your house?"

"Apartment. I haven't had time to house hunt."

But it sounded as if that were something he intended to do. For some reason—one she couldn't justify, given their relationship—she was pleased.

Because you're a glutton for punishment? Remember, this is a guy who couldn't bear to have you touch his cheek.

"It's not that I don't appreciate the offer—"

"But you aren't going to accept." He shrugged. "Up to you."

"Thank you. I mean that."

He made no response. They stood a few seconds in silence, both of them looking out over the relatively empty parking lot rather than at one another.

"It shouldn't take this long for them to get a car here."

He held out his hand. After a moment she dug her cell out again and placed it on his palm. He'd invited her to spend the night, and now it felt as if he couldn't wait to get rid of her.

Or maybe the man is tired and in pain and, having made his offer to protect you from all those thoughts that have been keeping you from sleep, he's ready to wash his hands of you.

Jace flipped open the case and began to dial. As he did, she turned to look out on the street once more.

"They're here," she said, tracking the cruiser as it approached the emergency entrance.

"About damn time." Jace closed the phone with a snap, handing it to her. When the squad car pulled up in front of them, he opened its back door, waiting for her to crawl in.

From the driver's seat, Rick Carlisle watched her slide across to make room for Jace. "Hear you all had some excitement at the ball game tonight. You okay?"

"I'm fine," Lindsey said. "A little smoke damaged."

"I can smell it. Shannon with you?"

"She didn't come tonight. I think—" Lindsey stopped, unsure what to say about her friend's decision. "Hard day at school," she finished softly.

"I heard about that, too. You just never know."

"Both our cars are back at the stadium." Jace interrupted their solitary conversation. "If you could take us there."

"You got it. Linds, if you'd rather, I can take you home and arrange to pick up your car tomorrow and bring it to you."

Before she could decide whether or not that was a good idea, Jace answered for her. "The stadium's fine. I'll make sure Ms. Sloan gets home safely."

Rick continued to look at her over the front seat. He seemed to be waiting for a response from her. The moment stretched, long enough to become awkward, as she weighed the two offers. In spite of her exhaustion, she went with her gut.

"That's okay, Rick. The stadium's fine. I might need my car earlier than you could get it to me."

And if I decide to make a run for it in the middle of the night, at least I'll have some means of transportation.

The deputy's lips pursed, but he didn't argue. He turned around instead and put the car in gear. "Stadium it is."

She stole a glance at Jace, but his face was turned toward the hospital. Obviously the scenery outside his window was highly interesting. At least more interesting than she was.

Of course, with Rick and his partner in the front, it was unlikely Jace would be willing to discuss either the events of tonight or Andrea's suicide. Or the church fires. Since those were apparently the only things they had in common…

As the car began to roll, she turned, looking out her own window. Whatever she had thought was going on between them the night they'd had dinner, clearly she'd been mistaken. Except…

He had been ready to break in to her house to protect her from an intruder. Fought a fire to rescue her. Invited her to spend the night with him.

She shook her head, denying the idea that might mean something. The invitation had come from his sense of responsibility. Because he'd gotten her involved in all this. Something he'd already confessed. The idea that he gave a rat's ass about her refusal was only wishful thinking.

And it was way past time she gave that up.

Fourteen

She turned into her driveway, Jace's headlights behind her, and pulled into the attached carport. As she killed the engine, she looked into the rearview mirror to watch Jace's lights go off. She waited for him to get out of the car, but when he didn't, she took her keys out of the ignition and climbed out.

Jace's door still hadn't opened. Maybe he was going to sit there until she was inside. Even if that was his plan, she should still say goodnight and once more try to express her gratitude for what he'd done. She punched the remote lock on her car and walked back to where he was parked.

As she approached, he lowered his window. In stark contrast to his refusal to make eye contract while they'd been in Rick's cruiser, he looked up at her, dark eyes unreadable.

"Carlisle a friend of yours?"

"Not particularly."

"But you know him."

"He and Shannon dated."

"Then why was he so interested in your arrangements tonight?"

"He was *interested* because he was worried about me.

Maybe he figured I'd be upset about my student's suicide," she said, not bothering to hide the sarcasm. "Or nervous about having been trapped in a burning building. Or about that snake I found in my house. Or maybe we just do things differently down here."

"Are you?"

"Am I what?"

"Nervous."

The easy lie was on the tip of her tongue. Something about the way Jace was looking at her kept her from offering it. "What do you think?"

"I think if you go into that house, you'll spend another night exactly like you've spent the last three."

Endlessly recycling every word and every action. Worrying. Sleepless. Guilty.

"If I do—"

"Go in, cut off the outside lights, and then come back out here in the dark."

She had told him her neighbors would talk. Clearly he had thought that concern was ridiculous—and at this point, so did she—but he was giving her a way around it.

If you go into that house, you'll spend another night just like you've spent the last three. It was a persuasive argument.

"They gave me a prescription for sleeping pills."

"You didn't stop to get it filled."

"The only place open is out on the interstate. I'll do it tomorrow."

"And in the meantime?"

She held his eyes, but he didn't say anything else. No attempt to coerce her. Just the offer he'd already made. And a way for her to accept it, despite the flimsiness of her excuse for not doing so before. "I'm trying to figure out why you asked me to go home with you."

"Because whatever's going on, I got you into it."

"So…basically your offer boils down to guilt."

"It's a powerful motivator."

One she knew about. If anything happened to her, Jace would feel just as she did about Andrea.

"I'll be fine," she lied.

"I'd like the opportunity to make sure of that."

By protecting her from the person who had put the snake in her hamper and set the fire tonight. Would that be wrong? Jace was a cop. And, as he'd said, he got her into this.

The problem was that, unlike somebody like Rick Carlisle, who might well have made this same offer, she was attracted to Jace. That alone changed the dynamics of the situation.

"I have no ulterior motive," Jace added. "If that's what you're worried about."

She almost laughed, considering the cause of her hesitation. "Believe me, the thought never crossed my mind."

"Really? I guess I should ask why not."

She'd left herself wide open for that one. "Because you don't strike me as that kind of man."

"You must not know many men."

Not like him. Something she'd admitted from the first.

The more she was around him, the more she recognized those differences. And the more she was attracted. A very dangerous attraction for her peace of mind.

"I really need to go inside."

There was no response. Clearly Jace had said all he intended to. The choice was hers. She could let him take care of her, or she could go into her house and spend another sleepless night wondering what would happen next.

Leaning down, she put her hands on the bottom of the window frame. "I know you don't want to hear this, but that doesn't mean I don't need to say it. Thank you for what you did tonight. For fighting the fire and for getting me out. Not many people would have—"

"You're right. I don't want to hear it. Get in the car, Lindsey. Go cut off your floodlights if you want. Then come back out here and get in the goddamn car."

"Why?"

"Because I want you to."

"And you always get what you want?"

"Very seldom. But in this case, it's what you want, too. You don't want to spend the night here. You've tried that, and it didn't work. You told me so yourself. All I'm asking is that you come home with me and get some sleep. I'll keep watch. I swear to God nothing else is going to happen to you."

It was the kind of promise her father had made when she was a child and had had a nightmare. *Go back to sleep, Lindsey girl. It's just a bad dream.* If only this were...

She removed her hands from the frame, at the same time straightening away from the car. She looked out over its top, conscious of the row of houses and the neatly mown lawns of her neighbors stretching to the corner.

Hers were the only lights on the street. That didn't mean that half a dozen people weren't looking out their windows to watch her say goodnight to whoever had followed her home.

Let them, she thought. *And let them think whatever the hell they want to.* Without giving herself a chance to change her mind, she walked around the front of Jace's car.

Before she reached the passenger side door, it opened. She slid into the seat. When she closed the door, the overhead light went out, providing a sheltering darkness.

"Now I know why you were chosen as the gifted co-ordinator."

"That isn't how it works," she said with a laugh.

"Well, it damn well should be," Jace said as he turned the key in the ignition.

She woke with a start, jarred out of the dream by its growing horror. Although she was aware enough to know it had been a dream, she was disoriented by the lingering images of the flames. Not real, she assured herself. None of it was real.

Except it had been, she thought, full consciousness returning in a rush. Real fire. Real danger. Real menace.

She took a breath, only now remembering where she was. And that she wasn't here alone.

There had been none of the awkwardness she'd expected when they'd reach Jace's apartment, which was in a complex on the edge of the downtown area. He'd shown her the bedroom and its adjoining bath. He'd opened a drawer and pointed out an unopened package of T-shirts. Then he'd left her alone.

She hadn't expected to sleep, but she had. Almost as soon as she'd closed her eyes. And now…

She turned her head, searching in the darkness for the clock on the bedside table. The digital display read 4:40 a.m.

More hours of uninterrupted sleep than she'd gotten in the last three days combined. And since it was Saturday, all she needed to do was to turn over and go back for five or six more.

She shut her eyes again, conscious of the deep silence that surrounded her. No sounds of traffic. Not at this time of the morning, despite the location. No noise from the occupants of the other apartments. Almost as if she were—

Alone? Her eyes opened. Ears straining, she lay in the darkness, trying to evaluate the quality of the stillness.

Jace was asleep. What he'd said about keeping watch had been metaphorical. He'd assured her that anyone who wanted to get to her would have to go through him, but that didn't mean he was *literally* out there watching.

She took a few soothing breaths, trying to return to that blessed state of oblivion from which the dream had pulled her. Instead, the images she'd fought through those sleepless nights at her house began to parade through her head.

Lifting the lid on her clothes hamper. Andrea standing in her doorway, fingers worrying at the cuff of her long-sleeved top. The reddish glow at the bottom of the door to the ticket booth. Jace's dark eyes looking up at her through the window of his car, the burn on his cheek obvious despite the darkness.

She wasn't sure why that particular image had been seared into her brain like the rest, but it was. At least it was far more palatable than the others.

She threw the covers off and crawled out of bed. She'd slept in her underwear and one of Jace's new T-shirts, but she wasn't going to go traipsing around his apartment looking for him like this. She grabbed her jeans off the chair she'd draped them across last night and slipped them on.

She hesitated when she reached the bedroom door. She had the urge to knock, although she was coming out of a room rather than going into one. Finally, she turned the handle and eased the door open.

There was a dim glow from the next room, the apartment's second bedroom, which Jace had told her he used as his office. Although the door was open, she was hesitant to walk in.

"Jace?"

"In here."

Emboldened by his response, she took the few steps that would take her to the doorway. His back to her, Jace was seated at a desk in front of a computer monitor. Apparently he *had* meant that "keeping watch" literally.

"Am I interrupting something?"

"I've been waiting for you to wake up. There's coffee in the kitchen. I drink mine black, so I'm short on amenities like cream. It's fresh, though, and I can vouch for its potency."

"It smells wonderful," she admitted, thinking caffeine might chase the remaining cobwebs—and the dregs of the nightmare—from her head.

Jace swiveled the chair around so he was facing her. The five o'clock shadow she'd noticed last night was darker, emphasized by the black T-shirt he still wore. If he'd been sitting here all night—

"I'll get you a cup while you take a look at that." He jerked his head toward the machine behind him.

"What is it?"

"You tell me," he said, pushing up out of the chair.

She had never liked guessing games. Her father said that was because she was afraid of being wrong. She'd always thought it had more to do with a fear of the unknown. Right now that's what the computer screen represented.

Jace walked past her and out of the room. An expanse of maybe twelve feet lay between her and whatever he had wanted her to see. *You tell me.*

She crossed her arms over her stomach, fighting a rush of nausea. There had already been enough this week. More than enough. Whatever this was…

Disgusted with her cowardice, she crossed the room until she was close enough to make out the central image on the monitor. She swallowed to control the nausea that climbed into the back of her throat. Then she closed her eyes and breathed deeply a few times to keep it at bay.

Jace wouldn't have asked her to look at this if it weren't important. That would take a cruelty he wasn't capable of.

She opened her eyes, deliberately focusing them on the

screen. As she took the final steps to the desk, she reached out with one hand to drag the chair Jace had vacated with her. She sat down in it, steeling herself for the emotional response she knew this site would evoke.

Surrounded by text and smaller pictures, a photograph of Andrea Moore centered the page. An Andrea Lindsey had never seen before. Her hair and makeup looked as if they'd been professionally done. Both the clothes she wore and the pose itself seemed deliberately provocative. Sexual in a way she had never associated with the girl.

Unconsciously, Lindsey shook her head, trying to reconcile the shy student she'd taught with this. Andrea looked as if she were trying to titillate the viewer. Or entice.

The thought was enough to make Lindsey's eyes go to the text at the bottom of the picture. It seemed innocuous enough. Name, age, the name of the school, favorite activities. Nothing more than the usual yearbook stuff.

Relieved by that normality, she continued to examine the page. On the right was a guest log, each entry accompanied by a photograph or icon or a slogan. Those had obviously been chosen by the individual posters, many of whom had left comments.

The column on the left of the photograph appeared to be a blog, the last entry dated two days ago. Twenty-four hours before Andrea had committed suicide.

Obviously this was what Jace had wanted her to read. Maybe he thought she could explain something Andrea had written. Something about her motives?

Why would you do that, Andrea? Why would you tell the whole world and then come to stand in my door and not tell me?

Somehow, despite the thick carpeting, she was aware Jace had reentered the room. She didn't turn, unwilling to reveal that she hadn't read what he'd wanted her to and was this upset.

He set a steaming cup of coffee down on the coaster beside the mouse. She picked it up, using the excuse to regroup. She took a sip, allowing the liquid to soothe her still-raw throat.

Only when she had taken two long swallows did she turn her head and look up at him. "Thanks."

"So what do you think?" He nodded toward the screen.

"I'm not sure I can do this. The last entry was written the day before she died. It's too soon."

"I can't ask her mother to read it, Lindsey. I don't know anyone who knew her better than you."

"That's just it. That's what you don't get. I *didn't* know her. *Obviously,*" she said, remembering Shannon's comment, "I didn't know her at all."

"Better than I did. All I'm asking is you read those pages and tell me what you think. It might be better to start a few days back. And look at the comments from that same time-frame."

"It seems… I don't know. An invasion of her privacy."

"She posted this on the Web. She *wanted* it read."

"*Before* she died. *Before* she made the decision to take her own life. Now… Now it seems as if we're ghouls, picking over her corpse." Exactly what Shannon had said yesterday.

"Picking over the corpse, as you call it, is how cops solve cases. I don't want to have to do that for another one of your students. I sure as hell don't want to have to do it for you."

"Andrea isn't a case, Jace. She committed suicide. The police aren't responsible for determining why."

"We are if her death has a bearing on another, on-going investigation."

So that, too, was part of the equation. Jace had implied Andrea's suicide hadn't been an isolated act. Not a coincidence that just happened to have occurred during the same week someone had attacked Lindsey. Twice.

"You still think all this is connected?"

"All this?"

"Me and the church fires, maybe." She had already conceded that because Jace was the lead investigator on those, they must have something to do with the attacks on her. "But Andrea? I told you that doesn't make any sense."

"Maybe not, but at least read this." He again indicated the screen with a tilt of his head. "All of it. All the comments. *Then* tell me it makes no sense."

Despite her reluctance, she knew that eventually she would have to do what he'd asked. If not tonight, then another night when she couldn't sleep. Alone. In a house that had become anything *but* the sanctuary it should be.

"Not with you here." She didn't want him looking over her shoulder, examining her every expression, reading into them things that she didn't want him to see. "Go get some sleep, Jace. I promise I'll wake you when I've read it all."

Fifteen

The fact that he didn't hear the bedroom door open indicated the depth of his exhaustion. It wasn't until Lindsey called his name that he began to climb out of the pit of sleep. By the time she said it again, the events of last night flooded back into his consciousness. Adrenaline roared into his system, bringing him awake and upright at almost the same time.

Lindsey must have been leaning over the bed. When he bolted up, the Glock he'd laid beside the pillow clutched in his right hand, she began backing away, her eyes wide.

"What's wrong?" he demanded.

Wordlessly, she shook her head, staring at the weapon.

No threat, he realized belatedly. That wasn't why she was here. Which meant… "You read it?"

She nodded, her eyes leaving the Glock to dart to his face. "And?"

He lowered the semiautomatic. His impression had always been that everyone down here was comfortable around guns. Based on Lindsey's reaction that wasn't true. Or maybe she just wasn't accustomed to having them pointed at her.

"She didn't do it."

Jace examined the sentence, trying to figure out the context, given that there were a couple of scenarios where the phrase "didn't do it" might apply.

"Didn't do what?" he asked carefully.

"That blog. Or any of them. Anything on that page. I'd bet my life that isn't Andrea's writing."

The wording was unfortunate, considering the stakes, but he ignored the unintended irony. "Writing a blog is a very different animal from writing an essay."

"I know. But there are all kinds of indications of authorship. In any kind of writing. The phrasing. Vocabulary. A lot of other things I probably couldn't explain to someone who doesn't read papers for a living. I've read Andrea's work for more than a year. She didn't write that filth."

He had set out to show Lindsey the image she had of her student as shy and retiring wasn't accurate. Now she was telling him that the person portrayed in the online profile he'd found wasn't just a different side of the girl she'd known. It had actually been created by someone else.

"Are you sure?"

It wasn't that he didn't believe her. She seemed too sure for him to doubt what she claimed as her area of expertise. He just needed some time to understand the implications.

"She didn't write it, Jace. I know."

"And the picture?"

Her eyes changed, losing their surety. "I...don't know. Photo-shopped maybe? Andrea's head on some other girl's body?"

Could it be determined if that had been done from a picture on the Web? He knew there were plenty of people who could tell about an actual photograph, but he didn't know how difficult that kind of manipulation, if it were well done, would be to spot on a computer screen.

"I don't know, but now that you mention it…"

He let the sentence trail as he got out of bed and crossed the room to the hall. When he reached the doorway to the second bedroom, he discovered his computer had gone to sleep while they'd been talking. He walked over and jiggled the mouse, only to find that Lindsey had clicked out of the site he'd left her to read. Her way of dealing with its graphic nature?

He sat down in the desk chair, still warm from contact with her body, and brought it up again. Even after a careful examination of the picture of Andrea, at this resolution he couldn't tell if it had been manipulated or not.

Whoever had put this up had to have a modicum of technical know-how. Most high-school kids these days had quite a bit, and he would be willing to bet some of Lindsey's students would qualify as experts. There were always a few who got off on this kind of stuff.

He couldn't think of anyone he could call on in the sheriff's department to verify her suspicions about the picture. A few of the deputies fancied themselves computer experts, but he didn't know if that expertise would spill over into determining if an image had been doctored.

"She wasn't that kind of person," Lindsey said from behind him. "Did you read all of that garbage?"

"Enough."

She moved nearer, so that she was standing in his peripheral vision. He glanced up at her, but her eyes were focused on the screen. She leaned down and toward the monitor, examining the image.

"Could this be a prom picture?" he asked. "Or a shot from a modeling portfolio? She have aspirations in that direction?"

Without straightening, Lindsey turned her head. They

were eye-to-eye, their faces in closer proximity than they'd ever been before. The urge to lean forward the few inches that separated them and put his lips against hers was almost undeniable. It seemed he could feel them under his. Soft and warm and open to his kiss.

"I don't know." She straightened, breaking the spell. "If she did, she never said anything to me about them."

"I'll ask her mother."

"Don't show her this, Jace. Not now."

"You don't think she might be aware of this already?"

"I can't imagine her knowing and not doing something about it. I can't imagine any mother letting this stay up."

Then she hadn't been exposed to the kind of parents he'd met. He'd known women who would have written that stuff about their daughters. And who would then have sold them to the highest bidder to satisfy their addictions.

"Andrea wouldn't do the kinds of things described here," Lindsey said. "I know you didn't know her, but…she really was shy. That," she nodded at the monitor. "That wasn't her."

"Then someone put the site up in her name."

"Can they do that?"

"All the time. These places don't require an ID. Anybody can get a space and then fill it with whatever they want."

"But why would they do that to Andrea? Why write things that vicious? All that sexual detail. As if she were nothing but a…" She stopped again, clearly unwilling to characterize the dead girl in the way she'd been represented on the site.

"As a joke," Jace suggested. "Hazing. Or bullying."

"It ought to be against the law."

Her tone said he was in charge of that. He doubted she wanted to hear all the reasons local law enforcement couldn't police both the Internet and the streets.

"It takes a while for the law to catch up with the technology, which is changing too rapidly."

"Do you think this had something to do with her death? That and the pregnancy rumor, maybe? Or that this is where that rumor originated? You did know about that, right?"

"Several people told me. Would she have come to talk to you about something like that?"

"About being pregnant? Or the site?"

"Either. Both."

"I don't know. All I know is she *didn't* talk to me."

"The kids ever talk at school about these profile sites?"

"Of course. Somebody will say something about what they've put up. Pictures or something. A blog. Some of them maintain their own sites, too, I think, separate from the group ones."

"Would you be comfortable asking your students about this?"

"Andrea's profile?" She had started shaking her head before she finished her answer. "All that would do is point it out to people who *haven't* seen it. Do you think we can get them to take it down? Considering the circumstances."

Considering the fact Andrea was dead.

Jace knew he could lean on the owners to accomplish that. *After* he'd leaned on them to find who'd put this up.

"I'll see what I can do. In the meantime I'd appreciate your help with your kids. If you don't want to ask all of them, then choose a couple you trust. Ask if this particular profile was being talked about at school. If they all knew about it. Or maybe more importantly, if Andrea did. Will you do that?"

He could ask those questions, of course, but they would be more forthcoming with Lindsey. Oftentimes, if a suspect trusted the interrogator, he'd add things he *wasn't* asked.

"I'll be glad to. As soon as it's down," she said, her tone

adamant. "I'm not going to take a chance on word getting out about this and having hundreds of people rush to view it."

He wasn't sure how quickly he could accomplish what she wanted. But Lindsey wouldn't have an opportunity to interact with her students until Monday anyway. Which reminded him of something else he needed to ask.

"You recognize any of the names attached to the comments?"

"Most of them don't *have* names. Just a nickname or a picture. Or some kind of icon. Those that did, the names were so common I couldn't connect them with any particular student."

"We need to make a list of them anyway."

"I can do that."

"And you'll talk to the kids about how many people knew about this?"

"I'll ask, but I'll be selective."

"Could you call them this weekend? Talk to them over the phone, maybe?"

"As soon as you get this filth about Andrea taken down."

He'd dropped Lindsey back at home on his way to the address David Campbell had given him over the phone. There had been half a dozen things about last night he knew he needed to follow up on. With the couple of hours of sleep he'd managed to grab while Lindsey read through the profile he'd shown her, he believed he'd remembered most of them.

First on his agenda was an interview with the kid who, according to the principal, had been charged with cutting off the lights. Campbell had assured Jace that his instructions had been clear that only the lights on the field were to be killed.

The principal had asked about Lindsey, saying that he'd tried to call her last night and had not gotten an answer. Jace had been noncommittal about the reason for that.

In his opinion, it was no one's business where Lindsey spent the night. With her concerns about her neighbors, however, and his own uncertainty about the culture of school politics in this district, he'd not been inclined to reassure her boss about her safety by telling him the truth.

He pulled up in front of a neat two-story colonial, checking the address on the mailbox against what he'd written in his notebook. According to Campbell, Steven Byrd was one of the most dependable kids in the senior class. A fine, upstanding young man who had applied to Duke and had a very good chance of being accepted. *And yet he can't manage to carry out a simple order without screwing it up?*

Putting his cynicism on hold, Jace climbed out of his car and walked up to the front door. He pressed the bell and then waited, idly examining the neatly trimmed shrubbery along the front of the house.

He turned when the door opened. The boy who stood just inside the threshold was heavyset, with a shock of brown hair in need of a trim. Behind the thick glasses he wore, the blue eyes widened when he saw Jace, a reaction that he quickly controlled.

"Steven Byrd?"

"That's right."

Jace removed his badge holder from the front pocket of his jacket, flipping it open to show his ID. "Detective Nolan. I'd like to talk to you."

The kid took his case, making a show of studying it.

"May I come in?" Jace asked when he finally handed it back. "I have some questions I think you can provide answers to."

"Is this about what happened last night?"

"That's right."

"Could we talk out here?" The boy took a step toward

Jace, pulling the door almost closed behind him. "My mom's asleep. She works nights."

"She work last Tuesday?"

There was no reaction this time except a slight puzzlement when the kid repeated, "*Tuesday* night?"

"PTA meeting at the school."

The kid looked relieved. "She went before work."

"And where did *you* go Tuesday night?"

"I didn't go anywhere. I was studying."

If Steven Byrd had been involved in putting the rattlesnake in Lindsey's hamper, nothing about his face gave him away. Jace didn't believe anyone this age could be that good an actor. Or that practiced a liar.

"I understand you're the one who cut off the lights at the stadium last night."

"Yes, sir."

"Who told you to do that?"

"Renee asked me if I could do it, and I said sure."

"Renee?"

"Renee Bingham. She's the head cheerleader."

"You talk to Mr. Campbell before you cut the lights?"

"Just Renee. She said she'd talked to him, and he'd said it was okay. They wanted to do the candlelight thing for Andrea."

"What did she tell you about the lights, Steve? Exactly."

"Just to cut them off. She said she'd signal me from the field when it was time. She said to watch her after the band got through, and she'd cue me when I was supposed to kill them."

"She didn't tell you *just* the stadium lights?"

"No, sir. I understood her to say all of them."

"You remember her exact words?"

"Can you cut off all the lights? Something like that." He

seemed less certain this time. "To tell you the truth, I didn't think it was important enough to memorize what she said."

For some reason that touch of sarcasm infuriated Jace. Maybe it was his exhaustion. Or the fact that, despite denying the need to fill the prescription for pain meds he'd been given last night, the burns on his chest and arms hurt like hell.

"You *did* hear what happened at the ticket booth while those lights were out?"

"Yes, sir."

Apparently the kid was bright enough to read Jace's face. The tone he'd used seconds ago was missing this time.

"Somebody set fire to it. With Ms. Sloan inside," Jace went on as if he hadn't spoken. "So I'm thinking that the instructions you received might be important enough for you to try and remember the exact words."

"I think that's what she said. I'm sure of it. 'Cut off all the lights.' That's what I did. If Mr. Campbell told her something else, you need to talk to Renee."

"Yeah? So you think she's the one who got it wrong."

"Yes, sir," the boy said, refusing to back down. "And I'm sorry about what happened to the booth. Ms. Sloan is my favorite teacher. Believe me, if I'd had any idea anything like that was going to happen—"

His eyes briefly considered the burn on Jace's cheek before they met and then held on his. There didn't seem to be any attempt at deception in their clear blue depths.

"Know much about snakes, Steve?"

Jace wasn't sure why he was pursuing this. Using every standard he knew to evaluate when someone was telling the truth, Byrd looked like a choirboy. Still, something bothered him about the boy's attitude.

"It's Steven."

"Okay, Steven, you know anything about snakes."

"*Snakes?* No, sir. Not much. I had a couple of ringnecks when I was a kid."

"No rattlers?"

"No, sir," the kid said with a grin, which faded pretty quickly when Jace didn't respond to it.

"How about Andrea Moore? What do you know about her?"

The boy's face settled into a properly serious expression. "She was a junior, so we didn't have any classes together. She was always quiet. Didn't come to a lot of extracurricular things at the school. I mean she was nice and all, but…" He shook his head. "I didn't really know her that well."

"Got a computer?"

"Yes, sir."

Again, there had been no reaction other than a slight puzzlement. Jace was beginning to feel he was making a fool of himself. "Know anything about manipulating images?"

"Like photographs, you mean?"

Jace nodded.

"A little. I can add a background and stuff."

"Put people in and out of the picture?"

The kid acknowledged his ability with a quick tilt of his head. For the first time since Jace had begun asking questions, Steven looked uncomfortable.

"You have a page on 'My Place'?"

"Everybody at school does."

Definitely defensive. And despite Lindsey's desire not to advertise Andrea's profile to her fellow students, Jace needed to follow up on that reaction.

He'd already called the company to have the page taken down, but he couldn't be sure it had been. And he couldn't afford to let the boy regroup. He needed to press him right now on what he knew.

Besides, there was always the possibility that Lindsey was wrong about Andrea's character. And he knew damn well she wouldn't like that idea, either.

"Did Andrea Moore have one?"

The flush started along the sides of the kid's neck, moving slowly into his cheeks as he tried to decide whether or not to lie. In the end, he made the right decision.

"Yes, sir."

"You read it?"

"Everybody did."

"I didn't realize she was that popular."

"It wasn't that." The kid again seemed to be weighing his answer. "It was pretty graphic. Her profile, I mean."

"As in having a lot of pictures?"

"No, sir. As in being sexually explicit." The color in the kid's face deepened, emphasizing every blemish of his skin.

"Was she that kind of girl, Steven? That's not the impression I've gotten."

"Like I said, I didn't know her all that well."

"You remember the central picture on her page? The big one of Andrea?"

Byrd nodded.

"You think it was manipulated?"

"I don't understand."

"Andrea's head imposed on someone else's body."

The blue eyes considered the idea, but after a moment the boy shook his head. "I don't know."

"But you know people who could do that."

"Some."

"Name them."

"Sir?"

"Who do you know that could manipulate a picture like that?"

Byrd laughed, shaking his head at Jace's naivety. "At least half the senior class. Probably lots of other kids, too. *Everybody* does that kind of stuff."

"Could you tell if somebody had?"

"If they had done it to Andrea's picture, you mean?"

Jace nodded. He wouldn't mind seeing what kind of setup Byrd had. Maybe he could tell something about his level of expertise from his hardware. And maybe glean some information about the boy's personality from his room.

"It's possible," Byrd said.

"Now?"

"You mean… I told you. My mom's asleep."

"Maybe we should wake her up. Tell her what happened last night. And about Andrea's profile. See what she thinks."

"You don't need to do that."

Jace knew he'd finally punched the right button. He could almost feel the panic emanating from the kid. He just wasn't sure if it was because of last night or because of Andrea Moore.

Part of his theory about the church fires had, from the beginning, been that whoever set them off had a curfew and someone checking up on whether or not they kept it. The fact that Byrd was so concerned about his mother knowing what was going on set off Jace's radar.

"We can go back to my room," the boy said. "I'm no expert—don't claim to be—but I can take a look at the picture for you. Maybe figure out if it's been shopped."

"Thanks, Steven. I really appreciate your offer to help."

Sixteen

"The kid didn't claim to be an expert." Jace's accent seemed more pronounced over the phone. "But he doesn't think the image was doctored. We printed a copy, and I'm going to show it to Andrea's mother to see if she recognizes the picture."

"You think that's a good idea?"

The woman had just lost her daughter. Lindsey couldn't imagine that she would be concerned right now about a picture of her that had been posted on the Internet.

"Steven said that everyone knew about that site."

"Oh, my God, Jace. If that's true… Do you think that's why she did it? Because people were looking at that and saying things about her?"

"I don't know. I do know that I want to find out who put it up. If someone else did it, then I want to know who."

"*If* someone else did it?"

"We won't know that until we hear back from the company."

"Can they tell you?"

"They'll give me what information they have. Whether or not we can trace it to the computer that was used to put the stuff up is a different question."

"I don't understand."

"We'd have to have pretty compelling evidence of who was involved to confiscate computers."

"Is that what you'd have to do?"

"I don't know. And I won't know until I find out what information the Web site host can give me. In the meantime, I'm going to see if this picture is really Andrea."

"I don't think her mom is going to like seeing it."

"Considering that her daughter is dead and this site may have played a role in her death, I think she'd want to know. With suicide it's the not knowing that's the hardest."

"Not harder than the loss."

"No, but feelings of guilt can make *that* harder to bear. In this case, it looks as if the mother did everything she was supposed to. I think she'd like to understand that it wasn't any failure on her part that precipitated this."

"You're right. Will you let me know what you find out?"

"I'll call you later this afternoon. The invitation's still open, by the way."

"Invitation?"

"My place. Tonight."

It sounded like a date, except they both knew it wasn't. "You have to sleep sometime."

"I thought I'd catch a few hours on the couch. If you're comfortable with that."

He meant if she were comfortable with him not staying up to keep watch. And she was. She knew she could sleep just knowing Jace and that gun were in the apartment. Whether that was a good idea or not was another thing entirely.

"Can I think about it?"

"All day."

"Thanks. And thanks for last night. For letting me stay,"

she added, wondering if he'd think she meant the fire. Not that she wasn't grateful for that. "Thanks for everything, actually."

"I think I liked it better when you didn't trust me. Or like me."

"I never said I didn't trust you."

He laughed. "I notice you didn't deny the other."

She couldn't. She'd been physically attracted from the start, but liking him had taken a while. "Fishing?"

"For compliments? Yeah, all those nice things you've been saying have confused me. I don't know how to act anymore."

"How about like a detective?" she suggested. "And let me know what you find out."

"I'll call you," he said again. "And Lindsey?"

"Yeah?"

"Watch your back."

"What does that mean?"

"Until we figure this all out, just be aware at all times that someone thinks you know something that's dangerous to their well-being."

She nodded as if he could see her. And then the connection was broken. She held the phone to her ear for a few seconds as Jace's warning reverberated in her mind.

Someone thinks you know something that's dangerous.

And if she did, she had no idea what that might be.

Although the video game he was playing usually calmed him—primarily because it allowed him to commit acts he couldn't get away with in reality—its virtual violence wasn't working today. Right now he needed to actually feel flesh split and bones crack and to know he'd caused that. This wouldn't suffice. Not for the level of his fury.

Shit-for-brains was going to get them all caught. And he

couldn't afford that. He couldn't afford to lose everything he'd worked for because of some puking, totally juvenile garbage.

He knew now that he should never have allowed himself to become vulnerable to someone else's stupidity. In the beginning this had all seemed like a game. Just like the one playing out on the screen in front of him. With what had happened last night, however…

Why the hell had that fucked-up asshole ever thought he could get away with something like that? They'd issued their warning, taking as much care with it as they had with the churches.

That…that had been something else. Impromptu. Careless. A petty act of jealousy that was going to bring the whole thing down around their ears. Just when it had been going so well.

He threw down the controller, walking around the room as he tried to think how to minimize the damage. It was too late to back away. Other targets were already in play, and once the campaign started, it tended to take on a life of its own.

That had been the beauty of the whole Suicide Club scheme. The fact that all they had to do was set things in motion and then let the forces they'd unleashed on the losers take over. There would be no one to blame. No one for the authorities to come after. Not until that idiot had pulled that boneheaded stunt at the stadium.

As long as he'd been in control, things had worked exactly as planned. And that was the key, of course. Being in control. Making the decisions. Manipulating everyone. What he needed to ensure would happen from here on out.

If he couldn't… If he couldn't, then he knew he'd have to take control of that, too.

* * *

Lindsey pushed the bell again, before she glanced at her watch. Twenty after eleven. Surely Shannon was up by now.

Of course, it was entirely possible she'd missed her. After what Dave had said about trying to get in touch with her last night, Lindsey had known she had to get over to her parents' house before they heard about the fire.

Although she'd downplayed the seriousness of what had happened and hadn't even mentioned the locked door, her mother had still been upset. Apparently neither of them had heard about the snake yet, so at least she hadn't had to deal with explanations about that.

She was about to try calling Shannon on her cell when the door opened. It was obvious by the nightshirt she was wearing and her bare feet that Shannon hadn't been up.

"Sorry," Lindsey said. "I thought you'd be awake by now."

"What time is it?" Shannon yawned, covering her mouth with her palm.

"Nearly eleven-thirty. You okay?"

"A.m. or p.m.?" Shannon stepped back to allow her to enter.

"A.m. You knew that."

"Yeah, even I'm not that far gone. You mad?"

"About what?"

"That I ditched the game last night."

"You can buy my forgiveness with a cup of coffee. All my folks had was decaf."

"You've already been over there?" Shannon threw the question over her shoulder as she led the way to the kitchen.

"Duty visit."

"Aren't they all?"

"So what happened to you last night?"

"I came home, had a couple of drinks, took some Klonopin, and went to bed."

"Not the smartest combination," Lindsey warned, easing up onto one of the tall stools on the opposite of the breakfast bar from where Shannon was measuring coffee into a filter.

"It was last night."

"Seriously, that's dangerous and you know it."

"Okay. No need to stage an intervention. I'll be good. So did you go?"

"To the game? Somebody had to sell tickets."

"You're a better woman than I am."

"You have no idea. Almost before I got out of the car, the cheerleaders met me, wanting me to ask Dave to okay a moment of silence for Andrea. They'd bought candles and everything. They wanted me to read a poem, but I told them I couldn't do that."

"Oh, God." Shannon's voice was rich with genuine sympathy. "I told you mine was the smarter choice. What did Dave say?"

"What could he say?"

Shannon inserted the basket into the coffeemaker before she turned to ask, "Was it awful?"

"I don't know. I didn't see it. I stayed in the booth."

"Wise move."

"Not really. Somebody piled trash in front of the door and set it on fire."

Shannon had been in the act of taking mugs out of one of the upper cabinets. As Lindsey's words penetrated, she turned, her mouth open. "Are you kidding me?"

Lindsey shook her head. Although she'd discussed the incident with her parents, she'd made it sound as if it had all been an accident. Putting into words the reality that someone had deliberately endangered her life had more of an emotional impact than she would have believed.

"Who would do something like that?"

"Maybe whoever put the snake in my house."

"Okay, that's enough of this shit. You call the police?"

"Jace was at the game. He's the one who put out the fire."

"So what did Sir Galahad say about the fire?"

"Don't call him that. He got burned in the process and ended up in the emergency room. If he'd waited for the fire department to arrive…" She shrugged.

"That's what the county pays him to do, Linds. Save lives. It's his job."

"Yeah, well, in that case, he earned his pay."

"You don't really believe somebody was trying to kill you."

"They locked the door, so yeah, I think maybe they might have been."

Her friend opened her mouth again and then closed it as she absorbed the information. "Shit," she said finally.

"I swear I'm not paranoid, but if you put this together with the other…"

"*Why?* Why would anybody want to hurt you?"

"Jace says they think I know something."

"About what?"

"The church fires. Andrea. I don't know."

"Do you?"

"Not that I'm aware of. Jace says I may have been the last person Andrea talked to, so maybe…"

"You said she *didn't* talk."

"*They* don't know that."

"*They* who? Who does your detective think 'they' are?"

"He's not *my* detective. And that's what he's trying to find out—who they are."

"Well, you know, he needs to get a freaking move on. You want to stay here? You know you're welcome."

It was tempting. As Jace's offer had been. "He feels guilty because he got me into this."

"Jace? He didn't have anything to do with Andrea coming to see you."

"No, but he targeted me as a source of information because he's convinced my kids were involved with the arson."

"Maybe he's right."

"I didn't think so, but… You said you suspected someone from the beginning."

"I didn't say that."

Lindsey couldn't remember her exact wording, but the implication had been that Shannon could believe what Jace was saying. "Words to that effect. You thought someone in the program was capable of that kind of mischief."

"Great and wise counselor that I am."

"You're a very *good* counselor."

"So good that one of my students went home and cut her wrists, and I didn't have a clue she was going to do it."

"Nobody did, including her mother. How could you have?"

Without answering, Shannon turned, finally taking down the mugs and setting them on the counter beside the coffee-maker.

"How could you possibly have known, Shannon?" Lindsey repeated. "You're being ridiculous."

"Do you know what I did all last week? I made out remediation schedules for all the turds who've sat on their asses for twelve years, doing no homework, ditching school whenever the mood struck them, acting like idiots in the classroom, and who now can't pass the grad exam. *Those* are the kids who got my attention last week."

"That's your job."

"So is knowing what's going on in the heads of the ones who need help the most. Like Andrea."

"None of us knew Andrea was vulnerable. We couldn't have. We weren't told."

"If I'd done my job, I might have found out. I could have called her in to talk about how she was doing. I might have established some kind of relationship with her besides asking which science course she wanted to take this year."

"She was seeing a therapist. You're a high school counselor. One with too far many kids to be responsible for—"

"*Responsible.* Bottom line. I was responsible for Andrea."

"No more than the rest of us. I was her special ed teacher. I filed an individual education plan for her every year. Met with her mom. Feel guilty if you want to, but don't think you have sole ownership of that."

"Oh, you're right. There's plenty of guilt to go around."

"And if we wallow in it long enough, we'll let the next one slip through the cracks."

"Not me," Shannon said.

"Meaning?"

"I can't do this anymore. It's not what I signed on for."

"None of us signed on for watching kids commit suicide."

"I don't mean that. It's all the other crap they're giving us to do. Testing, schedules, remediation plans. I swear I haven't had time to sit down and talk to a kid this year."

"It's always this way at the first of school."

"And it used to get better. Now it doesn't. We run from one test to the next. From one set of reports to another. I got into this because I wanted to work with kids. All I am now is a paper pusher."

"So what are you going to do that's better?"

"Wait tables. Be a greeter at the Wal-Mart. Anything but what I am doing. *Pretending* to help kids."

"Give it a few days. Give yourself a few days. You'll feel differently—"

"After the funeral?"

The word lay between them. In the aftermath of personal

threat, Lindsey had almost forgotten the next emotional battle.

"That's when the kids will need you more than ever."

"Maybe the county will send their grief squad back out."

"If they do, *you* need to talk to my classes. They didn't respond too well to the others."

"Yeah? What'd they say?" Shannon asked with a laugh.

No matter its cause, Lindsey welcomed the break in the tension. If she could laugh at the stupidity of the county, Shannon would probably crawl out of the dark hole she was in.

"That they treated them like babies. Talked down to them."

"Oh, I'll bet they did. Sanctimonious bastards."

"Which is why you can't quit. Because you aren't."

"Sanctimonious or a bastard?"

"Neither."

"I can't even imagine how her mom is dealing."

"I don't want to try."

"I thought about calling her."

"Me, too."

Shannon blew out a breath. "You think we ought to go over?"

Lindsey couldn't think of anything she wanted to do less, but Shannon was probably right. "Do you?"

"God knows I don't want to."

"If we do, you can't start that about feeling responsible. She doesn't need to hear that, and you don't need to say it."

"Are you trying to tell me how to act, Linds?"

"Yes."

"When's the visitation?"

"If Walt's right, Monday night."

"Why don't we do that instead?"

"Chicken."

"Just not a glutton for that much punishment."

"You think the visitation will be easier?"

"It will be *public*. People tend to be more restrained. And we can be in and out in a matter of minutes."

It was more tempting than a private visit. Besides, Jace had said he was going to see Mrs. Moore at some time today. Despite having spent the night in his bed—literally if not figuratively—she wasn't looking forward to seeing him again so soon. Maybe *because* she'd spent the night in his bed.

"I'm good with that," Lindsey said.

"I'm not up to the other. You want something to eat?"

"I ate at my mom's."

"Pancakes? You could have brought me some."

That was a Saturday morning tradition at her house. Pancakes with strawberries and whipped cream.

"If Mom had known I was coming over, she'd have sent them."

"You didn't tell her?"

"I didn't know. I just dropped by to check on you."

"I'm fine. You know me. I just needed to vent. You always happen to be around when I do."

"That's what friends are for."

"Yeah, but you get more than your share." Shannon took two slices of bread out of the package and stuck them in the toaster. "I appreciate your checking on me. I'll have to thank Lieutenant Nolan for rescuing you the next time I see him."

"Do that. He wouldn't listen to me express my gratitude."

"A saint as well as a superhero."

"In the emergency room last night—" Lindsey stopped, the image of Jace's bare chest too fresh.

"What?"

"He's been shot. A couple of times in the chest. I'm no expert, but it didn't look as if it had been all that long ago."

"In the chest?"

"The resident made some crack about him being lucky."

"Sounds like it. He get lucky last night?"

For a second or two, Lindsey didn't know what Shannon was asking. When she figured it out, she could feel the telltale color invade her cheeks, despite the fact that nothing had happened between them. "I barely know the guy."

"Not a hindrance. You need to sneak on over into this century, Linds."

"I'm in this century. I just prefer a little intellectual intimacy before the physical intimacy."

"Sounds like a crock to me."

The toast popped up, saving Lindsey from having to admit that it had sounded like a crock to her as well. She watched as Shannon spread both butter and jam over the bread, depositing each one onto a china plate as she finished with it. She brought the toast and her coffee over to the side of the bar where Lindsey was sitting and took the other stool.

"He likes you," she said, glancing sideways at Lindsey as she took a bite.

"He thinks I know something that could help him. If I did, at this point, believe me, I'd tell him."

Shannon shrugged, turning her attention back to breakfast. Lindsey let the silence build, trying to think of some way to change the subject. Only then did she remember she hadn't told her friend about the profile of Andrea Jace had discovered.

"The boy you suspect in the program? Does he have any computer expertise?"

"I never said I suspected somebody."

"Okay, the boy you think is capable of doing something

like the church fires? Can he manipulate images? Put up a fake profile of somebody?"

"You mean there's somebody in your program who *can't* do that?" Shannon licked jam off her fingers, eyes challenging.

"You're the one who says you know what they're capable of."

"I can Photoshop with the best of them, and I don't claim any kind of expertise. It ain't that hard, Linds."

"So the one you were thinking of the other day?" Lindsey repeated patiently. "He could do what I'm asking about?"

"Yeah. So what?"

"Somebody put up a fake profile of Andrea on one of those sites the kids all use."

"Who told you that?"

"I saw it. Jace showed it to me."

"So how did he know it was fake?"

"I told him."

"And just how did *you* know that, Miss Techno-wizard?"

"Because it was nothing like Andrea. It was very…sexually explicit. About the things she was doing with guys at school."

"That doesn't make it fake. Maybe she *was* doing those things with the guys at school. I keep telling you. They aren't the little darlings they'd have you believe."

"Andrea wouldn't have done the things that were described on the site. Besides, the writing wasn't hers. Give me credit for knowing my kids' writing styles if nothing else."

"And yet the experts argue over whether Shakespeare wrote some sonnet or other. Are you sure you could tell she wrote something from the kind of crap that's posted on those sites?"

"In this case, I could," Lindsey said stubbornly.

"Oh, *please*. Just because you don't want to think Andrea could be involved in that kind of stuff, especially now—"

"You didn't read it."

"And I don't want to. Not if it's upset you this much."

"It wasn't her."

"Okay. I believe you." Shannon took another bite of toast.

She didn't, but Lindsey couldn't see the point of arguing about it. "You still won't tell me who it is?"

"So you can tell Jace? I don't think so. Not because you think Andrea Moore is somehow different from ninety percent of the kids. Don't bestow sainthood on her because she's dead."

"I have a vested interest in trying to figure this out."

Shannon had the grace to look embarrassed. "If I really knew anything I thought would help you do that, I'd tell you, Linds. I promise. Or I'd call Jace. As of now, all I know is that there are a couple of kids in your program that I wouldn't put anything past. That's *not* enough to go to the authorities. At least not for me. That doesn't mean I don't care about what's going on. And I meant what I said about staying here. You're welcome anytime and for as long as you need a place."

"I know. Look, I'm gonna go," Lindsey said, sliding off the stool. She leaned over to kiss Shannon on the cheek. "Sorry about waking you up on a Saturday morning."

"Hey, it's the weekend. I needed to be up enjoying it. Neither of us is going to enjoy much about next week."

"We can talk Monday about the visitation, okay? I don't want to go by myself."

Shannon nodded, lowering her eyes to consider the remaining piece of toast.

"You okay?" For some reason, Lindsey was hesitant to leave, despite the Saturday errands she needed to get done.

Shannon looked up. For a moment it seemed as if she

intended to say something serious. Instead, she smiled, managing to make it look almost normal. "I'm fine. And remember what I told you."

Lindsey racked her brain, trying to think what she could be referring to. "Okay, clearly I'm not remembering."

"Jace and the twenty-first century. You ain't gettin' any younger, Petunia. Just remember that."

"Oh, please," Lindsey mocked. "Talk about stuck in the last century. I'm surprised at you, Hippy Princess."

"Yeah, that's me. Free love and nickel beer. Or was that century before last?"

"Gotta go. And *you* remember what I told *you*."

"What's that?"

"No more mixing booze and pills. It's stupid."

"I know. That's not a normal thing, you know."

"Well, once is too often. Promise me."

"Yes, Mother."

"Good girl. I'll call you later."

"Checking up?"

"Catching up. It's different. I care about you."

The silence was short-lived, but awkward. Shannon finally broke it. "If I think of anything that might help, I'll call."

"Thanks. Talk to you later."

Shannon nodded. She gave a half wave with a twist of her wrist as Lindsey walked toward the back door before she picked up the remaining piece of toast and brought it up to her mouth.

Seventeen

It was after eight when Jace's doorbell rang. He was feeling almost human after five hours of sleep and a shower, but he hadn't been expecting company. Nor did he want any.

He picked his holstered weapon up off the coffee table as he crossed the room. After he looked through the peephole, he laid it back down on the top of the TV. Lindsey was standing in the hallway, holding up what looked to be a grocery sack.

"I hope you like barbeques," she said, when he opened the door. "Something in the way of a bribe."

"For what?" he asked, stepping back to allow her to enter.

"You said if I needed to, I could come back tonight."

He closed the door, taking time to slip the chain into the slot before he had to face her. Despite what he'd told her, he hadn't thought she would take him up on the offer. He figured she'd either go to her folks or tough it out at her house.

Tough it out. What he'd do if he were scared. What any guy would do. But, rather obviously, Lindsey wasn't a guy.

Since she'd come back, he wasn't sure what she was expecting. It had been pretty clear last night that she was interested only in his protection. Tonight was an entirely different proposition.

Then, she'd been coming to terms with the reality that someone had attacked her again. He'd been mentally exhausted and in pain. Despite that, it had been all he could do to keep from issuing a different kind of invitation. Tonight…

He turned, surprised to find that Lindsey had moved only a couple of feet into the apartment. Although she was holding onto that same bright smile with which she'd greeted him, it seemed forced. And her eyes reflected that uncertainty.

"You were going out, weren't you?"

"Just to get something to eat," he lied.

He *had* thought about doing that when he'd gotten out of the shower, but hadn't been able to dredge up the energy. In the end, and only because he couldn't remember the last time he'd eaten, he had decided to nuke something from the freezer.

Now the smells emanating from the sack Lindsey carried were making his mouth water. And since she—and it—were here, there seemed no reason not to take advantage of one of them.

"But you've just made that trip unnecessary." He moved past her to head toward the kitchen.

"If you've got a date, just say so." She followed him, putting the sack down on the table. "I can stay with Shannon or go to my parents' house."

The fact that she was here was evidence she didn't want to do either. And if he were honest, he didn't want her to.

However, she was still emotionally vulnerable, operating from a sense of gratitude and a possible case of hero worship, both of which should put her off-limits. Neither of which made her any less appealing.

"I haven't gotten that far in the Randolph social scene."

"That far? To have a date? You've been here, what? Four months? Don't tell me you haven't had a date in all that time."

He took two plates from one of the upper cabinets and set them out on the counter. "Okay."

"Okay what?"

"I won't tell you."

"Because it isn't true?"

"Not exactly. It's been more like six months. This is not the easiest place I've ever lived in for meeting people."

That was the truth. As far as it went. There was little night-life, and what there was seemed to be limited to a few seedy bars on the interstate. He hadn't been interested in meeting the kind of women who made up their clientele.

It wasn't that he thought he was too good for them. In his profession, he knew the type too well and wasn't interested.

Because you're an arrogant prick.

"Soda, water or something stronger?" He set glasses beside the plates. Maybe she'd take the hint and let the subject drop.

"Sweet tea?" Her voice was hopeful.

"An acquired taste."

"One you *haven't* acquired, I take it."

"Sorry."

"Soda, then. Diet anything you've got."

"Silverware's in the top drawer." Jace tilted his head backward toward the cabinet next to the sink.

"I don't think we need any."

"I thought you said barbeque."

"*Barbeques.* Sandwiches. And onion rings. You do eat those, don't you? Or are they an acquired taste, too?"

"I think I can manage to choke them down."

He carried the glasses over to the refrigerator, filling both with ice. Then he popped the cans of soda, making two trips to convey everything to the table.

He looked around to find Lindsey arranging the sandwiches and sides on the plates he'd put out. She brought them to the table, placing one on one end and the other opposite it.

As she straightened, she met his eyes for the first time since their conversation at the door. Hers were still uncertain, maybe even a little apprehensive.

"You have a preference?" she asked.

He stepped to the end of the table where she was standing and pulled out the chair. "We can christen this," he said as she settled into it.

"The *table?*"

For him, mealtime usually consisted of something he'd grabbed on the way home or something that went into the microwave. And he ate it in front of the television, trying to catch up on the events of the day.

"Seems silly to sit in here when I'm eating alone."

"I know. I eat in the den."

He had already taken his place on the other end of the table before he realized there were no napkins. He'd expected those to come out of the sack she'd brought. He usually used paper towels or the hand towel hanging by the sink. Neither seemed appropriate tonight. "Napkins?"

"Sorry, they're in the sack."

He started to push up, but she beat him to it, slipping out of the chair and walking over to the counter. She was wearing jeans, maybe the same ones she'd had on the first night he'd taken her out. Faded with age, the denim emphasized the swell of her hips as well as the length of her legs.

Feeling his body react, Jace lowered his eyes to the sandwiches she'd put on his plate. Although the smell had made his mouth water earlier, another, stronger hunger dominated his brain and his body right now.

"Here."

He looked up to find her holding out a stack of paper napkins. He took them, unfolding a couple to lay in his lap and leaving the rest beside his plate.

"It's Country's. They're the best."

She was talking about the barbeque. Taking a breath in a fruitless effort to stem that sudden flood of desire, he picked one of the sandwiches up and took a bite. Although he was no expert, judging by the smoky tenderness of the meat and the sharp-sweet tang of the sauce, she was probably right.

"Good?"

He looked up to see that her smile was back, more relaxed and genuine this time. "Very."

She nodded as if she'd been vindicated and then picked up her own sandwich. They ate in silence, devouring the meal as if it had been days since they'd eaten. He was well into the second barbeque before she spoke again.

"I didn't realize how hungry I was. I didn't think about food today, and then when I started this, it was like I was starving. Did you hear from the Web site company?"

"Probably not until Monday, when they'll have the people who do what I need back in."

He had told her that this morning. He couldn't decide if she'd forgotten in the stress of reading Andrea's profile, or if she were just trying to make conversation.

"I told Shannon about the site and that we thought someone else had done it."

She had thought that, based on reasons he hadn't found totally convincing. And of course, he hadn't known then everything he knew now. "Her mother recognized the picture."

Her eyes came up, widened with surprise.

"Andrea had it done by one of those places that specializes in doing hair and makeup to make their subjects look like celebrities. Her mother went with her. Apparently there was a series of photographs, each made in different clothes and with different props. According to her mother, that particular pose was more of a joke than anything else. Mrs. Moore wasn't sure what had happened to it. She thought it would be in the folder in Andrea's room. We went to look, and it wasn't there."

"But… That just doesn't seem like something Andrea would want to do."

He'd said from the first that it was possible Lindsey didn't know the girl as well as she thought. Could anyone really know what went on inside a teenager's mind?

"The photographs, at least one of them, were intended as a birthday present for some boy. Not the shot on the site, but another much more 'ladylike' pose, to quote her mother."

"To a *boy?*" She shook her head, her lips parted in disbelief. "She had a boyfriend? Did her mom know who it was?"

"She told her mother his name was Todd. And that he didn't live around here. She met him at a college fair last spring."

"In Montgomery," Lindsey said. "I encouraged my kids to go. Several of them did, but… I don't remember Andrea saying anything about it. I could check. I'm pretty sure I gave extra points to those who attended. I could ask to see my grade book for that semester—"

"It doesn't matter, Lindsey. The important thing is that photograph is real. It hadn't been manipulated."

"Then you think he's the one who put up that profile? The boy she gave it to?"

It would probably be a relief for her to believe that. After all, that would mean none of her students had been involved. Unless that student was Andrea, of course.

"I don't know. Maybe, just maybe, it's exactly what it seemed. A profile Andrea put up."

"I don't believe that. She didn't write that stuff. You didn't know her, but… That wasn't her, Jace."

"You said that about the picture."

Her chin lifted, but she didn't argue. It was hard to cling to a set of beliefs when one of their central tenets had been disproved.

"So what did Shannon think?" His change of subject had been deliberate.

"About the site?"

He could tell that she was still dealing with the revelation he'd made. Lindsey been so convinced the Moore girl was as pure as the driven snow. Now she was trying to decide exactly what she could believe.

"Yeah. The profile."

"She didn't see it. I thought you were going to have it taken down, so I didn't suggest she look. She's far more technologically savvy than I am. I asked her which of the kids could have manipulated a photograph—" She stopped, obviously aware that skill was no longer central to this investigation.

"And?"

"She said almost all of them. She said she could do it, and she wasn't nearly as good as most of kids in my program."

"What about the writing? You said that based on Andrea's style, you didn't think it was hers. Using the same criteria, could you identify the writer?"

"Whoever did it was trying to make it sound like Andrea. Like a girl who would be involved in those things, but… I know you're going to think this is crazy—and I can't prove it—but I think a guy wrote that blog."

"Based on what?"

She shook her head, her eyes leaving his to look into the

distance. "The things that were said about the sexual activity. Those all seemed to be from a masculine point of view. A male's perspective rather than a female's."

He supposed that was better than saying the phraseology was masculine, but again, it failed to convince him. And it wouldn't convince any judge he approached for a warrant.

"That picture doesn't make her a slut." Her eyes, challenging, came back to his. "A lot of people have those shots made. Like her mother said, it was a joke. So what we're left with is the writing. Maybe if I gave you samples, you could have them analyzed to see if any of them match."

The idea of taking a bunch of schoolboy essays and trying to match them stylistically to the blog and comments on that site would be a nightmare. If any expert would agree to try. He could imagine what the sheriff would say to that request.

"I doubt that would be possible. Logistically, I mean."

"Meaning you don't think it's worth the effort."

"Probably not."

"Then what do we do?"

"At this point? Concentrate on verifying who put that page up. Maybe try to find Todd and see if he knew of anything that would make Andrea take her life. Find out if he knew anything about that rumored pregnancy."

Something happened in Lindsey's eyes. She opened her mouth and then closed it, as if she'd thought better of whatever it was she'd been about to say.

"What?"

"Nothing. *Probably* nothing," she amended.

"What kind of nothing?"

"When I went to ask Dave about turning off the lights at halftime, he was in the field house. He and Coach Spears usually eat together there before the game, but Coach had already walked over to the stadium, I guess. Dave was still in his office, though, talking to Walt Harrison." She stopped, her eyes losing focus again.

He waited, but she didn't go on. "And?"

"I don't know what they were talking about, but Walt said something to the effect that the rumors were out there and he felt Dave should know. Dave asked what he was supposed to do about them, and Walt said—" She hesitated again. "This may not mean anything. I don't want you to get the wrong idea."

"Why don't you just tell me what he said?"

"He said, 'I thought *you* should know.' And then something about there not being any secrets in this town."

"There aren't any secrets?"

"Or maybe it was more like 'You know how this place works.' I don't remember exactly, but I got the impression that whatever Walt had been telling Dave might be personal. That…" She shook her head again. "That it was about *him*."

"The rumors were about him?" Jace clarified.

She nodded.

"And my talking about the pregnancy rumor made you remember this? Do you think they were talking about Andrea?"

"I did at the time. But *I* was thinking about Andrea. I'd just talked to Renee. I was there to ask Dave's permission for the memorial. Maybe I just put the two together in my head."

"Have *you* heard rumors about Campbell?"

"No, but I'm not sure that means anything. I never heard the rumor about Andrea. If I had, maybe I would have done things differently that day."

"How would you characterize their relationship?"

"Dave and Walt's? Dave's the principal. We work under him. There's the normal amount of grousing about that, but Dave's a good guy. He's generally well respected."

"By the faculty?"

"Faculty. Staff. Community."

"Kids?"

"The bright ones. I'm sure you could find plenty who wouldn't have anything good to say about him. Their parents probably wouldn't, either, but that goes with the territory."

"Harrison do much of that grousing?"

"No more or less than anyone else. I've done my share."

"About what? In particular?"

"Inconsistencies. Generally they're small, but they make it hard to be sure how students are going to be treated if you send them to the office."

"Inequities in discipline?"

"That makes it sound more serious than it really is. There are certain kids who seem to be golden. Their parents are involved in the school or the booster clubs or just the movers and shakers in the community. Influential in some way. Or the kids are achievers, either academically or in sports. They get away with more than the normal, run-of-the-mill student."

"Probably no different than any other high school."

"I'm sure it's not," she said a little stiffly. "You asked me what people complained about."

"Is that it?"

For a moment Lindsey didn't say anything. Despite her silence, Jace knew there was more. Something that, for some reason, she didn't want to tell him.

"He's a flirt."

"With the students?"

"Not that I know of, but… It's just an attitude some men have in dealing with women. A lot of them would pass it off as teasing, but it's more than that. It's an awareness they convey that you're a woman and they're men."

"Campbell does that?"

"I don't even know if it's intentional. Maybe his father was that way. Maybe it's just a habit he had when he was young and single that he's never broken."

"He do that with you?"

"I don't think I'm his type." For the first time since they'd started this discussion, she smiled.

"Who is?"

There was another hesitation before she answered. "Shannon. For one. Anyone could see why he'd be attracted to her. Everyone is. Guys, I mean. Maybe because she's a little more—I don't know—more exotic than the rest of us, he seemed to think that kind of sexual innuendo is okay."

"It bother her?"

Lindsey laughed. "Shannon's used to having that effect on men. I don't think it bothers her so much as it annoys her. It's just inappropriate."

"You've seen this? Or has she just told you about it."

"A little of both."

"You think the rumor Harrison was talking about had to do with Campbell and someone associated with the school."

"I didn't. But looking back… Maybe."

"I better talk to Harrison."

"If you do, he'll know I told you."

"Does that bother you? Given what's going on?"

"What if that conversation had nothing to do with any of this? Not Andrea. Not the church fires. Not… Not the things that have happened to me. I'll feel as if I've betrayed a friend for no reason."

"I think the more important question, and the more logical one with the timing of what you overheard, is what if it *does* have something to do with any or with all of those things?"

"All of them?"

"My instincts say that none of those events happened in a vacuum. And trust me, Lindsey, neither did that conversation."

Eighteen

For a few seconds after she opened her eyes, Lindsey didn't know where she was. Then everything she'd tried to block from her consciousness during the last few days was back. She was in Jace's apartment because once more she hadn't been able to bear the thought of sleeping alone. *Sleeping alone…*

Looking up into the darkness, she replayed her arrival tonight in her head. Clearly, Jace hadn't been expecting her. That was hardly surprising, since she hadn't expected to come.

Shannon had offered her a bed. Her folks would have welcomed her. Yet she'd shown up at the home of a man she'd met less than two weeks ago. A man who'd sworn to "serve and protect."

There was nothing personal about Jace's concern for her safety. To him, ensuring that was nothing more than his job. So why the hell couldn't she get that through her head?

She turned on her side, punching her pillow into a more comfortable shape with her fist before she closed her eyes again, determined to go back to sleep. It was embarrassing that she kept intruding on him like this. Embarrassing and ridiculous and incredibly needy.

Which was exactly what Jace must think. That she was using this as an excuse to latch on to him. Why shouldn't he? She was an unmarried and unattached school teacher in a one-stoplight town who kept showing up on his doorstep.

She sighed, tired of trying to determine the proper social protocol for your actions when someone was trying to hurt or kill you. This was hardly the time to be worried about what the cop who'd gotten you into this mess thought about you. Yet she couldn't seem to get that question out of her mind.

Maybe because you're sleeping in his bed.

A bed in which the scent of his body lingered. Or rather the scent of whatever soap or shampoo he used.

Despite the smoke that had clung to his clothing last night, she had smelled this same masculine, highly seductive fragrance when he'd put his arm around her at the stadium. And even in the midst of everything going on, she'd responded.

She opened her eyes, glancing at the clock. Almost five. And the way she felt now, with everything rushing through her brain again, she probably wouldn't be able to go back to sleep. She had managed to do that last night only because she'd been exhausted. And because she'd felt safe.

Now all the things she'd tried to put out of her head were back. She could lie here, beating herself up or she could get up, get her clothes on and head back to her house.

Like an adult.

Maybe, if she was lucky, she could get out of the apartment without waking Jace. All she knew was that she couldn't lie in his bed another minute. She threw the sheet off and sat up on the edge of the mattress.

She'd slept in her own T-shirt tonight, choosing not to

borrow one of Jace's. That had been a little too intimate. *Like sleeping in his bed?*

She walked over to the chair where she'd again draped her jeans. In the interest of getting out of here faster, she stood on one foot, holding them out in front of her so she could insert her other leg into the opening.

In her hurry she lost her balance, bumping into the wall before she righted herself. She froze, listening for some response from the front of the apartment, before she quickly finished dressing. She used her fingers to comb her hair, refusing to use the mirror in the bathroom. She was leaving. What did it matter how she looked?

She reached for the knob and hesitated again, reluctant to put what had seemed like a logical plan only moments before into action. She didn't want to go outside and get into her car in the dark. She didn't want to walk into her empty house. She didn't want—

The door opened, causing her to step back. A dim light in the front of the apartment silhouetted Jace's body, his shoulders seeming to fill the doorway.

"You all right? I thought I heard something."

"I bumped into the wall when I was putting on my jeans. I didn't mean to wake you."

"You didn't. What are you doing?"

"Going home."

His eyes flicked to the clock on the bedside table. "Why? It's not even daylight."

"I know. But…eventually there comes a time…"

"A *time?*"

"I can't *live* with you, Jace."

This had all made sense when she'd been by herself, but now it sounded childish. At least he didn't respond with the obvious—that he hadn't asked her to live with him.

"I get that. It still doesn't mean you should go home in the middle of the night."

"What I meant was I can't keep coming over here. At some point I have to come to terms with what's happened."

"You might want to give yourself more than forty-eight hours. It would take most people a lot longer."

"You don't think I'm being an idiot?"

"Only in wanting to leave before daylight." His tone was slightly exasperated amusement.

"I didn't. Not really. I just didn't want you to think I'm using this—" She stopped because there was no way to say the rest without revealing more than she wanted to.

"Using what?"

He sounded as if he didn't have a clue what she was talking about. Maybe he didn't. Maybe the thought had never crossed his mind. Not until she'd put it there.

"It doesn't matter," she said. "I'm just… Look, I'm not usually this way. Anybody who knows me can tell you that. I'm normally very rational and calm and the last person on earth to get rattled. The last few days—"

"Someone put a snake in your laundry hamper and locked you in a burning building. Why would it be irrational to be rattled after that? I think that's a pretty rational response."

"To hate the thought of opening my front door? And to hate myself for giving in to that fear?"

"In all honesty, I would think you were irrational if you *weren't* afraid."

"I'd be just as safe at my parents' house as at yours."

"They're what? In their sixties? I assumed you didn't want to put them in any danger."

That was why she hadn't called her dad the night she'd found the rattler. When being used to remind her of that, Jace's tone didn't sound quite so condescending.

"Go back to bed," he advised. "If you're uncomfortable staying here, we'll work something else out in the morning."

"Like what?"

"We go to the sheriff with the evidence of the two attacks and ask him to provide round-the-clock protection."

"Would he do that?"

"He should. Is that what you want?"

Not unless you're the one assigned to protect me.

And if she were honest, she'd admit that had less to do with the fact that she knew a lot of the county deputies and wasn't impressed with their abilities and more to do with her growing feelings for the man who'd saved her life.

"Lindsey?" Jace prodded. "Would you be more comfortable doing that?"

"Is that what you think I should do?"

"I think you should do whatever makes you feel safe. If you're worried that people will talk because you're here—"

"I'm a grown woman. What I do isn't anyone else's business."

He was kind enough not to point out that was a direct contradiction of what she'd told him after the fire.

"Then why don't you tell me what's wrong with this arrangement? Wrong enough that you're going home in the middle of the night to a house you admit you're afraid to walk into."

She couldn't think of a plausible lie. For someone who had prided herself on always staying one step ahead of a bunch of very bright kids, she'd allowed herself to be trapped by her own words. The only thing left was the truth. Or part of it.

"I was afraid you'd think I had another reason for coming here."

"Other than to bribe me with food?"

"You know what I'm talking about. To the people in this

town, I'm what's generally known as an old maid. And all us old maids are supposed to be desperate to trap some eligible man."

Her eyes had adjusted to the low light from the hall enough to watch as one corner of his mouth tilted upward before it was controlled. He was laughing at her.

And he should be. Everything that had come out of her mouth since he'd opened this door was an absurdity.

"You're saying I'm what passes for eligible around here?"

"Eminently."

"Thank you. I think."

"You're welcome. That said, please believe that I'm not here because I'm trying to make a play for you. No matter how desperate you—or anyone else—thinks I am."

"I believe you."

"Thank you."

The conversation had now slipped from the absurd to the surreal, and she didn't know how to get it back to anything approaching normal. After this, she doubted normal would ever be possible between them again.

"Is that it?" Jace asked.

"I'm sorry?"

"Is everything straightened out? You aren't leaving?"

Was she? Not unless she had to, she realized.

"I'd really appreciate it if I could stay the rest of tonight. After that…"

After that, she supposed someone like Rick Carlisle would set up shop in her driveway or her kitchen. Which was almost as unappealing as staying home alone.

"So…you want some coffee?" Jace asked.

Since she didn't want to crawl back into his bed, the offer felt like a reprieve. A way to keep what little dignity she might have left. "I'd like that. Thank you."

"It's the least I can do since you fed me dinner."

"That was a bribe, remember."

"Then feel free to consider the coffee a bribe."

"For what?" She was grateful he had lightened the mood.

"To get you to stay."

"Look, I'm not really an idiot. I knew it was dangerous to go out before daybreak. I just felt as if I were intruding. As if I'd wedged myself into your life the last few days. 'Here I am. Take care of me, please. Whether you want to or not.'"

"Did you mean what you said?"

"About…?"

"Me being eligible."

"You *know* you are." Her laugh seemed strained, but at least she had managed one.

"I didn't. However, if you say so—"

Before she realized his intent, Jace stepped forward and pulled her into his arms. One second they were facing each other, a couple of yards between them. The next she was being pressed against his chest.

Her eyes lifted to his face. Her lips parted, the attempt to protest what was happening automatic. Unthinking.

And then she knew she didn't *want* to protest. She wanted to be exactly where she was right now. She had wanted to be here for at least a week.

"Uncomfortable?"

Wordlessly she shook her head. Her lips were still parted, now in anticipation of his kiss. As the thought formed, she began to doubt her instinct. But surely this was a prelude to that. Or to something more?

They were both adults—unmarried and, as far as she knew, unattached—alone in a bedroom with a bed conveniently near.

"Good," Jace whispered as his mouth lowered to meet hers.

Instead of the kiss she'd anticipated, the tip of his tongue trailed over her bottom lip and then slowly, teasingly, along the top. As it did, he shifted the hand that had rested at the small of her back, using it to press her hips into a more intimate contact with his.

Automatically she strained upward, trying to accommodate his height. With that encouragement, he moved his other hand to join the first. Cupping her bottom with his palms, he lifted her into the strength of his erection. Her lips opened again on a gasp, the sound quickly smothered by his mouth.

The kiss left no doubt about his expertise. It was everything she'd wanted. Everything she'd dreamed about. Sensual. Seductive. Inviting. And not nearly enough.

No matter what Jace thought about her motives in coming to his apartment tonight—no matter what he thought about her—right now she wanted nothing more than for him to make love to her. To destroy the memory of everything bad that had happened by reducing her to a state of mindlessness.

He broke the kiss, leaning back to study her face. Shadowed by the light behind him, she couldn't see his eyes well enough to read the emotion that was there.

"It's not too late," he said.

It felt like a withdrawal, as much as did the distance he'd deliberately put between them. "Too late for what?"

"If you don't want to take this where it's obviously headed, all you have to do is say so. But if you don't do that soon…"

She should be grateful for that consideration, she supposed. Never in her life had she been more emotionally vulnerable. And no one understood that better than Jace.

Despite the clear, physical evidence of how much he wanted her, if she stepped away, he would let her go.

Instead of doing that, she reached up, putting her hands

on either side of his face. The feel of the late-night whiskers under her palms was as sensual as the teasing caress of his tongue had been. She stood on tiptoe, her mouth seeking his.

When his lips again descended to cover hers, she was the aggressor. Standing taller, she tried to align her body with his, her breasts flattened against the wall of his chest, her hips straining to become one with his.

Without breaking the contact of their tongues, Jace lifted her, so that her feet came off the floor. Shifting her hold around his neck, she raised her body to wind her legs around his hips. Again she could feel the strength and heat of his arousal against the center of her need.

Her head fell back in response, allowing him access to her neck and throat. His mouth teased first along the sensitive skin beneath her ear. Then he suckled its lobe, before his tongue delved inside, sending waves of heat through her body.

He began to cross the room with her legs still wrapped around him. She had thought he'd lay her down on the bed. Instead he sat down on its foot, his mouth still caressing, teasing, driving her toward the mindlessness she'd sought.

His hands found the bottom of her tee and pulled it upward. Releasing her hold around his neck, she lifted her arms over her head to allow him to pull it off.

As soon as he had, he tossed it on the floor. Then his lips found the cleft between her breasts, the softness of his hair brushing against her throat. A multitude of sensations—all of them sensuous—threatened overload.

His palms enclosed the outside of her breasts, pressing them inward toward the seductive pleasure of his mouth. His tongue circled her nipple, which tautened under its touch.

Jace then switched his attention to the other breast. The sensation of cool air against the moisture-rimmed areola he'd deserted added one more torment to those his teeth had begun to inflict on his new target.

Passion ran hot and thick through her veins. Her fingers tightened over his shoulder, nails digging into the fabric of his shirt. In the maelstrom of need he'd awakened, she realized Jace was still dressed and that she didn't want him to be.

She wanted the hair-roughened skin of his chest against her breasts. They ached for more than the caress of his mouth, as enticing as that was. She wanted contact with every inch of him. Mouth to mouth. Skin to skin. Her body enclosing the driving power of his need.

She leaned back, putting space between them. He raised his head in response. In the dimness of the room, his eyes seemed distant, a little remote, as if he were already lost in that inevitable post-coital aloneness.

"What's wrong?"

"This," she whispered, her fingers working to loosen the buttons of his fly, to tug the tail of his shirt from his jeans.

His hands covered hers, stopping their movement. Surprised, she looked up, eyes questioning. "What is it?"

"Nothing," he said finally, freeing her hands. Without another word, he jerked his shirt out and pulled it off over his head. He tossed the garment onto the floor, and, in almost the same motion, drew her once more against the heat of his body.

The sensation was everything she'd imagined and more. Her breasts, already sensitized by his lips and teeth and tongue, were sweetly, delicately, abraded by the hair on his chest.

Before she'd had time to fully process that feeling, his mouth found hers. This time he didn't seek permission. His tongue pillaged, demanding a response. And receiving it.

Skin to skin. Mouth to mouth. The only thing remaining…

As if to match action to her thought, Jace stood. If he hadn't held her so tightly, she might have fallen as her feet dropped down to touch the floor.

Before she had time to find her balance, he was stripping off her panties, his mouth still ravaging hers. As soon as he'd taken them down below her knees, he released the bit of silk and lace, letting it fall to her feet. Then his fingers pushed between her legs, probing the wetness he'd created.

She gasped, bringing his mouth back to hers. He covered it with his lips, as if to taste the sensations his hand elicited.

She gave herself up to the building ecstasy, willing its culmination. Instead, he stepped back, looking down into her face as he touched her.

Despite her initial embarrassment, there was something so provocative, so tantalizing, about what he was doing, she never thought to protest. Her mouth opened instead, her eyelids falling as she drew closer and closer to fulfillment. As if he sensed the nearness of her climax, he lifted her, laying her on his bed.

Hungry for what he'd promised, she propped on one elbow, watching as he stripped off his jeans with the same efficiency he'd used to undress her. Then he reached into the bedside table drawer to retrieve a condom. He opened the package with his teeth, holding her eyes.

"Convenient." She smiled at him as he put it on, trying to ease the awkwardness of the moment.

"Hopeful," he corrected softly before he eased down onto the bed and moved over her.

There was no more foreplay. Nor was there any need. She was more than ready for him as he positioned her knees and then pushed into her waiting body.

She felt a momentary anxiety as she adjusted to his

entrance, before he filled her, driving downward until she thought she could accept no more. She must have made some sound. The pressure eased as he withdrew, raising his hips and then lowering them again, taking her to the edge of pain and then beyond. To something very different.

Another release of the pressure was followed by another stroke until the rhythm, older than time, began to build to its inevitable conclusion. The tremor started deep within her arching body. The spark for the conflagration that would consume them both.

It strengthened, fueled by the increasing frenzy of Jace's movements, as his body strained above hers. Then, as rational thought spiraled into the void of pure sensation, his release joined hers. Together they climbed and then slowly fell, exquisitely, into consummation. And when it was over, they lay a long time, their exhausted stillness disturbed only by the occasional shiver of aftershock.

Eventually Jace pushed onto his elbows, his shadowed eyes looking into hers. "Whatever you think, I didn't plan this."

"I'll believe you. As long as you believe I didn't come here expecting it."

"It might make it easier if I did."

"Easier?"

"You came to be protected. This doesn't qualify."

"It qualifies as forgetfulness. That's almost as good."

His lips tilted before he bent, brushing a kiss against her mouth. When he raised his head, she returned the smile.

"Regrets?" he asked.

"No. But that isn't to say that my upbringing won't provide some by tomorrow."

"Sometimes it's better to live in the moment."

"Then I vote we do that."

For a few heartbeats they were again silent. With one finger she reached out to touch the higher of the two puckered scars on his chest. His face hardened, causing her to curl that finger back into her palm.

"I'm sorry," she whispered. "I just…"

She couldn't think of an excuse. She'd been curious before and was even more so because of what had happened between them.

Jace shook his head, as if it didn't matter, but his withdrawal was obvious. Their bodies were joined, in the most intimate way possible for a man and a woman to be connected, yet they were suddenly miles, and perhaps years, apart.

"You don't talk about it?"

"A reminder of my own stupidity. Would you?"

"Sometimes talking helps."

"So they say."

"Look, I'm sorry. Just forget that I—"

"It's not something I'm proud of. I screwed up and other people paid the price."

"It looks as if you paid a price, too."

"In my case, it was deserved."

"Is that why you're here?"

"In bed with you?"

"In Randolph."

"As good a reason as any."

"Then… Since I don't know what happened, forgive me if I say that I can't be too sorry for it."

She knew that for someone like Jace to end up in a place like this would take some life-altering event. As meeting him had been for her. He had thrown her world out of the sameness in which she'd lived for the last ten years. Despite the pain and fear and disruption that had accompanied his arrival, she couldn't imagine going back to how things had been before. And unless he went back to wherever he'd come from…

Unable to bear the thought, she lifted her head, touching her tongue to the fullness of his bottom lip. As if grateful for the distraction, Jace opened his mouth, inviting her kiss.

And after a while, neither of them thought to worry about what had happened in the past. Or even about what might happen in the future.

Nineteen

"I tried to call you last night after I got home."

"Really?" As she pretended surprise at Shannon's inability to reach her, Lindsey wondered why she was keeping the change in her relationship with Jace from her friend.

"Sunday night, too. You sleeping at your folks, Linds?" Shannon asked, pushing her hair away from her face. "Not that I'd blame you if you are."

"I've tried to downplay with them what's been going on. If I went home, they'd know something was wrong."

"Guess we just missed connections."

"Anything important?"

"I wanted to whine about how much I don't want to be here."

With the county's permission, Dave had dismissed school at 1:00 p.m. on the day of Andrea's funeral. The thinking had been that Randolph-Lowen would have so many students checking out for the funeral there would be little point in trying to hold classes.

Since she and Shannon had gone to the visitation last night, they hadn't intended to come today. Not until Dave had made a point of asking the faculty to attend as a show of solidarity with the students and Andrea's mother.

The dismissal had obviously swelled the crowd making its way inside the sanctuary of the church. If the people milling around outside and lined up on the front steps were any measure of those inside, the building might not hold them all.

"Looks as if most of the kids are here," Shannon said.

"Didn't you expect them to be?"

"I just hope this doesn't turn into a circus."

Lindsey echoed the sentiment. Her gaze scanned those waiting to enter, looking for Jace. She knew he'd be here. He would consider this, too, a part of his job.

He would position himself so he'd be able to watch everyone in attendance. Looking for something—anything—that might give him the thread he sought to tie together Andrea's death, the fires and the attacks on her.

"It's already got the makings of one." Lindsey tilted her head in the direction of the cameras one of the Montgomery stations had set up on the lawn.

"Damn ghouls," Shannon said under her breath.

"Hey, Ms. Sloan. Y'all want to sit with us?" Renee was flanked by four other senior cheerleaders, their faces somber. One, Beverly Arnold, was already in tears.

"We'll probably find Mr. Campbell." Shannon took Lindsey's elbow to pull her up the steps and past the students dutifully lined up waiting to enter. "Excuse us," she said several times as she bulldozed her way toward the sanctuary doors.

"Shannon," Lindsey hissed.

"I'm not standing outside in this damn heat. You're not, either. Occasionally rank *should* have its privileges."

No one protested their progress and before Lindsey could object again, they were inside the cool, dark interior of the church. The scent of flowers was so heavy, it was sickening.

"Come on," Shannon ordered, leading the way down the center aisle, which was also lined with people.

Although Lindsey hadn't been able to see empty seats near the front, apparently Shannon's quick survey had revealed room on one of the pews about three rows back from the casket. She stopped at its end, waiting while other faculty and staff seated there made room. Then she motioned Lindsey in ahead of her.

As she sank down on the coolness of the uncushioned pew, Lindsey glanced to her right to smile her thanks to those who'd moved over. Walt Harrison met her eyes, his cold and hard.

Because she'd told Jace about his conversation with Dave on Friday night? Had Jace already questioned him about those rumors he'd mentioned and forgotten to tell her?

Not that they'd done much talking the last two nights…

Destroying that memory as inappropriate for the occasion, she quickly turned her gaze to the front of the sanctuary, still wondering about Walt's expression.

Before she had time to figure that out, Shannon leaned toward her to whisper. "Open casket."

She was right, Lindsey realized with a sinking feeling. Although that ritual was often dispensed with because of the funeral home visitation and viewing, apparently Andrea's mother or this congregation was of the old school.

As Lindsey considered the implications, one of the girls who'd reached the front of the church began to sob. The sound, and the sentiment it expressed, was contagious. Even the kids who had, up to this point, been standing stoically in the line began to cry. Both males and females.

"I was wrong," Shannon said under her breath. "This isn't going to be a circus. It's a freaking zoo."

"Shh…" Lindsey glanced to her right. If Walt had heard, he was pretending he hadn't.

"Standing room only. They're lined up in the back." Although Shannon had lowered her voice, she seemed determined not to be shushed. "Your friend's in the balcony, by the way."

Your friend. Lindsey had known Jace would be here. She tried to put that out of her head, concentrating not on the growing volume of the sobs, but on the blanket of pink sweetheart roses that lay over the bottom half of the casket. When the lid was closed, those would be pulled up to completely cover the top. *When the lid was closed...*

She denied the sudden burn behind her eyes, resolutely keeping them focused on the front of the church. She could hear the crowd behind her, shuffling into every empty space, despite the line that still stretched to the front and the casket.

"How long is this going to go on?"

She had no answer for Shannon's question, but she understood the fear that prompted it. This was what the professionals always warned about with teenage suicides. This public outpouring of grief and regret. The near-deification of the dead, which too often led other troubled kids to think that they, too, could have this kind of attention.

One of the girls at the front fell to her knees, her forehead resting against the bronze coffin. Sobs racked her body, drowning out what had, up to now, been the relatively quiet crying of the rest of the mourners.

"God, I can't take this. You can get a ride home, can't you?" Shannon glanced at Walt as she began to rise, apparently expecting him to offer.

Lindsey caught her arm, looking up at her imploringly. "Don't. Just wait until after the service—"

Before she could finish, Shannon turned her wrist, wrenching her arm away. "I'll call you later."

Without making more of a scene, there was nothing Lindsey could do but let her go. As Shannon slipped out of the pew, Lindsey crossed her arms over her chest, while the disturbance at the front of the sanctuary grew louder and louder.

"Get in."

Lost in thought, Lindsey hadn't been aware a car had pulled up beside her. She turned in response to that command to find Jace looking at her out the window of his county car.

She didn't argue. The funeral had been an ordeal, and with Shannon bailing on her, she'd had no one to talk to about the churning emotions it had evoked. Jace was the one other person with whom she could be completely honest.

She slipped into the passenger seat, relishing the blast of cold from the air conditioner. She was grateful he didn't ask her any questions as he put the car into gear, seeming to take her silence as appropriate.

It was not until he stopped at the next intersection that he glanced over at her. "You okay?"

The concern in his voice re-created the burn she'd fought at the church. "No, but given a little more time, I will be."

"Was that…normal?"

"The service?"

Based on her experience, it wasn't all that abnormal. Open-casket funerals were always difficult. People usually cried. Some "carried on" as her grandmother would put it. What had made this one so difficult, at least for her, was the age of the mourners. And the dangerous volatility of their emotions.

"It was…old South," she said. "Fundamentalist."

"Fundamentalist?"

"In a mainstream church, even here, things wouldn't have gotten so out of hand. The minister would have stepped in to stop it." She shook her head. "That… That was exactly what we were afraid would happen."

"The emotionalism?"

"Shannon called it a circus. And most of the kids seemed caught up in it."

"How about yours?"

She looked at him, feeling the same surge of resentment his constant questions about her students had brought from the beginning. "I thought I answered that a long time ago. They're not any different from the rest."

"You see a lot of them there?"

She nodded.

"Could you give me a list?"

She turned to look out the windshield. "So you can focus in on the ones who came? That won't tell you anything."

"Why not? You don't think the kids involved with Andrea's 'My Place' profile were there today?"

"I think the kids that were there were the ones who were able to convince their parents coming to that funeral was a good idea. Some of them wouldn't have been able to do that. Are you going to eliminate them based on the fact they were no-shows?"

He took his eyes off the street long enough to glance over at her. "I'd still like to know who you saw."

"I'd need my grade book. It's at the house."

She'd gone home to change for the funeral. No matter that she'd slept at Jace's the last four nights, she hadn't been comfortable bringing a suitcase over. Instead, every morning she'd gotten up early to go home and dress for school.

Not early enough, she was sure, to avoid neighborhood gossip. And it was only a matter of time before her mother would hear it and call.

Jace turned right at the next intersection, heading in the

direction of her bungalow. They rode in silence a few minutes, until Lindsey remembered Walt's reaction at the funeral.

"Did you talk to Walt?"

"Harrison? I told you I was going to."

"What did he say?"

"That you misunderstood what you heard. He said they were talking about some members of the booster club who'd taken it upon themselves to charge to the school the paint they used to spruce up the stadium."

She laughed, the sound bitter. "I didn't misunderstand, Jace. Not to *that* extent. Whatever they were talking about didn't involve boosters or paint."

"I figured as much."

"So why would he lie?"

"To protect Campbell. Or himself. Or because he thought that whatever they were talking about was none of my business."

"If it related to Andrea, it's your business."

"She wasn't pregnant, by the way." This time Jace kept his eyes on the road, perhaps to give her a chance to assimilate that information before he looked at her.

And she needed it. "Then why in the world…?"

"I don't know. But according to the coroner, the wounds on her wrists were all self-inflicted."

"Who else—" She stopped because she'd just figured out why he'd told her that. "You thought someone *killed* her?"

Despite the attacks on her, Lindsey had never questioned that Andrea's death was anything other than a suicide. Now Jace seemed to be suggesting that he had at least considered that it might be murder.

"That was always a possibility."

"And so we don't know any more than we did when this started." A girl was dead. Lindsey was afraid to sleep in her own home. Almost afraid to be alone. And it seemed the police were no closer to having answers to anything that had happened.

"The Web site wasn't put up from Andrea's computer," he went on. "Nor did any of the postings to it originate there."

Despite the overwhelming emotions of the day, she felt a sense of vindication. Andrea hadn't put up that profile.

"But even if they can give you information about the computer from which they *did* originate, you don't have the authority to search for it?" Jace had already told her no judge would issue a warrant based on guesswork.

"If I knew *why* they did it, I might be able to figure out the who."

"You said it before. A form of bullying. Harassment."

"But why Andrea?"

"Because…" She hesitated, unwilling to put what she was thinking into words. Not about the girl they'd just buried this afternoon. "Because they believed they could. They thought she wouldn't go to the authorities. And she didn't. Maybe that's why she came to my room that afternoon, but in the end—" In the end, she'd chosen to go home and permanently escape the persecution rather than tell anyone what was going on. "The bottom line is she was vulnerable," she added softly. "And whoever did this understood that."

"Are you surprised at the level of sophistication involved in that decision?"

"To target Andrea? To teens the kind of vulnerability the Andreas of this world display is like blood in the water. The sharks sense it long before anyone else."

"Not the analogy I would use," Jace said, "but for what it's worth, I think you're probably right. She was picked because she made the perfect victim. And I think she reacted just the way they expected. Just the way they wanted her to."

Twenty

"I just don't want any of you to get caught up in the emotions that ran rampant yesterday." Shannon was perched, as she had been for the last two hours, on the edge of Lindsey's desk, talking earnestly to her seniors.

Even before the funeral, they had agreed that the kids in the gifted program would probably be most in need of some extra attention today. And that, given their reaction to the county's grief counselors, Shannon was the ideal person to provide it.

"It may seem that Andrea is somehow better off, but you've got your whole lives in front of you, lives full of endless possibilities and opportunities. Tragically, hers is now over. You have to remember that suicide is a very permanent solution, especially for problems that are often only temporary."

Someone near the back of the room said something that elicited a spatter of laughter. It was so out of place in the prevailing atmosphere, even the students looked shocked.

"I didn't quite catch that, Justin. Would you care to repeat it for the rest of us?"

Although Shannon's voice seemed controlled, Lindsey had known her long enough to sense the underlying fury.

"Not really," the boy said, causing another wave of low laughter from the guys around him.

"I'd appreciate it if you would. No one likes being left out of the joke."

Lindsey wondered if she should step in. This was her classroom. She had an obligation to make sure a guest in it, which Shannon was today, would be treated with respect.

She hesitated only because she knew Shannon well enough to know she wouldn't see it that way. Nor would she appreciate any interference in the way she was handling this.

"Survival of the fittest," Justin said.

"I beg your pardon?" Shannon seemed genuinely shocked at the callousness of the remark.

"It's Darwin, Ms. Anderson. Theory of evolution. Those who are fit to survive do so. Those who aren't fit..." Justin shrugged. "It insures the continuation of the species."

"And how does that possibly fit this situation?"

Justin smiled, but he didn't bother to make any further explanation. The point he had made about Andrea's death—and her life—wouldn't be lost on this group.

"What exactly are you trying to say, Justin?"

Shannon slid off the edge of the desk and walked down the aisle toward him. Every eye in the classroom followed her progress, including those of the boy she was questioning.

"I think everybody got it, Ms. Anderson."

"I didn't. Why don't you explain to me what you meant?"

"I'm not into trashing the deceased."

"*Really?* I think you just did."

Justin's brows lifted, but his smile didn't fade. Not even with Shannon looming over his desk.

The bell rang, but for several seconds no one moved. Finally Justin picked up his notebook and reached under his desk for the rest of his books. When he had them, he started to stand, but Shannon stepped to the side of his desk so that he couldn't get out without physically pushing her out of the way.

Unsure whether or not her friend was trying to force him to do that, Lindsey decided it was time to intervene. She stood, pitching her voice so that it was clear she was addressing the entire class.

"Justin, why don't you stay for a few minutes? I'd like to talk to you. The rest of you can go."

As she had hoped, her request broke the tension. It took only a few seconds for the room to clear.

As the last of her seniors exited, Lindsey walked over to the door to stop the first of the next class from entering. "Y'all give me a couple of minutes. Okay? Just tell everybody to wait out here until I open the door."

When the two kids standing outside nodded, their eyes wide, she pulled the door closed, shutting off the noise from the hall. Then she turned to where Shannon and Justin were still engaged in their standoff.

"You'll give me a pass?" Justin asked Lindsey, ignoring the woman beside his desk. "I've got a calculus quiz."

"I'll give you a pass. Don't you think what you said just now was pretty insensitive?"

"It's biology. Suicide is stupid. Especially at sixteen. You both said it yourselves. She had her whole life ahead of her, and she threw it away."

"But to relate her death to Darwin?" Shannon questioned.

"Like I said. Suicide is stupid. Andrea's genes aren't going to contaminate the gene pool. Survival of the fittest."

"You little shit." The counselor's last word was hissed.

"Shannon!"

She turned her head to look at Lindsey, green eyes glistening with tears. Lindsey wasn't sure if those were caused by grief or anger. What she *was* sure of was that her friend was too emotional right now to handle this situation.

"Go," she said. "Get some coffee. Or go outside. Just... Get out of here for a little while."

She thought Shannon might argue, but she nodded instead. Without looking at Justin again, she walked back to Lindsey's desk and picked up her purse. "Can you handle next period?"

Lindsey nodded. "Go on. It's okay."

"And him?"

"I'll handle him, too. Go."

As Shannon walked past, she reached out and squeezed Lindsey's arm. Then she opened the door, again letting the noise from the hallway into the room. Not until it was closed again did Lindsey turn to face the boy she'd promised to "handle."

"I'm sorry," he said, surprising her. "I didn't mean any disrespect. I didn't even know Andrea."

"We're all on edge. Emotionally, I mean. But... What you said did come across as disrespectful."

"My dad says it. Not about suicide necessarily. Whenever anybody does anything stupid that costs them their lives, he says it's nature's way of protecting the gene pool."

"Except Andrea was very bright. Just very troubled."

"Look, I really am sorry. You want me to apologize to the class tomorrow?"

"Let me think about that. It might be a case of less said, soonest mended."

The boy nodded. "And Ms. Anderson?"

"Maybe in a day or two. Not today, okay? Think you can make calculus?"

"I can make it."

"Then go. And tell the others they can come in now."

Justin didn't meet her eyes as he walked toward the door. As soon as he opened it, she started toward her desk. She'd told Shannon she'd handle talking to her juniors. Now that she was actually faced with the prospect, especially after the tension of the last few minutes, she needed a moment to compose herself. Not that she was likely to get it.

"Justin in trouble?" Tim Harrison asked.

Maybe he should be, but surprisingly Lindsey believed his apology had been sincere. And she'd found herself responding more positively to him because of it than she ever had before.

She smiled at the boy. "Not really. How are you?"

"Okay. Rough week."

"Yes, it has been. We're going to talk about it." .

"Ms. Anderson coming back?"

The student grapevine had obviously spread the word that Shannon was talking to her gifted classes. Eventually it would also broadcast the incident from last period. There was nothing Lindsey could do to prevent that.

She wanted to go check on Shannon. Make sure she was all right. It seemed that since they'd heard about Andrea, her friend had been teetering on the edge of a breakdown. Right now, however…

"Not this period," she said to Tim. "She had some other things she's committed to."

"So it'll be just us."

"Just us," Lindsey said, smiling at him again.

"That's good."

For a fraction of a second, she wondered about the comment. Then, in the rush of incoming students, she dismissed the idea that the remark might have had any significance beyond the commonplace it appeared to be.

* * *

After school Lindsey stuck her head in the door of the guidance suite. No students waited in the outer part of the suite, and no sounds came from either of the offices.

She walked to the door of Shannon's office, which was open, but the room was empty. Her briefcase and purse were gone. After a quick scan of the room, Lindsey went on to the next. She tapped on the open door, causing Beth Taylor to look up from whatever she was working on.

"Hey. Looking for Shannon?"

"Yeah."

"She said you'd come check on her. She left about one o'clock. She said to tell you to come by her house this afternoon. And to stop at the state store on the way."

"Is she okay?"

"I think we're all holding it together as well as we can. All I know is I'll be very glad when this week is over."

"You want to come over, too? You know Shannon won't care."

"Wish I could. I have to pick Jason up and drive him to Dothan to get a shot. It's always something."

Beth had a three-year-old who stayed with her mother-in-law during the day. Her husband was the junior high football coach. Lindsey doubted she saw much of him this time of year.

"Is he sick?"

"He's fine. Booster. Wish it were any day but this. If you have any booze left, I'll join you tomorrow."

"Deal. Drive carefully."

"I'm not the one who's going to be drinking," Beth said with a smile. "Of course, you can always call the cops if you don't want to drive home, I guess."

"What?"

"Joke, Lindsey. The word is out."

"About what?"

"About you and that New York detective. You're still seeing him, aren't you?"

"We're…" Lindsey paused, unsure how to characterize their relationship. Put in the simplest terms, she was indeed "still seeing him."

"It's okay. I didn't mean to be nosey. More power to you. Good men are few and far between around here."

"You got one of them."

"Yeah, except this time of year. Then the team's got him. I shouldn't complain. As my grandmama used to say, at least he puts his shoes under my bed at night."

If the truth were known, Lindsey had always envied women with that surety. Despite that fact she was sleeping with a man she was admittedly in the process of falling in love with, she had no idea whether that kind of commitment was in her future.

"Y'all have fun." Beth's eyes fell to her papers.

Something she might need to finish before she picked up her son, Lindsey realized. "Okay, you take care."

"You, too. And see if you can get Shannon to talk. She's got all this bottled up inside. She needs somebody to listen."

"I will. I promise. See you tomorrow."

Beth's attention had already returned to her work. As Lindsey walked back through the suite, she took her phone out of her purse and punched in Jace's number. When she got his voice mail, she hit the off button without leaving a message.

If she ended up staying late at Shannon's, she'd give him a call. With the hours he'd been working, Jace wouldn't be back at the apartment until after 7:00 p.m. And he might actually like the opportunity to spend some time there without her.

Concentrating on putting her phone back into her purse, she almost walked into Jay Burke. The choral director caught her shoulders, preventing a collision.

"Heads up, Linds." Good friends with Shannon, Jay had picked up the nickname. "I've heard of walking around with your head in the clouds, but I've never seen it until now."

"I was putting my cell away."

"And just who might you be calling?" Jay arched a brow.

"I'm heading over to Shannon's," she said, avoiding a direct answer. "You want to come? There *will* be booze."

"Wish I could. I have rehearsal. Dave didn't want us to cancel any activities. Keep their minds on something positive."

That was probably a good idea. Her Scholars' Bowl team's match had been cancelled by virtue of the early dismissal yesterday. She planned to meet with them as scheduled on Thursday. Exactly one week after Andrea's visit to her room, she realized, which seemed to have taken place an eternity ago.

"Walt find you?" Jay asked.

"Walt Harrison? I didn't know he was looking."

"He came into the office maybe…ten minutes ago. Asked if you'd signed out."

She hadn't, she realized. She'd been too consumed with checking on Shannon. "Any idea what he wanted?"

She could guess. Despite what Walt had told Jace, they both knew she hadn't been mistaken about what she'd overheard. It had had nothing to do with boosters.

"You teach Tim. Maybe he wants to talk grades or assignments or some difficulty he's having with your course."

"There's little likelihood of that with Tim."

"Then…I don't have a clue. He'll probably find you tomorrow. Go have fun."

Jay was right. If Walt had something to say to her about the lie he'd told, he could track her down. She hadn't promised him confidentiality. And he shouldn't expect it.

Of course, Walt might not be aware of all that had happened or of the importance of telling Jace the truth about the rumors he'd been referring to. There'd been little talk about the snake incident or, surprisingly, even about the stadium fire. The first had been overshadowed by Andrea's death, and she herself had downplayed the latter, which had been blamed on faulty wiring.

Undecided, she watched Jay walk away in the direction of the choral room. Walt might still be in his room. Or, since she hadn't signed out yet, he might be looking for her in hers. She glanced at her watch. It was already 3:20 p.m. Walt had probably given up, and Shannon and the state store were waiting.

She turned toward the main office, walking quickly now that the decision had been made. Even Melanie had left for the day, she discovered when she entered. Dave's door was closed, but he often worked there long after everyone else had gone.

She signed out and then walked around the counter to the rows of teacher cubbyholes. As usual, hers was stuffed with tardy and check-out slips for her homeroom students and a few memorandums. She glanced at those, stuffing them back into the box for tomorrow. As she did, she noticed a folded piece of paper that had been hidden under one of the tardies.

She took it out, flipping it open with one hand. In neat block letters, someone had printed: IF YOU SEE THIS BEFORE YOU LEAVE, COME DOWN TO MY ROOM. WE NEED TO TALK. It was unsigned.

We need to talk... She replayed the conversation she'd overheard between Walt and Dave. Although, as she'd told

Jace, she couldn't remember it word-for-word, she also couldn't make anything about it match the story Walt had told him.

Maybe Walt felt he owed her an explanation, but after the last few days, she wasn't in the mood to hear it. Not now.

She closed the note and slid it back among the other papers in her cubbyhole. Childish, perhaps, but if Walt came back to see if she'd read it, he wouldn't be able to tell.

She thought about changing the time she'd signed out before she realized that, despite the fact that was after he'd left the note, Walt couldn't know that she'd come behind the counter to check her mailbox. She could talk to him tomorrow, she decided. Clear up whatever the misunderstanding was.

Except, if she left without seeing him, she'd wonder what he'd wanted. To come clean about the lie? If that were the case, it would be more appropriate to talk to the police.

Maybe he wanted to try and pressure her into recanting *her* version of the conversation. Or to explain why his version didn't match hers. In any case...

She walked around the counter and down the hall toward Dave's office. Surely Jace had verified Walt's story with the principal. And if he hadn't, she needed to do that before she listened to what Walt had to say.

She tapped lightly on the door. She waited several seconds before she tapped again, more forcefully this time. There was still no answer.

She reached down, her finger seeming to wrap of their own accord around the knob. She hesitated briefly before she tried to turn it and found it locked.

Dave was as exhausted as the rest of them. Maybe, like Shannon, he'd left early. If so, she couldn't blame him.

Although the faculty had had to deal with the still-grieving

students today, the responsibility for the well-being of the
entire school fell to the principal. If anything else happened,
Dave would be the one who'd be blamed, fair or not.

Five minutes, she decided. She could spare that much
time to look for Walt. And then she'd leave, feeling as if she'd
done the best she could with her own responsibilities.

Twenty-One

Lindsey decided the janitor must have started on one of the other floors this afternoon. The doors to the basement classrooms were all open, although the lights were off. Nor were there any noises that would indicate the cleaning crew was down here. The corridor seemed deserted, her footsteps echoing off the long expanse of tile and concrete.

She'd always been glad she'd never been assigned to one of these rooms, which she found depressing. When the school population had outgrown the building, the board had discovered that the cheapest way to add instructional space was to convert areas used for other purposes.

These windowless classrooms had been created from what had been the original basement. Pipes, ductwork, and beams had been covered where possible and left exposed when the cost to hide them had been prohibitive.

Some of the teachers who worked down here bragged about the fact that they were so distant from the office—and from supervision. A few professed there were fewer distractions. Others, like Walt Harrison, were so single-minded they would have been able to teach in any conditions.

She had already decided by the time she reached her destination that this was a wild-goose chase, but since she was this close there was no reason not to finish what she'd begun. Like all the others, the lights were off in Walt's room.

She stopped just outside the door, pitching her voice to carry inside. "Walt?"

There was no answer. A glance at her watch revealed it was now 3:30 p.m. He had probably decided she wasn't coming this late and had gone out the back.

What the hell was she doing down here? If Walt wanted to talk, he knew where her room was. And in the meantime, Shannon was waiting for a friend bearing booze.

Annoyed with herself, she quickened her pace toward the stairs, the click of her steps giving voice to her annoyance. She'd already reached out to grasp the metal railing when she realized there was another sound in the stillness of the deserted hall.

An echo of her heels hitting the tile? She stopped, holding her breath as she listened.

Not an echo. Whatever she'd heard was still there. Subtle and regular. Still unidentifiable.

For the first time, she felt a touch of unease. She was completely isolated down here from the other parts of the building. As she tried to rationalize her anxiety, she remained conscious of the sound. Soft and steady, it underlay the silence around her, like the beat of her own heart.

She lifted her hand from the rail and, careful not to make any noise, turned so that she was again facing the basement corridor. Its waxed tile gleamed under the overhead light.

Straining, she attempted to pinpoint the source of what she was hearing. And realized there was no question.

It was coming from the open doorway of the classroom

closest to the stairs. She took the few steps that would bring her back to that door, pausing again to listen.

From here, what she heard sounded like a squeak. The noise a wheel would make turning repeatedly past a place that needed oiling, the intervals between unvaried.

She stepped forward, her right hand feeling for the switch inside the door. The resultant buzz of the fluorescents masked whatever she'd heard, but as the lights came up, they revealed the source of the sound. And despite her growing horror, she couldn't pull her gaze away.

A rope had been looped over one of the exposed metal beams in the ceiling. The body hanging from it swayed slightly in the draft flowing out of a vent in the exposed ductwork. An overturned student desk lay directly below the dangling feet.

Since the face was turned away from her, she couldn't make an identification. Her impression was that this was a male, but she couldn't be sure. Not from here. With that realization, the paralysis of shock dissolved, allowing her to think again.

Maybe he wasn't dead. If she could get him down—

She rushed forward, frantically pushing aside the overturned desk in order to get closer. By then her eyes had found the face, blackened and distorted from the effects of the rope, unrecognizable still, but definitely a boy's.

She righted the desk, climbing onto its seat to grasp his legs. If she could raise him and ease that terrible pressure… Or somehow get him down…

She could do neither. Her stretching fingers couldn't begin to loosen that cruel knot. Not even when she put one foot up on the flat part of the desk to allow her a longer reach.

As she worked, struggling to do something that might change what was happening, she became aware of the sounds emanating from her own throat. They were guttural. Unintelligible. Like an animal caught in a trap.

And then finally—irrevocably—she knew there was nothing she could do alone. If she were to have any chance to save this boy, she had to get help.

She turned to climb down from her precarious perch only to have the desk literally tip over with her. She jumped, preventing herself from falling only by stumbling into another of the disordered desks.

Her purse lay near the door, exactly where she'd dropped it when she'd identified the noise. She ran to grab it, scattering its contents onto the floor as she frantically searched for her phone. Panting, she flipped open the case and pressed in 9-1-1. It seemed an eternity until the dispatcher picked up.

"Lowen County 9-1-1. What's your emergency, please?"

"I'm at the high school. Down in the basement. First room to the right of the stairs. A boy has hanged himself. I can't get him down, and I don't think there's anyone else down here."

That's what she should have done, she realized. Run upstairs for help. She knew there were people still up there.

"What's your name, ma'am?"

She swallowed to ease the dryness of her throat while she concentrated on the dispatcher's question. "Lindsey Sloan. I'm a teacher. You have to get somebody here right away. They'll have to cut him down. I tried to loosen the rope and—"

"This is at Randolph-Lowen High School, ma'am?"

"That's right. In the basement."

"And this person is still alive?"

Was he?

Her eyes went back to the body, still gently moving in the flow of the air conditioner. The image of the blood-suffused face was in her mind's eye, but she denied what it told her.

"I don't know. Please. Just get somebody over here."

"They're already on their way, ma'am. Maybe you could get somebody upstairs to direct them to your location."

"I don't think— Okay. Okay. I'll do that."

There was no point trying to explain. Beth had been in the guidance office minutes ago. And Jay was still here, although the choral room was at the other end of the building. Surely there would be someone closer. Someone stronger.

She needed to get upstairs and find someone. They could probably get the body down before the paramedics arrived.

"Don't hang up, ma'am," the dispatcher cautioned. "You stay with me until they get there."

"Okay, but I have to go upstairs. There may be somebody there who can help."

With the open phone in her hand, Lindsey scrambled up and began to run. As she reached the stairs, she began to scream, and she kept screaming until finally somebody answered.

Jace got to the school only a few minutes after the paramedics, but not in time to watch them cut the kid's body down. He did what he could to secure the scene, but everybody's focus was, as it should have been, on trying to save a life.

As the EMTs worked over the boy, Jace turned his attention to the room. He'd seen enough dead people to understand that nobody could help this kid now. At least not medically.

He hadn't seen Lindsey, but he knew from the dispatcher that she'd placed the original call. He hoped that didn't mean she'd discovered the body. He couldn't imagine what that would do to the fragile hold she'd managed to keep on her emotions.

When the paramedic finally looked up at him and shook

his head, Jace asked the question he'd been wondering about for the last five minutes. "Any ID?"

"Haven't had a chance to check."

Obediently the medic began searching for a billfold. He appeared to be not too many years out of high school himself. And currently green around the gills.

"Here you go." The EMT held a wallet out.

Jace weighed the risks of contaminating any evidence against waiting for the techs to arrive, which might be as much as an hour. He decided that, as quickly as news traveled in this town, he needed a name for the deceased. Besides, from what he could tell, there was no reason to think this was anything other than what it appeared—the copycat event everyone had warned might happen.

"Thanks." Jace took the billfold, allowing it to fall open.

The first thing he saw was the driver's license, with its smiling picture. The second was the name. *Tim Harrison.* He knew then that his first instinct hadn't been wrong.

Maybe this wasn't a crime scene. Maybe this kid had thrown that rope over the metal girder and put the noose around his own neck. Even if that *was* the way it had gone down, whatever had driven Harrison to that act was somehow connected to everything else that had happened in this town since that first fire.

And maybe, just maybe, this was the thread that would help him unravel all the others.

"What made you think this was from Harrison?"

Jace looked up from the note Lindsey had handed him to find her eyes clinging to his. She looked shell-shocked. Even more traumatized than the night of the fire at the stadium.

The urge to take her in his arms was so strong Jace deliberately broke the connection between them by looking down at the paper he held. Right now, Lindsey was a witness. And that meant their relationship was strictly professional.

"Jay told me Walt was looking for me. When I saw that," she nodded toward the note, "I assumed it was from him."

"And if you hadn't run into Jay? Who would you have assumed this was from?"

"Walt prints everything. I would still have thought it was from him. Maybe to clear the air between us, if nothing else."

"And when you got to his room, no one was there."

"I figured, as late as it was, he'd already left. I started back to the stairs and that's when I heard the sound. I don't know why I hadn't been aware of it on the way *to* Walt's room. Thinking about what he might want to say, I guess."

"What kind of relationship did they have?"

"Tim and Walt? They were father and son, Jace. They were close. They loved one another."

"They ever fight?"

"I don't know. I mean, I'm sure they did. Every parent and teenager fight. Ninety-nine percent of the time it doesn't mean anything. A kid trying to assert his independence."

"Was Tim doing that?"

"I didn't know them that well. All I can tell you is that they seemed close. Walt was very concerned about Tim after Andrea's death—" She stopped, her eyes locking on his.

"Why would he be 'very' concerned?"

"We were all concerned. About *all* the kids. Especially those in the program. It's a relatively small group. Most of them have gone to school together all their lives."

Every word she'd said was careful. Deliberately chosen. As if she didn't want to plant any ideas about Tim Harrison that Jace might take and run with.

"Did he have a history of depression? Any kind of psychological problems? Anything that would make his father feel he was especially vulnerable after Andrea's suicide?"

"Not that I'm aware of. If he *did* have problems, I couldn't tell from his attitude or his performance."

"Good kid?"

"Absolutely. Sharp. Funny." Her voice broke on the last, but then she outwardly controlled the emotion he could still read in her eyes. "This is going to devastate this community."

"You said Walt always printed. Did everybody know that?"

"The faculty certainly did. His students, too, of course."

"What if it were printed and phrased to make you *think* it was from Harrison?"

She shook her head. "Why?"

"To get you down there."

"You think Tim wanted *me* to find him? But…he wasn't *in* Walt's room. Why send me there, if that's what he wanted?"

Jace hadn't considered that Tim might have written the note, but it *was* a possibility. Something else Harrison might be able to clear up. And maybe it was better to let Lindsey think he'd been talking about the victim. Less frightening than the possibility he had been considering.

"The room by the stairs is the only one where they couldn't enclose the ducts without lowering the ceiling below standards. It's the only one left with exposed beams. Maybe he figured that if he could get you down here…"

"Why me?"

"Maybe for the same reason Andrea came to you. He knew you'd care."

Jace couldn't know if he was on track with either scenario until he'd talked to Harrison. After all, the history teacher might have written the note himself. Just as Lindsey thought originally.

Since Walt's car hadn't been in the parking lot, he'd sent two patrolmen to his house to deliver the news. Normally that was something he'd feel an obligation to do himself, but judging from the teacher's animosity when he'd questioned him about the conversation in the field house, Jace figured he'd be the last person from whom Harrison would want to hear this.

"If Walt *did* just want to talk, then I guess your being the one to find the body is another coincidence."

"I know you think this is all connected, but what if it's not? What if we just have two troubled kids—"

"I'd say there were more than two, wouldn't you? Unless you're implying that Andrea and Tim set the church fires."

"That isn't what I meant. I just don't think there has to be a connection between these suicides and the church fires."

"And the attacks on you? Any connection to those? And the fact that these two 'troubled' kids are in your program, Lindsey? Doesn't that tell you something?"

"It tells me you've targeted them from the beginning. You had made up your mind on that the first time we talked."

They were back where they'd begun. While the suicides had made him more convinced of the connection, they'd made it harder for Lindsey to accept it. Because that meant she was right in the middle of it all. And, just as he'd thought about Harrison, who could blame her for wanting to deny that role?

Twenty-Two

Lindsey had known Shannon would take the news of Tim's death hard, but she'd also known she should be the one to break it to her. She hadn't wanted her friend to hear it from someone who would have even less real information than she did.

"Oh, God. Oh, my God. Why?"

"Nobody knows."

She tried to reach out and hug her friend, but Shannon backed away to lean against the kitchen counter. Arms crossed over her stomach, she hunched forward as if she were in pain.

Lindsey withdrew, giving her the space she seemed to need right now. "Jace sent someone from the sheriff's department to notify Walt. He was going over himself as soon as he finished at the school. Maybe…"

Shannon looked up to ask, "He thinks Walt can tell them something that will explain why?"

"Jace asked me if there had been a history of depression."

"Like Andrea? Another one we let fall through the cracks?"

Lindsey ignored the bitter comment. "Did Walt ever talk

to you about Tim? Say that he was worried about him? Say *anything* that would lead you to think something like this was even a remote possibility?"

Shannon shook her head. "We talked about colleges. He wanted me to help them find money for that. Scholarships. Financial aid. Anything. I promised to start that process in the spring. Walt thought Tim should be able to get a band scholarship. Maybe with a combination of that and something academic… I swear, Linds, he never mentioned being concerned about anything else."

"He was concerned enough that he waited to drive him home the day after Andrea died."

"I got the impression he just wanted to be with him. To talk. To let Tim talk. I think most parents felt the same way that day. They just wanted to know their own child was okay."

"So you didn't take that as Walt being worried that Tim might…"

"Hang himself?" Shannon's laugh was mocking. "I think if he'd *really* been worried about the possibility of suicide, he wouldn't have let him out of his sight. And he did. I don't believe Walt expected this. Any more than the rest of us."

"If we didn't, we sure gave lip service to it."

"That Tim might commit suicide?"

"That there might be copycats. That's why the county sent out the grief counselors. That's why the two of us decided it would be a good idea for you to talk to my classes after the funeral."

Except Shannon hadn't talked to them. Not after second period. And not to Tim's class. Lindsey had done that herself, obviously as poorly as she'd dealt with Andrea that afternoon.

"You think that's what this is?" Shannon asked. "You think Tim thought this was a way to get attention? Did he strike you as being that needy? He had a father who loved him. And a lot of friends. Tim wasn't Andrea. He wasn't anything like her."

"I don't pretend to know what he was thinking. I'm beginning to believe we don't have any idea what *any* of them are thinking. All I know is that he's dead. By his own hand. And that he's the second one of my students who is."

"It could have been any of them. Any kid in the school."

"But it wasn't. It was another of mine. Jace is convinced this is all connected. That it started with the church fires."

"He can't think Tim had anything to do with those. You knew that boy. You *know* he wasn't involved in anything like that."

"Then maybe just connected to me. To what's been happening since Jace made a point of singling me out."

"I don't understand."

"Somebody left a note in my box this afternoon. I thought it was from Walt. It was block printed, and Jay had told me he'd been looking for me. I thought maybe he wanted to talk about the conversation I overheard."

"*What* conversation?"

"Last Friday night. When I went to ask Dave's permission for the ceremony at halftime, he and Walt were in Coach's office in the field house. Walt told Dave that the rumors were out there and that nothing could be kept secret in this town."

"What kind of rumors?"

"At the time I thought he was talking about Andrea. The rumors Walt had told us about in the lounge. I told Jace what he'd said, and he asked him. Walt said they were talking about some boosters, but that wasn't what I heard. I know it wasn't."

"Okay, maybe I'm slow, but I don't get what any of this has to do with Tim. Or how he's connected to Andrea."

"Maybe they aren't, but when I saw the note, that's what I thought Walt wanted to talk to me about. That conversation."

"You check to see if Tim has a profile on 'My Place'?'"

"What?"

"A page like Andrea's. Something out of character."

"I came straight here to tell you. I didn't want you to hear about Tim from somebody else."

"Then let's go see." Without waiting for a response, Shannon turned and headed to the back of the apartment where her computer was set up in a corner of her bedroom.

"Jace says Andrea's page wasn't done on her computer. Do you think—?" Lindsey realized she was talking to herself.

When she reached the bedroom, Shannon was already seated in front of her computer, typing in an address. Looking over her shoulder, Lindsey watched as she navigated the popular site with a skill that bespoke familiarity.

"There," Shannon said as the image of a smiling Tim, looking normal and completely happy filled the screen.

It was last year's yearbook picture. Lindsey had seen it a dozen times as she'd thumbed through the pages. He seemed ridiculously young. Innocent. Filled with potential.

All of it now lost. All gone.

They read together in silence. Lindsey wasn't sure what Shannon had been searching for when she'd pulled this up, but there was nothing here that reminded her of the travesty Andrea's profile had made of her life.

This was exactly what she'd thought at first glance. Normal. A portrait of an ordinary, small-town teen.

There were pictures of band practice. Posed shots of laughing friends. Scenes from the beach with the same kids. Family photos. Even the visitors' entries were appropriate for a sixteen-year-old's site. Nothing to raise any alarms.

"Walt probably had his password," Shannon said. "Maybe even parental control. There's nothing here."

"Did you expect there to be?"

"You said Jace thought they were connected."

She hadn't really meant Andrea and Tim were connected. She had been thinking of each of them being separately connected to the fires. Or to the things that had happened to her. But the two of them were connected in one undeniable way.

"Because they took their own lives," she said aloud.

"Is that what he meant?"

"I don't think so, but it's true."

Shannon turned, looking over her shoulder. "And he thinks the reason they did that is the connection."

It wasn't a question. As Shannon said the words, Lindsey knew she was right. She couldn't have articulated why, but it resonated with the ring of absolute truth.

"Because they knew something?" she suggested.

"About the fires?"

"Jace keeps saying that to me. That I know something they're afraid of."

"So…what would those two kids know that would make them kill themselves?"

They had discarded the possibility either of them could have been involved with the arson. It was so out of character that neither she nor Shannon could fathom that. Which left—

"Maybe they didn't," Lindsey said softly.

The words hung in the air between them a long time, neither willing to take the next step. Because that, too, was something neither could fathom.

"Does that mean what I think?" Shannon asked finally.

"I don't know. Maybe suicide was a possibility with Andrea. She had a history that would make it seem…possible. But *Tim?* It doesn't make sense. You said so yourself."

"That's quite a leap, Linds. I'd think long and hard before I suggested it to anyone else. Especially to Jace."

Jace was the one who'd first suggested to her the possibility concerning Andrea, but he'd discarded it with the results of the autopsy. In any case, Shannon was right. Thinking someone might have killed Tim was way out of bounds. Maybe the result of the guilt she felt about so many things.

"Sorry. I'm just…exhausted. And emotionally strung out. We all are."

"Yeah, well, we aren't all talking about murder."

"Forget I said it."

"That you can even *think* that—"

"I guess it seemed better than the alternative."

"The alternative?"

"I tried to get him down, Shannon, but I couldn't. The paramedics said it was too late by the time I got there, but I'll always wonder. Maybe if I'd gotten some help—"

"Stop it. You played this game with Andrea. I never realized you had such a martyr complex before."

"I just keep thinking that there might have been something else I should have done. In both cases."

"There wasn't anything you could do. They *chose* to end their own lives. And in ways that precluded intervention."

Which was also highly convenient…

Once the thought that they might *not* have committed suicide had formed, Lindsey found it difficult to get it out of her head. "You think any sixteen-year-old really wants to die?"

"I know two who apparently did," Shannon said.

"They threaten. They leave notes. They call people. They call 9-1-1. Neither of these kids did any of those things."

"Because they weren't posing."

"Tim Harrison wanted to die? Do you really buy that?"

"You saw some pretty graphic proof of just how much."

"I don't believe it."

She didn't, Lindsey realized. No matter how much it went against everything she'd seen and been told. She had known Tim. He'd been in her class today. And there had been no indication he was suicidal. For him to go downstairs only a few hours later and hang himself—

Shannon pushed up from the computer, leaning over to click out of Tim's page. "You don't *want* to believe it. I swear you're as bad as Jace. Is that what you get from sleeping with a cop? Conspiracy theories? Better than an STD, I guess."

"What the hell does that mean?"

"Oh, don't play innocent with me. I know you, remember. I knew the first night you slept with him. Not that there's anything wrong with that. About time if you ask me."

"I didn't ask you. It isn't any of your business."

"You're right. I just thought it might offer an explanation as to why you've gone off the deep end."

"*Me?* Hey, you're the one who claims to know kids who might be capable of setting those fires. I'm the one who defended them. But you know what? Things are getting way out of control. If Jace is right—and despite whatever you think about him, he is a detective—then the suicides, the attacks, are all connected to those fires. Isn't it about time you went to him with whatever information you have? We're past the point of protecting somebody from having suspicion cast on them."

"I don't have anything concrete to base it on. I told you that."

"Whatever you think, whoever you suspect, he'll keep what you tell him in confidence."

"Like he did with what you told him about Walt?"

"I never asked him to. I knew he'd have to talk to Walt. And at that point, I was beyond caring about the niceties. Getting locked in a burning building does that for you."

The stakes had started climbing when she'd found the rattler in her hamper. The fire at the stadium had pushed them higher still. Now, with the deaths of two students…

"I'll think about it," Shannon said. "I promise. My instinct was that going to the police with what's only intuition would be a betrayal of the student/counselor bond. But maybe you're right. Maybe that kind of ethical consideration is a luxury we can no longer afford."

"If Jace can narrow down the possibilities for the computer where Andrea's page was created, he might be able to get a warrant. I know he'd like to question its owner. If he has a chance to do that, something might come of it."

"And that might have nothing at all to do with the fires."

"Maybe not, but do you think it might have had something to do with Andrea's death? The fact that everybody in school knew about that garbage? For someone with her history, don't you think that might have been enough to push her over the edge?"

"I told you I'll think about it."

Lindsey knew if she said any more, Shannon's stubborn streak might kick in. "Fair enough. That's all I'm asking."

"So, is he any good?"

Despite the abrupt change of subject, she knew what Shannon wanted to know. "Yes, but if you're looking for details, you're going to be disappointed."

"Just trying to live vicariously." Shannon led the way out of the bedroom and down the hall, her words floating back in the gloom. "It's been a long, dry spell. I may have to call Rick."

"If you do, please don't blame it on me."

"Dumb and dumber."

"You said that. I didn't."

"I'll probably just settle for booze and my vibrator."

"Well, there you go."

They'd reached the kitchen where Lindsey had left her purse. She picked it up, leaning over to hug her friend.

"No pills, okay. Not if you're really going to drink."

"Don't worry. You were supposed to bring the alcohol, remember. I doubt I've got enough here for a good buzz."

"Good. Go to bed early and get some sleep."

"You think we ought to go over to Walt's in the morning?"

"The way he looked at me at the funeral, I'm pretty sure I'm the last person he'll want to offer him comfort."

"You found his son, Linds. At some point he's gonna want to talk to you about that."

She swallowed hard, thinking about the difficulties of that conversation. "Yeah, but I'm not sure I can do that tomorrow."

"He may not want to, either. The police can give him enough information for now. More than he'll want, I'm sure."

Lindsey nodded, grateful for the reprieve. She walked over to the back door. "Call me when you get up."

"I will. You going to your folks?"

Lindsey's hesitation gave her away.

"You're going to his place," Shannon guessed. "Good. At least I'll know you're safe."

"It's a good feeling."

"As I said, long overdue."

"Call me."

Shannon nodded. She threw the night latch on the door, holding it open as she switched on the porch light. Lindsey pushed open the screen, but before she could step out, Shannon's question stopped her.

"Were you really serious about what you said?"

"About what?"

"That they might not have killed themselves."

She could deny that's what she'd meant. Or make a joke of it. That's what Shannon wanted her to do.

Kids did stupid, impulsive things all the time. She had ten years of experience with them that proved that. None of it convinced her that Tim had written her a note, climbed up on a desk, put a noose around his neck, and stepped off.

"I guess it's like that intuition that leads you to suspect someone of the church fires. Mine says Tim wouldn't do that. Not to his father. Not to himself. And if *he* didn't…"

If he didn't, then Jace's arsonist and her attacker had crossed the line to murder.

Twenty-Three

As soon as he closed the apartment door behind him, Jace loosened his tie and unbuttoned the collar of his shirt. He pitched his jacket, which he'd shed before he'd gotten back in his car, at one of the chairs as he walked over to the credenza that served as his makeshift bar.

He took a bottle of Scotch out of the bottom and poured a couple of fingers into one of the glasses. Then he downed the liquor in one gulp, feeling the burn all the way to the bottom of his stomach.

He hadn't had to break the news of his son's death to Walt Harrison, but he could imagine few things worse about his job than the interview he'd conducted with the grieving father. Maybe if Harrison hadn't just been allowed to view the body...

He knew that with some of his questions he'd probably crossed the line between accusing the dead boy of knowing something about the arson and letting this pass as another troubled kid trying to find a way out of whatever was going on in his life. And other than infuriating Harrison, he couldn't think of anything he'd gained from doing it.

His cell vibrated in the pocket of his shirt. Probably someone from the department notifying him of the complaint Harrison had filed with the Sheriff about that.

He fished the phone out, holding it up to read the number before he flipped open the case. "Where are you?"

"Leaving Shannon's."

Lindsey's voice sounded remarkably normal, considering the afternoon's events. Of course, the person with whom she'd been discussing Tim's death wasn't as personally involved as Walt Harrison had been. "You okay?"

"Compared to what?"

To what your life was like before I screwed it up...

"To normal," he said aloud.

"I've forgotten what that was like. Where are you?"

"Home."

The silence that followed lasted several seconds. She was waiting for him to invite her over. God knew he wanted to. He just wasn't sure his reasons for wanting her here jibed with the reasons for which she would want to come.

"Are you in for the night?" she asked.

"Unless I get called out again."

Another silence, this one more awkward.

"Have you eaten?"

Lindsey's question reminded him that it had been a long time since the burger he'd grabbed at lunch. And the Scotch he'd consumed was reinforcing that realization.

"Not yet. Want to meet somewhere?" Meeting in public would be safe. Having her come here, given the effects of the alcohol, probably wouldn't be.

"I thought I might pick something up and bring it home."

Home. Her use of the word in this context should have bothered him. It didn't. She'd spent the last few nights at the apartment. He'd enjoyed having her here. And not only in his bed.

"Sorry," she spoke into his hesitation. "I shouldn't have said that. Your home. Not mine. It's just… I don't want to be alone tonight."

"Me neither."

That was the truth, he realized. He'd been looking forward to having her spend the night. Perhaps that was a confession he shouldn't have made, not at this stage of their relationship, but he was too tired right now to play "relationship games."

He wanted her. In more ways than just sexually.

"Thanks," she said softly. Her voice strengthened on the next question. "Any preference?"

"Just food. Lots of it."

"On the way. See you in a few minutes."

He was surprised at the speed with which the connection was broken. She hadn't given him time to say anything in response. Not even "Be careful," which is what he'd been thinking.

He considered calling her back before he decided he was being paranoid. She was going to be in a public place buying food, probably by going through some drive-through out on the highway. Then she would come straight here. There was no reason for the anxiety he felt.

Too much Scotch on an empty stomach. Or too much death, up close and personal.

He needed a shower and to get out of these clothes, which seemed to hold the smell of the morgue. He pulled off his tie as he headed to the back of the apartment. By the time he got to the bedroom, he'd stripped off his dress shirt and T-shirt.

When he turned on the light, he saw that Lindsey had made the bed before she'd left. Another bit of domestic tranquility that would normally have set his teeth on edge. The only effect it had tonight was to cause him to hang up his slacks and put his shoes on the floor of the closet. He carried the shirt and underwear with him to the bathroom, throwing them into the hamper before he stepped into the shower.

He'd been under the pulse of hot water only a minute or two, not long enough to have bothered yet with the soap, when the doorbell rang. Maybe Lindsey had gotten supper before she'd called. Or maybe she'd decided she wanted something more substantial than fast food.

He turned off the faucets and stepped out of the enclosure. Wrapping a towel around his waist and leaving a trail of wet footprints behind him, he headed to the front door.

Despite his state of undress, he never thought about checking the peephole. Instead he opened the door, prepared to let Lindsey in and return to the shower he'd begun.

Shannon Anderson stood on the threshold. Her eyes widened slightly before they crinkled with amusement. And then changed again with some other emotion he couldn't read.

"Obviously I'm interrupting something," she said.

"Just a shower." He'd realized by now that Shannon knew about the change that had taken place in his and Lindsey's relationship. If she expected him to be uncomfortable, she was in for a disappointment. "You looking for Lindsey?"

"Is she here?"

"Not yet. She's picking up dinner. You want to wait?"

He didn't invite her to join them for the meal. It wasn't that he objected to the idea. He just figured that since she was Lindsey's friend, she should issue any invitations.

"No, that's all right. Give her a message for me?"

"Of course."

"Tell her I've decided to take her advice. I just need to check something out first."

"She'll know what that means?"

Shannon smiled. "She'll figure it out."

Lindsey had said she was leaving Shannon's when she called him. This must be something related to the conversation there. If so, the cryptic message would probably be clear to her.

"You got it," he agreed.

"Thanks."

"Sure you don't want to wait?"

"No, I'm gonna go before you shrink the carpet."

"Look, you're welcome to stay. I didn't mean to be inhospitable. I just wasn't expecting company."

"Other than Lindsey. Or isn't she company anymore?"

He didn't answer, simply holding her eyes.

"Okay, forget I said that," Shannon said, looking a little embarrassed that her teasing had fallen so flat. "I apologize. It's been a really bad day."

He nodded. The air conditioner, set low because of the heat outside, chilled his wet skin. He didn't give a damn whether Lindsey's friend stayed or went. He just wanted her to make up her mind.

"I'll let you get back to your shower. Just give Lindsey my message, please."

This time she turned and disappeared into the darkness of the hallway. Jace wondered if Lindsey was going to be pissed he'd let her leave. He stepped into the doorway to call her back, but Shannon had already rounded the corner.

He closed the door, and from force of habit, turned the dead bolt and secured the chain. He hadn't yet given Lindsey a key, so he'd have to let her in.

Maybe the drive-through she'd chosen would be as slow as those places normally were. If he was lucky, by the time she got here, he'd have finished his interrupted shower. And if he hadn't, maybe he could talk her into finishing it with him.

* * *

Lindsey juggled her purse and the two heavy sacks she carried so that she could free one finger to stab the doorbell. Reaction had finally set in as she'd climbed the stairs to Jace's apartment.

This afternoon's adrenaline had faded, leaving her feeling as if she'd been run over by a truck. On top of that, she'd skipped lunch, hoping to find Shannon in the lounge. And the sense of camaraderie she'd felt at Shannon's had long ago evaporated. Everything, the emotional as well as the physical, seemed to be catching up with her. Fighting inertia so intense it felt like illness, she lifted her arm and punched the button again.

"Coming."

Her heart lifted just to hear Jace's voice. Which sounded remarkably normal. But then he was a professional, long accustomed to the kind of violent death she'd encountered for the first time this afternoon.

She listened to locks being manipulated before the door swung inward. Jace was wearing threadbare jeans and a faded navy polo, both of which emphasized the strength of his body.

"Hey," she said, her eyes drinking in the sight of him.

He leaned forward to relieve her of the sacks. At the same time his lips brushed the side of her cheek. As kisses went, it wasn't much. The kind people in the South gave all the time in greeting or in saying goodbye.

Tonight it said welcome home. And after her screw up on the phone, that was something she had very much needed to hear.

"Hey, yourself. Smells good." Jace turned and started toward the kitchen.

She hovered in the doorway, too emotional to make small

talk about the food. When he reached the door on the other side of the room, Jace realized she hadn't followed him. He turned back, his expression quizzical. "Is there something else?"

He meant more food. Maybe out in the car. She shook her head and stepped inside.

"Lock it," he ordered.

She took the opportunity to try to gather control. Once the chain was in place, she turned and found him watching her. She managed a smile.

"Are you sure you're okay?" he asked

"We had this conversation."

"That was a while ago."

"So if anything, I should be better, right? Not worse."

"It doesn't always work that way. Sometimes it takes a while for things to sink in. Want a drink?"

She shook her head. "I'd probably pass out."

"You can do that, too, if you want, but you ought to eat something first."

She nodded, reluctantly moving toward him. He didn't turn and go on into the kitchen as she'd expected. Instead his eyes examined her as they had at the school this afternoon.

With that memory she was suddenly back in that classroom with that limp, lifeless body swaying in the draft from the air conditioner. Sickness curled in the pit of her stomach, so strong she was forced to swallow against it.

"Did you find out about the note?" she asked.

"Yeah. No mystery there. Harrison left it for you. He just wanted to clear the air. He said—"

"What?" Whatever else Walt had said, Jace clearly didn't want to tell her. She could see the regret that he'd started this in his eyes, but she needed to know. If it would make sense of any of this...

"Tell me, Jace. Tell me what he said."

"That you were Tim's favorite teacher. He didn't want—"

She didn't know what her face revealed, but Jace reacted to it immediately. He set the bags on the hall table and opened his arms. That was the only invitation she needed. She walked into them as if that were the most natural thing in the world. As if she belonged there.

He smelled of soap and deodorant and shampoo. Clean. Alive. Normal. She took a deep breath, savoring the smell. Savoring the feel of soft knit under her cheek and the strength of his arms. Willing the other images in her head to disappear.

"Don't think about it," he said.

"How do you do that?"

"You just don't think about it. You concentrate on something else. Something good."

So, is he any good?

Think about something good. Something like Jace.

"Easier said than done." She didn't move her head from his chest. She felt as if she never wanted to move again.

"But it *is* possible. I promise."

"Help me," she whispered.

She felt his chin brush against the top of her head as he nodded. Having his arms around her was therapeutic. Feeling the solid warmth of his body against hers—

"You hungry?"

She shook her head. She knew she ought to eat, but she was unwilling to give up the security of having him hold her for food. She couldn't think of anything right now that was more important or more tempting than to be in his embrace.

"I know you're emotional right now. And vulnerable. I don't want to take advantage of that. You need to say if—"

"Take advantage? Like… Do you mean what I think you do?"

"I'm thinking of a time-tested way to make sure you don't have to think. Not about anything."

Something devoutly to be wished for right now. She pushed slightly away from him, keeping her palms against his chest so that she could look up into his eyes.

"I don't want to think, Jace. Not about anything."

"Good. Because neither do I."

Jace lifted his torso, propping himself on his forearms. She could hear his breathing, ragged from the strength of his climax. She was reluctant to open her eyes, afraid the oblivion he had promised—and had delivered—would vanish if she did.

Tonight had been nothing like the other times they'd made love. There had been no preliminaries. No foreplay. No courtship. Jace had simply taken her, his lovemaking hard and fast and controlling. And she knew now, though she hadn't at the start, that this had been exactly what she needed.

"You asleep?"

She opened her eyes to find him looking down into her face. Their bodies were still joined, their skins wet with sweat.

"No, but give me a minute."

She could feel his heart rate beginning to slow. The frantic pulse of hers was also returning to normal. She closed her eyes again, blowing upward a breath that stirred the damp, disordered hair on her brow.

What had just happened had been beyond the scope of her experience. A little rough. Almost painful. And her reaction had surprised her almost as much as his total dominance. She would never have thought she'd be the kind of woman who would respond to that. The kind who *could* respond to it.

"You need to eat something."

"Before I pass out?" She suspected the light-headedness

had little to do with food deprivation. Lack of oxygen, maybe. Or multiple orgasms.

He bent, pressing a kiss against her forehead. She opened her eyes again, finding his face still next to hers, their noses almost touching.

"Thank you."

"For what?"

"For coming here tonight. For this. For trusting me."

She did trust him, she realized. If this had been anyone but Jace… "You were right. So…thank you."

"Right about what?"

"It was consuming." There had not been one second when she had had to think about anything other than what was happening between them.

"I told you."

She nodded, wondering what they did for an encore. After all, there were physical limits to how long they could sustain this method of forgetfulness.

"Don't." He lowered his head so that his lips found the soft skin beneath her ear.

"Don't what?"

"Think." He whispered the word, his mouth moving upward until his tongue dipped into her ear.

Something hot and heavy moved low in her belly. As incredible as it seemed, given the number of times she'd climaxed, her body was once more responding.

"It's too soon." She hadn't intended to voice that realization aloud. Because, of course, the physiological restraints were not hers.

"Speak for yourself."

The breath needed to whisper those words stirred against the moisture his tongue had left on her ear. Sensation, pure and sexual, moved along all the sensitized nerve pathways of her lower body. Without any conscious direction on her part, her muscles began to tighten around his erection. Incredibly, he responded, making a mockery of her declaration.

Once more his hips began to move, the silken slide of flesh against flesh eased by their previous lovemaking. Despite that, she could feel the now so-familiar sensations beginning to build. She strained upward, her hips lifting into the downward thrust of his, trying to deepen his penetration.

She wanted all of him. As much as she could take. As much as he could give.

Jace lowered his chest so that muscle flattened her breasts. That sensation shivered erotically along overstimulated nerves. Her breath quickened as heat, molten, fluid, began to spread from her core throughout every part of her body.

Jace rocked above her, need fueling his driving tempo. She responded to each stroke with an exhalation, her breath sighing out of her lungs in increasingly short gasps.

And then, after a long time, her growing response became sound. Harsh. Wordless. Mindless.

An unbearable tension grew inside, screaming for release. "Too soon" echoed in her head, but this time in response to her own desire. She wanted… She wanted…

Her mouth opened, trying to express a need that seemed too cruel. Too demanding.

Then, without warning, she forgot to breathe. Forgot to seek. Forgot even what she'd been straining to achieve. Wave after wave of spiraling, cascading pleasure—dark and primitive and aching—flooded all her emptiness.

She was aware on some level that Jace still moved above her, but for an instant—an eternity—she was all alone. Removed from time and place. Lost in a distant reality that seemed totally disconnected from this.

And then, as Jace's release began, sensation trembling

once more through her ravaged body, she was connected to him again. Flesh to flesh. Exactly where she wanted to be. Needed to be.

When the last tremor had stilled, he put his forehead against hers. Once more she listened to his labored breathing, tracking it against her own. Matching the decrescendo of sensation as together they returned from the place the ancients had termed "the little death."

She turned her head, her lips finding his hair even as she rejected those words. She knew death now. As did Jace.

This… This was the opposite. The antithesis of what had happened this afternoon.

This was life. Made more precious, perhaps, because of the knowledge they shared.

"Go to sleep." His breath against her neck caused a shimmer of heat to slice through her veins like the last flicker of summer lightning after a storm.

Still he didn't move, the weight of his body on hers not uncomfortable. She lay beneath him, feeling his heartbeat slow and then steady.

Like the familiar pulse a baby hears in the womb, it spoke of security. Protection. Love.

Love…

She couldn't have pinpointed the moment when attraction had become something neither of them anticipated, but she no longer bothered to deny it. She was in love with Jace Nolan. Someone as different from who and what she was as night from day.

And despite the fact that tonight she would again sleep in his arms, she still had no idea whether his feelings mirrored her own.

Twenty-Four

There was a message from Dave waiting on her answering machine when she got home the next morning. Fearing her mother might be trying to reach her, she'd punched the button before going back to her bedroom to get dressed.

As soon as she'd heard what her boss had to say, she dialed Jace's cell. He'd still been asleep when she'd left the apartment, but this was something he needed to know.

While she waited for him to pick up, she realized there might be nothing he could do about this. Still, if nothing else, she wanted to talk to someone about it. Normally that would have been Shannon or someone from school. Now that Jace was in her life—

"Hello?"

It sounded as if he'd been awake, which made her feel marginally better about calling. In her rush to get home and dressed for school, she hadn't had time to think about the discovery she'd made last night.

It was too new to talk about, to Jace or anyone else. It was almost too new to examine inside her own head.

"The superintendent cancelled school for the rest of the

week. Dave left a message on my machine. I guess they began calling everybody on staff last night as soon as the decision was made."

The school had an automatic notification system that could be used to call both students and staff with emergency announcements. That Dave had called personally had been a courtesy to his faculty.

Jace didn't say anything for a moment. Maybe he was unsure if that was all she wanted to tell him. Or maybe, she realized, he didn't understand why she'd called him.

"I think this is the worst thing they could have done," she said, trying to fill up the silence, "but then they didn't ask me. And possibly none of the other teachers. They never do."

"You're concerned about the effect this has on the kids."

"I don't know that the grief counselors that they sent out before did much good, but just to let them stay home alone and stew about Tim…" She shook her head at the stupidity of that.

"You want me to contact the superintendent?"

It was the natural assumption for him to make. That she had called because she wanted him to do something.

"I just wanted to tell somebody. Even if you did call, I'm not sure how much listening they'd do. To you or anyone else. Maybe they talked to the counselors. Maybe this was a consensus. But my God, after two suicides—"

"Your friend came by last night. I forgot to tell you."

"My *friend?*" Only then did she make the connection to what she'd just said about counselors, which must have reminded him. "Shannon? She came to your apartment?"

She knew why Jace had forgotten to tell her. There hadn't been a lot of conversation between them last night. She'd pitched the two sacks of food they'd never gotten around to eating into the Dumpster this morning on her way out to her car.

"She said to tell you she'd decided to take your advice, but she needed to check something out first."

The only advice Lindsey could remember giving Shannon was that it was time to tell Jace, or someone in authority, if she really believed someone in the program was capable of setting the church fires. As for checking something out…

"Did she tell you what?"

"That's all she said, Lindsey. I'm just passing on the message. Belatedly."

"I need to call her."

There was a small pause, and then Jace said, "For what it's worth, I agree with you."

Not about calling Shannon. He was agreeing with her about the stupidity of closing the school.

"Then if you want to contact Dave, you can use my name. Tell him I told you what they'd done and that I'm concerned."

"Let me talk to the sheriff first. This may have come from somewhere other than the superintendent's office. I can't imagine they'd make that decision without talking to us."

It was possible Jace was right. Who was she to think she knew better than the experts?

The one who, in the aftermath of Andrea's death, had "counseled" Tim Harrison's class.

"I didn't think about that. Maybe they're right," she said, fighting her sense of despair and incompetence. "I honestly don't know what's right or smart anymore."

"Are you okay?"

An echo of the times he'd asked her that last night. Obviously, he was worried about the state of her mental health. Maybe he was afraid she was coming unglued under the pressure.

Maybe he's right.

"I'm okay. It's just that… All the way over here I was

psyching myself up to handle the kids. The closing came as a shock. I guess I needed to vent to someone, and yours was the first name on the list."

"I'll let you know what I find out."

She shouldn't have expected any expression of appreciation from him because he'd been the one she'd turned to. That he hadn't responded to her confession was only a guy thing.

Jace had a job to do, one that had been made more difficult by the events of yesterday. He'd comforted her last night when she'd really needed it. She couldn't expect to keep going back to that particular well or it was likely to dry up very quickly.

"Thanks. I'm going to call Shannon and see if the counselors were part of the process in reaching that decision. I'd feel better if that's the case." Besides, she wanted to ask about the message Shannon had left with Jace.

"Okay, then. I'll talk to you later."

Before she could say goodbye, the connection was broken. He had probably taken her saying she intended to call Shannon as a sign she wanted to end this conversation. Another of those natural assumptions, but this one left her feeling that the call had been unfinished. Especially since there had been no mention of when the "talk" he'd promised would occur.

She brought the phone down from her ear, vowing not to invite herself over to his apartment tonight. After Tim's suicide, no explanation would be required if she showed up at her parents' house.

The thought was tempting. Maybe she would head over there after she'd talked to Shannon.

Before she did either, however, she needed to get out of the clothes she'd been wearing for the last twenty-four hours and grab a shower. Once she had, she might feel more hopeful about the long, empty day, as well as the possibility of an equally long and empty night, that stretched before her.

After splashing water on his face, Jace glanced up into the mirror above the lavatory. He'd gotten a decent amount of sleep last night, but his eyes were bloodshot. The beard that darkened his cheeks added to the look of exhaustion. He needed a shave and a shower, not necessarily in that order, and then he needed something to eat.

He'd pretended to be asleep this morning when Lindsey slipped out of his bed. He'd lain there, eyes closed, listening to the sounds she made as she dressed.

He wasn't sure why he had hidden the fact he was awake. Because he wasn't up to dealing with the inevitable "morning after" dregs of emotion? Or because he thought it would be better if they both had some time—and some space—to think about what was happening between them.

For the first time in longer than he could remember, he allowed his eyes to examine the reflection of the puckered scars that marked his chest. A reminder, if he'd needed one, that there was no room in this job for emotion. Not of any kind.

He'd learned only later that the kid holding the gun in the drug deal gone wrong had been thirteen. He'd looked younger. Too frigging scared to ever pull that trigger.

Jace had had maybe half a second to make that determination. Instead of blowing the kid away, he'd screamed at him to drop the gun. The kid had put two bullets into Jace and one into his partner before they'd taken him down. Geoff hadn't made it. And there had been many times during the next year when Jace had wished he hadn't.

It had been a hard lesson. One he had believed he'd mastered. Until he'd let himself become involved with Lindsey.

Until this was over, that involvement was something he needed to rethink. His first reaction when she'd told him about the school closing had not been to wonder how that would affect his investigation, but to worry about how it was affecting her.

There were any number of ways he could justify the relationship he'd allowed to develop between them. Lindsey was someone he'd once believed possessed information he needed to solve the arson. Then, with the two attacks, she had become someone who might have been targeted because he'd deliberately singled her out. Someone deserving of his protection. All of those were still legitimate concerns, which made it difficult to put a necessary distance between them. At least until this was over.

Given the deaths of two students in her program, he didn't need further confirmation that he'd been right about her students being involved. He wasn't sure, however, that he had enough evidence to make a case to the sheriff that Lindsey should be assigned protection. If he couldn't, he'd have to figure out how to provide that and at the same time disentangle their developing personal relationship from their professional one.

And maybe you ought to start by not sleeping with her....

The lips of the man reflected in the mirror flattened until they almost disappeared. He wasn't sure how he'd gotten so deeply involved. All he knew was that until he figured out what the hell was going on in this town, he didn't need the distraction Lindsey had become.

Explaining that would be a bitch, but if he put the brakes on now, without making some attempt to do so, she'd believe exactly what his intent *had* been when he'd asked Campbell to arrange a meeting. That he'd been using her. He wasn't proud he'd intended to do so, but it was part of who and what he was.

And part of the job he'd undertaken. This—whatever was between them now—wasn't. But unless he did something about it—

His phone rang, vibrating so hard that it jumped against the hard tile of the counter. He picked it up, peering at the number before he flipped open the case. "Nolan."

"Looks like we've got another one," the sheriff said. "Corner of Oakmont and Locust. You need to get over there."

"On the way." And then, because he knew enough about the kids in Lindsey's program to want to know, "You got a name?"

"They're still waiting for an ID. Maybe by the time you get over there, they'll have one for you."

Lindsey listened to the rings, counting them until Shannon's voice mail message came on again. When it did, she brought the phone down, taking her gaze off the road long enough to punch the "End" button.

Maybe she'd decided to sleep in this morning. With the cancellation of school, there was no reason for her not to.

And she's probably muttering curses from under her pillow every time I call her.

That very logical explanation for why she was getting no answer didn't quell the nagging anxiety she'd felt since she'd left the first message. Shannon didn't have a landline, so she slept with her cell on the bedside table. She had always answered it in the past. Even the times Lindsey had called before she'd managed to drag herself out of bed on a weekend.

Like last Saturday. The morning she'd confessed to mixing alcohol and Klonopin. If she'd done something like that again…

As she maneuvered her car along the narrow, tree-lined

streets of the old neighborhood, she fought those circling thoughts. The ones that had fueled the apprehension that had driven her out of the house and on what she had told herself over and over was a wild-goose chase.

Shannon was fine. She had been okay emotionally when Lindsey left her house last night. And she'd come by Jace's apartment to leave a message, which meant she hadn't reacted to Tim's death the same way that she had to Andrea's.

Maybe they'd become too accustomed to that kind of news. Callous to the tragedy it represented. Or maybe—

As she turned onto Locust, she could see two cars parked along the curb near the end of the block. Within a couple of seconds, she'd identified the nearer one as a county cruiser. As she neared the house on the corner, she saw the emergency vehicle in the drive, its rear doors standing open.

The terror she'd managed to hold at bay during the last forty minutes flooded her mind. Her heart lodged in her throat and her hands trembling on the wheel, she guided the Honda to the curb on the near side of the drive.

A sheriff's deputy was leaning against the side of the patrol car. Although he was facing away from her, it was apparent he was talking on a radio. And the paramedics…

Her gaze flew back to the house. A dark rectangle marked the location of the front door. Also open.

From force of habit, she turned the key in the ignition, killing the engine. Although her knees felt too weak to support her, she fumbled for the handle of the door.

The deputy talking on the radio turned when she slammed it. She ignored him, her sole focus on putting one foot in front of the other until she'd crossed the lawn and gotten inside that house. At some point during that journey, she began to run.

"Hey! Hey, you! You can't go in there."

She heard the words, but their meaning was totally disconnected from the dark rectangle that beckoned her. She needed to find Shannon. She needed to know what was going on.

"Ma'am! Ma'am! You can't go in there."

This time she stopped, turning to watch the deputy sprint towards her across the lawn. "What's going on? What's happening in there?"

His face changed as he took in her state. He slowed, his mouth opening and then closing. Finally he shook his head. "I'm sorry, ma'am. I really am, but I can't let you go inside."

As she turned and again started toward the house, he reached out, catching her elbow. She tried to wrench her arm away, but his hold was firm.

"Ma'am. I'm really sorry, ma'am."

She was no longer listening. Instead she was watching as a man in uniform began to back out of Shannon's front door. He felt for his footing as he stepped over the threshold, carefully pulling a wheeled stretcher out with him.

Lindsey stopped struggling against the deputy's grip. Her world had narrowed to the two men maneuvering the unwieldy stretcher through the door and down the front steps of Shannon's house. As they made the turn to head toward the emergency van parked in the drive, she could see the pale blue fabric that covered whoever they were bringing out of the house. A corner of that sheet, along which Lowen County was stenciled in faded black letters, trailed through the grass, its edge darkened by the morning dew.

Almost against her will, Lindsey's eyes followed the drape of that material upward. And found that the sheet had been placed over the face of the person on the stretcher.

Her knees literally gave way. Although the deputy tried to hold her, she fell to the ground as the first sob tore through her throat.

The man beside her stooped down in an awkward attempt to comfort or lift her, but the paramedics didn't look her way. They continued toward their vehicle, the stretcher bumping over the uneven bricks of the sidewalk.

With the ease of long practice they began to put their burden into the back of the van. Lindsey realized that she had no idea where they would take the body. No idea if they had notified Shannon's family.

She looked up at the deputy to ask those questions and realized he was no longer watching the body being loaded. He was looking instead at the door of the house.

Jace stood on the threshold, his eyes on her. Her tears started again. Relief that she wouldn't have to ask for answers to any of those questions.

Jace would take care of everything. He'd notify Shannon's mother. That was his job. That was what he did.

And he'd take care of her, too.

Jace crossed the lawn, stopping just before he reached her. He nodded to the deputy. And then he bent, making sure they were on eye level, before he spoke to her, the words slow and clearly enunciated, as if he were speaking to a child.

"This isn't what you think, Lindsey. That isn't Shannon on the stretcher."

Twenty-Five

"But what was Dave doing here?" Lindsey asked. "And where's Shannon?"

She was sitting in the passenger seat of Jace's car, sipping from the glass of water he'd sent the deputy to get inside. She no longer looked as if she were about to pass out.

"I don't have any answers. Not to either of those questions. All I can tell you is that she isn't in that house."

Shannon's cleaning lady had discovered the principal's body in the back bedroom, but only after she'd collected the trash from the wastebaskets in all the other rooms and taken it outside. She had told the deputy who'd responded to her panicked 9-1-1 call that she'd wanted to get the garbage bagged and out on the curb before the truck came.

"I started trying to call her from the time you and I hung up," Lindsey said. "She *always* answers her cell."

He could tell by a sudden widening of her eyes that she'd thought of something. She didn't offer an explanation of what that might be, hiding that involuntary reaction by lowering her head to take another swallow from the glass she held.

"Can you think of somewhere she *might* be?" he prodded. "Somewhere she might have spent the night? Somebody she's involved with, maybe?"

"I don't know. Shannon doesn't hide the fact that she…" She stopped, touching her tongue to the center of her top lip before she started over. "She still sees Rick Carlisle occasionally. It isn't serious, but…you might want to check."

"To see if she's at Carlisle's?"

She nodded. Which meant Lindsey also knew that Shannon slept with the deputy "occasionally."

He opened his cell and punched up the dispatcher. When she answered, he said, "Nolan. Can you give me Deputy Rick Carlisle's home phone number, please?"

"You want me to contact him for you, Lieutenant?"

"I just need his number. And his cell if you have it."

"We don't usually—"

"Make an exception," Jace interrupted. "It's important. If Carlisle complains, I'll clear it with the sheriff."

"On your head then, hon," the woman said.

"Yes, it is."

"That number is 555-8219. I don't have a cell listed."

"Thanks." Jace pushed the "End" button and then put in the number he'd been given. He waited through the rings until the answering machine picked up before he pushed the button again.

"No answer?" Lindsey asked.

"You know how to get there?"

Like Lindsey, he was growing concerned about Shannon Anderson. He could find out if Carlisle was on duty today, but it seemed simpler just to show up at his place than to go through the small town bureaucracy again.

"It isn't far. I don't know that she's there. You said…" Lindsey took a breath, releasing it before she finished. "You said she told you she was going to check something out. Something that had to do with the advice I'd given her."

"That's what she said."

"The only advice I gave her, Jace, was that she needed to tell you or someone in the department about the kids she thought could have set those fires."

"Are you saying she suspected someone?"

"It wasn't that specific. There were a couple of boys she believed might be capable of doing something like that."

"Then why hadn't she come to us?"

"Because that's all it was. A feeling someone might be capable of that kind of mischief. She didn't want to ruin a child's life based on nothing more than that."

"You think she might have gone over there to tell Carlisle what she suspected?"

"She and Rick are close. Despite what you're thinking, it's more friendship than anything else. Whatever else—"

"I don't give a damn who your friend sleeps with, Lindsey. What I *do* care about is that we've got a rash of fires and three people, all of them associated with Randolph-Lowen, who are dead. And don't tell me Campbell was influenced to commit suicide by the attention those other two received."

"The last few days he seemed… I don't know. Disheartened. He'd put his whole life into this school. Dave thought he was in line to become superintendent when Dr. Burke retires. That's why he'd started working on his doctorate. With the fires and the suicides, he must have believed he'd never get that chance."

"Even if he were that despondent, why here? Why in Shannon Anderson's bed?"

He hadn't told her that detail before. Her eyes widened as she grasped the implications.

"I don't know. I can't imagine why he'd come here, much less…" She shook her head again.

"Then it seems the only person who can give us that information is your friend. Let's start at Carlisle's."

Jace stabbed the doorbell once more, listening as it chimed inside the brick two-story colonial Lindsey had directed him to. She was standing beside him on the front porch, her arms crossed over her chest as if she were cold.

"There's a garage out back," she said, glancing up at him. "You want me to see if his car's there?"

Before he had a chance to answer, Jace heard the lock being turned. The door opened to reveal Rick Carlisle, wearing nothing but a pair of rumbled jeans. It was obvious by his disheveled hair and the fact that he hadn't taken time to do up the button at his waistband that they'd gotten him out of bed.

The deputy's eyes fastened first on Jace and then settled on Lindsey. "Somethin' wrong, Linds?"

"Is Shannon here?"

His gaze went back to Jace. "Depends on who's asking."

"I am," Lindsey said. "I just need to know that she's all right, Rick. Is she here?"

The belligerence faded from Carlisle's expression to be replaced by puzzlement. "Why wouldn't she be all right?"

"Because we found a dead man in her bed," Jace said.

The deputy's eyes swung back to his face. For a moment he didn't say anything. Then, "She's here. Come on in."

When he stepped away from the doorway, Jace gestured for Lindsey to go first. As he entered the foyer, he automatically checked out the disordered living room adjacent to it.

A pizza box lay on the coffee table, a single slice remaining. Half a dozen empty beer bottles were scattered around the area between the couch and the table. There was a stack of unlabeled DVDs on the floor, and the doors of a massive entertainment center across the room stood open.

"What's going on?" a female voice demanded.

Jace turned to watch Shannon Anderson descend the stairs. She appeared to be wearing a man's shirt and nothing else. The garment ended midthigh, revealing a long length of tanned legs. Her dark, curly hair tangled around her face, and mascara smudged the skin beneath her eyes.

"Linds? What is it? What's wrong?"

"I thought… Were you here all night?"

"I didn't want to be by myself," Shannon said. "I'm sure you, of all people, can appreciate the feeling."

"Tell her what you told me," Rick demanded.

"What?" Shannon's bewilderment appeared genuine, as her gaze moved from one to the other of them.

If she knew about Campbell, she was wasting her time as a counselor, Jace thought. She should be making movies. If nothing else, the kind she and Carlisle had probably watched last night.

"When she arrived for work this morning, your maid discovered the body of David Campbell in your bed."

Shannon's lips parted and then stayed open as she attempted to assimilate the news. *"Dave?"*

"You have any idea what he was doing there?"

Shannon closed her mouth. Her eyes met Lindsey's briefly, before, slightly defiant, they came back to his.

"Probably waiting for me to come home."

"In your bed?"

"It wouldn't be the first time."

Jace heard Lindsey's inhalation, but he ignored it. Despite all the clues, including Campbell's attitude toward Shannon, which Lindsey herself had told him about, she'd obviously had no idea the two were involved.

"But you hadn't been expecting him last night."

Shannon shook her head.

"When's the last time you talked to him?"

She exhaled, her cheeks puffing out as she lifted her hands to rake her hair back from her face. "I don't know. He wasn't in the office when I left school yesterday. I thought he might call during the afternoon, just to talk, but he didn't. Then Lindsey came by to tell me about Tim and… I never thought about Dave again. Was it a heart attack?"

To Jace's ear the question seemed perfectly nuanced.

"He killed himself," Lindsey said softly.

"*Killed* himself. Are you saying—? No." Shannon shook her head. "Goddamn it, no. I don't believe that."

"Shannon—"

"*Not* Dave. He wasn't the kind."

Jace couldn't decide if that was denial or if it was based on her knowledge of the principal's personality. In either case, that statement, too, had the ring of absolute sincerity.

"Given what's been going on…" Lindsey began again.

"Have you told his wife?" Surprisingly, Shannon sounded as if she cared.

"The sheriff was going to get Coach Spears to go over with him. They should have done that by now."

"And his boys," Shannon said. "God, he loved those boys." *Implying that he hadn't loved his wife?* Jace wondered.

"Are they sure it was suicide?" It was the first question Carlisle had asked since they'd come inside.

Prompted by Shannon's disbelief? Or by the same instinct Jace had felt about Campbell's death since he'd walked into Shannon Anderson's bedroom this morning.

"Nothing at the scene to indicate otherwise."

"But?"

Maybe that *had* been implied by his wording. "The techs will check to be sure. And there'll be an autopsy, of course."

"Cause of death?" Rick probed.

"No visible injuries. There was a bottle of Scotch and an empty bottle of pills nearby." From the residue in the glass and on the surface of the bedside table, it appeared the medicine had been crushed and mixed with the liquor.

"What kind?" Shannon asked.

"Klonopin. The prescription was in your name, Ms. Anderson. You have any idea how many were left in that bottle?"

The counselor took a breath. "I'd had it refilled earlier in the week. Maybe…Monday."

"So you'd gotten a month's supply, which would be what—thirty pills?—on Monday. How many have you taken since then?"

Not that it really mattered, Jace thought. More than likely it had been the combination of medication and alcohol that killed David Campbell. However many pills were left—

"One for each night. I wouldn't have slept without them."

"And the Scotch? Any idea how much was in the bottle when Campbell arrived? Or would he have brought it with him?"

"Dave had brought a bottle over a while ago. Not my poison of choice, so I don't have any idea what kind of inroads he'd made on it before last night."

"What does it matter?" Lindsey asked. "*Whatever* was there was clearly enough."

Still, there was something about the scenario that bothered Jace. He knew from experience that if he let it go, stopped trying to figure out what that was, it would come to him.

"You realize you can't go back home until the techs finish," Jace warned.

"I'm not in any hurry." Shannon looked at Carlisle as if asking permission to stay.

He shrugged in response. The gesture fit with Lindsey's description of their relationship. They might sleep together, but the involvement was clearly casual.

"You can stay with me," Lindsey offered. "As long as you want. You know that."

For the first time this morning, the counselor's expression lightened. "I didn't think *you* were staying at your place, Linds."

"I'm going to my parents' for the weekend. But you know you'll be as welcome there as you would be with me."

In spite of Jace's earlier conclusion that his involvement with Lindsey was becoming detrimental to his ability to do his job, that announcement was like a kick in the gut. Not only had he not expected it, he didn't like it.

"I know I would," Shannon said. "And believe me, I'm grateful, but…I'm fine here. Really."

"What about what you told Lindsey?" Jace asked.

Shannon didn't pretend not to understand. "About her kids and the fires?"

He nodded.

"That's why I came last night. To talk to Rick about it."

"Why not talk to me when you were at my apartment?"

"I guess I felt talking to Rick would be less official."

"We're past the point of *any* information being 'unofficial.' And if there *is* some connection between those fires and the suicides—"

"Justin Carr," Shannon offered before he finished.

Jace remembered the name from the special education rolls Campbell had provided him.

"Because of what he said about Andrea?" Lindsey asked. "That's not fair, Shannon."

"Hey, you're the one who told me to come forward, even if I don't have proof. And it's not just because of that remark, although you have to admit it was typical Justin."

"He apologized. It wasn't directed at Andrea. He said his father says that about any suicide or death that shouldn't have occurred. And it certainly isn't original with Colonel Carr."

"Still defending them, Linds?" Shannon taunted.

"What did he say about Andrea?" Jace didn't look at Lindsey, addressing his question to Shannon instead.

"That her death was survival of the fittest." Shannon's chin lifted, as if daring him to say that wasn't significant.

"Anything else?"

"About Andrea? Not that I heard. You or Rick need to talk to the kids, though. Enough of them dislike Justin that they might be willing to tell you other things."

"You told me you suspected someone *before* Justin made that comment. Who were you talking about then?" Lindsey asked.

"Him, for one. His attitude sucks, and you know it. I'm not denying that he can come across as sincere and polite when he wants to, but that's an act. If you're around him long enough, it's evident that's *all* it is. His old man probably beat him until he could carry it off."

"If you suspected he'd been abused, you should have reported it," Lindsey said. "That's your job, remember."

"His father keeps a tight rein?" Jace asked, attempting to defuse the atmosphere.

"He's ex-military. Very strict. Very old school. Justin has siblings, but he's the only one at home. His parents are considerably older than the norm for our seniors. At least his father is. I got the impression Justin was an unexpected addition. Maybe an unwanted one. I can't remember the mother ever even coming to the school. Justin's dad handles everything, including making a lot of demands on the guidance office to procure his son a scholarship or an appointment."

"Justin will probably get an appointment to West Point,"

Lindsey added. "I know he applied. Both his grades and test scores put him in the top few percentiles."

"He won't if *I* have anything to say about it," Shannon said. "And I do. I wouldn't recommend that punk for anything."

"He's bright. He's polite. And he's not from around here." Lindsey no longer bothered to speak to her friend. Instead, she seemed to be lobbying Jace on the kid's behalf. "That's the biggest strike Justin Carr has against him."

Maybe she thought that as an outsider, Jace could identify with the boy's difficulties. The trouble with her supposition was that at this moment, he cared nothing about some kid's bruised ego, unless it gave him a motive for what had been going on.

"We have lots of military brats," Shannon said. "And most of them aren't. *This* one… I wouldn't put anything past him."

"You think his dad would be the kind to set a curfew? Check the mileage on the car?" Jace asked.

"That sounds just like him."

"Any run-ins with the department?" Jace asked the deputy.

Carlisle shook his head. "Not that I remember. Most of the kids around here are relatively well behaved. Especially when you hear about the stuff they do other places. If he'd been into anything serious, I'd remember the name."

"The snake even sounds like something he'd dream up," Shannon added. "He *is* a snake."

"Not the symbolism they were going for," Lindsey said. "And not an interpretation I can agree with."

She'd told Jace the snake was a warning. And a message that *she* was a snake in the grass because she'd associated with him, something her students, if they were involved, would view as a betrayal.

"And the fire at the stadium?" he asked.

Shannon shook her head. "I don't know. I can't imagine he'd take a chance like that. Not in that setting. As Lindsey pointed out, he's got a lot to lose."

"Can we find out if he was at the game that night?" Although Jace had couched that as a request, Carlisle nodded, recognizing it for what it was. "Like you, I can't remember anything in our files about Carr, but information about something that would put him under the control of the juvenile authorities in another location wouldn't necessarily be available. It would be sealed. How long's he been here?"

"He enrolled at the first of last year," Lindsey said.

"As a junior?"

She nodded, her face strained.

Regret that she was being forced to face these unpalatable truths stirred in Jace's chest. But Shannon was right. The time for protecting any of these kids was long past.

"I want to see the records from his previous schools, not that they're likely to tell us much."

"You got it," Shannon said.

"I don't think you can do that," Lindsey objected.

"You hide and watch me," Shannon said. "I don't know about Andrea Moore. Maybe she was just a time bomb waiting to explode. Tim Harrison? Hard to believe, but kids do crap all the time that nobody can believe. But *Dave?* Think, Lindsey. *Think.* Dave was one of the most stable people I know. He isn't going to copycat some sixteen-year-old's stupidity."

"He was unstable enough to jeopardize his marriage and the boys you say he loved by having an affair with you." Lindsey's voice was cold.

"That wasn't an affair, Linds. It was stress relief. Sex. Like minds. However you want to describe it, I don't give a damn. All I'm telling you is that Dave didn't kill himself by downing too many pills. Or any other way. That dog won't hunt. And it's past time somebody put an end to whatever the hell is going on around here. If you don't want to help him do that," Shannon said, nodding toward Jace, "then get the fuck out of the way and let me."

Twenty-Six

"The kid's clean," Carlisle announced, dropping a folder onto Jace's desk. "At least according to the locals where the family's lived before. We haven't gotten anything back from the Army. I don't know whether they're protecting their own or whether their bureaucracy is just slower than everyone else's. You talk to the dad?"

Jace had intended to wait for that interview until they'd gotten all the background information on Justin, but Shannon's surety, combined with his sense that things were escalating, had forced his hand. "This morning. I didn't get very far."

The description of Justin's father as "old school" had been on the mark. Judging by the colonel's weather-beaten features, Jace would have estimated his age in the late fifties, but the ramrod posture and snow-white buzz cut made it possible he could be off by as much as a decade.

Justin's mother, who had appeared to be younger than her husband, hadn't opened her mouth during the half hour he'd spent in their immaculate living room. Her eyes had been merely guarded where the colonel's had been openly hostile.

"I figured as much. He called the sheriff to complain that we were harassing his son. How about the kid?"

"The father refused to let me talk to him."

"Sounds like he knows something's up with the boy."

"Maybe, but he's also a guy who's used to calling the shots. I think he was making that point."

"You could bring Justin in."

"Not on what I've got. There's nothing to tie him to the fires or the attacks on Lindsey. I'm betting that if I try to lean on him, his parents will provide him with an alibi for each and every one of those occasions. I know they'd have a lawyer here before the boy opens his mouth. And, according to both Shannon and Lindsey, he's exceptionally bright, which means he'd be smart enough to know he doesn't have to talk to us. You find out who he runs with?"

Carlisle shook his head. "Seems to be pretty much of a loner. Most of the local kids don't like him, but he doesn't give a shit. He isn't breaking down any doors to get accepted. The consensus is he's smart, but weird."

"Weird how?"

"They didn't go into details, and I hated to try and pin anyone down. Just weird. Different," Carlisle said with a shrug. "Around here that could mean somebody who doesn't like football or NASCAR. It don't take much."

Over the course of the last forty-eight hours, Jace's opinion of the man he'd once characterized as "Deputy Dawg" had undergone a revision. Carlisle fit in well with the good old boys he'd grown up with, but underneath those folksy Southernisms was a native intelligence and the dogged determination of a better-than-average investigator.

"Can you think of anything we haven't covered?"

Jace's question seemed to surprise Carlisle, but he took it in the spirit of cooperation in which it had been rendered. Or maybe he recognized the request for what it was—a peace offering of sorts.

"You've talked to his parents and to the assistant principals. I've touched base with the guys I trust to give me the straight shit. Shannon. Lindsey. Not much left."

"That's what I've been thinking."

Jace had tried every one of those avenues, and other than Shannon's strong instincts about Justin's culpability, none of them had provided evidence the boy was anything other than a brilliant loner. It was frustrating because the longer he worked on this, the more convinced Jace had become that there was something to Shannon's assessment of the kid.

For one thing, she'd been in this business a long time. He trusted that, because of her experience in dealing with them, she would have a feel for the ones who spelled trouble.

And Lindsey wouldn't? After all, brilliant loners were her specialty. Carlisle's question interrupted that nagging caveat.

"You're planning to talk to Harrison again, right? Try asking *him* about Carr. About the relationship between him and his son. If there was one. And while you're at it, talk to Andrea's mother about Justin. If you really think the suicides are connected to one another and to the fires, that seems to be something to look at. Carr's association with the victims."

Justin's school records didn't indicate he'd had any personal dealing with Campbell, nor had the assistant principals Jace talked to. Still, everything from the two attacks on Lindsey, which had immediately followed Jace's first contacts with her, to the relentless and slanderous online assault on Andrea indicated there was a thread that tied these events together. And a controlling evil behind all of them.

"Hard to believe he could fool this many people," Jace said, touching the file Carlisle had pitched on his desk. "And

Lindsey, who's known Justin as long and as closely as anybody in this town, remains convinced he isn't involved."

"You met her folks yet?"

"Lindsey's?" Jace shook his head.

"If you had, you might understand her. Lindsey was brought up to believe the best of people. And she isn't cynical enough to have figured out that some criminals start young and fast. Sometimes it don't matter what type of home you come from or what kind of upbringing you had. Some people come into this world looking to hurt and destroy."

"The bad seed."

Carlisle shrugged. "You could put it that way. Lindsey wouldn't. She'd find some evidence that they'd been abused or neglected or something. You'd think with her training that would be Shannon, but she wasn't protected like Lindsey growing up. She's harder. If I had to bet on which of them was right, I'd be backing her gut about Carr."

Which was probably the smart thing to do, but something—maybe nothing more than his personal involvement with her—made Jace unable to disregard Lindsey's opinion. If she was right, he'd spent the last two days going down an alley that wasn't going to lead him where he needed to go.

"Talk to Walt and Ms. Moore," Carlisle suggested again. "We just might get lucky."

There was no way he was going to let this shit destroy everything he'd worked for. It wasn't his fault that whore had been sleeping around. Her car hadn't been at the house. He'd checked. So how was he supposed to know they were going to walk in on Campbell?

Once they had, there was nothing else to do but go through with what he'd planned. As emotional as the Anderson bitch had been lately, people would have bought into the idea that she'd felt responsible for the other suicides. So despondent over them that she'd reached the point of taking her own life. The principal, however...

He shook his head, knowing, as he had then, that scenrio was far less likely to fly. Not with that fucking detective who was determined to blame one of them for any and everything that happened around here.

There had to be a way out of this. All he had to do was think it through. Take control. Figure out which buttons to push—something he was very good at. If that didn't work...

If that didn't work, there were other ways to end this. And as far as he was concerned, right now none of them were off the table.

"I want to bury my son. He deserves that. *I* deserve it. And this community knows that."

Jace hadn't had time to explain why he was here before Harrison had begun again on the bitter, on-going battle about the autopsy.

"I respect that, Mr. Harrison, but it's the law. And as long as there is some question—"

"I don't have questions. I want to lay my son to rest beside his mother. The sheriff tells me you're the holdup. Maybe, since you aren't from around here, you don't understand what something like that means to us."

"I understand—"

"Then let me bury my son," Harrison demanded.

"Even if there are still doubts—?"

"You think that matters to me? My son's *dead.* Nothing you can do is ever going to bring him back."

"And if someone had a hand in his death? You don't want to know that?"

"Are you saying somebody put that rope around Tim's

neck and then pushed the desk out from under him? I saw my son, Lieutenant. I looked at his body laid out on that morgue table. There were no marks except—" Harrison faltered, his anger no match for the power of that memory. "If what you're saying were true, Tim would have put up a fight. He would have defended himself. There would have been some indication he'd fought for his life."

"I'm not sure it happened that way."

"Meaning what?"

"That maybe somebody *drove* him to do what he did."

For three or four heartbeats, Harrison was perfectly still, his eyes locked on Jace's face. The anger faded from them as he seemed to consider what Jace had said.

Jace hurried to press his advantage. "We know there was an orchestrated cyber campaign against Andrea Moore that may have played a role in her suicide."

"What kind of campaign?"

"An attempt to smear her reputation with her classmates by suggesting she was promiscuous. That she was pregnant, which was a lie. And that it wasn't the first time she had been."

He knew from Lindsey that Harrison had been aware of those rumors. And while Walt's interest gave him the opportunity to explain the theory he'd been working under, Jace was well aware that he couldn't prove any of that had led to Andrea's death. Not the kind of proof that would be required by a court of law.

"Somebody created a fake online profile for her," he went on, bolstering his case with things he could prove. "It detailed her supposed sexual exploits, although according to her autopsy, Andrea was still a virgin. As a result of that profile, she was openly derided in the chat rooms the Randolph-Lowen students frequent. And maybe at school. We know that in the last few days of her life, she received thousands of e-mails from classmates and others who'd read about her on what was supposedly her site. If something like that happened to Tim—"

Before Jace finished the sentence, Harrison turned and walked out of the room. Acting on instinct, Jace followed him.

He was aware that the "My Place" profile for Tim was genuine. If, in an attempt to prove him wrong, that's what Harrison was going to pull up, then he needed to acknowledge that. But it didn't disprove the rest of what he'd said.

Jace entered the hall as the history teacher disappeared into one of the bedrooms. Feeling that at this point he had no choice, Jace walked into the room in time to see Harrison jiggle the mouse of the computer sitting on the desk in the corner.

As soon as the screen came up, Harrison clicked on an icon on the desktop. Then he sat down in the chair in front of the monitor, waiting for the site to come up.

When it did, it appeared perfectly innocuous, just as it had the last time Jace had looked at it. Harrison scrolled through the pages, seeming familiar with the navigation.

"Nothing's changed," he said, continuing to review his son's profile and the messages there. "I watched Tim build this. That was the condition before I'd let him have a page here. Until he died—" Harrison's voice broke, but he strengthened it to go on, "I checked what was posted every night. It was a routine. Clockwork. And with the exception of a couple of things I thought might be questionable, there was never a problem. Tim's friends are good kids. All of them."

"Have you read his e-mail?"

Without turning, Harrison minimized the profile and

brought up the mail screen. Jace watched as he clicked on the inbox. Only when the dozens and dozen of e-mails began to download did Jace know that something of what he'd suggested to Tim's father must have been going on.

"Oh, my God," Walt said softly. "Dear sweet Jesus."

Feeling as if he was intruding on what was a private grief, Jace forced himself to move closer to the desk so that he could read the headings as the e-mails continued to flood the screen. The gist of all of them was the same, the phrases in which it had been couched differing only in their degrees of cruelty and vulgarity.

"Mr. Harrison?"

"You want to know if this is true," Walt said. "You want to know if Tim *was* all these things they're saying about him."

"No, sir. What I want to know is, if Tim saw those, would it have been enough to make him do what he did?"

"He was so worried about me. Because I teach. Because I'm a deacon at our church. Because of what everyone in town would think. Not about him, but about his mother and me. Worried they'd think *we'd* done something wrong. That we hadn't raised him right. Especially his mom."

"Tim was gay," Jace said flatly, knowing from what Harrison said that the basis of those hate-filled e-mails had been a secret long kept. And long feared.

"He told me last year," Harrison said, swiveling his son's chair to face Jace. His eyes, red-rimmed with grief, were more bleak now than when he'd opened the front door. "He said that however I took it, telling me would be a relief. But I think somewhere inside I'd known for a long time. Maybe always. At least…" Walt shook his head. "Having it in the open between us was a relief for me, too. And it made us closer. Like when his mom died. Just the two of us holding strong for one another."

"Tim never told anyone else?"

"Here? Where they preach from the pulpits every Sunday that homosexuality is a sin and those who practice it will burn in hell? Who *could* he tell? Who could he trust that much? Nobody. And believe me, Tim was smart enough to know that."

"Then…" Jace lifted his chin toward the e-mails that were still downloading on the screen.

"I don't know. Maybe they didn't know. Maybe it was like what you said with Andrea. Tim was kind. And sensitive, especially about the feelings of others. Everyone who knew him knew that. Maybe whoever did this just made something up they thought would hurt him, like with Andrea. And they got lucky."

"Do you know *anyone* who would want to hurt your son? Anyone who had a grudge against him? Anyone at school he'd had trouble with?"

Harrison laughed, the sound devoid of amusement. "You didn't know him. *Everybody* loved Tim. There wasn't a mean bone in his body. That kid didn't have an enemy in the world."

Maybe it was a comfort for Harrison to believe that. Maybe it was even true. If so, it made what had been done to him even more evil. More diabolical.

Andrea Moore had been chosen because she was vulnerable. Believing in her own self-worth had been a struggle she'd fought for years. Despite the progress her mother and her therapist thought she'd made, the ridicule and cruelty she'd been subjected to by her peers had destroyed whatever fragile foothold she'd managed to attain in that battle. After days of unrelenting pressure from the things that were being said about her, she'd gone home and cut again. And then, despairing, she'd cut a little deeper, severing the veins in her wrists.

And Tim Harrison? Had the cruel insults he'd just watched flash across the boy's monitor been enough to make him react by hanging himself?

"Maybe he didn't have enemies," Jace said aloud, "but somebody at Randolph-Lowen is behind this. Somebody is pulling the strings to make these things happen."

And Jace believed he knew why. Just as he had told Lindsey at the beginning. He had stopped the church fires, but they'd found another way to get the rush they'd once gotten from watching the flames they had set consume their targets.

Now they were targeting their classmates. With a few carefully placed sparks, they had managed to set off a firestorm of rumor and gossip. Then they had stood in the background and watched as those flames, too, had consumed their victims.

Twenty-Seven

"Somebody to see you," Lindsey's father announced as he walked back into the kitchen. He had answered the doorbell that had interrupted their dinner, assuming it would be for him.

"Did you tell them we're eatin' supper?"

"It's okay, Mom." Lindsey put her napkin beside her plate and pushed her chair back from the table.

She hadn't talked to either Jace or Shannon since their contentious discussion at Rick's. If either of them had come to see her, she was more than ready to heal the strains that day had created in their relationships.

"I showed him to the living room." Her father picked up his napkin, waiting for her to leave before he resumed his seat.

"Don't you be long," her mother cautioned. "Your supper won't be fit to eat if it gets cold."

Without responding, Lindsey left the kitchen and made her way toward the front of the house. Her dad had said "he," which meant Jace and not Shannon. That realization created a stir of anticipation, along with a nervousness over the way she'd acted the last time they'd been together.

It wasn't that she regretted defending Justin. She couldn't help thinking, though, that she could have made her case in a way that wouldn't have alienated the two people, other than her family, she cared about more than anyone in the world.

She rounded the corner the hall made with the arched entry to the living room. The expectancy she'd felt dissipated in an instant, to be replaced by an even stronger sense of anxiety.

Justin Carr stood in front of the fireplace, his torso bent so that his head rested against the forearm he'd placed along the top of the mantel. The pose emphasized his thinness, making her more aware than ever that, no matter his IQ, he was still a child.

"Justin?"

He turned and straightened in one motion, a rush of blood suffusing his cheeks. Lindsey wasn't sure if that was because she'd caught him in such a vulnerable pose or because of whatever emotion had sent him to see her.

"Your dad said you were eating. I can wait."

"It's okay. Is something wrong?" As she asked the question, Lindsey advanced into the room, resisting the urge to offer him some physical form of comfort, as inappropriate as that might be between a teacher and her male student.

"You have to talk to that detective, Ms. Sloan. My dad's going to kill me. If the Point hears about this, they won't touch me. Everything I've worked for will go down the drain."

"Justin—"

"If this is about what I said in your room that day, you have to tell them I apologized. I barely knew Andrea Moore. What I said was just something stupid my dad says. I didn't mean anything by it. Not about her. Even if it made Ms. Anderson mad, it's not worth ruining my life over."

"Nobody's trying to ruin your life." Lindsey couldn't think of anything that might sooth his angst. Everything he said echoed her own fears. "If you weren't involved in any of this, it will come out. Your name will be cleared, and things will—"

"*Who's* going to clear my name? You know how that works. Once people think you're involved in something criminal, it doesn't matter what kind of proof you offer of your innocence. Not around here. They're never going to forget that you were accused. If you're accused, then it stands to reason, you must have done *something*. They're ready to believe the worst about any of us. Especially about someone like me."

The bitterness of being an outsider—a bitterness Lindsey would wager had been created long before Justin Carr arrived at Randolph-Lowen—marked his words, but she couldn't deny them. The idea that someone who hadn't come from this small, close-knit community might have set those fires would be welcomed.

Justin wasn't even from Alabama. He'd grown up in locations all over the world, most of them far removed from the South. All those accusations of Southern-bred racism, which had swirled through the media during the last two months, would be more difficult to espouse if this boy could be proven guilty.

"And you have to know I didn't have *anything* to do with what happened to you," Justin went on, his voice more impassioned. "I'd *never* do anything to hurt you, Ms. Sloan. You have to believe me."

…with what happened to you…

Despite the efficiency of the local gossips, there had been little talk about either incident. Apparently her neighbor's version of how the snake had gotten into her house had been accepted. And although the fire at the ticket booth had been very public, it had been blamed on overloaded wiring. When she'd been asked about it, she herself had downplayed its seriousness, primarily to keep her mother from freaking.

"What do you mean, what happened to *me?*"

"The snake. The fire at the game."

She shook her head, trying to think if this were as significant as she feared. If Justin was clever enough to have gotten away with the arson, as well as those two attacks, surely he wouldn't be stupid enough to make this kind of mistake.

"How did you learn about those, Justin?"

The boy looked confused by the question. "The detective asked my dad where I was those nights."

"And did your dad know?"

"My dad *always* knows where I am."

"So…where were you?"

"God, not you, too."

"I'm just wondering how you knew about the snake."

For a fraction of a second, the boy seemed at a loss, but his recovery was quick. And plausible. "I heard somebody talking about it at school."

"Who?"

"I don't remember. They weren't talking to me. I just… heard it. In the lunchroom I think."

"What did they say? Exactly."

Justin took a breath, as if gathering his thoughts, before he answered. "That you'd called the cops because you found a rattlesnake in your house. That was it." His face suddenly relaxed. "They had a police scanner. They heard the dispatcher send the cops to your house."

"But…you don't remember who had the scanner or who you overheard talking about it."

"It was just…" He made a quick, negative motion with his

head. "I don't know. The only reason I listened was because they were talking about you."

She wasn't sure how to take that, but it didn't mitigate her uneasiness. She was accustomed to adolescent crushes and accustomed to dealing with them. For any young, single, remotely attractive teacher they were an occupational hazard. After ten years in the classroom her radar was fairly well attuned to the signs. She had never gotten that feeling from Justin, and despite what he'd just said, she didn't have it now.

"So you listened because it was about *me?* Should I be flattered?"

"I think it was Steven. Yeah, I *know* it was. I listened because it was one of the guys in the program and because he was talking about you."

"Steven Byrd?"

"He's got a scanner. He's into that kind of stuff."

"What kind of stuff?"

Justin shrugged. "All of it. Geek Squad. Cops and robbers. Technology. *CSI* crap."

She knew Jace had questioned Steven about the Web site profile that had been created for Andrea. He'd come away from that meeting feeling the kid had told the truth when he said he hadn't had anything to do with putting up that page.

Still, Justin was right about Steven's interests. And in spite having been born here, Steven was almost as much of an outsider as Justin.

"Do you remember *who* he was telling?"

Again the boy looked as if he were struggling to retrieve the memory, but once more he shook his head. "I wouldn't have remembered it was Steven if he hadn't been... You know."

"I *don't* know. If he hadn't been what?"

"So into you."

Lindsey was aware of what the phrase meant, of course, but it wasn't one she would have ever associated with Steven Byrd. Like Justin, by neither word nor deed or attitude had he indicated his feelings about her were anything other than those appropriate for their relationship.

"Steven?"

"You didn't know?" Justin laughed. "*Everybody* knows, Ms. Sloan. He doesn't have a girl, so… I guess fantasy's the best he can do. And his all revolve around you."

"He's never given me any indication of that."

"He's smart enough to know you'd do something about it."

"Like what?"

"Whatever teachers do. Talk to his mom, maybe. She'd have him up at the church altar confessing his sin before sundown."

Lindsey had no idea if that were a fair assessment. A good proportion of her students belonged to relatively fundamentalist churches, like the one Andrea had attended. Those kinds of public confessions might well be the norm.

"Will you talk to him?" Justin asked.

He meant talk to Jace, she realized. The information Justin had just given her about his classmate seemed to mean little to him. Not nearly as much as his quest to clear his name.

"I already have."

"You *knew* they thought I had something to do with this."

The tone was accusatory. As if Justin expected her to have warned him of the sheriff department's interest.

"They're considering a lot of angles," she said carefully.

"Does that mean they suspect other people, too?"

"I think suspect is too strong a word."

"Not according to my dad. He's already talked to a lawyer. Somebody well connected in Montgomery."

"I don't think that's necessarily a bad idea."

"Then they *do* think I had something to do with this crap. Shit. Just…shit." His face contorted as if he might cry.

"Justin—" Lindsey reached out, intending to touch his shoulder, but the boy twisted away.

"They're going to fuck up everything. And I didn't do anything, Ms. Sloan. Not the fires. Not to you. Why would I want to burn down a black church? Doesn't that sound more like your little homegrown redneck bigots? I guess it wouldn't do for anybody to accuse one of *them.* That might make everybody around here look bad. Especially when you all have got yourselves a perfectly good scapegoat."

"Justin—"

"I swear if those assholes screw up my life… I swear…"

Either he couldn't think of a threat dire enough, or he was too cautious to utter one. Instead he flung himself toward the front door, slamming it on his way out of the house.

The sound echoed through the hall, which was as far as Lindsey had followed him. She thought about trying to get him to stop, but there was really nothing more she could say.

"Everything all right in here?"

She turned to find her father standing at the end of the hallway. She nodded, fighting the temptation to run and throw herself against his chest to be comforted as she had as a child.

"That kid have a temper tantrum?"

"Something like that."

And not without reason. Not if she was right about Justin. And if she were, Jace and Shannon were very wrong.

"I need to talk to you." Even as the words came out of her mouth, Lindsey hated how they sounded. As if she had called him about some personal need. Sexual. Or even worse, emotional. "It's about Justin Carr."

No matter how important she thought it might be to try to convince Jace he was wrong, she didn't want him to believe she was calling him because of what had been between them.

Past tense?

"What about him?"

Maybe it was the distortion caused by his cell, but Jace sounded distant. Preoccupied. As if he didn't have time to talk. Or, and the thought was painful, as if he didn't want to.

"He came to see me. At my parents' house," she clarified, not wanting him to jump to any other conclusion.

"Are you okay?"

She took some small comfort from the fact that the first thing Jace asked when she'd mentioned Justin's visit was not about the case, but about her.

"Of course. He's upset that you talked to his father. And he's concerned that West Point or the congressman who recommended him will find out he's the subject of a criminal investigation. Which I assume he is." Although her inflection on the last part was inquiring, Jace didn't address it.

"What'd you tell him?"

"That you're investigating several people. I hope that's still true?" Silence was the only answer she received, but it told her all she needed to know. "He mentioned both the snake and the fire, Jace. He said you asked his dad where he was on those nights."

"That's right."

"I was surprised that he knew about the rattler. Nobody at school seemed to. At least they didn't talk about it to me."

"That may not mean anything."

She wasn't sure whether he was referring to Justin's comment or the lack of gossip. But neither was really pertinent to what she wanted to tell him.

"He said he overheard Steven Byrd talking about the

snake. That Steven has a police scanner." She waited for the information to sink in, but apparently it didn't make the impression she'd hoped for. "Don't you think that's strange?"

"A lot of people like to listen to the dispatches. It may be strange, but it's not illegal."

"No, but don't you think it's revealing? If you were tracking an investigation."

Another silence. A considering one?

"Are you talking about the arsons?"

"Maybe. He found out about the snake that way. He knew I'd made a 9-1-1 call and that the sheriff's department had sent someone out. What possible need would a seventeen-year-old kid have for a police scanner?"

"I told you. A lot of people have them."

"And a lot of people know computers. And a lot are in my gifted program. And a lot went to school with Andrea and Tim. I know that. I also know Steven Byrd is one of them."

"I felt he was truthful the day I talked to him."

"And *I* think Justin Carr is telling the truth. I didn't know that's what investigations like this turn on."

A sound like an exhalation came over the line. It took a second for her to realize it had been a laugh. "Is that funny?"

"I'm not making fun of you, Lindsey, believe me, but the reality is investigations often follow an officer's instincts. His gut. His sense of who's lying and who's telling the truth."

That was the way a classroom worked, too. You didn't always know the facts, so you relied on that elusive sixth sense you'd developed through years of dealing with kids.

"I don't think Justin's lying."

Again, Jace didn't respond, allowing the silence to become uncomfortable enough that she finally broke it.

"Have you found *anything* that would tie him to *any* of this? Anything in his past?"

"No."

"Has he even been in trouble before?"

"Not that we know of."

She had waited, dreading his answer, so that when it came, she closed her eyes in relief. "Then all you have to go on is what Shannon told you? Is that what you're telling me?"

"Right now."

"Well, for what it's worth, I believe she's wrong. I want to go on record as saying that. She's wrong, Jace."

"Or you are. And both of you can afford to *be* wrong. I can't. Three people are dead, Lindsey. And the more I find out, the more I know one of those kids is responsible."

"The more you find out?" He had told her they'd found nothing on Justin. This had to be something else. Something that he hadn't known the last time they'd talked. "Like what?"

"Someone had been cyber-bullying Tim Harrison."

"*Cyber*-bullying?"

"Did you know he was gay?"

"*Tim?* Who told you that?"

"His father. Supposedly *nobody* else knew. But for three or four days before he died, he got hundreds of very graphic e-mails detailing his supposed sexual activities."

"Like Andrea," she breathed. "Just like Andrea."

"Enough alike to establish a pattern. In Tim's case they didn't need to put up a profile. Apparently just the whisper of his sexual orientation was enough to set off the rampage."

"Oh, God. Poor Tim. Poor Walt."

"It doesn't explain everything, but…it's enough to tie the two student deaths together."

"And Dave?"

"We don't have results back yet from the autopsy or the evidence tests. Harrison did tell me the truth about something else."

"Something else?"

"You remember the conversation you overheard that night in the field house?"

"I remember."

"You were right. It wasn't about booster activity. And it wasn't about Andrea, either."

And suddenly she knew. As if Jace had already told her. "Shannon. Those were the rumors Walt was warning him about."

It explained so much. Dave's distraction. His despondency. His suicide?

"It wasn't Andrea and Tim he thought might keep him from getting that promotion," she went on, thinking aloud. "It was their affair. Maybe that's why he went over there that night. To talk to her about the gossip. To tell her they had to break it off. When she wasn't there—"

"He killed himself?" Jace's question was cynical.

"He had a lot to lose, Jace."

"And he knew that when he started with her. Besides, Shannon said he wasn't the type."

It rankled that he was again quoting Shannon's opinion to her. Until she realized why he had. "You don't think he killed himself?"

"They may be smart, Lindsey. They may be goddamn little geniuses. But I swear, *nobody* is that good. Or that lucky."

"I don't understand."

"They target three people who are vulnerable for one reason or another. And they succeed in getting all three to commit suicide? I don't buy it. Not three for three."

She waited, but he didn't go on, forcing her to ask. "What does that mean, Jace? That they aren't *that* lucky."

"I think at some point they stepped over the line. I think they went from pushing the vulnerable to take their own lives to helping someone along who wasn't quite so willing to cooperate."

Twenty-Eight

"Sorry to call so late, but you said you wanted the results as soon as they were available. I got in from the Gulf a couple of hours ago and came over to do the autopsy before I grab a few hours sleep and have to start operating on the living."

The county coroner's choice to do the autopsy, a surgeon at the regional medical center, had been out of town on a fishing trip when Campbell's body was discovered. At Jace's urging, the sheriff had requested the coroner's office make the principal's autopsy a priority, apparently prompting this Sunday night call.

"Not a problem." Jace laid down the permanent records Shannon had provided him to pull his notepad closer. "I appreciate your getting on this so quickly."

"Mondays are always bad. I knew if I didn't do it tonight, might be another twenty-four hours before I got to it."

"Anything interesting?"

His sense that there was something fishy about Campbell's death had grown over the weekend. Although he'd reviewed the photos taken at the scene a dozen times, he hadn't been able to put his finger on anything concrete to verify his suspicions.

"I got the coroner's notation about the Scotch and the pills. You were right about one at least."

"Which one?"

"The deceased consumed alcohol. Probably not enough that he'd even be tested if he'd been pulled over on his way home."

"He wasn't drunk."

"Not by any standard. One drink. Maybe two, depending on the strength of the mix and when he'd consumed them."

"No pills."

"I don't know what happened to the ones that were supposed to be in that bottle, but the victim didn't consume them."

"Victim?"

"We aren't dealing with suicide here, detective."

Although Jace should have been pleased by the validation, it was still a jolt to have it confirmed. "So what killed him?"

"Took a little digging, but I confess I got interested. There were bruises that couldn't be explained by lividity."

"Defensive in nature?"

"Probably. Suggestive of that, in any case. Enough so that they made me look harder than I might have otherwise."

"And you found…?"

"A needle mark. Just beneath his ear actually."

"Do you know what was injected?"

"Maybe. You familiar with KCl?"

"Not really."

"Potassium chloride. It's used medically to balance electrolytes. Given intravenously in high enough concentrations or injected too rapidly, it can stop the heart, which is why it's also part of the protocol in lethal injections."

"So death would appear to be caused by a heart attack."

The doctor laughed. "Except, as in this case, when you lack any evidence of heart disease."

"Then why…?" Jace's question ground to a halt, but the doctor knew what he was asking.

"Because, according to popular culture, it's undetectable."

"Is it?"

"It breaks down into its components, both of which are naturally occurring in the body. But high levels of either in the blood can be suspicious. Coupled with an injection site…"

Jace could almost see the shrug. "Why the charade of the empty pill bottle and the residue in the glass?"

"The simplest answer is usually the right one. Somebody wanted those pills."

Klonopin, Jace remembered. Shannon used them to help her sleep. Were they something that might prove convenient when administered covertly to an overly watchful parent?

"So how would someone obtain potassium chloride?"

"A hospital would be the logical source. Anybody who works in one could have access to the stuff."

"You've been a big help. I wonder if I could come by and get a statement detailing what you've found."

"This is preliminary. Just the bottom line. It's gonna take me a few days to write up official results."

"I understand that. I was wondering if you could give me enough tonight that I could get a warrant for a search."

"Sure. If you can be here within the next half hour."

"You got it. And Dr. Wayne, I appreciate this."

"I hear you're the investigating officer for the church fires. Could this have anything to do with those?"

"It's very possible."

"Then I'm doubly glad to help. Those fires made this

community look like something straight out of *Deliverance.* Bastards."

The last was a sentiment Jace could certainly share. And if Justin Carr were responsible, then Randolph would get a deserved reprieve from those accusations of racism.

A win-win situation. For everyone except Lindsey.

Justin's father opened the door the following morning, wearing a silk bathrobe over a pair of black pajamas. His wife, who was fully dressed, hovered in the hall behind him.

"I'd like to speak to your son, Colonel Carr." Jace nodded to the woman before he turned his eyes back to her husband.

"Whatever you have to say, you can say to our attorney. That's Phillip Stone. Cohen, Stone and Longdale in Montgomery." Carr began to close the door.

Jace put his palm against the wood. "David Campbell was murdered. We've received the autopsy results last night."

There was a momentary hesitation, but Carr recovered quickly. "As I said, talk to our attorney. Whatever kind of witch hunt you're on, detective, we don't intend to help you."

"I have an order signed by Judge Reynolds that allows me to collect Justin's computer as evidence."

"His *computer?* Evidence for what?"

"A murder investigation."

Carr laughed. "I told you. You're barking up the wrong tree. Justin's a good kid. He's been assured of an appointment next year. I warn you, if you continue this harassment—"

"If I need to, I can come back with enough deputies to take the computer by force. The smartest thing you can do for your son, Colonel, is to let me have it without the theatrics. And without getting yourself arrested. If you're right about your boy, then our examination of his computer will prove it."

He could see Carr was considering the idea. And like his son, he wasn't stupid. "Go get him, May," he said to his wife.

"Justin's not here, Paul."

Carr turned to look at her then. "Where the hell is he?"

"He's already left for school."

"This early?" It had been a few minutes before seven when Jace had pulled into their driveway. Judge Reynold's wife had refused to wake him last night, but she had agreed to have him call as soon as he was up. Jace had picked up the warrant on his way here.

"He had a project due today," Mrs. Carr explained. "He said he needed extra time to get it set up in the classroom."

"What kind?" A finger of cold ran up Jace's spine.

"I can't remember if he said. Science, maybe? He's had those before. He was working on it all weekend downstairs."

"Downstairs?"

"In the basement," Carr explained. "It's not finished, but when we moved here, Justin claimed the area for his own. He doesn't sleep down there, you understand. I drew the line at that, but the rest of the time—"

"How big was his project, ma'am?"

Jace's interruption seemed to surprise them both. Apparently when the colonel talked, everyone listened.

"I don't know." Justin's mother shook her head. "There were several pieces, I think. He had a duffel bag—"

Before she could finish the sentence, Jace was down the steps, running for his car.

Lindsey scrawled her name across the sign-in sheet and then turned to find Shannon at her elbow. Although her friend was as fashionably dressed and as carefully made-up as usual, her green eyes looked less confident than they normally did.

"Hey," she said.

"Hey, yourself. What are you doing here so early?"

Lindsey usually arrived at the school shortly after seven, using the time before the students flooded in to get ready for the day. Like most of their kids, Shannon raced the first bell.

Lindsey couldn't help wonder if her friend's being here so early had anything to do with the gossip about her and David Campbell. A way to avoid answering unpleasant questions?

"The county, in its infinite wisdom, has decided to send their so-called 'grief' counselors out again today. When they called me to set it up, I told them I was doing your classes. That we'd worked it out in advance. I hope that's okay."

Lindsey had been mistrustful of the county's decision to close the school after Tim's suicide. She had to admit that, despite David's death and the resultant uproar in the community about where his body had been found, nothing else had happened during that mandated closure. Now, after last week's two-day break and the weekend, they would all be back together once more, again comforting their kids in the midst of loss.

"You know it is."

Lindsey walked behind the counter to the row of teacher cubbyholes. Shannon followed, watching as she emptied hers.

"Look, Linds, I know we left things a little—"

"We had a difference of opinion. We've had them before. We'll have them again. That doesn't change things between us."

"Jace said you still have doubts."

The surge of jealousy Lindsey experienced at hearing Shannon refer to him as Jace was unexpected. She struggled against it, working to keep what she felt out of her voice.

"He came to talk to me. Justin, I mean. He told me he was innocent. And I believed him. I told Jace that. I suggested that he broaden the scope of his investigation."

"If it's any comfort," Shannon said as she turned to take the messily stacked papers out of her own box, "Jace said they'd found nothing to indicate he'd been in trouble before."

Lindsey nodded, but she kept her eyes on the photocopied sheets of announcements and reminders as she pretended to look through them. She didn't trust herself not to reveal how far from the truth her assertion was that nothing had changed between them. And now the gulf wasn't only about Justin.

"First, second, third and fifth periods, right?"

"That's it. I'll see you first period, then." Lindsey smiled, but movement of her lips felt stiff.

"Hey, it's gonna be okay." Shannon touched her arm. "As weird as it sounds, Dave's death will take away the mystique. It won't be cool to off yourself anymore. Not when the principal's doing it."

She was probably right. She usually was about the teenage psyche. Still, the dispassionate statement Shannon had just made about death of a man who had literally risked everything to be with her chilled Lindsey to the bone.

"I hope for *their* sake you're right."

Obviously she hadn't managed to mask her revulsion. Shannon's face changed, the beautifully sculpted features rearranging themselves into something less comforting.

"See you upstairs."

As soon as Lindsey was out of the office, she took a breath, trying to control emotions that threatened to overwhelm her. She would be no help to her students if she couldn't conquer her own feelings of loss, as well as her sense that the world she'd inhabited for the last ten years would never be the same.

She hurried up the stairs, fumbling her keys out of her purse as she did. There were two girls from her homeroom waiting outside her door. Their parents dropped them off early every morning on their way to work, and, although they were supposed to wait in the commons until the teachers arrived at the mandated time of 7:45 a.m., Lindsey let them stay in her room where they either studied or caught up on homework.

She smiled at them as she inserted her key, letting them enter the room while she removed it. She flicked on the overhead lights, thinking that the dimness fit her mood better.

She put her tote bag down on her desk before sticking her purse in her bottom drawer. Then she took out her lunch and walked over to put it into her wall cabinet. When she turned back, the girls had already taken their seats in the row by the windows, their heads lowered over their books.

Lindsey turned to erase the blackboard and found the janitorial staff had taken advantage of the off days to wash it. They'd also cleaned off the long-term assignments that she always left up in the right-hand corner. Replacing those would give her something to do. Something that might keep her mind off the last classroom she'd been inside.

Determinedly destroying that image, she picked up her desk calendar and carried it to the blackboard. She worked for several minutes replicating the assignments that had been erased. Before she could finish, a feminine voice interrupted.

"Ms. Sloan?"

She turned to find Jean Phillips at her desk. "Hey, Jean."

"I was wondering if we were going to practice today."

Scholars' Bowl, Lindsey realized. The team had a game tomorrow, one she hadn't thought to cancel.

"I'm thinking we'll take a break this week. I'm going to try to reschedule our match with Duncan."

"So when will it be?"

"I'm not sure yet. I'll put it up on the board when I've made the call. Okay?"

Jean nodded. "Can I stay here 'til the first bell?"

"Sure. Plenty of room."

Lindsey glanced around the room as if to verify that. Steven Byrd had come in and was sitting in the middle of the back row of desks.

The bright blue eyes behind the thick lens of his glasses had sparkled with amusement the last few times they'd interacted. This morning they were cold.

Had Jace talked to him after their phone call? If so, surely he wouldn't have used her name.

The uneasiness produced by Steven's glare increased when she realized he had no books out. She thought about telling him that if he were going to sit in her room, he needed to start studying, but for some reason she decided against it. She broke eye contact with him instead, turning back to Jean.

"You can sit anywhere."

"Thanks." Jean picked up the enormous backpack she dragged everywhere. She slung it over her shoulder and made her way, lopsided under its weight, to where Steven was sitting.

His gaze didn't shift to follow the girl's progress, but remained locked on Lindsey. Nor did he speak when Jean slid into the seat beside him. The girl leaned down into the aisle between them to unzip her bag, wrestling out a notebook. As she laid it on her desk, she glanced up at Lindsey.

"Something wrong, Ms. Sloan?"

Lindsey shook her head. She made herself begin to unpack her tote, but her hands were trembling. She refused to look up, imagining she could feel Steven's eyes on her as she worked.

He's into you, Justin had said. Was that what this was about? A manifestation of that crush?

Despite her intentions, she lifted her eyes from the books she was taking out of her bag and found Steven's gaze still focused on her. She looked at Jean, whose head was down as she thumbed through the notebook she'd removed from her backpack.

When she shifted her eyes back to Steven, his lips lifted at the corners, the motion hardly enough to be called a smile. More like a sneer, she realized. He was sneering at her.

Fury flooded Lindsey's body, increasing the vibration of her hands. Had he been the one who'd put that damn snake in her hamper? Locked her in a building he'd tried to burn down around her? Had he then targeted Andrea and Tim, hounding them to suicide?

Each memory fueled a rage she hadn't realized simmered so near the surface. She dropped the tenth grade anthology on her desk, taking a perverse pleasure from the bang it made as it hit. On some level she was aware the girls had looked up to see what was going on, but she was past the point of caring.

She marched down the center aisle until she reached Steven. She had to step around Jean's book bag to lean forward and put her palms on the wooden surface of his desk.

His eyes never left her face. And other than a slight widening as she bent down, they didn't change.

"What are you doing?"

"What does it look like I'm doing?" His voice was soft, the lift at the corners of his mouth increasing.

"You're supposed to be studying. Or you need to go."

"I *am* studying. My favorite subject in the world."

There was no doubting his meaning. With that realization,

Lindsey knew this was a confrontation that couldn't take place in this classroom. Not in front of the other students.

Steven shifted forward in his seat, bringing his face closer to hers. She recoiled, straightening and stepping back, only to stumble over Jean's backpack.

In the split second she had to react, she put her arms out, trying to regain her equilibrium by finding something solid to grab onto. Her right hand found purchase on the seat back of the desk in front of Jean's. As it tilted backward under her weight, Jean jumped up, scrambling, or so Lindsey thought, to get her bag out of the aisle.

By the time Lindsey managed to right herself, still hanging on to the seat back, she realized that both the boy and girl were bending over the backpack. A couple of books, which she assumed had spilled out when she'd fallen over it, lay beside the bag.

As Lindsey straightened, her balance restored, Jean began to pull something else out of the depths of the backpack. It took Lindsey too long to understand what she was seeing.

And far too long to react.

"Back up," Steven said, brandishing a gun that seemed to have appeared from thin air.

Despite the threat it represented, Lindsey couldn't keep her eyes off the object Jean had taken from her bag. The olive drab, rectangular-shaped package had a D-cell battery duct taped to its top. A tangle of wires protruded from it and the tape.

Eyes shining, the girl held it out as if she were presenting a gift. Something wonderful. Something miraculous.

Lindsey heard a gasp from one of the girls seated by the windows, reminding her of their presence. And of their lives. Her students' lives, which she was responsible for.

"Back up," Steven said again, gesturing with his weapon. "Do it *now,* Ms. Sloan."

She took a step backward and then another. She tried to hold his eyes, willing him not to use the gun.

Even as she did, she was aware of the far greater danger represented by what Jean held. It was clearly some kind of explosive. Maybe four or five pounds of it. And Lindsey had no idea what kind of damage something like that could do. Destroy this room? The whole wing?

Her eyes flicked to the left, to see if anyone in the hall was aware of what was going on. The door to her classroom was closed. Had Steven done that when he'd slipped in?

"What are you going to do?"

His smile widened. "I don't know. Got a suggestion?"

"Please don't do this, Steven. Whatever—"

He laughed. "We've come too far to go back now. You know that. You knew it when you told your boyfriend to start asking all those questions. You can't unring the bell, Ms. Sloan."

Neither could he. Whatever they were planning, Steven would understand very well there was no going back from this.

"You don't have to make it worse," she pled.

"Oh, yeah. Yeah, we do. Much, much worse for everybody. It's the only way to fly."

"That's insane."

"I'm sure that will be said. Aren't you sure, Jean? That they'll say we're nuts? But what's different about that?"

The girl laughed, her hands cradling the explosive.

"Put that down," Lindsey urged her, "and I'll talk to them. I'll talk to Jace. You know he listens to me."

"Jace listens, huh? And you talk?" Steven mocked, and then his voice hardened. "You talk to him while ya'll are fucking?"

"Steven."

"I forgot. Mustn't talk naughty to the teacher. You want to wash my mouth out with soap, Ms. Sloan? Well, believe me I'd like to wash you, too. Only not your mouth. 'Cause I don't mind if you talk dirty to me."

A distant rattling, like the noise of a jackhammer, came from somewhere outside. Jean laughed in response, the sound jarring and inappropriate.

"You know what that was, Ms. Sloan?" Steven asked.

Lindsey shook her head, afraid to speculate.

"That's our signal."

"Signal for what?"

"Signal that the *fun* has started. And it's time for us to join in. Go get your keys."

"What?"

"Get your keys." He gestured toward the front of the room with the gun he held.

"Why?"

"Because I said so."

The muzzle of his weapon swung away from her and focused on the two girls sitting by the window. The motion carried Lindsey's gaze with it. One of the girls screamed. The other laid her head on her desk, burying it in her arms.

"Steven, don't," Lindsey begged again.

"Keys. *Now.*"

She turned and ran for her desk. Before she got there, she had to come to terms with the realization that she might just have missed her chance. If she'd grabbed his gun in the fraction of a second while it was moving away from her—

Then Jean might have done whatever they intended with that bomb. If she had, they might all be dead. As of now, they were all still alive. And it was up her to see they stayed that way.

Lindsey stooped, pulling the bottom drawer of her desk

open. She tried to think if there was anything in her purse she could use as a weapon. She jerked it out, feeling inside for her keys. Her fingers encountered the cool metal of her cell phone. By policy, students weren't allowed to carry them on school property.

"Just the keys."

Her hand still in her purse, Lindsey looked up to find Steven standing on the other side of her desk, watching. She knew this was another crossroad. If she obeyed, and left the phone in her purse, she would be giving up her only means of communication with the outside world.

"Everything else stays in your purse and it goes back into the drawer," Steven ordered.

When she hesitated, he put both hands on the stock of the gun, tilting the barrel downward so the dark hole of the muzzle was aligned with her forehead. Then he lifted one brow, the movement obvious despite his glasses.

She found her keys and pulled them out of her handbag, letting him see them as she laid them on the desk. Preventing Steven from pulling that trigger was the important thing now. Not only to preserve her own life, but to keep him from crossing that barrier of killing his first victim as long as she could.

And which of the three already dead wasn't his victim?

That was different. Or at least she hoped it was. Driving someone who was vulnerable to take their own life wasn't the same as firing a gun and blowing out the brains of someone you knew. Someone you supposedly cared about.

How much of a role did Steven's infatuation with her play in all this? Had he seen Jace's questioning of him as a final betrayal of his fantasies?

She closed the drawer, sacrificing any chance of using

her phone to the hope that she could keep the unthinkable from happening.

"What are you going to do?" she asked again.

"That's for us to know and you to find out."

The childishness of the taunt reinforced the reality—and danger—of the situation. No matter how bright they were, these two were nothing but children. With a child's impulsiveness, lack of control, and inability to see consequences.

Their brains aren't done…

Yet in their hands were very adult weapons of destruction. Guns and explosives. And before them lay an entire school, beginning to fill with people who, because they suffered from the same faults, had not always spoken or acted with kindness in their dealings with these two.

Therein lay the seeds of Columbine and every other act of violence that had been perpetrated on an unsuspecting student body. Those seeds had been sown here, too.

And now, she feared, it was time for all of them to reap their harvest.

Twenty-Nine

As Jace put the car into gear to back out of the Carrs' driveway, he called the dispatcher, impatiently counting off the rings until she answered. He told her he wanted two patrol cars dispatched to the high school and that he'd meet them there.

There was a beat of silence before she asked, "Are those in addition to the one I just sent over, detective?"

The sense of dread he'd felt since Carr's mother had mentioned the kid taking his "project" to the school blossomed into something far worse. "You've already sent a car? For what?"

"One of the school's maintenance workers reported hearing what sounded like automatic weapons fire."

"Would he know?"

"Said he's a Vietnam vet."

"Jesus." Jace's response to that information was as much a prayer as an expletive. He increased his speed, eyes checking intersections he approached as he talked. "Where? *Exactly.*"

"He thought it came from the commons."

"The commons?"

"It's an area off the main lobby. A place for the students to congregate, mostly before school. In the same general vicinity as the lunchroom and the gym," she added helpfully.

"But the lunchroom wouldn't be open this early." Jace tried to remember the geography of the main building.

"Oh, they serve breakfast, too, mostly for the free lunch crowd, but anyone that wants to can buy it."

Crowd. The word reverberated in Jace's mind, reminding him of the swarm of teenagers that had poured out of the gym after the pep rally he'd attended.

"How long ago was the call?"

"I dispatched the deputies out about…three minutes ago."

"Send a couple more cars," Jace said. "Tell one of them to go to wherever they unload the buses. They need to stop anyone else from entering the building. Oh, and one more thing. I need the home phone number of a Colonel Paul Carr."

When the dispatcher provided that information, Jace dialed the Carr residence, again waiting impatiently through the rings.

Justin's father answered. "Hello."

"Jace Nolan again, Colonel. I need to know what weapons are missing from your house."

"If this is another accusation against my son—"

"You *do* have weapons there, don't you, Colonel? Have you checked them this morning?"

There was a slight hesitation before Carr said, "I keep my collection in a gun safe, detective. No one has access but me."

"That's great. Now go check and tell me what's missing."

"I just told you—"

"We received a report of automatic weapons fire at the high school. You have automatic weapons in that collection, sir?" The resulting silence was all the answer Jace needed. "Go see what's missing, goddamn it. And do it now."

"Hold on."

As he waited, Jace tried to think what else he should do. Turning the wrist of the hand he was steering with, he glanced down at his watch. It was 7:18 a.m. How many kids would be in and around the building at this time of the morning? And how could he make sure that no more were allowed inside?

"Three weapons are gone," Carr said without preamble. "An M9 Beretta, a 1911A and an AK47."

The latter explained what the maintenance worker had heard. "So now we know what your son's 'science' project consisted of."

"See here, Nolan—"

"You better get that high-powered Montgomery lawyer on the phone, Colonel. I suspect you and your family are going to need all the help he can give you very soon. And if you have any influence over your son, I suggest you call him. Try to convince him that whatever he's doing needs to end right now."

"Believe me, I'd be glad to," Carr said, "but they don't allow cells at the high school. Some kind of safety measure."

Christ, Jace thought. That meant there was no communication in or out of the building, except through the central office. And if they had already taken that out, as they should have in an assault, there would be no way for outsiders to know what was going on inside.

"Then you and your wife might want to start praying."

Jace broke the connection. Eyes shifting between his phone and the road ahead, he held the cell out in front of him, running down his contacts list until he found Lindsey's name. Carr hadn't mentioned if the ban on phones extended to the teachers, but Jace thought that was unlikely.

If he could reach Lindsey, she could clue him into what

normally went on at the school this time of the morning. Where the kids were. And maybe more importantly, where they weren't. If they could do anything to minimize the exposure…

When—after a half dozen unanswered rings—the voice mail message came on, Jace resisted the urge to snap the lid closed. Maybe Lindsey had her phone on vibrate. Or maybe it was off. Just because she didn't answer didn't mean she'd been caught up in whatever the maintenance worker had reported.

"Call me as soon as you get this," he said in response to the prompt. "If you're in your classroom, lock your door and stay there. Promise me, Lindsey. Just stay there." He hesitated, his mind racing. And then, knowing that despite what anyone could do, this could blow up in their faces, turning into the same kind of bloodbath Columbine and Thurston had been, he added, "I love you. Just… Just please, please don't let anything happen to you."

He closed the case of his cell with a snap and tossed it onto the seat beside him. Then, conscious of nothing except getting to Randolph-Lowen as soon as possible, he continued to drive too fast through the sleepy streets of a town that had, until this morning, thought nothing more tragic than the suicides of two teenagers could ever happen to it.

Jace went to the back of the school, because he assumed the first cruiser they'd dispatched would go in the front. He wanted to make sure his instructions were being followed and that students weren't being allowed to enter through the transported-student entrances. Judging by the two buses lined up along the sidewalk—

Rick Carlisle stepped out from between them and started toward him. The deputy was in uniform, his shoulder radio in place so that he would only have to turn his head to make contact with the dispatcher.

"What do you know?"

"Not much. I got here in time to stop this one. The other," he said, turning to indicate the first bus in line, "had already unloaded, but we've rounded up the students who hadn't gone into the building and got them back on it."

"You hear anything like the gunfire that was reported?"

"Not back here, but it was pretty noisy until we got the kids on the bus."

"You check with the dispatcher?"

"Yeah. Nobody's heard anything from the first responders, but given the timing they must be inside by now. We were close, so we got here maybe five minutes behind them."

Carlisle's attention was diverted by the arrival of another bus. He stepped around Jace, raising his hand to the driver.

Although the woman had been reaching for the lever to open the door, she must have caught sight of the deputy's gesture out of the corner of her eye. Carlisle walked around to the side. The driver completed her motion, cracking the door.

"Pull up beside the front bus in line. Don't let anyone off."

"Has something happened?"

"We don't know yet. It may be nothing. Just keep them on the bus until we find out."

She nodded before she pulled the lever toward her and put the bus in gear. Accompanied by the stench of diesel fuel, it rolled past Carlisle and into the place he'd directed.

"Where's your partner?" Jace called.

Rick stepped to his right and pointed in the direction he'd sent the woman driver. When Jace walked around the rear of the parked bus, he saw another deputy standing beside the first, in conversation with a man holding a briefcase. Teacher, Jace surmised, and possibly the driver as well.

"Tell those two to take over out here. They can call for backup if they need it. Tell them whatever they do not to let anybody into the building. You come with me."

Leaving Rick to make those arrangements, Jace turned and headed down the covered sidewalk toward the back entrance. Before he reached it, he was left in no doubt about the accuracy of the original information they'd received.

Although distant, the sound from inside the building was distinct enough to be instantly identifiable to anyone familiar with it. The combat vet who'd called in hadn't been wrong. Apparently Carr's son knew enough to be able to use the powerful assault rifle his father owned.

Jace drew his own weapon, and then positioning himself to the side of the glass panel in the door, he tried to see inside. Nothing out of the ordinary seemed to be happening in this hall.

After a few seconds, Carlisle, his department-issued .38 held in both hands, assumed a similar stance on the other side of the entrance. His brows lifted in question as he looked over at Jace. When he nodded, the deputy reached out to open the door. Jace slipped inside, leading with his Glock.

The hall was eerily empty. Maybe another of the early-arriving teachers had heard the gunfire and collected any students from back here and either taken them outside or secured them in a safe place.

He moved forward as quickly as he could without exposing himself to fire from the dark classrooms he passed. Carlisle followed, checking behind them as they navigated the hall.

Before they reached the end, there was another burst of fire from the automatic weapon. This time it was followed by the throatier bark of a semiautomatic.

Department issued? If so, that might mean that at least one

of the first officers who had been dispatched was still alive. That made at least three of them inside the building. And other cars should be arriving at any minute.

With the thought, he turned to watch as Rick ran toward his position. "Backup?"

"On the way. ETA maybe four minutes."

It should have made him feel better, but in any situation involving guns, especially automatic weapons, a hell of a lot could happen in a couple of minutes. None of it good.

"What about the first responders?"

Rick shook his head. "Dispatcher still hasn't been able to make contact."

Which made it likely both were dead, probably gunned down as they'd entered the building. The shots he'd heard, which he had taken as return fire, might mean someone was using their weapons. In any case, they were going to have to operate without any of the information those first arrivals might have provided them.

"Best guess where they'd be?" he asked the deputy. "Commons? Gym?"

"Depends on what they want. If it's maximum kill, then this time of day I'd say the commons or the lunchroom. If they want somewhere they can secure and hold, I'd go for the lunchroom, with the gym a distant second."

Maximum kill. Another of those phrases he'd rather not have in his head, Jace acknowledged.

At this time of the morning Lindsey would already be upstairs. If they could contain this—

More gunfire interrupted that hopeful thought. He wondered how many shooters they were looking at.

He'd always suspected at least two people had been involved in the church fires. That kind of mischief was more fun if you shared the high. Just as this would be.

The more people involved in this kind of assault, the better, from a strictly tactical aspect, for the shooters. And the bigger the nightmare in trying to contain them.

That was something they'd have to learn as this played out. Right now, the only choice they had was to concentrate on the area where gunfire had already been heard.

"Okay," he said to Rick. "How do we get there?"

"Follow me."

Without waiting for agreement, Rick moved into position in front of him. He peered around the corner, carefully checking out the cross hall they'd reached. Then the deputy stepped out into it, knees bent, his weapon moving in a 180-degree arc. When nothing happened, he glanced back at Jace and nodded before he took off to his right.

Taking the same precautions, Jace trailed him. Unlike the procedure Jace had followed in the hall, the deputy didn't bother to check out the rooms on either side, although there were lights on in some of them. Jace hoped the teachers who had unlocked those doors had by now relocked them. The best-case scenario would be that they'd gathered up any students they'd seen in the hall and brought them inside.

He knew from his initial visit that most of the kids congregated in the commons area before the opening bell. Because they'd been forbidden to enter other parts of the school at this time of day? If that was the case, Carlisle was undoubtedly right.

Maximum kill. Which meant they were going for a Columbine-type assault. Unless someone took them out—

Rick stopped again, pressing his back against the wall. He had reached the next intersection. The one that would lead into the lobby, at the very heart of the school. The office and stairs up to the second floor classrooms would be on the left; the commons, gym, and lunchroom on the right.

With his hand, the deputy motioned to hold up. Adrenaline had already been pumping like a drug through Jace's bloodstream. With the realization of where they were, it surged again. Sharpening his focus. Magnifying each movement made by the man in front of him.

Once again Carlisle leaned forward in an attempt to make a visual reconnaissance of the intersection ahead of them. This time, he jerked his head back immediately, flattening himself once more against the wall.

Mouth open from their recent exertions, Rick turned to look at Jace. Because he couldn't read the deputy's expression, Jace raised his brows, questioning. Carlisle shook his head before again looking back at the intersection.

Clearly he'd seen something that had bothered him out there. Or maybe *someone?* One of the shooters? If so, why hadn't he tried to take him out?

Because it would have endangered others. That was the only explanation that made sense of the deputy's actions.

Were the shooters holding hostages? Using them as shields? Whatever was going on, Rick had decided now wasn't the time to confront whoever was out there. The only problem Jace had with that decision was that time was a luxury they no longer had.

As if to prove his point, there was another burst of automatic weapons fire, the popcorn rhythm of it much clearer. More distinct. Obviously it was coming from the right, while whatever Carlisle had seen that had driven him back from a confrontation had been off to his left.

Tired of trying to figure out what was going on, Jace ran to where the deputy was, his back against the wall. Although he'd attempted not to make any sound, Rick had turned his head to watch his approach.

As he came to a stop beside him, Jace hissed, "What? What'd you see?"

"Two of them coming down the stairs from the second floor."

Jace started to move past him, but Carlisle used his forearm to push him back. And then he said the words that were guaranteed to stop Jace in his tracks. And to stop his breath.

"They've got Lindsey."

Thirty

"**W**hy are you doing this?" Lindsey asked again.

Steven continued to hurry her along, gun in one hand, the other wrapped around her upper arm. Since they'd left her room, she'd formed a dozen plans of action and discarded them all.

She couldn't decide if Jean was capable of setting off the explosives she carried. She wasn't as afraid of Steven as she was of that totally unknown element. After all, the boy had made her lock the door of her classroom, leaving the two terrified girls unharmed.

"I'm not going to spend the rest of my life in prison."

"Then stop this *now,* Steven, before it's too late."

"It's already too late. It was too late when you butted in." He jerked her arm, dragging her forward, almost causing her to miss her footing on the stairs.

What Steven had just said had to be a reference to Jace. Despite his attitude on the phone, he must have taken what she'd told him seriously. There was little consolation in the thought that she'd been right.

"Where are we going?"

This time Steven didn't bother to answer, his hold tightening as they made their way down the few remaining stairs to the main floor. The assistant principals would be in the office by now. And Melanie. One of them would have called the sheriff's department when they'd heard the gunfire.

The lobby was deserted. Lindsey lifted her eyes to look across to the double set of doors that opened to the commons. That area was also empty, its gleaming tile stretching to the lunchroom at the other end.

As Steven guided her past the elevator, she tried to look back at the door to the office, where she'd signed in less than twenty minutes ago. It was closed. And a smear ran down its central glass panel as if someone had dipped their hand in red paint—

The realization of what that must be caused her steps to falter. Steven jerked her arm again, forcing her to keep moving despite her shock.

She turned to look at him, surprised to realize how tall he was. As tall as her father. Or Jace. No longer a child.

Glancing down, he laughed at her expression. "Did you think I was kidding?"

"Who...?" She couldn't complete the question.

"Whoever was in there. That was the one place we couldn't afford to be lenient."

As he had been upstairs?

"I don't understand. Why are you doing this?"

"I told you. Better to go out in a blaze of glory—"

"By killing innocent people? Is that your idea of glory?"

"Hey, don't try to blame me for this. Blame your lover. Blame yourself. What we were doing wasn't hurting anyone. And we wouldn't have. Not until he decided to get involved."

"He got 'involved' because that's his job. You know what you were doing was wrong. How can you blame someone else—"

"Shut up," he demanded, shaking her. "Just shut the fuck up. You aren't in charge here, *Ms.* Sloan. We are. So don't try to tell me what I can and can't do."

They were past the elevators, approaching the intersection with the hall that lead to the back of the building. The hold Steven had on her arm strengthened as his anger grew. The closer they got to the commons the more aware she was that the time to act was running out. If she was going to make a move—

She tried to pull her arm from his grasp. In answer, Steven not only tightened his grip, he turned the gun he held so that the muzzle was pressed against her temple.

"Stop it. Stop it now," he hissed, his voice no longer amused, "or I swear I'll kill you. I'll blow your brains out."

She stopped struggling, convinced from the rage in his voice that he was so far over the edge he might really pull the trigger. As he had done in the office?

She closed her eyes in despair, allowing him to pull her forward. Only when she felt the pressure of the metal against her skin lessen did she dare open them again.

Steven had taken the gun away from her head and was in the process of moving it so it once more pointed in front of him. Before he completed the act, something warm and wet hit the side of her face, followed by a sound she would identify only later.

Steven seemed to stagger forward, pulling her with him. Then, his fingers still clutching her arm, he fell to his knees, dragging her down. As she automatically put out her hand to break her fall, Lindsey glanced to her right to see what had happened to the boy who'd compelled her here at gunpoint. And understood the significance of the moisture she'd felt.

As Steven's body continued to fall forward, his grip released. Although he'd carried her down to the floor with him, she began to scramble up immediately, a reaction to the horror of his head wound more than fear of what might happen next.

She just wanted to get away. Away from Steven. Away from the blood that continued to spill out onto the white tiles.

She'd made it up into a crouch before she remembered Jean and the bomb. She turned her head, trying to locate the girl.

Jean was standing slightly behind them. Her mouth had opened, her widened eyes fastened on the dying boy. The block of explosives was still cradled in her hands, but so far she hadn't attempted to pull wires or turn switches or to do whatever she had to do to set the thing off.

Lindsey's head continued to turn, trying to find the person who'd fired the shot that felled Steven. Jace stood at the foot of the stairs leading to the second floor. His knees were bent, both arms extended in front of him, hands wrapped around the butt of a pistol.

"She has a bomb," Lindsey screamed.

As the words echoed through the empty lobby, she realized her warning had brought the girl out of her trance. Then, almost simultaneously, she realized there was no way in hell Jace could reach Jean in time to stop her from setting it off.

Instinctively, she sprang to her feet, lunging at the girl. Jean reacted by backing away, but she still made no effort to set off the explosives.

Emboldened by that and by the adrenaline flooding her system, Lindsey grabbed both sides of the package to pull it to her. Finally understanding what she intended, Jean tried to retain her hold, but in that fraction of a second surprise had bought her, Lindsey was able to wrest the thing away.

She brought it around with her as she turned toward Jace. He had managed to close perhaps half the distance between them, coming at a dead run. Behind him Rick Carlisle brought up his weapon to take aim at the girl by her side.

For Lindsey, the realization that she might be holding a bomb was beginning to sink in. All she wanted to do now was get rid of it. To have someone who knew what they were doing take it out of her hands and dispose of it. If that someone were Jace—

She caught movement in her field of peripheral vision and turned her head in time to see Jean start toward her. "Do it, and I'll tell him to shoot you, too."

"Don't." Jace's shout came almost on top of her threat. "Step back. Now."

He'd slowed enough to bring his weapon up again. Jean's face crumpled, anger replaced by fear and then surrender. And just as she always had, she did as she was told. She took a step back as Jace continued to advance.

That threat eliminated, Lindsey once more turned imploringly to him, holding out explosive. "Is this real?"

"Just stay calm." He slowed, almost to her.

"Is it *real,* damn it? Just tell me."

"It may be. It looks like C4."

"I don't know what that means."

"Plastic explosive. Something the army uses because it's relatively stable."

Stable sounded comforting. If it was true. "How stable?"

"It's probably not going to explode just from holding it."

Not going to explode… Probably… Whatever comfort she'd taken from the first was destroyed by the delayed import of the other. "What do I do with it, Jace?"

"You give it to me."

It was what she thought she wanted. To have someone who

knew what he was doing take this thing out of her hands. And now Jace was telling her he was about to do exactly that.

"What are *you* going to do with it?" She wanted to give it to him—God knew how much—but there was something about this she didn't like. Something she didn't trust.

Jace was no more a bomb expert than she was. He obviously knew more than she did about explosives—anybody did—but disposing of bombs wasn't his job, any more than it was hers.

He's a cop. It's his job. Whatever this is, it's his job. Just give the thing to him.

"I'm going to dispose of it." His voice was too calm.

"Do you know how?"

"Do *you?*"

She shook her head. Her hands had started to tremble both from fear and the overload of adrenaline. First that had made her brave. Now it was making her sick.

"Then give it to me."

He put his gun back into the holster under his suit coat. He took a step toward her, holding out both hands, palms up, perhaps six inches apart. They looked strong. Capable of anything. And rock steady.

And all she had to do was to place the explosive on top of them, then step back, and let Jace take care of all this. Let him take care of *her.* She lifted her eyes to his. They, too, seemed steady. Reassuring.

She took a breath before she moved her hands, raising them so that they were only a couple of inches above his, still outstretched before her. Then she began to lower the block of plastic explosive, the trembling of her hands becoming more acute the closer she came to putting it on his palms.

Suddenly the wail of multiple sirens, all of them seeming to converge on the school, made her freeze. With the cacophony, they both turned to look out through the glass doors of the main entrance. She watched, her hands still hovering above Jace's, as a half dozen county vehicles roared into the parking lot.

Taking advantage of the distraction, Jean bolted toward the commons. Without thinking about what she held in her hands, Lindsey turned, her eyes following the running girl.

"Stop her," Jace shouted.

Surprised, Lindsey turned to look at him. *Rick*, she realized. He'd been talking to Rick, who still stood, arms extended, tracking the progress of the girl with his weapon.

"She can warn them," Jace said. "Shoot her." And then in almost the same breath, he said again, his voice low and calm, "Put it down, Linds."

Behind her she could hear Jean's sneakers slapping against the tile. She was probably across the commons by now. Going to warn whoever had fired the shots they'd heard upstairs?

"Put it down," Jace urged again.

She expelled the breath she hadn't known she was holding and placed the explosive on his palms.

"Now let it go and step back. Then run to Rick and stay there." He raised his voice, his eyes holding hers, "Rick?"

"Yeah."

"Tell them I'm bringing this outside. I'm going to walk it to the middle of the parking lot and put it down. I don't want anybody to approach me. Tell them that after I come back to the sidewalk, they should cordon off the lot and get somebody out here who can disarm it."

"You got it."

"Release it, Lindsey, and step away," Jace said again.

"Don't let anything happen to you."

"I'm not planning on it. You tired of staying with your folks yet?"

She nodded, her throat thick with emotion.

"Good. Now turn this loose and go to Rick."

"Jace—"

"I can't get it out of the building until you move out of the way. We need to do that, and then we need to find out what they're doing in the lunchroom. They've probably got students in there, Lindsey. Maybe a lot of them."

She nodded, moving her hands away from the sides of the homemade bomb. It ought to have been a relief to give it over to Jace, but it felt instead as if she were abandoning him. Choosing the coward's way out.

"Now go," he ordered.

"I love you." She hadn't meant to say that. Hadn't been aware she was thinking it before the words were between them.

Not that it wasn't true. She just didn't know whether saying that to him now was a kindness or one more burden to be added to those the situation had imposed on him.

For a long heartbeat Jace didn't say anything. In the now absolute silence, she could hear Rick conveying the instructions he'd been given via his radio to the deputies outside.

Finally Jace nodded. "Go on."

This time, having nothing else to offer him, she obeyed. Only when she was enclosed tightly by Rick's left arm, which had opened to welcome her as she'd approached, did she look back.

Jace was halfway to the main entrance, the explosive carefully carried on his outstretched hands. Before he reached the row of glass doors, one of the deputies stepped up to open the central one, moving to one side as Jace came through.

Suddenly Rick released her, shoving her hard to the side. The blow was powerful enough that she fell against the wall. Shocked, she turned to see Rick bringing his weapon up again to focus on something beyond the opening that led to the commons.

Still crouching beside the wall that had broken her fall, her gaze shifted to find whatever he was targeting. A figure ran toward them from the open lunchroom door. Her identification of Justin Carr was instantaneous.

In his hands was what appeared to be a rifle. She had time for only those two thoughts before the weapon he carried began to spray bullets toward the place where she and Jace had been standing only seconds before.

Rick hadn't moved, other than to return fire. The sound of the exchange echoed through the lobby. The intermittent bursts from Justin's weapon. The heavier bang, bang, bang of Rick's gun as he methodically squeezed off round after round.

Bullets struck plaster and tile, shattering both and sending debris raining down. Instinctively Lindsey tried to protect her eyes and face, shielding them by putting her arms over her head.

There was literally nowhere to go. No cover she could reach without exposing herself. Hunched against the wall, she waited for an opportunity to get out of the line of fire.

Then the deputy's hands flew out to his sides. Without any attempt to break his fall, his body slammed backwards, his head striking the floor hard enough to bounce.

She turned away from the relative safety of the wall and started to crawl toward Rick. Bullets swept the tile a few feet in front of her, so close that she felt bits of it sting her legs. They drove her back to the wall, but as she had realized before, there was literally nowhere to go.

Justin was still advancing, but he was no longer concentrating on the deputy. And no longer firing, since it must be clear by now that she was unarmed. He held the weapon nonchalantly. Confident of his control.

"Don't do this, Justin. Don't make it worse."

She hated the pleading note in her voice. Hated that she'd been so wrong about him. Hated that she'd been lied to and lied to and had bought into all of them.

"Act Three. Like in Shakespeare. Who do you think will be left alive, Ms. Sloan? Who's the ranking character? Who's going to be around to restore order when this is over? You?"

"This isn't a play."

"It's all a play, Ms. Sloan. You know that. The old king is dead. Long live the king."

Some infinitesimal shift in the posture of his body warned her he was about to apply the pressure needed to send another burst of bullets from the muzzle of the powerful weapon he'd used to shoot Rick. And this time she would be the target.

Her eyes left his, looking beyond his thin body, now silhouetted against the wall of glass at the front of the school. Through the still-hazy air of the lobby she could see the flashing lights of the cruisers parked beyond the entrance. And then she focused on another figure, this one also outlined by the sunlight coming through the glass doors behind it.

Jace. No longer carrying the explosive on his outstretched hands. Instead both were wrapped around his weapon, knees once more bent, arms extended.

She would never know if she'd made some sound. A gasp or an intake of breath. Or had her eyes betrayed what she saw?

Justin turned, bringing the gun around with him. His finger must have tightened over its trigger before he had even identified the threat. An arc of bullets shattered the glass of the office, including the blood-smeared panel in the door, tracing an unmistakable pattern. One leading directly to the man now standing in front of the outside entrance.

Thirty-One

Jace blocked the image of Lindsey crouched on the floor from his mind, concentrating on his target. To his right, glass shattered as the boy began to swing around to face him.

His movement narrowed the kill zone by changing the angle of Justin's body in relation to Jace's stance. It would be difficult, if not impossible, to hit his torso, presented now in profile like some nineteenth-century dueler. And if Jace missed, his shot could strike Lindsey, directly behind Carr.

There was no time to yell at her to get out of the way. Nor would she hear him over the noise of the automatic weapon and the growing symphony of sirens outside.

In that terrible split second's realization, Jace knew that all he could do was to wait until Justin completed his turn, unwittingly positioning himself again so that his body would shield Lindsey from Jace's bullet.

As he waited for that to happen, time telescoped so that it seemed as if the boy were moving in slow motion. As did the path of destruction wrought by the assault weapon he brought around with him. Jace tracked its progress strictly by sound, listening as bullets impacted the glass wall of the front office and then swept ever nearer to where he stood.

Carr's turn occupied a heartbeat. Maybe two. Yet in that span a thousand images invaded Jace's mind. The weeks he'd spent in the hospital after he'd been shot. The endless pain and, far worse, the resulting disability. The loss of control over his life. The long rehabilitation, undertaken in a failed attempt to get his job back. And then, finally, the decision to start over. To flee to a place where there were no ghosts. No echoes from a past he'd rather not remember.

He'd come here, a place as foreign to him as another country. And yet somehow he'd come full circle. To this moment. This wait.

As the heartbeat thundered in his head, memories began to speed like the shifting patterns in a kaleidoscope. Meeting Lindsey. The nights they'd spent together. The resurgence of all the fears he thought he'd left behind.

As the kid's shoulders began to square, aligning for the shot Jace had to make, he fought the almost irresistible need to take his eyes off his target for one more look at Lindsey. Her face still stained with tears. Her eyes telling him far more than the words she had whispered.

But time had returned to those normal split seconds. All you were ever allowed in which to make the decisions that really mattered.

To squeeze off the shot that would end Justin Carr's worthless existence.

If he failed in that, there were a dozen deputies outside prepared to do it. They'd take care of the boy if he didn't. Eventually. What Jace had to do was take care of him now, before he could turn around and gun down Lindsey as he'd gunned down how many others today.

Now. The command of his brain had been coldly rational,

calm even, despite the stakes. Jace's finger closed over the trigger. Fragments of plaster and shards of tile from the wall to his right hit the side of his unprotected face and neck.

He saw the boy's body jerk in response to his shot before his mind relayed the information that he had exerted the necessary pressure. He continued to squeeze off rounds, watching the impact of each as they struck Carr's body.

After the third, Justin's knees buckled. The lean of his body changed the trajectory of his bullets. Instead of striking the wall, they gouged chunks of tile from the floor before ricocheting off into a dozen different directions.

Please, sweet Jesus, Jace prayed. Not for himself, but for the woman crouching on the other side of the vast, echoing lobby. He couldn't bear it if they had come this far only to have her hit by one of those distorted slugs. Or more cruelly, by a piece of flying debris. He'd seen men die from one of those same pointless ironies in this kind of shoot-out.

Jace pumped one more round into the falling boy, watching as first the weapon and then his body stuck the floor. Arms outstretched above his head, Justin didn't move again, although Jace waited a long time, long enough that the fog of smoke and shattered plaster began to clear and the echoes of gunfire fade.

At last his gaze lifted from the boy's lifeless body to find Lindsey. She was still hunched against the wall, arms over her head. His eyes traced over her, searching for a telltale stain of red. When he didn't find it, he began to breathe—once and then again—until the familiar pattern was reestablished.

He became aware of the shouting behind him. The doors opened and men rushed past, the soles of their shoes crunching over the debris field of the lobby. One of them stooped down over the body of the boy, but Jace walked past them, his weapon extended as if the threat still existed.

Intellectually, he knew it didn't. Not from Carr. He'd put too many shots into the area that would have been outlined in black on a shooting range target. In Jace's mind that's all he'd done—put his shots into that vulnerable area of the human body, the one that contained the vital organs. *Kill zone.*

Using the wall behind her for support, Lindsey struggled to her feet as he approached. He allowed his left hand to release its grip from under the right and then let both of them fall, finally lowering the Glock.

Lindsey closed the last few feet between them, throwing herself into his arms. His left encircled her, crushing her to him. Only with the warmth of her body did the ice that had encased his heart begin to thaw.

She was alive. And she was safe.

Jace was again aware of the sounds that swirled around them. Squad cars and emergency vehicles continued to arrive out front, the scream of their sirens blending with the shouts of the men already pouring into the building. Half a dozen, weapons drawn, rushed through the lobby toward the lunch-room.

You aren't in charge of this operation, Jace told himself. The deputies knew there were probably other explosives in addition to the one he'd carried outside.

Whatever the plans for the assault had originally involved, the ringleaders were dead. He had no doubt that Justin Carr and Steven Byrd had been the driving force behind this and everything else that had happened in Randolph. The evil genius he'd long suspected and discovered too late.

Their reign of terror would be over with the rescue the SWAT team was mounting. All that was left for him to do was take Lindsey outside. Walk with her into the sunshine. Away from the blood and the bodies and this place, which for her, as

Seneca had been for him, would never again be the same. Whether she could come back here or not was something only Lindsey could decide and that might take a while. In the meantime…

"Let's go," he said.

"Where, Jace? Where do we ever go from here?"

"Right now, outside. Eventually… Eventually we go home."

Whether that was something they'd do together was one more thing only Lindsey knew the answer to. And all he could do was wait for her to figure it out.

"Most of what we know came from the Phillips girl, who on the advice of her lawyer is being very cooperative. She's got nothing to lose and maybe leniency, given her age, to gain."

Jace had had one of the deputies take Lindsey to her parents' house while he'd stayed behind at the school to put together the timeline and motivations for today's attack. Apparently his role had included interviewing those who'd been involved in the lunchroom standoff, including Jean Phillips. Although it was almost four, he'd told her this was the first chance he'd had to call.

Jace had already given her the death toll. Each victim someone she'd known. Someone she'd interacted with every day.

One of the assistant principals, Lucas Colbert, who'd been unlucky enough to encounter Justin as he was bringing his "project" into the vocational wing of the building, had died from a single shot from Colonel Carr's Beretta. Melanie Perrin, the registrar, who'd entered the office through its back door, had been killed as she'd unlocked its front. The two deputies who'd responded to the call from the maintenance man had been gunned down as they'd entered the building. Other than Steven and Justin, only one student, Mary DeWitt, had died.

Colbert's intervention had put the timetable of the attack off track. Most of the students the three had targeted hadn't even arrived at the school before it was all over. Those names, according to Jace, included kids prominent in school society—popular, involved, attractive. Many of them were among Lindsey's students.

"What could those students have possibly done to them to justify the kind of rampage they planned?" Lindsey questioned. Renee's inclusion was especially hard for her to understand, given the girl's innate kindness.

"Some perceived slight. Simple jealousy. But in most school shootings, no matter the targets, the ultimate victims hinge primarily on opportunity. Mary DeWitt was the unfortunate exception."

"I thought there was some kind of budding romance there. Between her and Steven."

"Byrd did, too. The Phillips girl says Mary had rebuffed his attentions, so he put her on the list the three of them composed over the weekend. He knew she got to school early. He was waiting for her when she got out of her car."

"And he shot her?" The first shots she'd heard occurred after Steven came into her room, but maybe in the parking lot—

"He stabbed her, pushed her body back into the car, and locked it. Then he came into the school to wait for Justin. We didn't find Mary until we were clearing the lot."

Then Steven had killed Mary before he'd come to her room. The barrier she'd worried about had already been broken.

"Steven said he wasn't going to spend the rest of his life

in jail. That they were going out in a blaze of glory. What changed? Was it because you talked to Justin again?"

"It started to unravel when they killed David Campbell. To give them credit, they were smart enough to know that."

"Then why *do* it?"

"We think he surprised them inside Shannon's house. There's precedent for that, remember."

The snake in her hamper. Lindsey wondered briefly what they'd planned to do at Shannon's. Another warning? Or had the drug they'd brought with them been intended for the counselor?

"Do you think that what they did to Dave they intended to do to her? Because Justin knew she saw through his act?"

"Jean says she wasn't involved in Campbell's murder. She may not have been. Like the others, her parents apparently kept her on a tight leash. We're trying to determine if Steven's mother was working that night."

"You think he's the one who broke into my place?"

What role had his supposed crush on her played into that? Or any of this? Assuming, of course, Justin had been telling the truth. It was clear he'd been trying to divert attention from himself and willing to throw Steven to the dogs to do it.

"Probably. According to the coroner, the drug he believes was used on Campbell is a staple in hospitals."

"And Steven's mother is a nurse."

"That's *not* reflected on his permanent record, by the way."

"She probably wasn't working when he provided the information. They do that at the start of their sophomore year. Steven's dad walked out on them sometime around that time, and she was forced to go back to work." Although emergency contact cards were updated at the first of school, other than posting grades and disciplinary actions, the permanent records weren't. "But…she wouldn't have stolen drugs for them, believe me."

"Steven's been doing some volunteering there. He was familiar with the medication system. And we've verified his mom had keys to the cabinets, based on her position."

"For the community service component of his scholarship applications," Lindsey spoke her realization aloud.

"What?"

"That's why he volunteered at the hospital. Scholarship committees want someone who's well-rounded. For kids who aren't athletic, and Steven wasn't, the other things they look at can become more important. His mother probably helped him get the position."

"I haven't talked to her yet, but I will. And to Carr. I understand he's concerned now that someone might sue because his guns were used. He's called the sheriff twice to detail his security arrangements, but he has yet to say he's sorry for his son's actions or take responsibility for them. Or the weapons."

"My bet is he won't. I'm sure that in his book he did everything he was supposed to. We'll be the ones to blame. Justin was bullied or belittled or misunderstood. We failed to protect him until his only option was to strike back." Lindsey made no attempt to hide her bitterness. She'd heard that, or some variation on the theme, too many times before.

"With the church fires as a prelude, he'll have a hard time making that case. Justin liked to demonstrate how much smarter he was than everyone else. Who do you think he learned that from?"

Jace was right. That sense of superiority had been taught at home in innocuous doses like the "survival of the fittest" comment. Shannon had been right in thinking it was significant.

And once more she'd been wrong. Tragically wrong.

"And Andrea? Tim? Was that what they were doing when they targeted them? Trying to prove how brilliant they were?"

"In a way. And it seemed foolproof. No one would know where those rumors had originated. If they didn't work, they'd lost nothing but a little time. If they succeeded, they couldn't be blamed for that success. And it would have been a good substitute for the rush they'd gotten from the fires."

"Two for two. Were they really that smart?"

"Jean knew about Andrea's depression. Even the cutting. They went to church together and had been close at one time. When their friendship fell apart, she was able to use what she knew to do the damage. Apparently she even suggested the youth minister at their church talk to Andrea about her promiscuity. All out of concern for her friend's soul, of course."

It was exactly as Jace had characterized it. Diabolical.

"And Tim?" According to Walt, no one had known about his son's secret. They both had felt there was no one in this community who could be trusted to keep it.

"Jean says that came from Justin. I'm not sure how he knew…could have just been a lucky guess."

Despite not having been raised here, Justin understood this community's mores well enough to push all the buttons that must have driven Tim to think he had no option but take his own life.

"So damn needless."

"Tim's death?"

"Everything. All of it. All of *them.*"

Their brains aren't done…

"You need to let this go, Lindsey. Let them go. The sole responsibility for what happened here lies with the three who set this into motion."

And two of them were dead. "What will happen to Jean?"

"She'll be tried, probably as an adult. They're sorting through possible charges. Although she didn't fire any shots today, she was certainly an accessory."

"I heard on the news that she didn't set off the explosives in the lunchroom. That must count for something." As the words came out of her mouth, Lindsey realized that she was again defending someone who no longer deserved her defense.

"They weren't real. That's probably what Justin had been putting together in the basement this weekend. Thankfully, being the son of a lieutenant colonel didn't give him access to C4. Still, they needed something to control the hostages they planned to take in the lunchroom, so they faked it."

"Then the bomb I took away from Jean—"

"Was a box wrapped in several layers of newspaper."

More deception. And she'd fallen for all of it.

"I have to go," Jace said. "I'll call you later. You're going to be all right there, aren't you?"

"I'm fine." Her parents had been glued to the television, but she'd had to take the coverage in small amounts. It was still too real. Too up close and personal. It always would be.

"Why did Justin come out of the lunchroom? I've thought about that all day, and I still can't figure it out. Why not stay there and make them come in and take him?"

"I don't think there was anybody in there Justin really wanted. Nobody whose death would give him a sense of achievement. None of that glory Steven talked about."

That had been their avowed goal. Was that why Steven had come upstairs to get her?

"Was I on their list, Jace?"

"Does it matter? Whoever was on it—"

"Were you?" Like poor Mary, had she unwittingly made Steven feel rejected? Because of her relationship with Jace? Could they have known how serious that had become?

In a town where there are no secrets? she mocked her own question. *I knew the first night you slept with him, Linds.*

"Lindsey—"

"Never mind." Did she really need to hear him say it?

"I'm sorry."

"For what? For saving my life? And who knows how many others. You have nothing to apologize for. Not to anyone."

"Neither do you. You need to believe that."

"I'll work on it. I promise. And now I need to let you get back to work."

"I'll call you as soon as I can."

"Thanks."

"Don't let this change who you are."

She smiled, thinking about all the ways it already had. "I'll work on that one, too. And while I am, you take care."

She didn't add the words she'd said to him this morning. He'd heard them then. If they'd meant anything to him, then the next step was up to him.

Jace had tossed his jacket over a chair and headed straight for the cabinet where he kept the Scotch. Then, decanter in one hand and a glass in the other, he'd been about to pour the first drink of what might be several, when his doorbell rang.

For a second or two he considered ignoring it, but there were too many loose ends that hadn't been tied up to his satisfaction. If someone had come up with the answers he'd posed in the debriefing, he wanted to know about them.

Setting the Scotch and the tumbler down, he walked over to the door. After looking out the peephole, he turned the dead bolt and opened it to Lindsey.

"I thought you might not have had time to eat."

The smell emanating from the sack she held reminded him that he hadn't. And of the last time she'd brought takeout.

He stepped back, gesturing her inside. Considering what had gone down today, she looked a whole lot better than he felt. He'd thought about going by to check on her on his way home, but had finally decided, as late as it was, that it would be an intrusion. Not to Lindsey, but to her parents, whom he'd never met.

"Are you all right?" she asked as he secured the door.

"That should be my line." He turned, taking time to verify his initial impression that she seemed better than she had on the phone.

"I haven't been working on this all day. Despite my parents' obsession with Fox, I've had some distance."

"The more time and space, the less consuming it becomes."

"The voice of experience."

"Unfortunately."

He led the way to the kitchen, setting a couple of plates down on the counter. Lindsey watched as he did, but made no effort to put whatever she had in the sack onto them.

"Soda okay? Or something stronger?"

"They finally brought me my purse," she said. "Steven made me leave it in my desk drawer, and I knew they weren't letting anyone back in. I called and asked them to go up and get it."

"If you'd told me—"

"I didn't want to bother you. Actually, I thought it was a little…strange that I even thought about it, but it had my driver's license, of course, so I couldn't drive. And my cell."

As she said the word, the message he'd left on her phone played through his head, the words etched on his memory by the emotions of the moment. He'd been so afraid he'd lose her. Afraid that he'd been too slow to figure it all out. Once again too slow to stop what he knew was going to happen.

And he almost had. When he'd seen that punk put the muzzle of his weapon against her temple, everything he'd managed to rebuild of his shattered life had hung in the balance.

One chance. And this time he hadn't hesitated.

"I don't know whether your message was from the stress of the moment," she said. "If so, I understand. All you have to do is say—"

"Was that what it was for you? The stress of the moment?"

When she'd whispered the words she was trying so hard to give him an out for, she'd just laid a bomb on his palms. Did she regret saying them? Or was she just afraid he did?

"No," she said simply.

"Truth be told, Lindsey I'm *not* particularly eligible. Not by anyone's standards. You've probably figured that out by now."

"No," she said again, her eyes holding his.

He laughed. "Then you aren't as bright as I thought."

"A quality that just might be overrated. I think sometimes... You said important things sometime turn on a feeling. An investigator's instinct. From the first, as much as I resented *why* you were here, I was glad you were."

"I don't know that this can ever be home. I can't go back to the place that is, but I know how important home is to you."

"*You're* important to me. And if you meant what you said in that message, then nothing else really matters."

"It will. Eventually. Your family. Friends. Your job."

"The irony is that until today I might have agreed with you. Now..." She shook her head. "I just want to grow old with you. Somewhere safe. Somewhere we can send our kids to school and not have to worry if they'll come home. Where we can walk into our house at night and not be afraid of the dark."

"The dark's always out there, Lindsey. There isn't any place where those things don't happen. Even here."

"That's why what you do is so important to you. I understand that now. Important enough that whatever happened to you before didn't keep you from going back to your job."

"Maybe another quality that's overrated. What I did was for me. I needed to know if I could face what I feared. I needed to know the next time I wouldn't make the same mistake."

"Did you?"

"No."

She nodded. "And now that you know that?"

"I have to decide if I need to do it again. And if there are other, better reasons for it if I do."

"I don't know that I can do that. I don't ever want to go back to what happened today. Or to the weeks before it."

"Nobody will judge you if you don't."

"Maybe you won't, but to me, it's the coward's way out."

"You're not a coward, Lindsey."

"I don't know if I can ever walk into a classroom without wondering which of them is capable of what happened today."

"Fair enough. You don't owe anybody. Do something else."

"Be a greeter at Wal-Mart."

"What?"

"That's what Shannon always threatens to do when she can't take the little darlings anymore. Right now…"

"Right now, you need to give yourself some time."

"How long did it take you?"

"I'm a slow learner."

"Sorry, that's not my specialty."

"What is?" His grin emphasized his meaning.

"You know all of them. Such as they are."

"That's right. You're the *gifted* coordinator. Highly gifted, I might add."

"Thank you. Actually, thank you for everything."

"Don't get grateful and serious on me. Neither one of us needs that. Not tonight."

"Barbeque?"

"Eventually," he said, taking the sack from her and putting it down on the counter.

"I've got to stop bringing food over here. It's a waste."

"I thought it was a bribe," he said as he took her into his arms. "Police corruption."

"As long as it works."

His lips closed over hers, swallowing the last word. And it was a long time later before either of them spoke again.

"I liked the part about sending our kids to school." Jace ran his thumb over the moisture left on her bottom lip.

Maybe not in Randolph, given the memories that would haunt both of them here. But not so far away that those children she'd mentioned wouldn't have grandparents. Someone who would love them and nurture them and help them become the kind of person Lindsey was. Someone to balance his cynicism. And someone willing to babysit for the occasional weekend away.

"Boys or girls?"

"Which is less trouble?" He leaned back to see her face.

"Depends on the age, but…you need a little girl. One who will wrap you around her finger."

"I thought you'd already done that."

"Just wait."

"Okay, but…not too long. Time has a way of getting away from you. You never have as much as you think you will."

"We'll have enough. We'll *make* it enough. I love you, Jace Nolan. I always will."

"That isn't gratitude talking, is it?"

"Desperation. I told you. So if you have any thought of getting away…"

He didn't, he realized. No qualms. No doubts. Nothing but an absolute certainty this was how it was supposed to be. Maybe from the beginning.

And certainly—absolutely—to the end.

* * * * *

If you've enjoyed THE SUICIDE CLUB,
don't miss Gayle Wilson's next spine-tingling
romantic-suspense novel,
VICTIM
Available in February 2008
from MIRA Books.

Turn the page for an exciting preview.

Don't talk. Just shoot.

The words careened through her brain as her hands and her eyes continued to track her prey. Dan must have said them in a hundred darkened movie theaters through the years. Transfixed by what was occurring on the screen, he would whisper those words, offering his warning to countless heroines tremblingly holding a gun on the bad guy.

Shoot him. Don't talk to him. Just shoot him, you stupid bitch.

That was exactly what Sarah had planned to do. She had even uttered Dan's words over and over, preparing for this moment.

Now, despite what her intellect was telling her—had told her from the moment she had thought of this—she knew that she needed him to know. She needed Tate to understand for which of them he was dying. In some sense, perhaps, what she was doing would be for all of them, but the only way it would ever make any difference to her was if Tate knew *her* son's name.

"Daniel," she shouted.

The dark, well-groomed head turned, everything happening in slow motion. She had time to watch his eyes meet hers before they fell to the gun. When they rose again, they were slightly widened, but there was no panic in them. Fastened on hers, they were exactly the same pale, clear blue her son's had been.

"His name was Daniel Patterson," she said, no longer shouting, because he was near enough that she knew he could hear her. And because she had his full and undivided attention.

His head moved up and down. In agreement? Did that mean he had known Danny's name? Or did it simply mean he understood for which of them he was about to die?

Tate's descent had begun to slow, his gaze still locked on her face. *Shoot, don't talk.* Now she could. Now she could kill him, because she had told Tate Danny's name.

Her finger closed over the trigger, beginning the slow deliberate squeeze…

* * * * *

VICTIM by Gayle Wilson
February 2008

The stunning debut by sensational new talent

JASON PINTER

I moved to New York City a month ago to become the best journalist the world had ever seen. To find the greatest stories never told. And now here I am—Henry Parker, twenty-four years old and weary beyond rational thought, a bullet and one trigger pull from ending my life.

I can't run. Running is all Amanda and I have done for the past three days. And I'm tired. Tired of knowing the truth and not being able to tell it. Tired of knowing that if I die, this story will die with me.

And if I die tonight, the killing will have just begun....

"A gripping page-turner you won't be able to stop reading."
—James Patterson

*Available the first week of July 2007
wherever paperbacks are sold!*

THE MARK

GAYLE WILSON

32361 BOGEYMAN   ___ $6.99 U.S. ___ $8.50 CAN.
32320 THE INQUISITOR   ___ $6.99 U.S. ___ $8.50 CAN.

(limited quantities available)

TOTAL AMOUNT $ _____
POSTAGE & HANDLING $ _____
($1.00 FOR 1 BOOK, 50¢ for each additional)
APPLICABLE TAXES* $ _____
TOTAL PAYABLE $ _____

(check or money order—please do not send cash)

To order, complete this form and send it, along with a check or money order for the total above, payable to MIRA Books, to: **In the U.S.:** 3010 Walden Avenue, P.O. Box 9077, Buffalo, NY 14269-9077; **In Canada:** P.O. Box 636, Fort Erie, Ontario, L2A 5X3.

Name: _____
Address: _____ City: _____
State/Prov.: _____ Zip/Postal Code: _____
Account Number (if applicable): _____

075 CSAS

*New York residents remit applicable sales taxes.
*Canadian residents remit applicable GST and provincial taxes.

MGW0707BL